Lovers
in a
Small Café

Part II of The Ice Meadows

EDMUND BURWELL

PAGE PUBLISHING, INC.
Conneaut Lake, PA

First originally published by Page Publishing 2020

ISBN 978-1-6624-1207-3 (pbk)
ISBN 978-1-6624-1208-0 (digital)

Printed in the United States of America

Introduction

THIS BOOK IS a work of fiction. Names, characters, places, and incidents are products of the author's imagination and are used fictitiously. Any resemblance to actual events, locales, or persons, living or dead, is coincidental.

Chapter One

I N THE ARSENAL of wonders that is the Metropolitan Museum of Art, there is a photograph called *Lovers in a Small Café in the Italian Quarter.* The great Brassaï sometimes staged his images, but whether this one was staged or candid has made little difference to an enchanted world for over seventy years. It is very much early thirties, romantic, bohemian, European, and perhaps to an American, lusty in an intimate, Latin sort of way. It has the ephemeral look of the Paris so cherished by writers and artists, the fabulous, chic decadence of a place like no other and at a time that is wholly lost. There must be many who see this affecting picture and hope, though the time and place have vanished forever, that its intimacy and sweet joy can still be found somewhere.

The scene is clean and well lit, though dark enough to be romantic, and too early for the storm gathering outside to affect the interior shadows. It is a picture of security of sorts—a moment of private safety on a darkening plain where confusion, struggle, and flight are near and ignorant armies will clash as though any victory they may achieve will be determinative of anything.

He had come across a copy of Brassaï's great photographs during college, and Joe had kept a copy of *Lovers in a Small Café* ever since, tacked up near his desk in a place where he could see it but not have to explain it to anyone. When he was younger, he felt he shared something with the young Brassaï, coming from remote

5

Transylvanian forests into the light of Montmartre. Then he grew older and began to wonder if his journey was the other way around.

The counseling Kate had faithfully agreed to that night at the kitchen table with him and their friends the Gallaghers never happened. For six months, Joe waited patiently for her to tell him when her counselor said he could join in. Again, he worried that Kate's silence on a major matter meant she had something to hide. When he asked her early on, casually and with extreme care, how she was getting along with the counseling, she had replied at length by trying to describe the architectural style of the building where the appointments took place. After several more months, when he sat down to pay the family bills, he asked her when the counselor would send a statement. She had replied that she didn't know and that maybe her school insurance company was holding matters up. Since then, she had never mentioned counseling again.

After waiting for six months, Joe called the counselor's office to inquire about making payment. A polite young receptionist answered. She explained that she had just started working there and, if he would bear with her, she would try to find the file. A few minutes later, she returned and informed him that there was no record of Kate returning after the initial interview, which was "free," as far as she knew, so although she was not 100 percent sure, she figured he did not owe anything. As a lawyer, Joe realized that the girl had innocently given him confidential information. He wanted to question the counselor herself but was reluctant to do so for fear of getting the girl, who had tried to be helpful, into trouble with her new boss. Besides, he knew the counselor would not tell him anything without Kate's permission.

He thought it over for a day. He did not want to accuse Kate unfairly, in case the girl had made a mistake. Kate would blow up at him if he confronted her, an indiscretion he knew he would have to pay for in dozens of small ways over time. If he confronted her unfairly, however, it would make the matter worse. To his amazement, the counselor herself provided an answer. She telephoned him the following day, introduced herself, and said, quite professionally, that it had come to her attention that her new secretary had exceeded their legal authority to provide information. She apologized for both of them and assured Joe that the girl was just getting started and that she had been trying to be helpful. Joe spoke briefly in the secretary's behalf and assured the doctor that he understood entirely. Then, encouraged by the counselor's conciliatory tone, he lamented that his wife had not followed through.

"Yes," replied the counselor. "We planned a whole series of appointments to fit her teaching schedule, but we never saw her after that. And that's about all I can say. I know you understand, Mr. Stephenson."

Time went by, too, while Joe waited for Kate to let him know when they would be moving into the farmhouse on the school property. She had been so positive about it. When the place she referred to as "my house" had been given to a new teacher, she was entirely certain of being able to live in the farmhouse "as soon as they finished painting it and cleaning it up." It was part of every teacher's contract, she told him. "So give me a break and be patient." He had been patient, thinking all the time how helpful it would be to go ahead and put their house on the market.

Over the years, she had lamented her small salary, sulking for weeks each spring, when contracts were prepared for the following academic year. She reasoned, with Joe's complete support, that her salary should be higher since she saved the school money by not occupying the faculty housing that was reserved for her. "Father" always told her that the school was contractually obligated to provide housing for teachers but there was no provision for raising the salary of a teacher who did not take advantage of faculty housing. He realized she had to pay for gasoline and the other teachers did not, but he could do nothing about it. If she ever decided to move to St. John's, her house would be waiting for her.

Joe waited patiently through the winter, prepared to act when she gave him the word. He spoke with a real estate agent, who called him every week or so, wanting to know when she could list their house and assuring Joe she could have sold it by now. He met representatives of local moving companies at the house and had compiled a list of their bids. He calculated the savings they would have when they no longer had to pay the mortgage and figured out which bills to pay off first. He talked to Kate about paying off their credit cards first, and then the cars. They could add to Ted's college account, and they would be in a better position to put a new roof on the Wicomico house whenever she and Ray worked out the details.

As the weeks passed, he found himself paying more and more attention to small things around the house and the lawn. He stood at the kitchen window more often to watch the birds at the feeders and sat for many minutes in various rooms on his days off, just looking around. He spent more time in picking up and straightening the rooms than usual, and shopping for groceries. He was conscious of an unsentimental realism about every detail. Then, in changing the beds one Friday morning, he grew emotional. He remained composed, but he was conscious of how easy it would be to cry. He examined the nooks and corners outdoors where he had planted crocus, seeking any sign of their emergence. He had always forced forsythia and plum, and this year he had placed some in every room, big graceful branches that filled the house with glorious color. A friend let him clip branches from her star magnolia to take home. He lingered in the garage, cleaning the shelves and discarding things nobody had used in years.

He would miss this house, the place where Ted had grown up into a teenager and they had celebrated birthdays and entertained friends. He had loved to be at home wherever they had lived. At one time, he had thought himself the most domestic man he knew, but age had taught him he had a world of company. Most of his close friends, and all the men with whom he fished and hunted, were at home as much as they could manage. Most of them spent their days, when not at their jobs, around the house, tinkering, fixing, repairing, planting, painting. They were not good about cleaning or ironing, but most of them cooked as well as their wives, and some were even better. Many of his friends thought it peculiar that Joe did not know how to cook. He liked to make soup, although Kate and Ted seldom ate any of it. And one day, he wanted to learn to bake bread, not in a machine, but in the old way.

In the spring, Kate began talking about moving to Wicomico for the summer and complained that her schedule for the following fall required her to teach an extra period each day. She made no mention of moving, something that would have required a great deal of planning and preparation. It would not have surprised Joe to find that moving was something she intended to leave up to him while she was away at her beach house. So knowing he was risking days of irritation and brooding, he brought the subject up again. She sighed and told him that "Father" had reserved the farmhouse for another teacher. That teacher's former place was an apartment. Hervey had graciously offered it to Kate, but it was not large enough for a family. Joe was surprised when she admitted, without him having to draw it out of her, what Hervey had said when she reminded him of what he had always told her about faculty housing.

"He looked right at me and said, 'Mrs. Stephenson, don't ever believe what you're promised in a job unless you get it in writing.' Can you believe that? After all I've done for him? For that school? I'm not trusting him anymore. After all I've done! He lied to me. For years! And they wonder why people work there a few years and go on to another job. People are so fake!"

Joe was so surprised and angry he could not speak. After a moment of clearing his throat and swallowing, he said, "When did he tell you this, Kate?"

"When! What difference does that make? A couple of months ago. So what?" Her very animation meant she was already defending herself from what he was going to say.

"You knew I was waiting to know…to put the house on the market…to…"

"Oh, Joe, I told you. When I got home that night, remember? You were sitting right there at the kitchen table, and I said—"

"You did not tell me, Kate. I'm an intelligent man, and I would certainly remember a conversation about our family moving from one house to another."

"Well, there you go again. Why is it always my fault, Joe? Why am I always the one to blame? You have no idea what I do all day. I'm busier than you are. I've got more to do than you do, Joe. And I work harder than you do." She raged and stormed, finally turning off the kitchen light and leaving him alone in the dark as she stomped fussily upstairs to the bedroom.

His every lawyerly instinct was aroused against Hervey and the school, but he was so angry with Kate, at her impenetrable wall of denial, that he felt he could vomit. He knew he could make a case for breach of contract against the school. The mere threat of legal action might have brought some reason into the situation, but he immediately rejected that preposterous thought. It was his anger affecting him, not his legal expertise. He turned on the light and thought about it all while Kate thundered about on the floor above. He was very upset at the way Kate had been treated and at how she had once again treated him. He knew better than to try to think clearly or make plans while feeling so angry. How dare that bastard Hervey treat her that way! And she was still unwilling, after fifteen years of marriage, to simply open her mouth and tell him the truth and do it without him having to coax it out of her. And how much of the truth did she ever tell him, anyway? He did not know.

He got up and stared blindly out the window into the pool of light where Cory was watching like a fan expecting the appearance of a screen idol. He began to twitch about and thump his tail when he saw Joe. Despite his anger, Joe smiled at his friendly little dog, sending Cory racing away into the darkness, from which he returned in seconds, bearing a stick and dancing in the pool of light.

* * *

Neither Kate's brother nor her best friend called Joe again following his pleas for help at the time of the intervention. A few weeks following that weekend, Joe was in the kitchen one night when Kate, reclining on the couch in the den, took a call from Fawn, Ray's wife. Kate did most of the talking in telephone conversations, but in this call, she listened in silence for about ten seconds and then said, "Oh, fine. I'm fine. No problems. A lot of work to do at school. But no… no problems. Can't wait to get to the beach. Exams begin on…" From what he could overhear, there was no further mention made about her, personally. She hung up five minutes later and continued to watch *Inspector Morse*. She was aware that Joe could hear every word from where he was washing dishes, but she had nothing to say.

About a month following Fawn's call, as they were going to bed one night, Joe and Kate were talking and he asked her, routinely, innocently, how she was feeling. She told him she was feeling fine, but then she began to grow indignant and told him she did not appreciate his talking about her "personal business" to "strangers." When he asked her what she meant, she said he had called Ray, Karla, and his parents about her. Her face had taken on the color of a ripe tomato, and she had even closed her book, always a prelude to turning off her light. He explained quickly that he had spoken only to Ray and Karla because he was desperate with concern for her, that he had talked to them once and only once and had been waiting for them to give him some advice. He assured her he had not spoken to his parents. At this, she sat up a bit and adjusted her pillow in apparent relief.

"You're my wife, Kate. I'm your husband. Your drinking affects us all. I'm doing my best to cope. I know I make mistakes, but talking out of court isn't one of them—as your husband, as a lawyer, and as somebody ordained. I have never talked about it except anonymously in Al-Anon, and with the family counselor. It is nobody else's business. It was very hard for me to call Ray and Karla that night. But your health, our marriage...I was desperate for help. He is your brother. She's your best friend. They were the only ones I could turn to. Neither of them ever called me back."

"You can't blame Karla for not calling you back after the way you talked to her, Joe!" She was indignant again. She described how offended Karla had been by the mean things Joe had said to her, and about her, and about Kate herself.

Joe explained as carefully as he could exactly how the conversation had proceeded, trying to repeat every word, hoping Kate would see how he had handled it. Kate listened carefully, even putting aside her paperback book and looking at him the whole while. Although she tried to hide it, he saw her amazement when he told her that Karla had admitted to him that she was an alcoholic too. Could these two best friends, who had spent so much time together, truly not know that the other was a problem drinker?

When he had finished his explanation, Kate was silent for a moment. She asked him questions to confirm once more that he had talked to nobody else and that he had not spoken to his parents. He answered her fully and truthfully, and she gave every sign of being relieved. Joe surprised himself by being surprised that she appeared to believe him. She did not contest anything he said, including his assurance of the tone with which he had tried to reason with Karla. She was more cheerful and chatty for a few minutes, until Joe told her again how pleased he was for her that she was following through with counseling. It would be another four months before he learned the truth. At his mention of therapy, she nodded in reply, opened her book again, and was quiet until they went to sleep.

* * *

The food, medical care, and personal interactions in the nursing home restored Catherine to better health than she had enjoyed for many months. She continued to need a wheelchair for moving any distance, but she was able to propel it herself, an achievement that astonished both Kate and Joe. Kate visited her every few days and was soon coming home with stories about the ancient gentleman with whom Catherine had struck up a friendship. Kate was amused, Joe was delighted, and Ted was full of jokes about the two of them roaring away in a cab to the airport and sending postcards from Las Vegas or the Bahamas. Joe visited and brought Communion, which Catherine, although a Baptist, seemed to find meaningful. He had asked the clergy closer to the nursing home to visit her too. When the weather allowed it, the three of them took Catherine out to dinner. Occasionally, they arrived to find Catherine seated in the big room, watching television with other patients. Whether any of them could understand one another as they commented on the complexities of soap opera intrigues, no one could be sure.

After six months, Ray stopped sending his half of the monthly payment. Joe could not induce Kate to call him about it; there was always some excuse why it didn't suit her just then. Joe tried to call him, but Fawn or the children said he was out, or asleep. He never returned the calls. Joe left messages at his office. As the months passed, the Stephensons' savings account was depleted. When Joe informed Kate that unless she resolved the matter there would be no money around for the seven or eight hundred dollars she always took with her to begin the summer at Wicomico, she called Ray at work from St. John's. For two months the checks arrived, although Ray sent nothing extra to make up for the missing months. Then, as before, the checks stopped arriving, with no explanation.

One evening, Kate returned from work and said that Ray had told them to move Catherine into a less-expensive place. She said she reminded him they had found the only place they could afford and that it was a good one. She said she reminded him she was driving almost an hour each way to visit Catherine. She was vague on how their conversation had ended, or what more was said, and Joe could draw nothing else out of her. Over the years, he had become very guarded about accepting anything said in conversations between Kate and Ray, and in anything related to him by Kate about what the two had discussed.

Joe wrote Ray several letters explaining the financial difficulty they were getting into because he had stopped paying. He received no reply, but Kate received a call from the manager of the nursing home saying that Ray had called to say he would be coming up at the end of the following month to move Catherine to a place in Georgia. Kate called him, again from work, and reported to Joe that Ray had found a "cheaper" place in his town, where Catherine would be "just fine." Kate was clearly angry and predicted that Ray would not take care of Catherine with anything like the attention she and Joe had for her.

As difficult as Catherine had been for so many years, and as hostile toward him for the slightest reason, Joe found himself deeply concerned by this forthcoming move to Georgia. For the first time in fifteen years, Catherine would be out of their day-to-day family life. Given her age and health, he knew that this time she would not be sent back to them within weeks, as had happened every other time she had visited Ray and his family. He told Kate that he feared it meant he would not see Catherine alive again. Kate said he was probably right. He found himself moved by this thought.

Ray would be coming for Catherine after Kate had departed for the summer. She was prepared to make the long drive back to pack her mother's possessions for the trip south. Joe offered to do it for her, and she agreed.

The day before Ray's arrival, Joe carefully nestled into boxes and two large suitcases Catherine's clothing, personal items, books, and other things. He took down Kate's handmade curtains and folded them carefully into one of the suitcases because he feared that Ray would not do so, even if he left him a note. He set out clothing for the following day's travel, as well as an additional set of clothing in case a change was needed on the long ride to Georgia. He left a sealed letter for Ray tucked into the suitcase handles, reminding him about Catherine's daily medicines and a few foods for which she recently had developed a liking, and listing the expenses they had paid and for which they still needed reimbursement. Catherine observed all this with interest, speaking up now and then to advise him how to fold her sweaters or blouses—exactly the way he had folded them the first time—and sending him down the hall to the rooms of other residents with magazines and books she did not want to take with her. He knew that when she departed the following day, she would pass right by her neighbors without a glance. The thought of it made him sad.

He found saying goodbye excruciating. He said a prayer, asking God's blessing upon Catherine and Ray for a safe journey, and praying for Catherine in her new residence. He thanked God that their lives had touched and that through their meeting Kate had come into his life and together they had brought Ted into the world. He said the Lord's Prayer for both of them, as Catherine never joined in. For what he knew was the last time, he administered to her the consecrated bread and wine from his small Communion case and made the sign of the cross over her and said *amen*. Catherine endured all this quietly and attentively. When he kissed her on the cheek and told her he loved her, he thought she said, "I love you too," but he wasn't sure.

Chapter Two

DR. O'CONNOR'S PILLS made a difference. It was hard to say exactly what it was, but there was a difference, and it was good. Joe wondered if the parishioners and clients whom he had urged to use medications over the years had been blessed with a similar feeling. He hoped so. It was healing. His focus was sharper. He was more hopeful. He told his family counselor that he had sat through dinner without the old sadness as Kate had questioned Ted a hundred times about who had said what to whom or done this or that at St. John's that day. Instead of brooding on his exclusion from their conversation, he told himself that Ted was a teenager acting his age and that Kate was his wife and he would accept her ways with serenity. He told himself he was a blessed man to be eating dinner with the people he loved safely in his own home. He reminded himself that high school was something his wife and son had very much in common, it was where their interests were, and perhaps Kate was reveling in experiences she had missed in her own teenage years. If that was the case, he was glad she had this chance to catch up. Clyde Candler, his most recent family counselor, a short, bespeckled man whom Joe liked and admired, listened carefully to all this without much comment.

Like a farmer in drought reminding himself that it had always rained before, Joe found himself trusting again in eventual change in his marriage. He had always remembered Robert Louis Stevenson's words: it is better to travel hopefully than to arrive. He had enough common sense to focus on the journey for the time being. He would make a good home for Ted. He would continue to work on his own issues. He would pay no attention to small matters or troubling disappointments. He would be cheerful with Kate and continue to feel his way forward in the confusing territory between enabling and true love.

He tried again to attend every event at the school. He took Kate to dinner at her favorite Chinese restaurant as often as she wanted to go. He listened to her talk about her favorite subjects. They talked about Ted and his future. He let go of the whole issue of homelife. For years, he had tried to keep down the disappointment like a tubercular patient controlling a cough. Now he did his best to let it all go. He continued taking care of things on his days off and said no more about it.

He tried to be more tolerant of Kate and found that it required having patience with himself as well. He committed himself to being calm and nonjudgmental in the face of old behavior patterns whose outcome he knew too well. Kate continued to live as she always had, doing and saying things that had almost always led to conflict before. It was as if she was heedless and unconcerned by design or calculation and that whatever did not concern her personally did not exist. He had seen it all before, but he had been too close, too reactive. The medicine had helped him gain a little distance now, and he made better choices. He could minimize conflict by softening his own reactions. So long as he was patient with himself and kept it all in perspective, moments of potential conflict passed without incident. When she surprised him by starting to dress for something at the school on a Friday or Saturday night and swore she had told him about it weeks before, he made a quick change in plans and began to get ready to go too. When he examined the checkbook and found she had spent a lot of money without saying anything to him, he delayed paying several bills for a month and let it go. He continued to iron for everyone, pay the bills, keep the house straight between the cleaner's visits, go to some social gatherings alone, and all without questions or complaints. Except for getting away for a few days in the spring and fall to fish, he had no time for himself, not even to read, but he kept quiet about it. In not complaining, and certainly by not attempting to discuss differences with Kate, he seemed to have discovered a key to tranquility

Kate gave not the slightest sign of noticing any of this. Joe wondered whether she dwelled occasionally on her old allegation that she worked harder than he did and had more to do than he had. She accepted what he did as only what was naturally due her. He still worried about drunken driving, an emotional breakdown, a financial crisis hidden from him until too late. His worry that she would hurt herself was relieved largely by Ted's age and perception. Joe knew that Kate knew that Ted, who was so close to her, would notice immediately anything bizarre in her behavior. Although Ted's disposition raised few concerns for Joe, he still worried that his son might inherit the compulsion to drink.

They were all lonely worries and could have driven a person mad, but Joe was in good company, and he knew it. His family counselor, spiritual director, and companions in Al-Anon continued to be a blessing in his life. He valued their views and example. He continued to see them as blessings, sent by God to help him cope, and he was grateful.

Divorce never entered his mind. Occasionally, he daydreamed about starting over knowing all he knew now. He was certain he would make fewer mistakes, that he could rise above the ignorance and poor judgment he had brought to so many crises in the past, that he would be a better husband and father. He was older now, more experienced, and aware of what others were dealing with in their lives. Perhaps the medicine allowed him the tranquility one needs for self-assessment, like turning off a radio in the background so he could concentrate in silence. He remembered his own past mistakes, the chances lost through his own impatience, things done and said and—what was far worse—left undone, unspoken, and he easily could have become depressed again. Instead, he was hopeful. Every regretful memory renewed his determination to handle himself differently in the future. He was changing, and he would continue to change.

He told himself that Christ had never misled anybody by suggesting that obeying the rules and doing one's best would lead to success or fairness in this life. Could he really blame Kate for doing whatever had worked for her? Denial and alcoholism were diseases like Parkinson's or malaria, or conditions like Down syndrome or allergies to peanuts. They weren't choices. Nobody goes out and signs up for them any more than gays elect to be gay or twins choose to resemble each other. He told all this to himself with the best of intentions.

Yet none of his learning or rationalizations or excuses or experience could make sense of the complete self-centeredness of alcoholic denial, its thoughtless ruination of surrounding lives, its cruel insensitivity to everything that failed to support its own existence. He knew that in this sort of analysis, this endless inquiry into motives and rationale, he was slipping back into disappointment, which would close about him like quicksand. Even if he took Kate to the best psychologist or psychiatrist in the world, there was no assuring that she would participate willingly and in good conscience. And even if she did, whatever motives or physiological complications there were might still be beyond discovery. Who was he to try to understand what the best physician might fathom? He would destroy the joy of life by trying. His part was to focus on changing his own shortcomings.

What is peace? He prayed and wondered. As he went about his hospital calls, committee meetings, and the many community works in which he served as leader, he thought about it constantly. Peace. In every personal counseling session with people from the community, in each Bible study group, surrounding him in every worship service he conducted in retirement homes, he recognized the same question in the words and faces around him. "Make sense of all this for me!" they said in one of ten thousand ways. "If God loves us, why is all this happening to us?" they wanted to know, in so many words. "Why did God take John? He had finally been able to retire." Where is peace? they wanted to know. "My trophies," they cried, "if you can call them that. When can I lay them down?" Peace.

There is none, he knew. God's peace does not fit the human conception of cessation of hostilities or surcease of want and sorrow. Such a human peace is precluded by what we do to one another. It comes from within us. Can we change ourselves? Is that why we need a savior? God's peace is unfathomable, unimaginable. First principles, he told himself. What do I perceive before me? What is reality? Contemplating holy mysteries wearied him in a world where rock stars and immature athletes, most of whom couldn't print their names, prospered and thrived, while the poor were always with us. It could be overwhelming. Just as Kate insulated herself in denial, he felt at times like doing the same thing. He counted his blessings and gave thanks for feeling better.

Joe could count among his blessings Kate's love of Ted. Their son was the only star in her narrow, exclusive band of night, and she doted on him. She spoiled Ted. That was clear to Joe and to many of their friends, some of whom commented to him about it, in the lightest and friendliest of ways, from time to time. He knew Ted was influenced by his mother's example of ignoring responsibilities and whatever else annoyed her. Like Kate, Ted took no responsibility for their home. The chores Joe required of Ted were invariably forgotten in the more important activities at school or elsewhere. Unless Joe was there to remind him, Ted would hear no reminders. Kate always covered for him, making excuses for Ted the way she made them for herself. And Ted accepted it gladly, not because he had no conscience, but because he was a teenager going through the busy changes and development that were entirely natural. Though soaking up his mother's attentions and examples, he remained good-humored and easygoing and, Joe believed, genuinely caring toward those around him.

Kate did not see a child's responsibility in fulfilling simple chores as having anything to do with building character. Managing an allowance, saving a bit each week, writing notes of thanks for gifts, taking initiative in the tasks of family life—none of it was important enough for her to demand that Ted follow through. However, the teacher in her rose up and pushed Ted appropriately in academics—more vigorously, Joe believed, than occurred in other households.

Joe was appreciative for this, and Ted's solid B average reflected it. He would have liked to take part, but Kate preferred to handle Ted's homework and special school projects on her own. After a few years of grade school, Ted leaned naturally toward Kate in all matters relating to academics. When Joe provided help to Ted on evenings when Kate was attending faculty meetings, it led invariably to Kate's readjusting matters on the following evening in line with what she would have done had she been there. Joe saw the resulting confusion in what he had meant to be helpful for Ted. And giving Kate her due as a professional teacher, Joe thought it made sense to let her have her way. He made himself available to Ted, but Ted always turned to his mother. Even in matters in which Joe could have clearly been of help to him, Ted turned reflexively to Kate. And she could be counted upon at any time to express an opinion, reflexively and immediately, and provide "answers" to every question on any subject, no matter how unrelated to her training in biology. Whether it never occurred to her to turn to Joe in certain fields, or whether her competitive nature overrode such an inclination, she carried on as though only she and Ted were in the house. When son and mother were together, Ted followed her example. Without being rude, neither of them acknowledged Joe's presence. Except in the most egregious circumstances, where a want of accuracy would damage Ted's composition or project, Joe did not interject corrections. It avoided arguments or confrontations with Kate in Ted's presence. Instead, he waited until Ted had gone to bed and tried to point out to Kate what had occurred. She listened, returned to her paperback mystery, and proceeded to act in the same way the next time.

Ted was Kate's child, and she smothered him with her love, becoming his friend and confidant and giving him eventually what he wanted. As Ted grew into his teens, Kate's love for him included complicity in circumventing Joe. Where fatherly expectations collided with teenage preferences, Ted could count upon Kate as an ally. Joe was ignorant of this growing pattern. He no longer completely trusted Kate, but it never entered his mind to question her intentions concerning Ted. Most of the reason and cooperation he drew from her always came in their mutual role as parents. In other things, she might ignore Joe, denigrate him, and actively work against him, but when he tried to reason with her about Ted's overall welfare, planning for his future, raising him with standards, she listened and engaged in the conversation. Following through with agreements was another matter entirely. If erring must take place, her erring on the side of spoiling Ted was preferable, he supposed, to the alternative. It was an attitude he would come to despise himself for later. For Ted's high school years, though, it seemed a reasonable and harmless compromise with a wife whose obstinate self-absorption had defeated his every effort to compromise. Although he would never have analyzed it in such terms, Ted saw his mother increasingly as an indulgent older sister, a contemporary who was as cognizant of high school intrigue and gossip as any teenager in his class. She was an ally in the clash of wills that every normal boy experiences with his father. But his son was healthy, popular, and making good grades, so Joe continued to count his blessings.

Al-Anon took on additional meaning as Joe began to feel better. In facing dreadful situations, he had always found it inspiring to observe composure in others. All his life, he had welcomed humor as a healthy lubricant in decreasing tension, and keeping issues in proper perspective was calming in itself. He continued to see Clyde Candler, the licensed family counselor with whom he had worked weekly for several years. The therapist was at a partial disadvantage because he had never met Kate, in spite of all efforts to encourage her to participate. Their time together was instructive because Joe welcomed the therapist's confrontation. In Joe's view, it was always appropriate and necessary whenever it happened, strengthening, clarifying, and enabling him to cope better. If Kate had agreed to participate, Joe knew that one minute of confrontation over matters she was not prepared to discuss would send her storming from the room, and he told this plainly to Candler. But as she never agreed to attend, the issue was never tested.

The monthly visits to his spiritual director were also affected by his lighter mood. Dr. Lewis Batterton was only five years older than Joe, but he had been ordained while Joe was still in law school and was a man of much and varied experience. His children had graduated from college. He served a very small parish in an economically depressed region, where he fulfilled the duties of priest, parish secretary, and youth director. He still found time to work on his latest book, a history of the church's scant efforts to convert Native Americans along the frontier of the thirteen original colonies. His experience and knowledge of ministry was more mature than that of Joe, who willingly drove many miles to a neighboring diocese for these appointments. He often pulled to the side of the road on the way back home to make notes on their discussions.

They talked about the faith life and its special meaning for ordained ministry. They discussed their own sinful lives earnestly and with careful attention to Scripture. They explored the private regions of their thoughts, prayers, and personal struggles to be faithful to their calling, a very hard course at times in a world headed generally in the opposite direction. They discussed God's expectation of them for their families and the people they served. Since their first meeting, Joe had believed Lew Batterton possessed the indispensable quality for maintaining a faithful balance in the broken world, a sense of humor. As he was conscious of feeling better himself, he discovered subtleties and nuances in his spiritual director's conversation that he feared he had missed before. Batterton perceived meaning and purpose in brokenness. He could discern the presence of the cross in the whole chaotic spectrum of sinful humanity. He discussed Origen, Aquinas, Rahner, Barth, and Chardin as though he had known them personally, and his intimate appreciation of their teaching, and that of dozens of other theologians, astounded Joe. In him Joe recognized a character type that transcended culture, ethnicity, learning, and time. He was a thoroughly civilized human being with a compassionate appreciation for reason and order. In Batterton's case, it was a reflection of his belief in God. Joe had known his type before in other times and places: friends of his youth with whom he still fished and hunted each spring and fall, certain teachers over the years, many of his colleagues in law, and some members of the clergy. They all came to be themselves through varied paths, but each was a man or woman who lived with integrity. He counted it a special blessing that Harry Campos, the senior warden at his beloved Redeemer, was this type of human being. He thought of his parents, the secretaries in his law office, the family who toiled on the farm next door when he worked as a teacher. It was the quality he admired in Clyde Candler, whose path to truth, through the social sciences and counseling, resonated in Joe's theological meditations with Lew Batterton. Neither pious nor sanctimonious, they were all people of rare quality, without illusions about success or rewards in this transitory life. He believed his spiritual director would make a splendid bishop. At the same time, he had been ordained long enough to know that Batterton was too much a theologian and not enough a politician to be selected for that role.

Though his spirits had lifted, life was often still as stormy as the tropics in August. Whatever difficulties arose for Joe, however, sunlight and clarity broke through when he thought of Ted. The very sound of his son's voice was soothing. In the relentless disappointments of an alcoholic marriage and his frustrated hopes for Kate's recovery, he still had Ted. Ted had come of their marriage, and it was all good. His bishop's cool distance, the poverty of diocesan life, and the unending diocesan travel that always coincided with important family occasions were occupational hazards that he could bear. The negative handful of parishioners who despised him, and their peculiar ability to gain the bishop's ear, was manageable and unimportant when he thought of Ted. The perpetual balancing of limited time and resources and the chronic struggle and juggling of personalities and priorities were worthy of his most conscientious energy when he thought of Ted. His son was a gift of God to parents who loved him unconditionally. Something good and decent was coming into the world in Ted, a kindness and courage, a strong character who would be a blessing to everyone whose life touched his. It was a marvel for Joe, an inspiration at the core of his wondering fatherly heart and mind. He had his precious son for a time, he knew, in trust. It was his duty to send Ted out one day, prepared as well as Joe and Kate could manage, for what he would find.

* * *

Joe had tried to treat Catherine with the same respect and kindness he accorded his own parents. It was how they had raised him and what they expected of all their sons and daughters. He had failed along the way more times than he had gotten it right, a source of continuing personal anguish and guilt. Catherine had made it excruciatingly difficult. He had always acknowledged her consistency, even in that. She would mumble to his face the same sarcastic, painful falsehoods she said about him behind his back. When he tried to make peace between her and Kate in their pitiless competition and bickering, Catherine would seize the opportunity to join Kate's side against him every time, even when he tried to resolve disputes in Catherine's favor. It had been a hard relationship, a triangle in which he had assumed his position before he knew it. If he kept quiet and let the two of them go at each other, the whole atmosphere at home became bitter and filled with tension, Kate's part of which, in due course, was directed toward him. Raising Ted in such unpleasantness was wrong, and he would eventually intercede to preserve a kinder atmosphere. He told himself that relationships between mother and daughter were better at their beloved Wicomico Island. The vacation mood of the place and Ted's ability to play outdoors and roam the beaches and dunes made it less tense.

The only factor that diminished Catherine's contempt for Joe was age. The older she became, and feebler and more dependent, the happier she seemed at his attention. By a year or so before her move into the nursing home, she had grown too feeble to secure and use alcohol. She seemed to understand that a drink or two might be all it would take to kill her. So the last year had been easier on all of them. When Ray packed her away to Georgia, he found a weaker, quieter, more compliant, vastly older mother. Joe bought a half-dozen books of postal cards, scenes of flowers and birds, historical places on the East Coast, lighthouses, ships—subjects that appealed to Catherine. He left the collection depicting the Italian wine industry, with its merry scenes of women and children stomping grapes, and the series of vintage Scotch Whisky labels, in the store. Every Sunday night before bed, he wrote out a card, bringing Catherine up-to-date about Kate's health and teaching and Ted's schoolwork and athletics, and mailed it on Monday morning on his way to Redeemer. He made Ted write to his grandmother every few weeks, which he did obligingly and quickly.

In the week following her departure, Kate advised that the nursing home manager had called to ask them to pick up Catherine's television. Ray had left it behind, and they learned for the first time that private sets were not allowed in Ray's Georgia nursing home. It was bound to be jarring to Catherine, for whom television and a remote control had long provided her only entertainment. When Kate inquired about it, Ray assured her that the new place had a television "in the big room, where they'd all go during the day." Did this mean she sat up all day with a few dozen others, at the mercy of attendants who drifted through now and then and changed the channels? No, said Ray, and besides, "people that age all like the same sort of shows anyway." As to further details, he was vague.

Kate accepted it and never mentioned it again. Joe found it lingering in his mind, the increasing value of small kindnesses and courtesies, the heightened significance of small comforts to the elderly and helpless, the need for extra care and attention that grows in everyone in old age. He had visited parishioners and friends in a hundred elderly care facilities. They were cheerful and very well-run, most of them. Where someone—a manager, director, nurses—set a standard for warmth and courtesy, it was often evident as soon as one entered. Others, though clean, were managed by business types intent upon meeting state and federal standards and not much more. He recognized such places by a cool silence that became apparent soon after entering. He prayed that Catherine's was not such a place.

Kate drove down for a visit after six months, during her spring vacation. Joe encouraged her to fly, but she preferred to drive and have the car at hand. She stayed at a motel, where she spent the visit reading by the pool when not seeing Catherine. Eventually, she telephoned Ray and Fawn and ended up going by for a short visit on the day she departed.

Kate reported to Joe that every one of his postcards was lined up like trophies on her mother's bureau and the windowsill beside her bed. Catherine informed her cheerfully that Joe wrote to her every week, as though she might not know. Kate had found Catherine seated in a wheelchair in a corridor with other patients. She shared a small tidy bedroom with another resident, who slept all day. Kate was satisfied that the place was adequate, although by no means as bright and comfortable as the one they had found.

She said that when she left, she realized that she might not see her mother again and had thought about it on the drive back. It was touching upon a matter far more personal and emotional than it was in Kate's nature to express, and Joe was genuinely touched. He saw her contemplation of her mother's death as healthy, realistic, preparing her for what was to come by facing reality while the waters were still relatively calm. He encouraged her to talk more about it and gave her plenty of time to do so. Whether she realized that he was trying to be helpful, or whether she just needed some comforting after her long drive, he did not know. But she came to him and sat beside him on the living room sofa and allowed him to hold her hand while she talked. He was grateful. Although much of what she said was travel observations, he knew the whole journey must have been strenuous and emotional. He listened while she said everything she wanted to say.

Six months later, Kate was suffering from a bad cold, and running a slight fever, and sleeping in the guest room for a few nights so Joe wouldn't catch it. She didn't hear the phone at 7:00 a.m. She and Ted were used to Joe receiving calls at all hours. The night nurse in Georgia informed Joe kindly that Catherine had "passed. She passed in her sleep. Mr. Stephenson. Never woke up. It was peaceful. We all liked her so much. She was a pretty little lady."

He went down to the kitchen and prepared a Coke for Kate, who did not like coffee, before waking her. He gently explained what the call was about and kissed her. As soon as he said the words "the nurse at...," she sat up quickly and asked, "Did she die?" They talked a while, and Kate cried a little, silently. They went downstairs. As Kate was preparing to call Ray, the phone rang. He had just been informed and was calling to report the news. He was vexed to learn they had been called before him.

Chapter Three

I N HIS FIRST year of college, lonely and with little money, Joe accepted an invitation from a chaplain to join a student retreat at a mountain lodge in the Blue Ridge. The spiritual dry spell he was in had lasted since halfway through his senior year in high school and had gone on so long he could barely remember the days when he took God more seriously. He had no interest in anything to do with the church. In this, he was like all his best friends, except that their disaffection had begun long, long before his. He found it impossible to pray, and pointless, and when he did recover the elusive ability, for brief periods, he poured out prayers of escape—from bad grades, longing for his high school girlfriends, life with no money, constant anxiety over disappointing his parents, his grandmother, his brothers and sisters. He accepted the invitation to this retreat because the chaplain had been friendly to him and he feared that this rotund young priest, who had spent much time organizing the retreat, would be hurt by a low turnout. Everyone believed the chaplain was queer; his fussy animation provided standard fare for jokes and mimicry. But everyone agreed he was a decent sort anyway. They regarded him as entirely harmless, sincere, and a bit embarrassing.

But Joe joined the retreat largely because he was lonely. His friends from home had joined fraternities, which cost money. Joe had no money, and first-year students were not permitted to hold jobs. He knew that the small amounts sent him by his parents and grandmother represented sacrifices by good people who were getting along on little and who were proud of being able to support his education. He winced each time he cashed their checks, generous contributions of five or ten dollars to his well-being. In those days, he could eat for a week on five or six dollars. Life's smallest expenditures—a toothbrush, a hamburger—caused him guilt and shame, knowing what the people at home sacrificed for his being where he was.

The retreat was "free," which Joe took to mean that the cost had been covered by the chaplain's fund or a local church or the bishop, perhaps.

A rented school bus chugged the noisy group up rocky switchbacks into the mountains along a dirt road constructed many years before for horse-drawn carriages and, later, touring cars. The old bus was twice the length of the hotel vehicles that had once borne guests up from the railroad station by the river. In a few places, the patient driver had to back up and ease forward on a sharper angle to make the turn, undistracted by the raucous cheers and chatter in the seats behind him. The big bus rocked and lurched slowly upward, mountain laurel and rhododendron scratching at its sides and an occasional low limb making a noise on the roof like a snake slithering away. Through the dusty windows, Joe could see way down the slopes to the flat land and the distant ridges beyond, and several times he caught a flash of sunlight reflecting on the river below. Even above the gaggle of voices, he could hear the whine of cicadas in the trees along the road, singing their hymn to the coming autumn.

The vast rambling mountain lodge stood in a lofty saddle between two higher ridges. A grove of magnificent oaks, many of them several hundred years old, clustered around the sagging main building and among its smaller dependencies, and the whole complex was surrounded by a pleasant meadow that curved gently upward to the thick forest on the north and south. On the east and west, the land fell off and away, affording dazzling views of the distant blue valleys and mountains that impressed even the jocks and business majors in the group. The meadow had been mowed earlier that day, and the wide porches around the hotel had received a new coat of green and white trim earlier in the season, and the whole effect was entirely inviting. Generations of families had retreated here in the days before air-conditioning, seeking breezes and waters and respite. Like most of the other venerable mountain hotels, this one had a mineral spring, whose copious outflow could be heard crashing through the forest a few hundred yards away. These days the elderly owners booked only special groups: hunting parties, art clubs, hiking associations, and an occasional wedding. They had accepted these rollicking college students into their antique bedrooms and rustic dining hall because the leadership of a chaplain seemed a guarantee of decorum. They all agreed it was a beautiful place. The chaplain signaled his enthusiasm by shuffling a few yards into the meadow and back, whooping and waving his arms, embarrassing everybody.

The church had rented the place before, because in the drawer of his bedside table, Joe discovered a blue hardbound copy of William Temple's *Nature, Man and God.* He was alone in his room after compline, following which the group of forty or so young people had dispersed, some to drink alcohol down by the noisy stream, some to cuddle and have sex in the abundance of secluded places, and a few, like him, to nurse their loneliness in their rooms. He knew a couple of girls on the retreat but was too shy to approach them.

He did not yet know if he would have to suffer with a roommate, the room assignments having been hastily made by the young chaplain on the way up the mountain. He expected to be interrupted suddenly at any moment, while he was masturbating beneath the sheets or having succeeded finally in getting to sleep, by a drunken upperclassman who would fall on the opposite bed and snore hoarsely through the night.

Joe took a long shower and brushed his teeth. He sat outside in an Adirondack chair on the flagstone terrace in the moonlight in his pajama bottoms, listening to the music of the night. The distant cries of revelers drifted up from the rushing stream. He desperately hoped the chaplain would not happen by. The rough, cool stones felt good beneath his feet, and the warm night air was arousing. In the trees and along the darkened paths, mournful insects sang in unison, making their incessant best of the last few balmy nights before the autumn chill.

One of the girls in the group had appealed to him fiercely. His erection had lasted the whole way up on the bus, and he almost shot off at the delicious casual slap of her hand on his shoulder. As she moved up and down the aisle, her gardenia scent floated along with her like incense. She had bantered hysterically from the moment they boarded until they thundered off in front of the wide hotel veranda. Jocks crowded around her, responding with inanities and grins, scrutinizing her every quiver as though they would like to eat her. Her image made him horny again, and he considered pulling down his pajama bottoms and jerking off in the warm moonlight. The mere thought of it was arousing, but the voices in the hemlocks below made him hesitate. The thought of the chaplain emerging from the shadows as he ejaculated, or spies in the trees recounting the lurid scene to everyone at breakfast, was withering. He could already imagine himself memorialized in college folklore, being expelled, and disgraced before family and friends. Rattled with nerves, he decided to trade the sensuality of the dark for the protective custody of his bunk. Always too cautious, too careful, too cognizant of disappointing those who had sacrificed to send him here. Perhaps his father was right: *The trouble with you is, you think too much.* He could imagine the look on his parents' faces as they read the chaplain's dreadful letter: "I regret to inform you that, unfortunately, it has been necessary to ask Joseph to disassociate himself from our fellowship. On a recent spiritual retreat, he was interrupted in the most compromising circumstances. Although of no potential harm to anyone else, his proclivity easily can become the source of much personal grief for him if not tempered by appropriate counseling…" And no doubt the well-meaning chaplain would be up to the task, if only his parents would order Joe to avail himself, and so forth.

As he had no female companion, and not enough courage to wander off into the woods, what could have been a solitary pleasure gave way to discretion. The others had whiskey, he knew. He had smelled it on the bus and on his companions at dinner. He would have loved to have some. He could have guzzled it without ice or water, straight from the bottle. But he had none, and he was too shy to join the group carousing by the water.

Sometime between ten and eleven, he went into his room and lay down on the bed. In the small bedroom, with the door held open by a round rock and window sashes propped up with sassafras sticks, the sounds of the early-autumn night flooded in. He could not hear the party crowd from inside, but he could hear a screech owl pleading in a tree nearby, and what he thought was a distant whip-poor-will. There were no books around, and he had brought nothing to read. Television in such places was unheard of then. He considered putting on his jeans and going to the lobby in search of a magazine but was reluctant to risk meeting the chaplain and having to chat with him for a while. In the drawer of the rickety bedside table, he found Temple's book. He opened it and began to read at the preface.

The most agreeable experiences in life are those which are marked by a coincidence of duty and pleasure.

It was tedious. It made little sense. Who was this Temple, anyway? He had vague memories of the name, perhaps from sermons as he crouched in the pews as a child, staring at the girls in the pew in front of him and nursing his erection. For inexplicable reasons, and despite his fatigue and better judgment, he read on.

All my decisive thinking goes on behind the scenes; I seldom know when it takes place—much of it certainly on walks or during sleep—and I never know the processes which it has followed.

Ah, here's something that makes sense, he thought to himself. What is it about dreams? Something from *Moby Dick.* "Never dream with thy hand on the helm! Turn not thy back to the compass." Well, what little helm he had managed to grasp in life never stopped his dreaming, and he was still waiting to find out where the compass was. Shit. He read on. And on.

In time, the shouting by the stream died down to silence together with the night noises of the forest. The big September moon brightened the treetops and rock breaks along the ridge above the lodge. Cool air flooded in through the windows and door. A critter of some sort, a raccoon or possum, rattled something outside and scampered off into the woods. No drunken roommate appeared. By the time the blue dawn began to glow in the windows and door and the songbirds had begun their cheerful matins, Joe had arrived awake and alert, as he had never been before, at The *Sacramental Universe*. He read on.

> *We are confronted therefore with this fact: in many forms of religion, and conspicuously in the most extensive tradition of Christianity, prominence is given to rites in which the spiritual and the material are intimately intertwined. That proves nothing, but for those who on other grounds expect to find in religion guidance for the ultimate interpretation of reality, it is suggestive.*

As the sun gladdened the treetops, he finished Temple's book. Stunned, whether from the book or something else he could not have said, he wandered along the terrace and down the steep path to the cold, bright stream. He was barefoot on the rocks, but he did not notice. On a wide flat boulder, he pulled off his pajama bottoms and flung them aside with no thought to where they landed. A mist drifted above everything and followed the noisy water down the narrow gorge.

He eased his skinny body into the water and lay on the bottom with his head upstream, propped against a rounded stone. The stream, not as cold as he might have imagined, plunged over his shoulders and around him in a cleansing surge, drenching his hair and sleepy, sunburned face when he hunkered down. Through the shade of his narrowed eyelids, he could see his toes breaking the surface downstream, as though miles from him, brown and still against the receding torrent. He allowed his eyes to close. A crow called in the distance.

*Rites in which the spiritual and material are inti-
mately intertwined…to find in religion guidance
for the interpretation of reality.*

Emerging and receding in the darkness behind his closed eyelids were the yellow fields of Arles, Monet's blossoming meadow at
Argenteuil, Renoir's luscious *Nude in the Sunlight.* Reality.

*Once out of nature, I shall never take my bodily
form from any earthly thing…nor beauty born out
of its own despair.*

After a little while, he got up and sat on the flat rock in the sun
until he was dry. He was not tired, although he suspected he would
be later in the day. Somewhere, a bell incessantly signaled breakfast.
Quite uncharacteristically, he walked halfway up the path before he
realized he was naked. He returned to the rocks for his pajamas in an
old sense of propriety that was even then fast changing into something far less conventional. He could feel a movement, clarity.

Nobody paid him much attention for the balance of the retreat.
Formerly, such anonymity would have suited him entirely, but now
he took no notice of himself. It left him free. During small group
discussions and during the chaplain's talks, he listened and watched.
Joe was already quite used to watching. He drank in details with the
urgency of one who anticipates his own compulsion to draw or paint
his surroundings. He consumed lines, forms, spaces, textures, and
always colors, the infatuating tints and hues of reality, like a parched
man gulping water or a connoisseur savoring wine. He found himself
listening now in the same way. A way of observing that had grown
in him for eighteen years was suddenly paired with another perception that seemed to have occurred in him overnight, and with equal
intensity. It was the closest he would ever come to revelation, and
he might have even missed it in a less-conducive context. To anyone
who noticed him, nothing was different. He was the same short, thin,
quiet type as before, a nonentity who would have been good-looking
but for his constant expression of sadness and perplexity.

But something in Joe had quietly and calmly turned a corner. With Temple's book, he had altered course on a small angle that grew wider and more profound as he moved forward from that night, largely unknowing, on an inexplicable, new trajectory. A gradually unfolding, internally consistent transformation had begun and would continue for the rest of his life, undramatic and imperceptibly slow, but relentless and infallible. His was not a conversion experience, but a long, slow movement in a homeward direction, a journey fraught with wrong turns and false starts, detours into cul-de-sacs and long periods off his lead, like a bad rider on a green hunter, and the way continually interrupted by obstacles and hazards. In later life, he would see it as a wonder that he had stayed the course, but he would grow to understand how every setback and slipup, demoralizing and discouraging as they surely were, made him stronger and, in the end, wiser.

The human dilemma. A spiritual dimension. The church was a repository of moral and ethical guidance that allowed human beings to come as close as was conceivable in this world to understanding ultimate meaning. It all fit into an immeasurably larger reality: the whole of creation and its Creator.

Despite its troubled history and his own ignorance, Joe had viewed the church as a pool of sanity in a crazy world. He saw its leaders, with all their frailties and unfashionable alienation, as guardians of truth and all the other qualities that make life sacred. He did not always understand theologians, but he saw them, in the world and in his own confused life, as inviolable bulwarks against the crashing seas of sin and ignorance. When at last he answered the call to holy orders after years in the law, he entered the church with a liberating sense of approaching, as closely as one could in this world, to truth.

He saw his birth, family, marriage, wife, son, and friends—all the blessings of his life—as preparation and validation for spending his days in ordained ministry. Witch hunts, Alexander VI, the Inquisition, persecution of Jews, the Black Hundreds, destruction of the Cathars, conversion of Native Americans by the sword—he knew about it all. He concluded that such infamy was behind the human race now, where the church influenced the course of things.

In no sense did he imagine himself a leader in the church. Had he been single and childless, he would have served a parish in a ghetto or the missionary field, where he knew such idealism as still afflicted him would meet the gritty hide of reality. He could not have expected Kate to accept such a life, and he was not yet faithful enough to subject his child to such suffering for the sake of his own ideals. Let others lead and administer. Had he yearned for that, he would have stayed in the law. He would spend his time as a parish priest in America, as hazardous an outpost on the front lines of the kingdom as any assignment in Columbia or Borneo.

These convictions bore him up through years of turbulence. He remained faithful in the trials of parish ministry, a troubled marriage, difficulties in his extended family, physical suffering, and emotional fatigue. Diocesan responsibilities, superimposed on his shepherding one of the largest parishes in the state, with no assistance, and an uninvolved, faultfinding spouse took their toll. He believed God would not give him more to bear than he could stand. He tried to carry on with honesty and competence. He paid as little attention as possible to small matters, apologized for his errors and moved on, and tried—with better success than average, he supposed—to be cheerful in outer and inner turmoil. On the whole, he was more successful in his vocation than in his marriage, an acknowledged failure that always troubled him deeply. But he loved his wife, son, and friends and found great validation in them all and in his calling. He trusted the church. He believed that those who endure to the end would find their way home.

Chapter Four

ALMIGHTY GOD, MAKER *of all things, Judge of all human-kind, I know that this is reaching your heavenly throne, and I know that you hear me as a good parent hears his child's pleas. Please forgive my sin and my ignorance and listen to my prayer. I need to tell you I am losing hope. If you want me to go on, to keep trying, you will have to step in now and take away from me my confusion and frustration, make me clean and whole, and show me what to do. I can't handle it. I never could. I am powerless over any of it. Kate is your child. You created her. For me to fulfill my vows to her and to you, I need you to take over now and do whatever it is you are inclined to do. And whatever that might be, and whenever you might be pleased to do it, I confess to you that I can no longer be of service to her and to you, feeling as I do. I have no power over anything but myself and very little over that. I know you can change me, heal me, improve me, repair me, and make me clean and whole and acceptable to you. I ask you to strengthen my self-control, drain away my frustration, cut the disappointment out of me like coring an apple, and cleanse me of impatience and bitterness like gutting a fish. And most of all, in the name of our Lord Jesus Christ, take away this burning anger that sickens me. Take it away. Wrench it from my life. I am failing. I want to give it all to you. I plead with you, as a sinner trying hard to follow your commandments. I am not asking you to change Kate or the world. I am praying for you to give me the tools to change myself. I thank you for all the blessings of my life, my family, friends, and neighbors. I thank you for everything, and I pray you will have mercy on me, a sinner. Please hear my prayer, and in the name of Christ, please act now. Amen.*

Like a patient emptying his bedpan, he poured himself out on a cold November night in his quiet house as sleep came over the people he loved in their beds above him. Then he got up from the kitchen table and proceeded to what he needed most to do at the moment. He put on his running clothes and shoes and went out into the night. He ran down the winding drive and out along the country road, gulping in the air as though the clean, cold darkness would scour him of his ugly flaws. He ached to be free to cope with kindness. For a little while, he needed to put aside thoughts of God and Kate and his own brokenness and the whole damn weight of worry he had known since shortly after his wedding day.

As he ran, he revived for the first time in many months an old mechanism for relaxing. Since childhood, he had been able to replay in his head his parents' old LPs, records of classical and popular music that had filled his early years with an unrecognized joy. It was yet another blessing taken for granted by him and his brothers and sisters as they grew up with their parents in their tiny home. He could reproduce from memory the vanished sounds of the Hi-Lo's fantastic range, the golden tones of the Four Freshmen, Frank Sinatra, Ella Fitzgerald, and Billie Holliday. He could resurrect the style of different conductors or specific orchestras.

He began to hear Wilhelm Furtwängler conduct the Amsterdam Concertgebouw in the first and second movements of Beethoven's Seventh Symphony, a favorite of his parents, recorded while his young father was fighting the great conductor's countrymen in the thankless fields of France. In the poor, crowded household of his youth, with parents who gazed at the stars, he was being blessed in ways that supported him all the days of his life. They were private gifts, like this thrilling recollection of music, known only to him.

He marveled as the *Vivace* section of the first movement thundered and heaved while he paced his flying steps in unconscious ways to the basses and cellos and howling horns. The melancholy, solemn wistfulness of the second movement ("Sounds like a funeral march," said his mother. "It's too fast for that," replied his father, "too…uneasy") flowed in his mind without a hint of peace. He needed peace, and with the lemon taste of the clarinet melody lingering inside him, he began to pray the Jesus Prayer, coordinating the ancient syllables to his footsteps for almost a mile, a moving mantra, thumping out the petition mechanically, an unthinking admission of who he was and what he craved. *Jesus Christ, Son of God, have mercy.* Over and over, his footsteps keeping pace obediently, the soothing words revolved within him. For a mile or two, as he had done long ago in running track and jumping rope, he counted his steps, oblivious of his direction or the distance between him and home.

He was suddenly at the lonely junction of two unmarked country roads. The spur to the left led off through dark fields toward the home of one of Ted's school friends. This was a corner he had turned many times in taking his son there to visit, or in picking up Ted's friends to bring them home for weekends. A hundred faces and voices stirred within him, welling up in the stillness as he bent over, facing the gravel, a torrent within and around him as though somewhere a dam had given way. Through the chaos, like a swimmer surfacing into the light, his son's precious image came forward to meet his inward eye, smiling, with the look Joe knew meant he had heard something amusing and wanted to tell him about it, a bit of shadow darkening his upper lip, wearing his favorite baseball cap. Kate appeared, looking through to him, as she was during summers by the sea, relaxed, calm, and satisfied. Even at this lonely place and late hour, Joe felt tears rising within him. They gathered to his eyes, and he coughed a little and put his hands over his sweating face as he bent forward in the dark, conscious of the pain that had troubled his insides for days.

Where were you when I laid the foundations of the earth? boomed a voice in his head, a reply late but distinctly pertinent. It echoed in his imagination with an awful clamor and seemed to burst out and disperse in solid pieces over the dark fields.

"How about a little 'comfort ye, comfort ye, my people'?" he said aloud in the night. For a few seconds, he surprised himself and laughed at the absurdity of the scene. He was glad there were no witnesses.

See what I have done for you? You! Out of all the world! And will you caution me? I made Behemoth as I made you! Inseparable. Purposeful. One. I understand the way. I know the plan. It is I who do all these things...

Leaping forward like a deer, he set out toward home, his feet seizing the broken asphalt with a reckless purchase, distance and ground disappearing behind his long lanky strides, outrunning the presence in his mind. Miles of jogging had brought him to the crossroads, but strange adrenaline urged him homeward at a speed he had not experienced in years. He ran the hills of the undulating, crumbling road like a smooth straightaway, slowing for nothing, sidestepping a few late pickup trucks, and outrunning hysterical dogs that burst in spasms from darkened farm lanes. He felt he could have crossed the rugged fields and jumped the fences and creeks like an Irish hunter. In what seemed mere minutes, Cory was leaping toward him near his mailbox and accompanying him merrily along the drive to the house, sniffing his shoes and sweatpants carefully for news of his journey.

He reached home in half the time it took him to run out. Leaving his wet clothing draped on a drying rack in the garage, he turned out the lights and went up quietly to the shower. When he came out, he found his flashlight and checked on Ted, set his alarm clock, and got into bed beside his sleeping Kate. His usual course was to lie awake, hoping for sleep. Whether from the exertion of his body or the fatigue in his mind he could not say, but he must have fallen asleep immediately. The next thing he knew, his alarm clock was emitting its noxious whine.

For days thereafter, he went about his homelife and ministry with as little thought of God as possible. Closing God completely from his mind was like trying not to breathe; it was never entirely possible and was only effective—more an appearance than reality—for a short time. But he supposed he had come near enough to need a little recuperation. He could imagine the disappointment of the bishop and the incredulity of his brothers and sisters in clergy at the thought of such insolence and disregard, the shameful challenging that surfaced in his rambling prayers. It made no difference to him; it was what he needed at the moment, whether anyone understood it or not. He was confident that God understood, just as he himself had understood when his infant son had become discomforted and cried as a baby.

In the following days, he had to buy gasoline for a three-hour drive to and from a two-hour regional clergy meeting. Kate had the checkbook. The greasy old owner of the service station, whose wayward daughter Joe had visited in jail several times at her father's embarrassed request, allowed him to take the gasoline on credit, a thing he had not done for anyone else in fifteen years. At home that night, after preparing dinner for Ted and himself, he sat down wearily to pay the monthly bills and accepted as a sign of progress his own calm recollection that Kate still had the checkbook. His schedule would prevent him from paying bills for another three nights, and he was a little late this month already, but it couldn't be helped.

It was the time of month when Joe worked on the family bills, but Kate nevertheless held on to the checkbook for days. It was her practice to make him ask for it. He knew what he would find when he received it, but he had not asked for it this time. He was certain the need to manage his own foreboding was more important than whatever surprises she had for him, or penalties they would be charged for overdrawal. By not asking for the checkbook, he was conscious of behaving in as juvenile a way as Kate. It was ridiculous for grown people to play such games. After all these years, her inexplicable unwillingness to simply talk with her own husband about money and future finances remained a mystery to him. He knew the theological issue was control, but how to understand the psychology of her behavior was beyond him.

When she returned home late one evening following a faculty meeting, he listened patiently while she talked about the irritating positions various people had taken on the school budget and related financial issues and the ridiculous responses made by Hervey to their suggestions. A few nights later, in preparing a few things for the next day, he found the checkbook beneath his briefcase on a dining room chair, where he was supposed to see it as he departed for work the following morning. He did not examine it until he went to the service station the following day to pay for his gasoline. He saw that

Kate had not recorded two checks and that a third one was noted but without an amount. A fourth had been written to cash for two hundred dollars, without explanation. He simply put it away and, that night, when he sat down to pay the bills, mentioned that he had to balance their account and asked her quietly to record her checks. She rummaged around in her pocketbook for a moment, went quickly out to her van, and then handed him several long white sales receipts. She walked away without comment. He thanked her and said no more and tried to match the missing checks with the receipts.

He spent most of the following Saturday raking leaves around the house and away from the heat pump and wheeling big barrows of them way down to the end of the yard to the compost pile. Kate did not offer to help, nor did he ask her. She sat inside all day, reading, watching television, and trying to telephone the one friend she had in the community whom she knew well enough to call for a chat. He could imagine the bishop's angry, corrective advice. "You should go in and sit with her and listen to whatever she has to say. Forget the leaves. They'll wait." Maybe so, he thought, but three more weekends would pass before he could tend to the yard again—two Saturdays spent in diocesan meetings. He knew if he directed Ted to rake them, their son would appeal to Kate in his absence and she would find something to justify letting him off the hook.

He raked and thought, his mind working as steadily and forcefully as he swept his wide rake, gathering in leaves and ruminations together. He recited "Sailing to Byzantium" and as much as he could remember of "A Prayer for My Daughter," a poem he had always loved, so much so that strangely he found it harder to remember than works he favored less. He spoke out loud a poem by W. H. Auden that he though was called "If I Could Tell You." He sang aloud "The Man Who Shot Liberty Valance," "Knocking on Heaven's Door," and the theme song to *High Noon*. He listened for a while in his head to part of Mozart's *Quartet for Piano and Strings in G Minor*. He reviewed in silence the following day's sermon. He thought about last spring's fishing trip and the fun he'd had seeing old friends.

On the following Monday, he tried to organize dinner with friends at a restaurant for the following Friday evening. Kate announced she could not go because of a student dance at a nearby girl's boarding school. She was going along on the bus with Ted and the St. John's students as a chaperone. "Remember?" When they had coordinated calendars two weeks earlier, as Joe insisted they do toward the end of each month, she had said nothing about a student dance or any other commitment on Friday night. Years in the law had made him a careful keeper of his calendar. Had she really said something? Had he gotten it wrong? He had not written anything down for that evening, and he said so, calmly and without emphasis. When she became nervous and began to defend herself, her memory, her calendar, her schedule, he listened and did not argue. Would she be able to go the following night, Saturday? His calendar showed nothing for her then either. Yes, she said, as long as she wouldn't be too tired for the next day. Wearily, like a put-upon servant, she explained she had to get up early the next morning and be at the St. John's alumni Sunday service by eleven o'clock. "I have to work, remember? And on one of my few days off!" This, too, had not been mentioned before, or if it had, he had uncharacteristically failed to note it on his calendar. Nor did he understand her distress about her "early" Sunday morning. For years, he had risen at 5:00 a.m. and left the house by six, a regimen she carefully ignored when waiting impatiently for him to accompany her somewhere upon his return in the afternoon. But he did not argue and went ahead with making the arrangements for Saturday night. He would have preferred to go out on Friday, but he would go Saturday night, without objection.

He suggested she call some of her colleagues at St. John's and invite them too. They could all meet at the restaurant. He knew the risk of dinner conversation turning into a catty discussion of student personalities and school politics between Kate and other teachers, but he enjoyed many of her colleagues; they were friendly and fun, and their spouses were often very good company. Including a few couples from Catoctin Springs would safely enlarge the talk.

Kate was opposed to asking anyone from St. John's and, as usual, would not elaborate. She would complain later that the people from Catoctin Springs were his friends, not hers, and that she found them boring with their talk of sports, international news, politics, and movies. But no, she would not invite the people she worked with. It was another of the mysteries he was still seeking to understand after seventeen years of marriage. He tried to encourage her to relent, suggesting everyone could meet at their house for a drink before going on to a restaurant. But no, she would not agree. She was tired and had to get up in the morning. "I have to work. Remember?" She did, however, take interest in who he might invite from their side of the river. He suggested a few couples. None of them seemed quite right to her. With her usual predilection for determining character from mannerisms, she discounted each suggestion because of something said once, somebody's accent, or a small misunderstanding. He began to analyze her objections, wondering whether these people—professionals, most of them—made her feel threatened somehow, or bored. But as soon as he realized what he was doing, he stopped and accepted what she said and moved on.

* * *

For many years, Joe's summer vacation days were planned for the middle of August so that he could help with closing the old beach house, packing up the family belongings, and moving everyone back home in time for Kate to prepare for fall classes. His summer vacation with his family in Wicomico should have been relaxing. Everybody assumed it was, including Kate. For years, Joe pretended that it was, too. In truth, although it had its pleasant moments, it always turned out to be a time of stress.

By the time he arrived at the old house, Kate was filled with irritation at the cumulative frustrations of renting to vacationers and disappointed at having to leave the beach and return to work. He understood that she was exasperated and wanted to stay. Anyone would have felt the same. The weather in late August was usually glorious. The great cumulus clouds piled up for miles into the sky above the islands like mountains of meringue, and the blue of the sea and the distance was scintillating. Especially lovely were the nights, whether moonlit or filled with stars, when balmy breezes washed through the wide porches among the rocking chairs and the nearby surf made a delicious crushing sound in the dark. One was tempted to sit out all night long, enjoying the rarity of being there. Joe longed for a month like that together with Kate and Ted, with nowhere to go and nobody to wait on, uninterrupted days to enjoy one another, with the beautiful old place to themselves. He dreamed of when they were both retired and could spend as long together in the old house as the weather allowed. Visions of Ted and his own family visiting them there made his heart feel warm and alive. He talked with Kate about it as he daydreamed during the year, and she agreed that retirement was something she certainly looked forward to. Whether it was purely his imagination, or whether he detected something that even Kate herself did not mean to convey, he always thought he heard in her responses a feint exclusionary note, as though his imagining his retirement in her house was, somehow, presumptive.

By the time he arrived at the old house in late August, year after year, Kate was disgruntled and agitated and in no mood to understand anyone else's situation. What Joe wanted desperately was some time to do nothing but relax. It was a troubling combination.

Days he longed to spend wandering the beach—when he accomplished some of his best thinking and planning and praying—he passed in boutiques and shopping malls with Kate as she searched the end-of-season sales for new clothes. He went along because she asked him to go, and he had been away from her for weeks and wanted to be with her. He went also because she had, by then, spent all her summer earnings and was drawing upon family finances. How much her summer earnings amounted to, or what she did with them, she would not say, disguising the subject in dozens of clever ways and refusing to provide any explanation when, months later, she paid taxes and insurance out of what Joe had saved from their salaries. She would spend three or four times as much if she were on her own, so Joe went along on these end-of-season shopping trips, which lasted most of the day. They always lunched in good restaurants and browsed leisurely in department stores. But for the proliferation of flip-flops and swarms of fat people in bathing suits, it was no different from being in the big stores back home. He told himself all this was important to her—she loved to shop, and it seemed to relax her and cheer her up—and he was her husband and this was what she needed at that moment. Any fatigue or discouragement he experienced was his own fault. Other husbands and wives sacrificed for their families. He could do it, too, and he would. Still, as they traipsed about the shopping malls, he longed to be on the beach.

He had largely given up trying to discuss important matters or his own feelings with Kate. It was so much easier not to do so and, as much as possible, to give in and become a part of her self-absorbed rush and routine. Her obsession with school schedules, lesson plans, and the world of St. John's School was the last thing he wanted to hear about in these precious few days by the ocean with his family. It never occurred to Kate that he had been working hard, whether as attorney or priest, or that he needed a rest, some days to relax without demands or schedules, some quiet time. She interpreted his efforts in these directions as signs of his abandoning her, his own wife, and she responded with a blend of anger and hurt. She took no notice of demands upon him. She forged ahead mindful largely of herself and Ted and living as though everyone else composed a supporting cast. He could never escape the conviction that he should have been capable of finding a way to some loving truce with her over the years and that his failure to do so was another of his faults.

They would spend a couple of days packing up, cleaning out the refrigerator and the house, returning library books, going to the dump, washing the final loads of sheets and towels, and assembling all the porch furniture in a pile in the breezeway between the house and the old detached kitchen, where it would be protected from storms. Later, when Joe began to come down for a week in early September and after several attempts by somebody to break in, they began leaving the porch furniture in place as a sign that someone was coming and going.

Upon their return home, Kate would disappear into the world of St. John's like a cabinet officer taking charge of a department of government. Sometimes she would not even unpack her bags until October. Chairs and the guest room beds would remain draped with summer clothes and beach accessories until the weather got cold. Clutter proliferated throughout the house, jarring Joe's sense of visual order and stirring up his emotional longing for harmony and discipline.

As his inner distress grew more frequent and painful, Joe was compelled to act in his own behalf, going down to the old house for the first week of September, after Kate had returned home. The peace and quiet were soothing and restorative. No matter what weather prevailed in those precious days, he stayed happily at the house and read, drew in his sketchbooks, wrote songs and stories occasionally, or swam and walked the beach. He fished in the early morning and late afternoon, although it would be many weeks before the bluefish and the occasional striped bass would run again. Kate brought their big color television from home to the beach with her each summer and took it with her when she departed. There was a small black-and-white TV in the dining room, which he turned on now and then to hear a weather report. Otherwise, he paid no attention to it. Except for a few trips to the grocery store, his car remained parked in the drive the whole time. To others, it might have seemed a boring, uneventful "vacation." To Joe, it was exactly what he needed.

Kate had stopped cleaning about mid-August, when school began in the southern jurisdictions and the summer renters began to return to their inland homes. By his arrival, the window screens were opaque with dust and brine and dust drifted in fuzzy clumps beneath the beds and furniture. "There is no dust at the beach!" she had told him for years. "There's no dirt, just sand. So there can't be any dust." In spite of his allergies to house dust, he was not prepared to clean upon arriving for vacation, although it made it hard for him to sleep in the house. The neighboring cottages were blissfully empty, so no one was disconcerted when he set up a cot on the wide porch and slept outside.

Long walks on the lonely beach worked on him like a seda-tive. His quiet mind filled with ideas for stories and novels, solutions to problems, creative plans for the fall and winter, and always with thoughts of the people he loved. He prayed in thanksgiving for his family and for guidance in the future. He wanted to paint again. He would begin his novel this fall and establish a routine; he thought it would suit him best to write in the morning, before work, but was uncertain how to manage it. He looked forward to Ted's games and other school activities, and to having him home again after the absence of summer. He thought about his parents and hoped they would come for a long visit. It would make Kate happy, too, because she loved them dearly. They were delightful company, good sports, and adored their big far-flung family. Kate looked upon them as parents and best friends and cherished her time with them. They would all have to plan a visit as soon as he returned home.

He spent hours on the porch of the old house, drinking coffee and thinking, dreaming, watching the sea and the birds, and returning the waves of occasional passersby. For days he was not called upon to speak to anyone; Kate notified the phone company to disconnect service before she departed. At night, he ate, sometimes for the first time all day, read books he had saved for months, watched the stars, and slept with the sounds of the surf in his ear. With nobody around to fuss about it, he cleaned up at night in the open outdoor shower, where the summer guests rinsed off before coming onto the porch from the beach. Sometimes he sat naked on the porch steps, facing the sea in the dark, drying in the warm wind. Except for glimpses of him during the day, and the glow of his cigar on the porch at night, nobody would have guessed the house was occupied.

From the peace of these calming days, Joe returned home invigorated and determined to be a more attentive and patient husband and father, a more faithful priest, a friend of deeper sensitivity, a better teacher, a preacher of more clarity and humor, a better son and brother, neighbor, everything. Kate made no secret of her thinly veiled suspicion about what he could possibly have been doing in the off season all day for a week, why he insisted on going down after she had left, why he couldn't visit while she was there, like other husbands. Any real explanation offered would have only made matters worse. How could he explain to one who terminated any discussion at the slightest hint of disapproval that, as much as she meant to him and as devoted to her welfare as he was, her disposition and denial were wearing him down?

He had tried to make it clear in the past. He remembered rushing around and making all the arrangements for a visit to Wicomico in late July one year. His necessary preparations for leaving their home for a week, and his ministry, seemed hopelessly beyond Kate's comprehension. When she left for any length of time, her responsibilities were suddenly out of mind and she never looked back. In a way, it was an ability he envied. He supposed a touch of it would have made him more normal. He was always left behind to deal with everything.

The weeks preceding his final July visit had been filled with difficult, unavoidable situations. He had accompanied two families through their dying relatives' final hours and officiated at the two subsequent funerals. In one of them, a guilty out-of-town relative who had waited too long to visit and arrived following the death had tried to take charge of the funeral arrangements. Joe had experienced this sort of interference with weddings but had never before had it happen with a funeral. Although a nominal member of another denomination and not a regular churchgoer (said the other relatives), she believed herself to be entirely capable of orchestrating the funeral and clearly expected to be deferred to. The distracted, grieving family appealed to Joe, who informed the relative gently but firmly that he was in charge and arrangements would proceed as already planned. Like a bird of prey flocking to its own kind, the relative had complained to her old friend Lottie Bascomb, and together, they had telephoned the bishop himself to complain about Joe's high-handedness. The bishop, seriously displeased, had called Joe to inquire why he was being so insensitive to the needs of a grieving family. He requested that in the future Joe treat people of other denominations with due courtesy. Joe carefully explained the behavior of the relative and the exasperation of the grieving family at her unwanted meddling. He suggested once more that the bishop weigh anything reported to him by Lottie Bascomb with the greatest of care. He would have said more, but the bishop, who had listened in silence up to that point, told him there were people waiting to see him and to carry on.

At the second funeral, the deceased's distant cousin's husband, a Baptist minister, with the family's cautious consent, had asked to speak during the service. "For five minutes, Reverend," he said, "and not a second longer." He had droned on for a half-hour. His dia-tribe included several references to the unpardonable sin of homo-sexuality, plainly understood by everyone present as a reference to the deceased's distraught teenage grandson, whom everyone knew was gay and who was seated with the family in front of the pulpit. Following the service, Joe had spent hours with the boy, helping him begin to heal from his double wounds, and almost as long to con-vince his father not to seek out the preacher and beat him to a pulp.

The neighbor girl who had promised to feed Cory during Joe's time in Wicomico decided the day before his departure to go with friends to Ocean City, forcing Joe to call four kennels before finding one, forty miles from home, that had room for Cory. A middle-aged parishioner called from her doctor's office and asked Joe to join her there immediately. He dropped everything and went to the medical center, where he sat with her and her weeping husband while her doctor explained a diagnosis of breast cancer. She recommended sur-gery immediately, and it was scheduled for the following day. After the wife had been admitted to the hospital, Joe left her there with her husband and went straight to their home. The children would be returning from school, and he had agreed to stay with them until their father could see that his wife was safely settled in the hospital. These were popular people, very well-known in the community, and word of the situation would soon become known. Joe knew that being alone with the three children in their home would violate the church's stern guidelines against unaccompanied clergy being alone with other people's children. None of their neighbors were available to stay with them. The other parishioners he called did not answer. This was the sort of infraction on his part that Lollie was certain to report to the bishop, whose recent displeasure was fresh in Joe's mind. So when the children had all arrived home from school, he told them their father was on his way home and he went out and sat in the swing on the front porch while they came to the front door every three minutes to ask him to come in and play their new video game with them. When the father arrived, Joe joined them all for the explanation of their mother's situation. Then, at the father's urging, Joe walked around the block a dozen times with the emotional middle daughter. He answered her questions and searched for ways to relieve her anxiety over her mother's predicament, a situation he himself—remembering the doctor's explanation—viewed with foreboding.

None of this was unusual. It was the ordinary stuff of parish ministry, together with that morning's surprising leak in the new roof of the nave, yesterday's exciting gift of two thousand dollars from an out-of-state donor, a parishioner's unmarried teenage daughter's delivery on Monday of a dangerously premature baby, and the call from a priest in a distant parish—a man Joe had particularly admired for his handling of some sensitive diocesan issues—who advised Joe of his decision to retire from ministry and accept a teaching position on the West Coast. But each of these usual matters needed attention, prayer, pondering, and especially, listening. In every case, somebody needed to be listened to about something.

He slept a little late the next morning for fear of dozing off at the wheel during the long drive and deposited a woeful Cory at the kennel on his way through the mountains. By the time he got to Wicomico, plowing through the weekend traffic and concentrating as best he could on where he was going rather than upon the issues he was leaving behind, it was early evening. A new restaurant had opened, and Kate and Ted wanted to give it a try. In his happiness at seeing them, he would have agreed to anything, and he stepped immediately from his car into Kate's big van without even taking out his suitcase. Rentals everywhere were ending and beginning for a new week, and the roads were choked with traffic. They drove for miles, stopping and starting again in the stifling heat with no air-conditioning. It had stopped working as soon as Kate had arrived for the summer, and she told him that early the next morning, she wanted him to follow her fifty miles to an appointment at the nearest dealership to leave the van and bring her back. At the restaurant, they waited in line for a half-hour while Kate cheerfully told him about people he knew who had visited already or who were coming down later in the summer. Her face was tanned and relaxed and happy, and her voice, or as much of it as he could hear over the din of waiting customers, was music in his ears. Ted sat on his knee, facing away from him, observing the crowd, and Joe rubbed his bony back. Finally, they were seated at a table next to seven noisy young African American men, who behaved as if they had never before eaten at a table.

Again, none of this was out of the ordinary. It was life as usual. He knew his experiences were like everyone else's. He sat in the deafening din beneath the new restaurant's one inoperable ceiling fan while the others revolved sluggishly at a quarter speed, and ate a bite or two of his cold crab cake when it finally arrived. He couldn't take his eyes off his wife and son, whom he could see but not hear very well. He thought how much fun it would be to dine with them in the relaxed and friendly environs of the Third Base. It crossed his mind how pleasant it would be to have a fortifying glass of wine, and briefly he wondered if this was how Kate felt before she began a binge. He looked at his son's happy brown face and at his wife's lovely complexion, like the blush of ripe peaches, and drank in her healthy summer glow. She was cheerful and animated in her busy way as she explained how bright the moon had been the week before, whom she had seen in the grocery store, and about the many books she had read.

He was where he wanted to be, with his family, but his insides burned with an intensity that alarmed him. He was compelled to say apologetically that his stomach hurt and asked for Kate's car keys so he could go out and lie down for a moment. Kate and Ted looked at each other with wide eyes. Neither of them said a word. Kate said nothing as she fished her keys from her purse and handed them to him. He squeezed her arm sympathetically as he got up, knowing that he was destroying the happy mood. He couldn't help it. He went out to the van and opened all the windows and lay down on the back seat in the heat and closed his eyes. What breeze there was drifted through the windows above him, leaving him in a sweltering confine below. The neighboring cars were parked so close he could not open the van doors. He shut his eyes and slept for a bit despite the pain, and after forty-five minutes, Kate and Ted came out. They got into the front seat, talking busily, and drove home through the traffic without looking back at him or saying anything. He was used to this sort of thing from Kate. Ted's ignoring him seemed very odd, however. He attributed his son's indifference at that moment to his absorption in his mother's conversation. Still, it hurt almost as much as his side. It was so unlike the anxiety and sorrow he remembered as a child when he and his brothers and sisters perceived any sign of sickness in their parents.

When they arrived at Kate's house, he left his suitcase in his car and walked to the house with Kate and Ted while the two of them discussed which of the two rented videos they would watch that night. As they came up on the porch, Ted began to consult several barefoot children, guests for the week, about the evening's entertainment choices. Kate began to talk immediately with an older woman who, despite the evening hour, peered at them all through enormous dark eyeglasses.

Joe passed through this animated group quickly and went up to the family bedroom and lay down on the bed. It was soothing to lie in the darkened room with his eyes closed and feel the refreshing land breeze that stirred the lacy curtains. Sometime later, Ted bounded to the top of the steps to tell him they were starting the video, if he wanted to watch it with them. He got up and went downstairs and found a place on the sofa where he could prop his feet up on a cassock, almost like lying in bed. From this position, he could see the television clearly. A few feet in front of him, Ted sat in an ancient rocking chair, with his smiling face lit up by the glow from the screen. It was an excellent seat, he thought to himself, whether the movie was any good or not.

Chapter Five

JOE BELIEVED HE was living his life and coping with his marriage as honestly and decently as he knew how to do. In many ways, he was correct. His mistakes were as honest as his efforts, and he was able to learn from them and alter his course as he went forward. There was disappointment in the results of his striving, but with the striving itself, he believed he was doing everything he knew how to do. He had no doubt that other men could have handled it better, shown more sensitivity in opening the doors of communication and empathy, and been better listeners and sympathizers. He accepted advice willingly and tried to put it to work in his life. He planned ahead and put his wife and child first in everything. But despite everything, and especially his many friends, it was a lonely existence. As a clergyman, he would have been lonely anyway. It came with ordination. But striving to keep part of his battle a secret, even a secret for someone else's benefit, only enhanced his life's solitary feeling. Because he was astute enough to recognize that his life was largely a series of personal choices and that he alone was responsible for them, he did not fall into the seductive trap of self-pity. On the contrary, he perceived himself as blessed as any other man he knew. He felt actively and positively loved by God and therefore interpreted the universe as essentially benevolent. He sensed divine favor flowing into his life through his family, friends, and neighbors. If one area of his existence continued to be troubling, like an infected wound, he had only to look at the world around him to be reminded of how fortunate he was.

That perplexity hovered about his marriage—and his marriage was the most important relationship in his life—meant that everything else was influenced by it. He was wise enough to realize what was occurring, but too distracted and negligent to identify the consequences in all their ramifications. He lost his overview in the day-to-day details of living and coping. The result was that some of those close to him recognized small signs of stress and discontent without understanding their meaning.

Part of his dilemma, painfully evident to him, seemed to have no good solution. After seventeen years of marriage, he understood how useless his efforts had been to control Kate's drinking. He understood how Catherine's presence increased his own anxiety for what eventually would happen to Kate unless she accepted sobriety. He understood his own anger toward Kate for not realizing what her drinking was doing to their relationship, and he was able to forgive himself for it. Over the years, he had gradually achieved an understanding of how to manage his own life so as to leave Kate free to accept sobriety if she wanted it. He had learned the value of detachment with love, accepted the healing properties of courtesy, and acknowledged the absurdity and harm of trying to force solutions. His understanding of humility had matured, and the need for focusing on progress rather than perfection. Above all, rising above his role of enabler had confirmed for him the healing power of prayer, a spiritual experience as healing and comforting as anything he had ever experienced in church.

How had he acted out his God-given knowledge? By preventing Catherine from picking Ted up from his crib while she was drinking. It had meant talking sternly and graphically to Kate to convince her of the consequences to Ted of being dropped to the floor by his drunken grandmother. It meant preventing Kate from going out with Ted in the car during her own spells of drinking. As Ted grew older and more perceptive, Joe was less anxious for his physical safety but increasingly concerned for his emotional health. There was no doubt in Joe's mind of Kate's love for Ted; it was her judgment, her pattern of thinking, or not thinking, that drove him wild, and the unlikelihood of her maturing so long as alcohol continued to be a crutch in her life.

Joe was perplexed by Kate's scant concern for others' feelings and lack of guilt over her own conduct. Her want of empathy toward Joe and most others, and her difficulty forming long-term friendships, alarmed him. Was she able to feel empathy? Sympathy? He had thought so, but he had witnessed things done and left undone over the years that made him wonder now, and the uncertainty was terrible. He knew Kate manipulated him, and often he was not aware of it till long after the fact. He was confident that the longer she lived in the adult world, the more all this would be modified by normal interactions with mature people. She was intelligent. She would mature. But what was he to do in the meantime, during their precious son's formative years? Ted would have no second chances to be eight, ten, or twelve again.

Kate's refusal to accept responsibility for their domestic life and spending took place in front of Ted. He was a bright child, for whom Kate certainly shared credit, but was he not also being shaped by her superficial glibness? Many others perceived it, and dismissed it, even to Joe, as Kate "just being Kate." Wouldn't Ted perceive it, too, and take unintended guidance from it? She demonstrated an amazing blindness to sadness and other emotions in others. How could Joe let her learn from her own mistakes, if learning was in fact the right way to put it, while their son was doting upon her and growing up under her influence? What was the right thing to do? How should he handle it? He was entirely responsible for Ted.

For this dilemma, nobody could offer him specific guidance. Counselors taught Joe ways of encouraging Kate to join in therapy. None of it made any difference. They taught Joe how to identify his own faults and ways to go about changing himself, rightly believing that change in Joe would necessitate change in Kate. In some small ways, this worked, but the issues it resolved were rather obvious and external. If Kate's part of their clothes closet was a jumbled mess, he could encourage her to straighten it up by rearranging his own things in a different order. Although he kept his clothes in good order, the mere fact of his rearranging them would in time have Kate in the closet straightening up, folding sweaters and hanging up blouses. But what was happening in her interactions with Ted when Joe was not around?

Although he did not know the answer to this, he saw traits in Ted that reminded him of Kate. He ascribed them to the natural relationship between mother and child. He did what love compelled him to do. He worked at setting a good example for Ted, encouraging all those qualities he so desired for his son, and using all the tools of compassionate, positive reinforcement he had learned in his years of teaching. Ted responded with a cheerful, willing attitude toward Joe that attracted the attention of others. From early on, Ted was agreeable and obedient with Joe, so much so that Kate allowed Joe to manage matters in public that were likely to lead to small tantrums if handled by her. In social situations and restaurants, she silently deferred to Joe in feeding Ted vegetables or taking him away to change his diaper. When Joe put him to bed, Ted smiled and settled down and was asleep within a minute or two. Kate putting him to bed often meant arguing, a half-dozen trips to the bathroom, and fighting over each little responsibility. Kate's voice grew more strained and exasperated by the moment until both mother and son were so hyperactive and aroused that nobody in the house could get to sleep. For Joe to step in and settle them both down meant peace and quiet for the rest of that particular evening, but whatever example he had hoped to set had no effect upon Kate's parenting. She would approach it all the same way the next time.

He discussed his own responsibility in all this with his spiritual adviser, family counselor, and Al-Anon companions. He found he could not talk *about* Kate for very long with others, even others dedicated to guiding him, without beginning to feel guilty, as though participating in a shameful act of betrayal. She was his wife. Other people had rocky marriages, too, and got through them all right. Husbands and wives were meant to work out these problems in family life. His prayers were filled with pleas for guidance, understanding, patience, and wisdom.

And so it went for years with very little change except in his own behavior, his own attitudes, and his own thinking. Covering for her had become second nature to him, and he was aware increasingly of the toll it had taken on his disposition over the years. The fault was his and his alone. He should have been able to handle it better. The only one over whom he had any control was himself. The only person he could change was himself. But why was she disdainful of his efforts at doing what she clearly wanted him to do?

"Remember what we've learned about denial," said Clyde Candler. "For her to show any recognition that you are covering up for her means she has to acknowledge that there is something, after all, to cover up. Someone who wants to appear perfect has nothing to cover up. For you to cover for her reminds her of what she doesn't want to face, and you become the bad guy for being the reminder."

Although he could hardly imagine it, would Kate turn on their son if he knew her secret, the way she had turned on Joe in the early days of their marriage? Clyde Candler, his spiritual adviser, and his Al-Anon friends all reacted to his anxiety for Ted in the same way, sometimes even with the same choice of words: "Don't kid yourself, Joe. He already knows." Joe could not believe it, would not accept it. That his son sensed that something was not right in their family was as much as he could bring himself to suspect. "He knows," they all said, kindly. "He knows."

* * *

The hours of driving that came with rural ministry provided Joe ample time to think, sometimes more than he would have liked. In cruising the summer roads between banks of chicory and Queen Anne's lace, or passing the brittle stubble of frozen winter fields, home was always on his mind. Love. The Greeks had words. He thought about love a lot.

He knew the basics, an understanding that not even all clergy have and that few others understand either. The kind of love Jesus teaches is not about emotions. Although all love has some emotional content, the love Jesus teaches is something very different. It has nothing to do with the "warm fuzzies" and "hugs" that simplistic people mistake for Christianity, as though the faith is a blend of feel-good romanticism and folksy civic togetherness. It is not the superficial affection of the temperamental, an enthusiasm that can turn quickly to anger. It is not even parental love, or the emotional attachment of siblings, or kindly affection. To love as Jesus teaches, to promote the other's highest good and preserve one's own integrity in the process, is a matter of the mind. Not the emotions. It is hard work. He supposed that is why there is so little of it in the world.

Joe was raised in a society in which the common good was taken seriously. History provided examples. It was implicit in business, medicine, politics, and the law. He had known lawyers, mostly old-timers, decent men and women who had seen it all and had a vivid working consciousness of justice. Often their vision was coupled with a hearty sense of humor as if they recognized a certain truth about the human condition. They regarded despair as a seductive waste of time. In his younger, more woefully idealistic days, Joe could not have said why this might be. The venerable men and women he recalled could shift easily and sincerely from jokes or talk of hunting or other sports to Jefferson, Madison, the Constitution, or Magna Carta and discuss them all with unselfconscious passion. They believed in the system. They had a working sense of fairness. They shared a marvelous ability to intuit the mood of a witness, a jury, a crowd, strangers. The sanctity of an oath was a serious matter. Truth transcended personalities. He had always admired such people and valued their example, especially when in later years he squared off against them in court. Going to the matt with such men and women was vastly harder and immensely more challenging than facing legal bullies or regional prima donnas. Truth and justice are hard. Emotion is so much easier. It requires much less self-confidence. *The years that bring the philosophic mind,* he wondered.

He drove home on a windy Friday night in late fall, thinking about the world and his temporary part in it all. He made a conscious choice to set it all aside, and the thought that he was nearing home made him smile. He turned on the radio and heard the voice of Janis Joplin, and he began to sing with her. One old song led to another.

Kris Kristofferson. Bob Dylan. Willie Nelson. You were always on my mind.

You were always on my mind. He longed to be home. Kate would be there, and Ted and a few of his school friends, no doubt outtalking one another about their new learner's permits and how soon it would be before they were out in their cars on nights like this. He wanted to see his family and his son's friends. He wanted them all to have dinner together. He wanted to see Kate.

He drove along the alley of white pines that wound through his neighborhood in tall splendor. The big trees waved in the wind like vast night creatures signaling to one another, roaring above his car against the icy blue heavens. He paused at the foot of his drive to gather the mail from the big leaning box and continued quickly onto the house. He pulled up to the garage door beside Kate's big van and then backed up into the corner of the parking lot and pulled forward a little until he was facing down the drive. How wonderful it would be to have a good snow. He switched off the lights and got out of the car and, before he could shut the door, was suddenly the subject of Cory's joyful attention. The feisty little dog, seeking clues to his day's activities, examined his shoes and trousers lightly with his inquisitive nose, inspected the tires and the car door, and satisfied that all was well, bounded back and forth over the asphalt like a happy child. After receiving a quick ruffling of his ears, he raced into the darkness and returned dragging one end of a long stick. Joe threw it like a spear down the drive several times, and Cory fetched it quickly, his blond bush and silky feathers bobbing about in the dark in the light from the house like the rump of a white-tailed deer. As Joe went in, Cory lay down on the walk with his stick, expectantly facing the door, content to wait with happiness if it took all night for Joe to return.

He expected to hear voices when he went in, but there was silence. It seemed every light in the house was turned on. In the family room, he found Kate asleep on the sofa. Ted and his friends were not upstairs, and the basement was dark. As he took off his coat and tie, he looked again at Kate. He called out her name, but she was sleeping soundly and did not respond. Her head rested on the back of the sofa, facing the ceiling, and her mouth was open. She was breathing heavily, and her nose was red, and a rosy flush colored her cheeks just below her closed eyes. Anxiety began to stir within him, and he returned to the kitchen and sat down at the family table. He had gotten better over time at mastering his feelings. He sat for a moment and felt calmer. One should not draw conclusions. It was unfair. He could deal with anything after all these years.

While Kate slept, breathing loudly, almost snoring, he looked about for a note from Ted but found none. He made a sandwich and poured a glass of milk. He sat at the table and ate and read the day's *New York Times*. It crossed his mind several times to examine the old pie safe to see if the bottles had been rearranged, or to go down to the cellar and search among the piles of clutter. He rejected both ideas immediately as unwarranted and unfair. Besides, after the intervention with the Gallaghers, there was little chance of discovering evidence anymore in so obvious a place.

After some forty minutes, he heard her yawn. "Wake up, sleepyhead!" he called.

There was another long yawn, and no immediate response. After a moment, she said, "When did you get home?"

"Almost an hour ago. You were sound asleep." "Ummmmm."

"Where's Ted and Josh and whoever?"

After a protracted yawn, Kate said, "Oh. They're spending the night at Josh's house."

"I thought they were going to be here," said Joe. He stood up and walked into the family room and sat down beside her. Immediately, she stood up and walked over to the high-backed chair, where she routinely deposited her coats, bags, and schoolbooks. She began to gather up a random armload in preparation for going upstairs. He watched her. It was evident she was not going to say anything else. The old impenetrable walls were in good repair, firmly in place.

"Well, how about you and I do something? We could go to your Peking Garden. Have you eaten?" He was not hungry, but he would have gone gladly.

"Oh," she said, in a peculiar way he did not quite want to understand. "I'm so tired. I think I'll just go on up to bed."

She walked into the kitchen and looked briefly at the mail on the table, set down the things she had picked up from the chair, and still yawning, walked through the dining room toward the stairs. Joe came in and sat down at the table, watching her. At times in the past, she had begun drinking following trouble at work, an argument with Hervey or one of the other teachers. He wondered if everything was all right.

"Kate?" he said, lightly. "Are you okay? Everything all right?"

"Of course," she replied, rubbing her eyes with the heels of her hands. "I've just had a long day at school. I can't wait to get in bed and read." He heard the peculiar explicitness of someone trying to maintain control.

"Honey," he said, "do you feel all right?"

"Yes," she said, without emotion.

"Are you worried about anything? Did something happen?" He was asking too much, and he should have realized it.

Her voice took on the sharpness that preceded anger. "I. Told. You. I. Am. Fine!"

"Well, I just wondered. That's all. Your speech…and your nose is red…I just wondered if you'd been drinking. If everything is okay."

"Oh! No. Gosh! No, no," she said, sounding a little surprised and a little annoyed, her voice trailing off and becoming dismissive, as though he was suggesting something that had never, ever occurred before.

"All right, all right," he said, calmly and quietly, trying very hard to convey that he accepted her answer and would not bring it up anymore.

She went quickly up the stairs without saying more. He returned to his newspaper and had not yet turned a page and hadn't even begun to think back over their conversation when a heavy thundering cascade startled him, as though a half-dozen people was descending the stairs. Alarmed, he was just turning to stand up, the paper still in his hands, when Kate stomped heavily in and bent down, bringing her face within an inch of his ear, and shouted, "You should have heard what Ted and his friends said about *you* tonight!"

61

In an instant, the surprise and sting of her words, so unexpected and sudden and filled with ridicule, cut into him like a hot needle. She had come at him this way before, but never using Ted's name as part of it. The sound of their son's name within the menace in her voice was like an electric shock, and before he knew it, he had straightened up and slapped her full on the cheek with his open hand. He had lost his temper as he had never done before. She backed rapidly into the pantry door, her eyes and mouth wide open in shock. He heard himself saying, "Don't you ever bring his name into something like this!" He had never slapped her before, never even imagined he could do such a thing, but her bringing Ted into her words to him seemed to fire up years of hurt that had smoldered inside him like live coals, now blown into fire by the wind of her words.

Her every word and movement, clarified by her crisp anger and what he later supposed was the sting of his slap, took on an instant cold determination. Gone was the weary irritability of a minute before. She stomped into the family room and picked up her pocketbook and coat from her usual chair, walked quickly back into the kitchen, where she jerked a paperback book from the pile she had deposited on the table minutes earlier, and shouted at him, "I'll see you across the river!" She burst out the door into the garage, and in the following seconds, he could hear the shriek of tires on the drive as she roared away.

For five minutes, he stood against the wall, staring across the kitchen table. In the dark window above the sink, his reflection gaped back at him like a ghost peering in from the night. He was stunned—at himself, his own egregious behavior, everything. He knew he had just lost it and done the worst thing he could have done. Remorse flooded through him like runoff in a storm drain. He felt like vomiting. He went into the first-floor bathroom and leaned for a minute over the toilet with his hands braced against the wall, but all he could do was spit into the bowl. He drank a glass of water, and then another. He sat down at the table and ran his fingers through his hair. He considered trying to find Kate, but where? Where would she go? Who would she seek out? He could telephone around. She didn't really know anyone nearby except the faculty at St. John's, but he couldn't imagine her confiding in one of them. It crossed his mind to call Hervey, but he concluded immediately that he was the last one she would go to. Fears of her on the road after drinking, although he had dealt with them many times before, made him sick now in a new way. He had slapped her. He had caused her to go out on the road. She would be angry as well as...

What could he do? He wanted to apologize, to tell her what a bastard he was, how much he loved her, how it would never happen again, how he would do better. He went into the family room and sat down by the phone. What had he done? He had hurt his own wife. He had slapped his wife. He had struck another human being. He had not done such a thing since childhood. He had slapped his own wife. He had slapped a woman. Sour bile rose up in his throat, bitter, like sludge with slivers of glass. He got up and walked again to the toilet and tried to vomit, but nothing would come. As he turned, clearing his throat, he spied himself in the mirror, the last face in creation he desired to see, and he saw that his cheeks were wet. He was a wretch, and he knew it.

He walked the house and waited. Finally, he lay down on their bed and shifted the telephone to a position beside him, close by his folded hands. He closed his eyes and listened to the sounds by which an old house communicates. Sadness and self-loathing had sharpened his every perception, and his memory buzzed with clear images of a thousand times she had shocked him before. He had always handled it better, God knows, than tonight! He had slapped her, his wife! He had violated every decent principle. He had done it, and he felt sick inside himself and sorry for Kate. Why had she brought Ted's name into it? She had never done that before. They had never vowed not to do it, but probably because their son was too sacred to them to dream of using him as a weapon. It had been a few years since she last talked of divorce, but she had never given an indication that her feelings had changed. He got up and walked to the door of Ted's room. He stood for a few minutes, staring at the clutter. At that moment, his son's room seemed so completely, horrifyingly empty, and he a wretched, scrofulous, profane interloper there, in the whole house, with no right to be in Kate's and Ted's sacred space. He returned to their bedroom and lay down. He was weary with guilt and sadness, a fatigue that stretched back across the years of his marriage, over hurts and disappointments and betrayals and embarrassments, all of them rattling out of control now like battered cars plunging over a cliff.

Despite the turmoil in his mind, he must have slept. He became aware of the rattle of dishes and the sound of water running in the kitchen sink below him. It was 3:00 a.m. He went down immediately and found Kate washing dishes at the kitchen sink. In the following days, looking back, he would recall the scene with great curiosity—after so painful an incident finding her uncharacteristically and almost calmly engaged in a domestic chore. She didn't turn around.

"I'm sorry about what I did," he said. "I apologize. It was his name that got me. I'm sorry. Let's hold things together until he gets through high school. That would be best for him if we can do it. Then we can get a divorce and you can do exactly what you want."

She did not speak but turned her head slightly toward him. He should have kissed her, but he did not, because after what he had done, he felt he had no right, and also because he was sick to death of their constant problems. He was not going to try to discuss them with her any more. He went upstairs and got ready for bed. While brushing his teeth, he looked at himself in the mirror once and was careful to avoid doing it again. He turned on Kate's bedside light, turned his off, and rolled over and stared at nothing. Where had she been? What had she been doing? What was going through her mind now? Would she stay with him until they got Ted into college? Would she come to bed? He couldn't imagine life without her, but neither could he conceive of going on without some kind of change.

He closed his eyes, and his mind raced about in the deceptive darkness that settled in. They both owed it to Ted to keep a home. Joe would do better. He would no longer anticipate change, but that was all right. After all this time, he could manage for a few more years. He was glad he did not hate her. He didn't even dislike her. He loved her still, in so many ways. But who would believe it if they had seen him tonight? He wanted nothing bad to happen to her. To any of them. But at the same time, he was worn out with it all.

At some time while he slept, Kate came upstairs and got into bed. He was so tired that he did not wake up when she came in. Her light was off and she was beside him, asleep, the next morning, when he awakened early from disturbing, half-remembered dreams. He got out of bed feeling like a man who had done the worst thing possible to the person closest to him in life.

Chapter Six

I N FIVE SECONDS, he had violated every code of decency he valued. His remorse was like nothing he had ever known. That his own wife was the victim made his action a thousand times more wicked and split the heart of everything dear to him. His regret for her and loathing for himself stained him with a shocking and thorough shame. He knew he was a man forever changed. He had turned a corner and left behind something clean and whole, which he had always taken for granted. He was going on now sullied and diminished.

Sick with guilt, he had spent the next day in distracted prayer. It had not helped and had only increased his heartache. His confessions to his spiritual adviser, Lew Batterton; Clyde Candler; and his Al-Anon companions were equally as depressing. In confessing to other human beings, especially people he respected, he knew he was doing the only right thing that could happen at that moment. Confession allowed some of the spiritual poison to leach out with his very words. These good people were especially helpful—they would have been in any case, but were especially so now—because they listened without trying to comfort him. They heard him out with no consoling interruptions, but it was all he could do to look at their faces. He felt his very presence, and his evil actions poured out to them like bile, were affronts to their goodness and decency.

When they did speak, he faced their reactions squarely. He wanted to hear from each of them something to confirm what a bastard he was, but they did not say it. As hard as he tried, he could not detect severe condemnation in their replies. All of them asked about Kate, as though she was someone they knew personally. They did know her, in their own way, and their concern was genuine. Joe knew it and was grateful.

Facing the women in his Al-Anon group—he had been the only man for almost two years—was the most difficult. He perceived in them the blend of understanding and weary revulsion that came of their own years of experience. He listened to every person who spoke, maintaining eye contact and never interrupting. He accepted their criticism and whatever else they granted him like the guilty man he was, mortified by his own conduct and accepting the punishment, any punishment, he knew he deserved.

Nobody condemned him, but they were clearly alarmed and quite careful to express their surprise and disappointment. Clyde Candler had heard it all before, having dealt with just about everything in his years as a licensed therapist. Of all the responses, his was the one tinged with empathy, a vicarious participation in Joe's anger confined to remarking that fifteen years of coping with alcoholic denial was bound to have its nasty moments. As Joe poured out his confession to the attentive therapist and listened to his careful responses, an inner voice mocked him, taunted him, reminding him that years of therapy hadn't prevented him from committing an unpardonable sin. Candler, calm and earnest, did not excuse Joe's behavior but proceeded to focus on preventing it from happening again.

No one needed to worry that Joe would escape without penance or punishment. His sorrow burned a hole inside him. He did not sleep through the night for many weeks. His days began with shame, flooding around him with the sound of the alarm clock and reinforced when compelled to look at himself in the mirror when he shaved. His every priestly act became a reminder of many new and unspeakable things, a refresher course in heartbreak and sullied gifts. He grew unspeakably sad and eventually was forced to remind himself, in order to get through the day, that he had made a mistake, an acutely vile mistake, but one he had never committed before and would never repeat. He loathed himself for it. When he closed his eyes, he saw Kate's face, eyes open wide with surprise, and his parents' faces, and Ted's, and he was sick of himself. After a few weeks of nearly immobilizing guilt, he began telling himself what he would have told parishioners or clients or his students: Everybody makes mistakes. It is part of being a human being. There is no peace. Only patience and tolerance. He forced himself to admit what his conscience kept rejecting; he felt he deserved no healing. God had been so good to him. He loved his wife. He had a son, a home, and friends. Instead of his being grateful and understanding, look at what he had done.

Everybody—clergyman, psychologist, and twelve-step members—told him that they knew he was a peaceful man. They saw him as someone pushed too far, who had lost it, although nobody said so at first for fear of diminishing his entirely justified self-condemnation. They allowed him some latitude to feel bad about himself because each of them, in his or her way, believed he should live the consequences of his own bad behavior. Punishing himself was what he should be doing.

Joe's own past made his shame blacker. He remembered the humiliating days when his father, re-enacting a parenting tradition stretching back over generations, disciplined him and his siblings with a razor strop. His years in the law and teaching had not made him a pacifist but had quickened the natural abhorrence of violence he shared with most people and taught him much practical sympathy for human frailty. Having recognized and appreciated his own second chances in life, he had always been willing to give other people a break. His duty as a public prosecutor had been to see that justice is done. Striking the right balance was often difficult, but his conscience troubled him if he felt he had not achieved it. The bad guys sometimes came with mitigating or extenuating circumstances like everybody else. Where to draw the line or harden one's stance could wreck peace of mind and keep conscience in turmoil in those whose experience and common sense were limited. He had done the best he could, and with a good measure of objective clarity, but it all grew dim and dark now that he was in the dock.

As an ordained person, he was exceedingly revolted by his betrayal of his spouse, his spoilage of their home with such an indefensible act, and the stain he had placed on his son's own portals. He should have been able to handle the situation, any situation, better than that. She had frustrated and disappointed and shamed him a thousand times before, with hardly a second thought that he could discern. Over the years, he had responded with everything from confrontation to quiet reasoning to acceptance of things he could not change. Her vindictive introduction of their son's name was bound to have happened eventually. After so many years of coping with her and Catherine and their family anger, he should not have been surprised at anything. But he had been surprised, shocked, and he had acted reflexively. He had lost it. It was his fault. Kate was sick. She had a disease. It had desiccated her disposition. His wretched act was rather like striking out at a disabled child. He could not forgive himself.

Kate was quieter for several days following that terrible moment. She seemed to be listening more. She appeared to choose her words with care. He was almost unnerved by it, but these differences had vanished by the following weekend. Several times he approached her, wanting to talk, but years of marriage had taught him that this, like everything else he would have discussed with her, would elicit nothing more than a noncommittal stare. At least he had already apologized and done so the moment she returned home. Although he should have attempted a discussion regardless of his experiences of the past, he feared her rejection would deepen his inner gloom, so he kept quiet.

Where had she spent those hours after leaving? Why had she paused in the kitchen to wash dishes upon her return? And above all, what did she mean by "You should have heard what Ted and his friends said about you tonight"? Had they said something bad about him? What was it? What had he done to make them say anything? Whatever they had said, what had she said in response? He pored over the preceding weeks and months, searching for something he had said or done to arouse the anger or scorn of Ted and his friends. He could think of nothing with Ted that even approached punishment. He was an amiable boy who very rarely needed correcting. He could recall several times when he was late picking up Ted and his friends from the movies or the skating rink. He insisted on speaking to parents first before allowing Ted to spend the night at a friend's house. Apparently, few other parents did so these days, and he knew this was a source of embarrassment for Ted. But could things such as these have generated the kind of talk Kate had so bitterly implied? He loved Ted, and he loved his son's friends, and their families. What had he done? What had he said?

Or was she making it up? He was used to her fabrications, but even after all these years, they continued to take him by surprise. He had learned to listen to her with a measure of caution, but he did not, could not, relate to her as if her every statement might be false. Living like that would be impossible or, at the very least, grossly unfair for both of them. But years of marriage had taught him that Kate would go to any lengths to shield herself from perceived threats. When he caught her in a falsehood, it always confounded him, as though it was occurring for the first time.

Several years before, they had spent a few days with Kate's friends Rachel and Kevin and their children. Rachel's parents had rented rooms at Wicomico when she and Kate were children, and now her family continued to rent for a week every few years. On the first morning of their visit, while Joe was showering early in the morning, Kate came into the bathroom to put on her earrings, and they chatted for a few minutes about what they were all planning to do that day. As Joe turned off the shower and as Kate was leaving the bathroom, she told him in an unhurried, offhand way, as though only just remembering it, that everyone else was ready to leave the house and was putting on their coats to go out and they were all waiting for him.

Joe raced to dry off, threw on his clothes, and rushed upstairs without shaving. There he found Rachel in her nightgown in the kitchen, preparing coffee, and the children in their pajamas on the floor of the adjoining family room, playing a video game. Rachel's husband, Kevin, had not even gotten out of bed. To Rachel's amused surprise, Joe had rushed into the kitchen with damp hair, still buttoning his shirt. He was astonished, so much so that he blurted out, surprising himself—it was the sort of thing experience had taught him there was no use pursuing—what Kate had just told him in the bathroom. Rachel handed him a coffee mug and, looking straight at him, said with a smile, "Well, I think that's just Kate." Kate, observing all this from the kitchen door, turned and immediately walked out of the room without a word. He looked at Rachel, who shrugged her shoulders slightly, almost imperceptibly, and continued to smile. The children's video game emitted a series of atomic blasts.

As a guest, instinctively wanting to avoid a scene with this friend whom his wife had known since childhood, Joe did not call after Kate or follow her. He thought it better manners to let it go until the ride home. In any case, he knew Kate would tell him plainly and defensively that she had never said anything to him in the bathroom. After years of marriage, he could almost predict her words. "I didn't say anything, Joe! You were in the shower with the water running, so you wouldn't have heard anything even if I had said something. Remember?" It was inexplicable, the sort of frustration that had occurred hundreds of times over the years.

Was her stomping into the kitchen and speaking about Ted another example of the same? Was it something she couldn't help? Had he reacted so vilely to a psychological problem? Her behavior had been consistent over the course of their marriage. What had changed was Joe. No longer did he rationalize her behavior by blaming his own misunderstanding, his faulty memory, his inattention or stupidity. But why did she do such things? Was it intentional? Did she want to hurt him? Was it unconscious? Was she hiding something? Was this why she refused to enter counseling? These thoughts amazed him, because after so many years, he had no answer to them.

Whatever the answers, none of it excused his slapping her. Words alone, even Ted's name used as a weapon, were never enough. He was at fault. He accepted responsibility.

He faced the future determined to be a good father. He would strive to make Ted's final years at home the best any of them had known and send him into the world confident and prepared. He would continue to keep his own counsel about his relationship with

Kate, still believing Ted was too young to understand it fully, and too young to *have* to understand it. Preserving his son's respect and love for Kate was in Ted's interest, and everybody else's, too. He would not sully his son's relationship with his mother and compound his own miserable conduct by committing another egregious crime

Joe abandoned any lingering expectation of change in Kate. She had not followed through with counseling after promising him and the Gallaghers that she would participate, and it had been necessary for him to find out about it on his own. Apart from Kate cutting off communication with their old friends, the intervention had come to nothing. He suspected that even her memory had been comfortably cleansed of it in her denial. She had rejected AA long ago; it was ancient history in their relationship now. She had nothing in common with "those people." Her expectations of their marriage and of him had been clear all along, and so long as Joe conformed to them all would be well in her eyes. His own hopes and expectations were what troubled the waters of their lives, a conclusion in which he was beginning to join her, although for very different reasons from hers.

There were no other channels through which to work. Her brother and oldest friend were unresponsive. She shut everyone else out when they came too close. His parents loved her, and she might have listened to them. But what if she did not? They were growing old, and after raising six children, they were tired now and deserved peace. If seeing Kate as a loving spouse helped their peace, he would do nothing to spoil it for them, or for Kate.

She had not contradicted him when he spoke of divorce. He accepted her silence as a confirmation that he was expressing what were still her desires, as well as his own conclusions. She had expressed herself on the issue of divorce before, but he had never wanted to take her seriously. Perhaps in this, too, he had long been at fault. He was willing to accept it now. He would strive to be decent and kind, but apart from protecting Ted, he would let her have her way. And somehow, despite everything, he was determined to continue trying to make a happy home, a determination that seemed to him as only natural and reasonable. One thought of Ted was all Joe needed to know this was the only right course. And surely, Kate, regardless of her feeling about Joe or authority or anything else, must see it this way as well.

But Kate Stephenson, in matters she perceived as affecting her own welfare, was a woman of single-minded determination.

Chapter Seven

BLUE-COLLAR CATOCTIN SPRINGS, with its dilapidated charm and stubbornly self-reliant citizens, worked on Joe an unexpected magic as the years passed by. Respect grew in him for the whole region, so very old yet inexplicably new and so unlike neighboring states in its resigned self-effacement and reticent suspicion. Regional problems continued to alarm him—the lack of civic responsibility, the shameful exploitation of a lovely landscape, and pedantic regional rivalries. An unwillingness to take risks and join together in creative planning was especially troublesome, until newcomers led the way forward. But Joe was a good learner and willing to be flexible. With his growing understanding came a true affection. Among outsiders, especially his old friends, his became the first and often only voice raised in defense of the state and its people when the hurtful comparisons and cruel jokes were repeated, as they inevitably were.

Many a fishing and hunting excursion in distant places included surprisingly spirited debate on the inaccuracy of regional stereotypes and the impact of poverty on education and progress, with Joe on one side and everybody else on the other. At such moments, the faces of his neighbors and parishioners rose in his mind and their life together, with all its good qualities, made him defend them like family. He came to regard the whole diocese as one accepts an eccentric, well-meaning relative, set in her ways and a bit old-fashioned, but admirable and lovable for a thousand reasons. He found himself loving his new home because of its peculiarities and not in spite of them. The stubborn regional attitudes that had dismayed him early in his tenure grew easier to understand, if not always more acceptable, as he continued to learn the history.

Most of the people responded with the same affection, accepting Joe in a surprisingly short time as one of their own. They welcomed him into their homes and shared the sacred stories of their lives, intimate treasures meant to be revealed only to those who were respectful, who understood. It was this mutual esteem that drove him to deplore the exasperating regional willingness to reinforce every negative stereotype that outsiders liked to believe. When an atrocious calendar appeared in local convenience stores for sale to tourists, with poor-quality, staged photographs for each month depicting family drunkenness, incest, outhouses, and poverty, Joe began a local campaign to remove it from local stores. He contacted the producer, a small advertising agency in the center of the state. The company president, at first amused by Joe's concern, grew irritated and defensive that an outsider wanted to interfere in his making a living. The wonder and sorrow of self-respect traded for tourist dollars would remain with Joe for years, reinforced every season by another destructive calendar or coffee mug or bumper sticker.

He continued to be incensed by the overnight proliferation of sidewalk litter and the casual dumping of garbage in the most scenic, secluded places, an anguish that appeared to trouble few locals. He began to understand the crippling process by which poverty, and the accompanying distrust of outsiders, had shaped the self-perception and expectations of an entire region. When he looked at the rest of the world, his comprehension grew of poor and conflicted lands everywhere. None of this understanding raised even a hint of contempt or condescension in Joe. In fact, it strengthened his esteem for his new community. It made his affection for his new neighbors more intimate somehow, and though he did not understand it, he knew they sensed in him exactly how he felt about them.

Like other outsiders, Joe had been alarmed by what he took to be a statewide, weary disinterest in the common good, an apathy that abated only when the state college football team played a distant school. As with Italy and Spain on the other side of the globe, local internal rivalries seemed to be born in the soil and imbibed with mother's milk and prevented the formation of a healthy state identity. Those in the next county or on the other side of the state warranted no more concern than people in Bulgaria or the Ukraine. A low tax base and scarce public funds converted every economic and fiscal issue into a battle of local self-concern. With only so much to go around, the fights for power and revenue grew messy.

A loose defensive unity emerged when outsiders came snooping around, historically seeking minerals or timber or a chance to buy into the power structure. Political offices could be purchased, and the only qualification needed was membership in the correct party. Nepotism and hypocrisy were tolerated so long as they were lucrative. One-party loyalty was the highest ideal, more precious than progress, and those who went to Washington rolled over shamelessly on every partisan issue. The majority was convinced that nothing could be done about problems and that speaking up was futile and so reserved their views for a life of grumbling behind the scenes. There were exceptions, of course, localities with reputations for conscientious people in public office. Joe came to realize that the corner of the state around Catoctin Springs was such an exception. And it paid dearly for it, quite literally, when state revenues were allocated.

The Redeemer congregation and its neighbors were decent, faithful, hardworking people, and most of them were genuinely pleased by Joe's presence among them. They treated Kate and Ted with the most encouraging kindness. They sensed Joe's open-ended commitment to the community and treated him as one who planned to stay. And so he was. For his own part, only a crisis in Kate's and Ted's welfare would have compelled him to leave before God called him out. In his first interview, a member of the search committee advised him that the congregation wanted someone who would become a part of their lives, teach them about the faith, and represent them in the community. Nobody had mentioned the word *pastor*, but it was clear that a pastor was what was wanted. He had tried to serve in that manner.

A century of hard work by fine laity, clergy, and dedicated bishops had left the diocese in an indigenous melancholy of which only newcomers appeared to be aware. Staying a while meant becoming unwittingly a part of it. Joe found the diocesan clergy of his small denomination well-educated, faithful, capable people, most of whom were commendably practical and who, in their first months of service, perceived many of the reasons for the cultural malaise. Because they were realists, they devoted themselves immediately to their parishes, service that if correctly managed left little time to focus upon large diocesan or regional problems or anything else. Early in his ministry at Redeemer, Joe gained much esteem for the diocesan bishop, himself very much an outsider. The bishop made careful efforts to educate the new clergy in the cultural ways of their new home. Many secular outsiders arrived with ideas of what they considered improvement, or development, and stayed so long as the profits continued to flow. The bishops and clergy had been different. Their spiritual and emotional dedication to the people was commendably long-focused, and Joe was very glad to share their company.

Decades of poverty can dull the hope and weaken resolve in people anywhere, but by the time of Joe's arrival, as more good people were becoming educated, many who did not depart for greener fields were beginning to look for solutions beyond the interests of their own town or county. Satellite communications and cable television were revealing to everyone just how closely the region was tied to issues beyond its borders. And with new awareness came the inevitable painful comparisons.

The young people felt it. Many of them were ashamed of where they lived. At the diocese's popular summer camp, teenagers assured Joe they would leave after high school or, if they attended the state college, as soon as they graduated. The longer they stayed in local schools, the greater many of them longed to move away. It was not the cramped schools or hardworking teachers who made them want to escape but the unavoidable comparisons sharpened by education and a growing understanding of the wider world. Professional people moved away to retire, departing with relief and exasperation over things that never seemed to change. By the time of their departure, most of them no longer confused native passivity and distrust with commendable self-reliance.

The diocese might have served as a hopeful alternative to regional depression. Like the national church of which it was a part, however, it had gradually renounced its distinctive historic identity. What should have been a healthy, evolving awareness of the Spirit's presence in a changing world had been only a growing reflection of its own cultural surroundings. For this reason, almost a third of diocesan membership had vanished in the twenty years before Joe was called to Redeemer, a percentage of loss that equaled that of the national denomination. Historically, the bishops of the diocese had found the challenges overwhelming. They had been well-meaning types who came into their positions intending to make a difference. After years in circumstances wholly beyond their control, they began to lose confidence in their laity and, in time, their clergy as well. This had led to governance styles in which domination and manipulation replaced the guidance and pastoral direction that characterized the episcopate in certain other places. None of the bishops recognized his own rejection of God's voice in the laity. It had led to trouble in every episcopate. For many years, the church had been run like a medium-size business, where employees and customers were assumed to be inept. In fact, in its purely business aspects, the diocese had become a commendable example of careful stewardship. Mission and ministry were conscientiously funded by the low-income, dwindling faithful. Parishes faithfully paid their dues to the diocese, and the diocese, unlike some of its vastly wealthier counterparts across the nation, paid every penny of its yearly apportionment to the national church. Especially under the bishop who was serving when Joe came to Redeemer, diocesan funds were managed with professional discretion and care.

But converting people to Christianity requires more than generous stewardship and social action, as in Joe's denomination, or the presence of band music, expensive sound systems, and buildings the size of high schools, indulgencies favored by some of the self-proclaimed more pious, fundamentalist churches. But for better or worse, Joe had come to the priesthood trained as a lawyer.

His training and experience, their value ascribed by popular culture notwithstanding, had been a fundamental and meticulous search for truth. His faith had clarified for him that there was one truth. All else trickled down with varying measures of integrity. Joe knew his duty was to know the source and make the source known in the world. He believed that all people hungered for God, even those unaware of why or for what they craved. Reverence for God is the beginning of identity, and it comes before all else. Devotion to politics, issues of gender, liberal social action, the denomination's obsession with race and sex, health care, the environment, and all else must have their beginning in the character of an individual's relationship with God. Clergy had a positive duty to make Jesus and the Bible known first, regardless of how many Muslims or secular humanists might take offense. The great cultural issues would follow, rather than serving as the entryways to faith. And some causes, it must be said, are more compelling for a Christian than others. Joe was not well understood by the clergy in his denomination, although the laity had little trouble with his convictions. He was no zealot; he was glad to do his part with patience because he knew that God had it all in hand anyway. Church leaders, when they thought of Joe at all, viewed him as odd and limited, especially when he began to talk about conversion. To many of them, the word seemed an embarrassment, as though birth in America was alone an inclusion in the Christian fold. Joe not only believed in conversion but also had the troubling habit of saying so.

"Conversion? Again!"

"Conversion," repeated Joe.

His friend Jarrett, one of the oldest priests in the diocese, grinned and scratched the side of his massive head like a bear. Hoping the bear would say something insightful, Joe gave him time and allowed his own head to loll over the back of his chair, affording him an unobstructed view of the office ceiling. While he waited, he closed his eyes and peered up into the mathematical order of Guarini's chapel dome in the Cathedral of Turin and, after a blink or two, into the decorative discipline of Tiepolo's Würzburg Residenz ceiling. He opened his eyes and frowned, as though trying to remember something. It was not his friend's presence he minded, or any other particular thing,

79

but the whole tiresome world at the moment. As though to give him a moment or two more of respite, into his mind came images of the painted walls and fireplaces at Charleston in its Bloomsbury days, and he reflected a minute on how conversation there would have dwelled on Jarrett, who would have reveled in directing shocking observations to the brainy sophisticates. Virginia Woolf would write to friends, "How he burst on, rather like an Italian, and spoke out-rageous comments and stared at one, awaiting reply. Hugely ursine. How very odd." Joe closed his eyes again and smiled. To the cogitat-ing ursine, he said, "There is no other word for what we should be doing."

Jarrett laughed like a man surprised by an old joke. He was used to Joe's talk of conversion, but whenever they discussed the subject, he had the peculiar feeling he was hearing about it for the first time.

"Conversion! There's your topic again. You must be careful with it. You'll scare the piss out of people. I've told you that before, you know."

"And make them hopping mad, too," said Joe. "The first reac-tion is 'Wait a minute. I'm already a Christian. We've been mem-bers of this or that church for a hundred years!' Or clergy will smile and promptly turn the conversation to the real business of minis-try. Ecumenism. War. Race. Women's issues. Politics. The dreadful unfairness of incarcerating criminals. That's all right. I understand it. John Wesley had been ordained thirteen years when he went to his meeting in Aldersgate Street."

Jarrett cleared his throat, and Joe hoped he was about to say something profound. Joe had spent the morning in a monthly meet-ing of the county ministerial association, trying to plan the yearly Christmas party for needy children with some fifteen clergy of a half-dozen denominations, none of whom had shown up with their calendars or so much as a notepad. Affable, good-hearted, and habit-ually unprepared, they were lovable and aggravating, much like some of the teenagers he used to teach.

"Go ahead and plan it for whenever you want, and I'll be there if I can. I mean, if nothing comes up, you know," a dozen voices had assured, a chorus still reverberating in his head like the sound of a distant traffic jam. Joe had long ago begun to accept the things he could not change, but he would have appreciated something enlightening from Jarrett about now.

Jarrett was an old, overweight, monumentally ugly man of remarkable intellect and unconventional insight about expressing which he had happily abandoned all reservations long before entering seminary. Eternally florid and disheveled, he was the antithesis of the young, attractive, politically savvy, and socially catty priest so favored by bishops in the belief they would attract new members. Jarrett thrived on biblical theology and scholarly examination of history and science. He was keenly aware of current events and trends and loved to discuss the state of the world, which he could do for hours without straying into the cul-de-sac of denominational politics. He was no longer taken seriously by his colleagues or bishop, who viewed him as harmless, irrelevant, and irreverent. Joe admired him and valued his insights, which, on many occasions, had rescued clergy meetings and diocesan conventions from endemic ennui. In the loneliness of ordained life, conversations with Jarrett worked on Joe like transfusions. But his old friend only sighed now, the sound of someone examining an idea and discovering in it a disappointing revelation. Slumped vastly in a chair, he appeared to fill a quarter of Joe's office.

"What's happened to us?" Joe asked. "Redeemer is growing, but the whole church is shrinking all over, here and everywhere. The connection between leadership and the pews gets thinner with every national meeting. Youth ministry, Christian education, evangelism— the other denominations do it all better than we do. We've always been a compatible, reliable bunch. God knows we're not prudes. But why is it breaking down now?"

Jarrett cleared his throat. "Up until the sixties and early seventies, bishops were pastors, a sort of corrective force, keeping the flock on the orthodox path. But about then, they began to see themselves as activists. The sixties, you know. Civil rights were adventurous, hands-on. They got a taste of the spotlight. Clergy too. More and more they began to accept social action as more constructive than theology for bringing in the kingdom, you see, and soon they got so they couldn't stop. Clergy got to be the same way. Then the seminaries."

"That's not all bad," Joe interjected. "In fact, it can mean—"

"Courage. Conviction. Leading by example. I know. But for us it seemed to gradually take the place of what clergy should be doing. Teaching, preaching, and healing. Too ancient, too irrelevant, much too exclusive, like the whole biblical narrative. Even clergy are skeptical of the Bible now. What can you teach and preach if you aren't sure, and how can you heal without teaching and preaching? Christianity has become one of a variety of equally valuable perspectives on the universe. There is no single truth and, God only knows, nothing important enough to fight for. Look where that got us. Read a history book. Accept everything as containing some validity and learn to live in the tension. The modern world is so fragmented, culture is so splintered and commercialized, that the path to God becomes like that, too. It becomes impossible to say what the truth is. Look back over history and see the endless catastrophes that resulted from standing up for one way or another. The thing now is diversity, multiculturalism, and inclusiveness. We cannot say that this is right and that is wrong anymore, because somebody else might hold that position and feel devalued. Everybody is a victim. How does a man or a woman preach Christ crucified in a culture that won't allow His name mentioned in a public school? Pastoring—as our Baptist friends like to say—has become an exercise in making people feel good. Biblical theology and all manner of outdated orthodoxy flies in the face of inclusiveness. Clergies become anachronisms. When that happens, the ministry of the laity loses its distinction too."

"The center doesn't hold," said Joe.

"Mere anarchy is loosed upon the world. Political activism is commendable, of course, except the world needs its pastors. We've got enough social activists for every cause under the sun. It became fashionable for bishops to fit that modern mold too. The people in the pews and some of the clergy wanted pastoral guidance and spiritual direction. The bishops and most of the clergy wanted a different role, political, skeptical, ethically relative, and culturally diverse. The culture began to influence Christ, rather than…"

"But that doesn't describe them all," said Joe, shaking his head. "Bishop Spencer, who ordained me, is a spiritual leader as much as an administrator. But most of them...hell, I don't *know*. I don't even *know* them, only what I read. It's an issue of authority. That's why we should be about Bible study, prayer, preaching, planting new churches, encouraging small congregations, meditation, youth ministry. People want to touch the sublime, the unseen world..."

"And the solutions to life will follow," said Jarrett. He slouched in his chair and wagged his head a little. "And it happens with us. We have a spiritual tradition, ancient, orthodox, but there's precious few around to teach it anymore. We still have a good record, in spite of the great decline. We must pay a price, though, for insisting on reason as a gift of God and not a barrier to God. People want immediate gratification, Joe. That means emotion. With us it takes a healthy dose of reason. Not many people can put in the work, or stand the waiting and the spiritual formation, without pastors, teachers, and if you'll pardon the word, *theologians* to help them. Especially in what we used to call the Christian West. Sentimentality and politics are so much easier. And God knows, the results seem quicker, more relevant, if you will. Big bands are so much more fun. Being told what to do creates much more security. It's so pleasant not to have to think."

"Everybody who could be teaching the meaning of *agape* is too busy climbing, running for bishop, being first," said Joe.

Jarrett was quiet for a moment and then said, "People trained as civil engineers should practice civil engineering. They have a perfect right to challenge land use, conservation methods, and building codes. But to do all that and be taken seriously, they must be good civil engineers first." He grinned as he spoke, like someone enjoying good food.

"First," said Joe, after a moment.

"Being first is an outward and visible sign supporting a claim to relevance."

"And of breaking with what came before. And some of that breaking is good, long overdue. God is probably saying 'Finally!'" Joe raised his hands and bowed his head. "The first to have a woman. First to have a black. First to have a black woman. First to have somebody divorced. It's good politics. Get the form right. Substance will probably follow."

"It's just a matter of time before we'll have the first gay," said Jarrett.

"Hell, George, we've had plenty of gays," said Joe. "Some of them have been better leaders than the straights."

"I agree," Jarrett said slowly and reflectively, "but the political point is not an individual's ability. It's iconoclasm, a collective ego that feels more confidence in asserting its political daring than its spiritual guidance. The language of ambiguity and relativism has less to do with freedom than with plain old politics. And in politics, it's important to be first."

"But, George, it's a little more complicated than that. It's arrogance to address spiritual issues in political ways. The people in the pews want spiritual guidance first, substance first, the biblical dimension opened up to them first, because that is where meaning begins. They come to church to connect to God, to know their lives are part of something grander than what we perceive with our five senses. We can say, yes, we learn about God in politics, sociology, and quantum mechanics…everything. But we can't begin in those places. Unless it begins in biblical understanding, the kind of evidence they'll deal with along the way will make no sense." He paused to clear his throat, and he observed that Jarrett's big face glowed with a hearty grin. "Don't say it, you old bastard! I know. I'm preaching. I know how preposterous I am. I don't know how to walk and chew gum at the same time. But the church isn't helping. It's all academic, every drop of revelation has been drained off, and mystery has become an embarrassment." He examined the ceiling for a while. "I don't know, George. There's so much and too little guidance. And I'm a novice, an asshole. How can a man doubt anyone who is trying, or even honestly thinks he's trying, to be faithful to God in the world of Pol Pot and Stalin and Mao? Does knowing the Bible ease the pain of AIDS or put food in children's mouths? And as for quantum theory or pre-Columbian art or linguistics or Hinduism, 'One glimpse of it in the tavern caught, better than in the temple lost outright.'"

"Ah!" Jarrett said with animation. "Now we're on home field. Having some home cooking. Come, St. Augustine!"

"No! Go another step forward," said Joe, lifting his hand as though encouraging someone to stand up.

"An Aristotelian restatement," began Jarrett, grinning and clearly pleased, quite composed, like a veteran theatergoer whose favorite scene is about to begin.

"The creation tells us *something* about God. What did he see in his vision? Before the straw," said Joe. "Can you guess?"

A burst of noise swelled suddenly in as Milly put her head in at the door and said, "Man's here to fix the women's toilet. Says what we really need is a new one. I told him we don't have no money to buy a new one, but he wants to speak with you anyway on account of how much it's going to cost to do what he's got to do. So do you want to come out and see him and go in there with him, or should he wait, or go ahead and start, or what? Wait a minute..." The telephone had begun to ring raucously, and she retreated quickly to her desk.

Jarrett stood up and bellowed, "Good heavens, man! Get on with your priestly duties, why don't you? We can't sit here talking theology when womenfolk don't even have a place to pee in this fallen world. Get on now with what gives life meaning!"

* * *

Joe believed that any parish that relied on pledged income alone would have to close its doors in another twenty years. He saw youth ministry as a positive duty for every Christian. He believed that people craved good preaching because they could understand it and put it to use. He saw pastoral care as critical. He perceived widespread biblical ignorance as afflicting both society and the church. Most people couldn't find the book of Genesis and didn't know the Hebrew Bible from the New Testament. Yet this woeful lacking was far less destructive than the fundamentalist televangelists who knew just enough to sound credible. Their exploitation of Scripture filled him with dread, like watching someone who has read a book on first aid attempt to perform a lobotomy. He speculated upon their own dread when one day Christ would remind them of the consequences of leading his little ones astray.

He spent his days helping the good people of Redeemer plan creatively for the future, talking about wills, charitable remainder trusts, and other means of long-range stewardship. He knew that a downtown church without parking, one that had expanded to the limits of its small parcel, would be in trouble in another generation, and he explored ways to acquire contiguous property. He took his youth group and Ted on trips, to movies, the National Cathedral, swimming, canoeing, white-water rafting, getting to know them, and becoming a part of their lives. He attended special events at their schools. He devoted himself to better preaching, studying Scripture like a compulsive gambler poring over the *Racing Forum.* He struggled to comprehend for himself and illuminate for others the astonishing revelation always present in everyday life, glittering like sapphires and emeralds among footprints on a muddy path, lighting the way to hope and glory. He counseled those seeking marriage, worked with prayer groups and Bible studies, and tried to serve the walk-ins as conscientiously as he served his parishioners.

There was never an end to it, never a lull, not even after big holidays. He was always on call, and there was something new every day, at times every hour, that required his attention, presence, or prayers. He was always ready to listen. He grew weary and discouraged sometimes like everyone else, but he never lost confidence in the rightness of what he was doing. His every word and move was guaranteed to offend somebody or become the subject of unfair misinterpretation by his eternal small group of detractors, but he was never a traitor. He went about his life and calling with all the courage and kindness he could muster, balancing hour by hour his duty to family, parish, and diocese (in that order) as fairly as he could. He seldom felt the Holy Spirit's movement in the details but perceived instead the presence of a forward flow in which he was caught up like a raft in the current, the power of which dispersed across the world and fulfilled a magnificent design. He perceived his life and ministry as part of it all, with himself as a small plain skiff, a miniscule and temporary vessel by whose choppy progress the general flow could now and then be discerned. He felt himself on the breast of the great swells as life poured onward, moving up and forward on powerful surges that roared in his ears and humbled him, frightened him, with power and wildness. In the rare moments when he seemed to gain the crest and spend a second or two quivering in wonder before the plunge, he looked out over the expanse ahead and felt entirely vulnerable, forced to draw comfort from the perception of his right direction alone. Though the sea was wild and could be terrifying, disorienting, he was sure at least of being propelled in the right direction, on a proper course, and in the end, of arriving at a safe mooring. Balancing giddily, sometimes unconsciously, on the great crests was always a prelude to a downward surge into the yawning troughs beyond. The depths were fixed in the elemental order of things and were the only way forward to a new ascent. He wondered that his forward progress seemed more plunging and darkness, with mountains rising up thunderously fore and aft, and the light above sometimes obscured as the frenzy closed around him. Chaos seemed to rule, and at times, only his turbulent forward progress reminded him that a deeper, hidden force had ahold of him. Was this reality? Did he perceive the cosmos with any accuracy at all, any clarity? Or was it his own nascent misconception, his unreliable perception, which misinterpreted the evidence through his lens of ignorance, melancholy, selfishness, doubt, anxiety, guilt, fear, or any one of a dozen other afflictions and weaknesses he had always recognized in himself? He loved truth, beauty, compassion, adventure. Why was the search for them so difficult and disappointing?

In one way, he knew there was nothing to do but journey on, negotiating all the swells and troughs, seeking rare glimpses of the horizon when he could get them, and giving thanks he was still afloat. And his loved ones were with him. He would gladly drown for them if he had to.

One could not anticipate the moment of descent into the deep places. But they were there always, yawning reliably ahead, and they could be anticipated like the furrows running between the hillocks of a plowed field, the one creating the other, giving existence to neighboring convolutions. Swells and troughs, bars and sloughs, unpredictable but always, unfailingly ahead—one learned more and more how to sail forward, or one gave up and slipped beneath it all. Joe knew himself to be neither an accomplished sailor nor a strong swimmer. But it was not in his nature to give up, and slipping below was something for which he would never, ever receive permission.

He would look back one day in amazement and recognize the crest he had been on.

He had achieved a sort of truce with Kate. Ted was driving now and more and more with his friends, independent and cheerful. It seemed to Joe his heart would burst with joy over Ted's maturity, pleasing personality, intelligence, sense of humor, and the other good qualities that Joe so admired in him. The anxiety that had plagued Joe when Ted was younger was largely gone. No longer did he fear that Kate would drive him around while intoxicated or that her temper would erupt and Ted would hear her say terrible things about his father. Ted was old and perceptive enough now to recognize if something was "different" (as people sometimes said) about his mother. Joe knew Ted would ask questions, and he knew that Kate knew that Ted would find her out. For this reason alone, she had increasingly controlled both her drinking and her temper, to Joe's tremendous relief.

She was no more cooperative or communicative than before, still refusing to plan with him for the future, talk about personal feelings or finances, or cease her criticism of him and most of those close to him. But she was less volatile toward him. How she behaved at work was something over which he knew he had no control, nor was it right for him to have any. He was disappointed that she spent all her time at St. John's. He accepted that she was not interested in their home and would take no part in its care. He took her to dinner on weekends and occasionally during the week, when she was not required to "supervise a table" at dinner. They sat in rural restaurants, appearing to observers like lovers in a small café, always ones she preferred, so she would eat and speak after they got there, and he listened to her talk about her work. Except for Ted, and occasionally Joe's own parents, the only other subject she would discuss apart from her job was Wicomico. In the spring, she talked about moving there when school ended, and in the fall she reminisced about the past summer until about Christmas. He listened and talked with her about these subjects willingly and with concern, because they were precious things they had in common, but also because they were all she could talk about. From time to time, he asked her about books she was reading, her murder mysteries and detective novels, and she would tell him, usually adding something about television shows she liked. When she was at home, she watched television or read, rarely moving from the sofa or the bed. At least it was peaceful.

He had given up trying to talk her into saving the Wicomico house. As far as she was concerned, she owned it. She (meaning herself and Joe) paid the taxes on it and the rest of the expenses, so of course she owned it. The fact that a deed somewhere reflected that long ago her mother had conveyed a half-interest in the place to both her and Ray and that Ray's wife had an interest in it too made no difference. A few years before her death, fearing Ray would sell his interest, and as though she had never made the prior conveyance, Catherine had signed a will leaving the place to Kate. That was enough to satisfy Kate in her denial. Years of trying to get her to seek legal advice and settle the title had come to nothing. Joe's legal opinion was completely irrelevant. It was her house, and she was the expert when it came to knowing anything about it.

The roof continued to deteriorate, the plumbing was failing, every storm carried away a few more brittle asbestos shingles, and each year the tide line grew closer and closer as the beach wore away toward the southwest. North and south of the old house, the careful neighbors had moved their own venerable cottages back from the sea and raised them onto newer and taller pilings. Creaking bulldozers had pushed up mountainous dunes between these houses and the narrowing beach. Kate's house, older than the others and which had been built originally a quarter mile from the surf, was left far forward of the rest of the neighborhood, sitting out on the beach like a great box washed up by the encroaching surf. Joe had always been willing to secure a loan to move the house and make all the necessary repairs, if she would only take the simple steps to settle the title. The equities were on her side, and he tried to reason with her. They had a son to put through college. They were not affluent people, and half of any

89

money they spent on the house would go straight into her brother's pocket unless she established ownership. Joe could close his eyes and hear Ray's voice. "I didn't ask you to spend anything on that house. Hell no, I'm not paying half of anything! Let's sell it. And I want my half of the money, with no deductions!"

But Kate would not act. She owned the house, and Joe was being a bastard by refusing to save the thing she loved most in the world, next to Ted. It made no difference to her that Joe was a lawyer and just might know what he was talking about. It was her house, and she knew. She would not budge. He tried to reason with her, for Ted's sake, arguing that she should want to preserve it so that her own child would inherit it one day. She replied that her own child *would* inherit it if his father would only stop being such a prick and give her the money to repair it. Joe had given up. A sort of stalemate had set in, a peace of sorts. Years passed. While the old place decayed and the waves grew closer by the month in Wicomico, at least some tranquility prevailed at home.

The congregation was growing, youth ministry and giving were healthy, worship services were filled, people who hadn't been in church in years were participating in worship, and a real sense of fun and community had developed around parish activities. Lay leadership was beginning to flourish. Joe was asked all the time to participate in events in the wider community.

An order of nuns had moved into the diocese recently and settled near Catoctin Springs. Joe had been particularly glad to help them get started in this new place, so different from their former home and, in many ways, so hard for an outsider to break into. He had contacted people on their behalf, introduced them to the bishop, worked with them in resolving a few small legal matters, and did all he could to make them feel at home at Redeemer. There were four of them, one quite elderly, two middle-aged, and one in her twenties. He welcomed them as neighbors and admired their fresh, gentle spirituality.

Within the Redeemer family, he was grateful for the good feeling that prevailed. He began to think he had outlasted the small nasty group that had despised him since his arrival. He had struggled to relate decently and fairly to each of them, absorbing their insults and slights with equanimity and praying that they would change. The friendly majority of parishioners winked at him, shook their heads, and assured him that it was in the nature of his detractors to be angry at authority figures, especially priests. Joe had a hard time thinking of himself as an authority figure, but he knew from the practice of law that nobody can please everyone. He hoped and prayed for his enemies and begged God to take away the anger he felt toward them now and then. Two of Lottie Bascomb's cohorts had taken their anger to other churches, even leaving the denomination to show how thoroughly they detested Joe. A few remained, but with the exception of their mentor, they had become civil and even indicated a guarded willingness to work with him. Joe suspected the change resulted only from their fear of being left behind by their friends in the growing and gregarious Redeemer congregation who liked Joe and supported his ministry. It didn't matter. As with Kate, he accepted any change, no matter how shallow or grudging, with gratitude.

His relationship with his bishop had improved immensely. Joe had gone about his diocesan duties with the same determination that marked his parish ministry. He had not been entrusted with anything momentous, but he had worked diligently and maintained a sense of humor in what he had been assigned. He spoke the truth plainly and politely to the bishop in all matters, even where he knew his words ran counter to what the bishop preferred to hear. He accepted criticism dispassionately and moved on. After a few years, he had been accepted by the longtime diocesan clergy and especially by the senior clergy, who were close to the bishop. With the gradual recognition that Joe could be relied upon to follow through, and at the diplomatic urging of the senior clergy, the bishop had begun to accept Joe as a responsible man. Joe knew the ice had thawed when the bishop took a moment to sit down beside him during a coffee break at a meeting. The two of them sat with folded hands, looking across the room at nothing in particular, long enough for the bishop to say quietly, "Just want you to know that when Lottie fills my ear about you, I just listen without comment and get away as soon as I can. I understand now. You're doing a good job. Keep it up."

It had relieved Joe's anxiety, and together with some peace with
Kate, he had begun to sleep a bit better and look forward to better
days. Having the bishop as a friend, and not an adversary, re-estab-
lished a right order to things. In the past, he had regarded superiors
with care and tact. Where he had failed, he had been quick to apologize. There was nothing in the least servile about him, but he was
used to according superiors their due. He did not expect to become
friends with them all. Especially in the law, it was right to maintain a
polite and respectful professional distance. Judges played a different
role, and lawyers had to remember it, avoiding even an appearance of
impropriety so that no relationship or emotion could damage one's
ability to represent a client. In the few phases of his life in which
Joe had been other people's superior, those people had treated him
decently and with respect. He had always remembered it and was
grateful.

Joe was particularly saddened one winter day to learn from a
colleague that the bishop intended to retire. He was taken totally by
surprise by this unwelcome news. Having waited so long for a good
relationship with him, and having found in him many good qualities,
he regretted to see this bishop go. He didn't understand all the diocesan issues that contributed to his decision to retire. After his attempts
to gain clarity had been politely rejected by some of the senior clergy,
he had been content to let the matter rest. He went about his service
at Redeemer while the machinery of transition geared up around the
diocese in preparation for a change.

The bishop's final months were the subject of intense planning,
and a retirement reception and other festivities began to be discussed.
A large committee was formed to search for a new bishop. The chief
criteria for membership were how well one's gender and race fit into
the mosaic that constituted the face the national church was striving
to adopt. Within these categories, persons well-known in the diocese
were selected to serve. Joe was alarmed to find that Lottie Bascomb
was one of them. By then he was used to the politics of the diocese
and knew there was little he could do about it. It comforted Joe to
know that Bishop Spenser was still serving his former diocese faithfully and well.

Lottie had a furtive way, partly ingratiating and partly dishonest, of gaining favor with leadership in the diocese while, on the home front, doing everything possible to destroy the ministry and reputation of her parish priest. For some years, it had been common conduct in which neither she nor her several friends on the diocesan staff or at Redeemer saw the least inconsistency. Joe had been plainly warned about her by former Redeemer clergymen, two retired bishops, and other clergy in the diocese. With Lottie's *modus operandi* apparently familiar to so many, Joe found it astonishing that a small coterie of women at diocesan headquarters and a few like-minded female clergy continued to secure positions of responsibility for her. Power was what she craved. He recognized that she certainly possessed some skill and talent, but her stiletto tongue and cruel suspicion of those who differed from her made people want to avoid offending her. Thus, she thrived in the old-girl network that was a factor in diocesan life. It amused Joe that one could find it so important to gain control and influence in a small denominational community like his diocese. It was saddening, too, to acknowledge that the church of God, in many ways, functioned like a political party or a franchise of small businesses. It amazed Joe that Lottie continued to serve on the seminary board, engaged in supervising the education of new clergy while doing all she could to bring down her own parish priest.

Chapter Eight

LIKE AN OLD engine jolted suddenly to action, the diocese geared up to call a new bishop. Committees, the essential genetic components of the body of Christ, began to flourish with excitement and innate short life expectancies. Everyone wanted matters done decently and in order, and as fast as possible. A profile of the diocese was carefully assembled, experts from the national church were enlisted for guidance, and nominations began to arrive from distant places. National church officers searched about for a retired bishop to serve the diocese in the interim. Canon law provided a plan for all this activity so that mission and ministry could proceed uninterrupted. It was a system designed by faithful people who had long sought a reverent balance of human responsibility and the widest possible latitude for the work of the Spirit, in the belief that in it all God's will would be made known.

Until a new bishop could take charge, leadership would be divided between two large groups. Both were comprised of clergy and lay members, all elected. The executive committee would make policy decisions normally made by a bishop, and the administrative council would manage the budget and day-to-day program of the diocese. The interim bishop would advise both groups and fulfill certain sacerdotal functions specifically reserved to bishops.

For five years, Joe had served on the administrative council. He knew and admired the other members, clergy and laypersons from across the diocese, good people who went about their duties with reverence and common sense. He did not know all the members of the executive committee, the real governing body next to the bishop. He had confidence in them, however, arising from the conviction shared throughout his small denomination that the Spirit guided the church and her officers in fulfilling their duty.

Divine will was made known in elections, appointments, ordinations, volunteering, and all aspects of ministry to which the church summoned her servants. Once in place, people were empowered in their work by the Holy Spirit, who moved in the church's ministry in cleansing and creative ways. Ordinary people, lay and ordained, gave up precious time from their families, businesses, and parishes to serve the world in God's name, believing that something more than their own volition and sacrifice was in operation. Confidence in the unseen world was expressed in presence and service and nourished in liturgy, which opened the doors of reason for the faithful and let through a gracious light.

Bits of negative gossip attached naturally, occasionally, to one or another of the diocesan leaders, but it made no difference to Joe. He had seen it in every parish he had served, every job, every club, each group, all his life. It was human nature to gossip and to be the butt of gossip, and he knew he came in for his own share like everyone else. He, too, found certain personalities easier to serve with than others. He never doubted their place in God's economy, however, because God's ways were different from humankind's. What human committee would have selected St. Paul to guide the churches or placed its chips on Thomas Aquinas or Gandhi? It was in the natural order of things for people to make mistakes, rub one another the wrong way, or interpret the Word differently. There was more, infinitely more, beneath the surface of personalities and situations than could be known in passing. Often in the law, he had seen good people standing before the bench for an uncharacteristic lapse of judgment or fit of anger. Nothing renewed his reverence more for Anglo-American jurisprudence than to see such cases handled with justice and dignity. It was what he felt he owed to others, and all human beings owed to the world, as expressions of the faith that was in them.

A well-respected lawyer who had volunteered faithfully in the church for years chaired the executive committee. Joe saw her as a model of lay ministry—kind, reasonable, spiritual but not precious, and willing to take risks. By canon law the administrative council was chaired by the diocesan bishop. An interim bishop was not authorized by canon to serve as chair, and council members were obliged to select a leader from among themselves. So it was that, upon the retirement of the outgoing bishop, the council members elected Joe as their leader.

In almost any other diocese, Redeemer would have been served by several clergy. The congregation was keeping pace with the growth of robust little Catoctin Springs, and Joe's own ministry expanded to keep up, stretching his attention and time thinner by the month and pushing his diplomatic skills to new strengths. He was loath to neglect anybody. He was of the diminishing class of clergy who visited regularly and spent a great deal of time with individuals, families, and small groups because he believed that after his own family table, visiting was the next level of parish ministry. Christianity was about relationships, he said in sermons. He never had any free time. He had not read a book in years.

Ted was a growing teenager, more and more focused on friends and sports. He was pulling away from Joe, a time of life Joe remembered with his own father, in his own youth. He was sad, but he knew it was natural and a necessary part of Ted's developing character and personality. In the busyness of life, with its worries and stumbling blocks, Ted was a bright light in Joe's heart.

Kate's self-absorbed life was more and more a world that excluded him. He watched her grow more isolated from him and from other people, more set in her ways, taking less and less initiative outside her own job and comfort. She had not been out with him socially for months, opting for student activities at her job, where she was in control and knew everybody. With Ted safely under her eye at St. John's, she had no need to dwell on matters outside herself and her work. What took place in Joe's life and how he allocated his time made little difference to her, except that she continued to express annoyance that he was never around at St. John's, where he should have been if he loved her. She craved news of things in general from him so long as it afforded some amusement, which was all she seemed to want. Joe could no longer tell whether she was drinking or not. Her behavior and thinking were the same whether she was or wasn't. There was nobody around anymore to confirm it for him, as the Gallaghers had several years before. He had given up trying to convince her to join him in counseling or believing that her brother or old friend would come out of their own denial long enough to help. Abandoning those efforts had brought a little peace to the time he spent with Kate. Kate was following the same path her mother had trodden so blindly before her, into the same social isolation and suspicion of everything outside her narrow vision. Catherine's alcoholic decline, such a profound source of anger and stress for Kate for so many years, was slowly becoming Kate's own story, with the same damaging subplots for those around her. Where Catherine had been rather brazen and uncontrolled in her drinking, as though daring anyone to defy her, Kate was careful and much more secretive. But Catherine had unknowingly bequeathed to Joe a helpful gift. Kate's conforming to her mother's pattern had helped Joe, working with his counselor and Al-Anon companions, to let go of the depressing guilt that he was somehow to blame for his wife's ways. He loved Kate still. He knew he always would. His love had turned, however, and so gradually that he had been unconscious of the change, from what it had been into a desire to protect her and Ted from the consequences of her behavior. Although he did not dwell on it much, he was encouraged by the hope of a smoother relationship with Kate when they could both retire and spend time with each other without the responsibilities of ministry or teaching.

A new bishop would be called in a year. It was the duty of every priest to serve the church beyond the parish. He had made a vow to God at his ordination to do so. He felt right about saving for Ted's college years, keeping Kate's car in good repair, maintaining a clean home, paying bills and saving for the future, and so many other things that most of the married men and women he knew were quietly doing with their spouses in their own lives. Although his family came first, a similar regard extended to his service in the church, and especially among the people of Redeemer. If Kate's health suddenly required a move to a dry climate, he would pack up and go.

There was no possibility of Redeemer affording an assistant priest. Only he knew of his marital problems. For all the anguish that came of having no support from Kate, she was his wife and it was his duty to her to keep quiet about their private matters. As a priest and a lawyer, he had a muscular dual ability to maintain confidences. His lonely efforts to keep their home together were invisible to the outside world. In fact, Joe suspected they were also largely invisible to Ted, who doted on his mother and was preoccupied with his friends. It was all so complicated.

"A tempest in a teapot," Joe said aloud to himself as he drove between appointments along the rural unmarked roads of his adopted state. Millions of men and women lived harder lives than his, had infinitely more to manage, more worries and troubles to distract them. Most of the people of the world found it hard even feeding their loved ones. It was even true of people in Catoctin Springs, of people living within a mile from his house. Compared to the anxieties of others, his issues were small. He was blessed in a million ways. He was not a complainer. He saw it as an act of faith, a positive duty, to count his own blessings. He was thankful for so much. Fulfilling his vows was a way of giving thanks in life.

The council found his leadership style differed from that of the former bishop, who had chosen to lead by consensus. It was rule by unanimity and concurrence, and Joe had found it fair enough, but the lawyer in him had been frustrated by the endless conversations over issues that should have been resolved quickly. Consensus was one of the new ways of doing things in the church, probably introduced at a bishops' conference or training session by people who seldom conducted meetings. Everybody's two cents' worth of input had been heard and discussed *in extremis* and *ad nauseam*, with some meetings adjourning with issues, which should have been resolved quickly, left hanging until the next time. Joe returned to the old up-or-down vote after what he deemed a fair amount of discussion on matters he saw as appropriate. He tried to move the proceedings along, fairly and politely, and keep to the schedule as much as possible. Most other council members were satisfied, and all of them appreciated leaving on time for their long drives home.

Soon after Joe's election, the chair of the executive committee telephoned to say she had just been informed that an interim bishop had been appointed. The proposed interim's name was Morris LaBelle. The executive committee chair diplomatically asked what he knew of Bishop LaBelle. In her voice was a hint of caution that implied a need for consultation. "Have you ever met him?" she asked.

"Briefly. A long time ago." Joe was quiet for a moment, thinking, searching his memory for something.

"And?"

"I suppose we have no choice. I mean, I wonder if there's anybody else," Joe replied, after a pause.

"Why?" she asked. Then, before he could answer, she said, "They tell me there's nobody else right now. He is the only retired bishop who can do it. That's what Warren Jones says." Joe knew Bishop Jones, a national church officer, both personally and professionally, a great deal better than he knew LaBelle. He had confidence in Jones, whom he had always found professional and competent since the days they had worked together in Joe's previous diocese.

"Well," Joe said, "if that's what Warren says. I just wonder about the...fit."

"What do you mean?"

"I have friends who served under Bishop LaBelle, clergy and lay, who had bad experiences with him. I think his latest assignment was as interim at that big church in Delaware, where they had the sex trouble with the choir director. You remember?"

His colleague chose to cut short the preliminaries. "What do you know about his lifestyle?"

"The word is he's gay."

"That's exactly what concerns me," she said.

"That he's gay?"

"Yes."

"That has nothing to do with his administrative skills."

"It's not that. It's the reaction here," she said. Joe understood her. In their rural state, where everything seemed to be forty years behind surrounding jurisdictions, a leader's lifestyle could quickly become a source of controversy. LaBelle would never have been elected here, and now he was about to be appointed.

"I wouldn't worry about it," said Joe. "He has been a bishop for a long time. He must be eighty. He's bound to be competent. Warren Jones wouldn't send him here if he weren't. How long will it be? A year or eighteen months at the most. And whoever his companion is, you can bet they both understand the stakes. He'll keep his personal life out of diocesan matters and out of the politics here. I think we'll be all right."

"You're sure?"

"He's probably more stable than some of the straights they could send us."

"Well," she said, "he's the only one available right now. But I hear you. I'm sure you're right. That's my feeling too. I just wanted to bounce it off somebody else. This is not exactly New York or San Francisco. Anyway, we have no choice in it."

"Don't worry," said Joe, with a laugh. "Bishop LaBelle will probably turn out to be just what we need."

The following day, Joe was contacted again on the same matter. The caller, whose cautious manner seemed entirely sincere, was a stranger. It appeared from the start he was trying to be helpful. He was a priest in a diocese in which Bishop LaBelle had served briefly, as an assistant to an ailing bishop, before taking his more recent assignment in Delaware. The caller first explained that he was calling Joe because they had a mutual friend, a very competent woman with whom Joe had studied in seminary, who had provided Joe's name and number. The caller and their mutual friend had been in recent discussions about the church and their own ministries. The caller asked if Joe was temporary chair of the administrative council in his diocese. Then he asked if Bishop LaBelle was coming to them as an interim.

Joe listened in amazement as the caller urged him, for the good of his diocese, to do what he could to get somebody else assigned in LaBelle's place. He went on to relate in some detail the experience of his own diocese, where LaBelle had alienated many of the clergy. He referred vaguely to similar matters in other places and implied that he was calling Joe after consultation with certain unnamed others.

Joe assured him that he had no personal knowledge of LaBelle, a brisk reply that seemed to make the caller unwilling to say more. That was fine with Joe, because he did not intend to listen to any more. After a brief exchange about their mutual friend, Joe thanked him for his interest and hung up.

He sat still for several minutes, troubled by this surprising call. It was not what the caller alleged that he found so disturbing but the fact that the call had been made at all. What want of professional judgment and good taste could have led the man, who said he was a member of the clergy, to call a stranger and warn against having anything to do with a retired elderly bishop of the church? It had the feel of something shabby, of professional impropriety. Was this the way things were done now? The seconds ticked by while he scowled at the phone, as if it were a varmint suddenly crawled up on his desk. Bishops were drafted by God into their difficult and lonely roles. What possible good could come of the caller's behavior, or information, or intentions? It smelled of prejudice, or character assassination. Had it not been the church, and if LaBelle were black, he would have considered the likelihood of racism. Was it some bias against him because he was a homosexual? The caller had never brought that up, had confined himself to talk of professional relationships with clergy. In any case, Joe had no idea whether any of it was true. The man had talked only about professional relationships, ways of relating to other people that could have applied to someone of any background, any lifestyle. Still, he wondered if sexuality had been behind it. Was it the same thing some people had against women in certain positions, Jews, Latinos? If that was it, the caller had disguised his true motivation quite well. He thought back over the conversation as he had once reviewed testimony at trial, searching for indications beyond the obvious in the way one reads body language and eye contact. He could find nothing except the call itself that indicated anything but sincerity.

Still, it was odd. Had it been somebody Joe knew well who happened to meet him on the street or in, say, a business conference, and in the course of conversation LaBelle's name had arisen naturally, and Joe's confidence had been requested, he would not have found it so objectionable. He might have understood, perhaps. The topic would have arisen spontaneously. But to call a perfect stranger and volunteer this sort of thing? Regardless of their mutual friend, Joe found it distasteful. He wasted no more time thinking about it.

A month later, the representatives of the churches met in convention to bid farewell to the retiring bishop and conduct yearly business on behalf of the faithful. Three members rotated off the executive committee, and new members were elected to replace them. Joe was sorry to see that his friend the chair was one of those whose terms had expired. He would miss working with her; he had appreciated her candor and trust. The world of church volunteers included many conscientious people whose good intentions came wrapped in warm, fuzzy forgetfulness and undisciplined enthusiasm. Joe always appreciated working with professional people who knew the value of schedules and setting priorities, respected proper procedure, and faithfully followed through when they took on a task. She had been one of them, and he would miss her.

His disappointment deepened a month later, when the new executive committee convened and the Reverend Kirby Porter rotated loftily into its chairmanship. Nobody liked Porter, and few of the clergy trusted him. Joe had known him since coming to Redeemer and had never felt any closeness. Among the clergy a general hesitation toward him was evident, a tacit recognition of his veiled aggressiveness. Porter saw himself clearly as a man on his way up, the sort who had begun to run for bishop in his first year of seminary. The other clergy recognized a big ego when they saw it and were sensitive to misplaced anger.

Joe agreed with the rest of them that Porter would step on his own grandmother to advance himself. While still a young man, he had become the rector of one of the few large churches in the diocese, and what he saw as the prestige of this position had energized him for a good five or six years. Now it was time for something more, a position that would fit what he saw as his considerable skills. He welcomed the executive committee chairmanship as an opportunity to strengthen his political platform. Of all this, the laity was largely unaware, while the clergy, including Joe, merely looked on with caution and amusement. In the day-to-day scraping stress and loneliness of parish ministry, they all had enough to do without worrying over Porter and others like him.

Chapter Nine

I N HIS NEW position, Joe traveled the roads of his rural diocese more often now. It troubled him to be away from home and the parish, doing what was expected of him but feeling the inevitable backward pull to the places of his dearest relationships and responsibilities. As his aged Japanese compact cruised the endless roads of poverty and disinterest, his mind raced with the ancient questions, conscience and reason lurching about in him in an awkward, lonesome balancing of duty and desire. The great uncertainties churned as he journeyed hopefully, exploring along the rural roads the best answers revealed so far to human reason, treasures left in the world by those who had come this way figuratively before him. His seminary education had been excellent, so good that it had raised in him a million questions, enough to ponder if his duties had led him a dozen times around the world. He fulfilled his tasks and listened eagerly to the deep and lively din that moved in him like a far sea. The more immersed he became in the concrete realities of life, the louder did the inner dialogue grow. And there were others. He could see them in his inner eye, gazing into the attic skies or walking the streets of the Holy City and longing for understanding within the wonder, clear and humbling perception that would temper doubt and confusion with truth, unity, and concord. Glimpses of the light excited him. He pondered revelation, the reaching down of God, the rising up of human intellect, the momentous grasping of human nature with favor and goodness by the divine, and the unfolding of truth. He heard what he thought was Irenaeus, Origen, John Chrysostom, Augustin. At least the words were theirs. Humankind had them in books. But the voices? The extrapolations? And they grew more provocative and challenging the more he struggled with the many small sadnesses of life.

Everywhere he went, decent, well-meaning laity and clergy struggled with faith and doubt and looked for light on the horizon. Most of them were kind people, practical and willing to make sacrifices. He longed to be like them. He recognized their problems and anxieties because they were his own, and his empathy and admiration for them grew as he fought the great battle beside them. As much as he worried for his wife, as remote and needy as Catoctin Springs was, and as much as Redeemer struggled with the costs of ministry, he knew his lot was far easier than that of most of his colleagues. Their faces emerged and receded within him as he traveled home from meetings and conferences, their hardships filling him with sorrow and making him grateful for his own blessings. He prayed for them as the lovely, depressed landscape sped by, and for days thereafter, the way he prayed for his family and close friends. He never discussed it with anyone. It was nobody else's business but God's. Although listening to his colleagues was part of his duty and he had no power to change anything, he found himself spending much of his time hearing them out when they were together. He listened with great care, an emotionally and physically exhausting exercise, as his brothers and sisters talked about their ministries and their lives. Their familiar words resonated in him like a chorus of frogs, the description of each incident and dilemma rousing new croaks from some part of his own wilderness. Their words filled him with an empathy that many of his colleagues appeared to sense. He could offer no solutions. He could not fix anything. The blessing was that he knew it.

The lawyer in him was becoming more patient as people talked on and on, consciously or unconsciously avoiding the facts and real issues until finally revealing their underlying theological conflict without recognizing it. In most cases, their experience was richer and had come at greater cost than his own. He took them seriously and accepted more and more the value to them of being heard and given generous latitude in getting to the point. If process was what others needed, he was glad to be able to give his patience and time. His somewhat-irreverent sense of humor often came across as comforting, helpful in going on, although he was less aware of it than his companions. Later reflections on these conversations deepened his awareness, always just beneath the surface of his faith, of his own deficiencies and imperfections. Listening was one of the few things he was good at, a legacy of his years in the trial court, and if it had value for others, he was very glad.

Sometimes he feared his clergy companions had begun to share their flock's assessment of life in these depressed regions, a listless resignation instead of Christian hope, a cautious suspicion in place of confidence in God's purpose and goodness. It was there in the people's own quiet acceptance of being left behind, an attitude that hid resentment in pride and concealed anger in a misguided idea of individuality and independence. It saddened him, and he found himself occasionally struggling against it too. There were churches that had not seen a baptism in twenty years. He listened to lonely priests struggling with meager budgets and low compensation, and he saw soup kitchens and clothing banks where donors were little better off than recipients. Clergy from distant places were at first grudgingly accepted by the locals because they had no choice. Little money could be found anywhere, a crumbling diocesan camp and conference center needed refurbishment, and tiny congregations limped along where churches should have been closed decades ago and consolidated with neighboring parishes. Sunday schools had disappeared because parents did not bring their children to worship.

All churches faced the same problems in this proud culture. From his colleagues in other denominations, he heard the familiar complaints and ideas about how to keep the churches going and what to do about the young people. At times he felt ashamed for not finding answers and, at once, recognized the arrogance that made him think he could succeed where others were failing. But Redeemer was growing. His parish had more young people serving as acolytes alone than churches of other denominations had in their entire Sunday schools. His reaction was to praise God and move on.

He asked himself how he could do otherwise. His ordination vows were clear. Yet all around him complications of culture, economy, geography, and history congealed in the faith life like infection in an open wound. Speeding along the rural roads, he thought of Armenia, Poland, Uganda, and a hundred other places where faith had suffered terribly. He thought of Stalin and Mao, each murdering more people than Hitler and Pol Pot combined, and it was suddenly hard to hear the inner conversation of Aquinas and Chardin.

God so loved the world, the whole world, and not just his little mountainous part of it, and not just Christians in their struggles. It was in that Christian conviction that he felt his greatest anguish. What was happening around him was already complete in other places, older places where the faith had been nourished for two thousand years. Christians were disappearing from the Holy Land. The cathedrals and churches of Europe were empty, and architectural significance and historic preservation had replaced belief as justification for their preservation. Among the educated and economic Western elites, secularism and humanism had prevailed since the fall of Berlin and Tokyo. The middle and upper classes especially viewed the faith life with disinterest and condescension, as irrelevant in the modern world as orders of knighthood. Where has God gone? Is he here, or have you and I killed him?

He recognized that the church is growing in poorer places. Millions grow in faith where stability has never come with governments or political structures. All the crudest expressions of tribal and cultural self-sufficiency can flourish within the church's fold. He thought of Gregory the Great counseling missionaries to Britain to celebrate Christian feasts during pagan festivals and choosing the Roman winter solstice as the date for Christmas. Hadn't the faith always advanced in some similar way, usurping the inevitably primitive, developing its splendid fullness out of the chaos of survival?

Comfortable religiosity that had appeared to validate the rational had crumbled into two world wars. What was left of it had eroded with Western affluence. A malaise of abundance obscures questions and answers alike in postmodern minds. What is a human being? What is the meaning of life? What is the meaning of *my* life? The answers of popular humanism are elusive and temporary. God is an obstacle to progress. Mention of him in public discourse becomes an embarrassing sign of pedantry and irrelevancy, the last refuge of the confused and desperate.

On all sides, Joe looked upon the direst poverty in the land. Only some of the Indian reservations were worse, and inner-city ghettos like the South Bronx. The dilapidated tar paper shacks and rickety trailers on the hillsides, spilling refuse down slopes into streams, looked almost quaint, even picturesque from a distance, a distance that yawned between the occupants and those driving by in vehicles that started when one turned the key, with fuel in the tanks and somewhere to go.

He saw obese women and fat children on ten thousand unsteady porches and men nowhere in sight. Working? Maybe.

He glanced at scrawny, detached men in denim and baseball caps leaning on one of a half-dozen immobilized pickups and petrified sedans parked by the road or lined up like rusting coffins in the weeds along the tree line. A look down leafy lanes revealed simple dwellings, painted white, if at all, with a leaning outbuilding or two, a clump of *rose of Sharon* or lilac perhaps, and a satellite dish. When they were glimpsed in passing, momentary charming impressions could arise like mirages, brief illusions of bucolic havens nestled in the folds of hills that glowed with cherry and redbud in the spring and all the colors of a coral reef in autumn.

Who would understand it? The boys who leave school and run away at twelve; unwed girls who give birth for the first time at thirteen; supplemental security income checks spent on cheap whiskey and beer, heroin, and crack, which are easier to come by than medicine and jobs; the chronic respiratory illnesses; mineral treasures that generate corruption as a way of life; child abuse; opioids; domestic violence; shuttered businesses; and abandoned mines—who could imagine that these people are materially better off than lawyers, doctors, and engineers in much of the rest of the world? Poverty is relative, like time.

When he stopped for coffee or a sandwich, he liked to choose local places rather than fast-food franchises. Seated in a rusty folding chair on the front porch of a rural store, drinking milk and watching buzzards sail in the distance, Joe thought of Burma, Mexico, China, Zimbabwe. Blue mountains receded in the distance ridge after alluring ridge, and upon his inward eye flashed visions of the incomprehensible, unimaginable: the Belgian Congo, where human hands were added up the way Indians counted out scalps for the French, and German East Africa, and Turks exterminating Armenians. Sobibor. Treblinka. Caligula. Islamists. Jihad. *God so loved the world.* He blinked his eyes and was ashamed of himself. The space and color and dazzling light before him took the breath away. The blue void of the endless sky, the soft-blue rounded mountains, the silvery blue of the streaks of clouds in the west, their white tops riding the blue world like clusters of sea foam drifting on waves, thrilled his heart and drove him to take up painting again, in his mind. In the distance the silent buzzards sailed on the thermals like music. Despite all the problems, in a very strange way, difficult to explain, *because* of the problems, he loved this lovely, troubled land. "I love these people," he said to himself, "but they don't know that."

God's definition of love, *agape*, is a mystery. Where *is* God? What must have gone on in the great, mysterious mind as Americans ate Spam and watched *I Love Lucy* and the Chinese killed twenty million of their own people? Was God asleep when Communists murdered millions of Ukrainians in a land where many now long for the Soviet past? Where was God in Auschwitz? Where was God in Rwanda? Constantinople? Where was God in Constantinople?

Three chubby children, a girl and two boys, emerged from the rural store into the hot morning sunlight, the screen door slamming behind them. They paused and began to examine their purchases— mammoth soft drinks, honey buns, candy bars, and bags of Doritos. They dropped their plastic shopping sacks casually onto the porch, where a slight wind caught them and drew them out over the highway. They bounced along for a hundred yards until they were sucked crazily, one after another, over the precipice into the blue distance. The girl, standing less than a foot away from him, had the sweet, tender face of a ten-year-old and the enormous breasts and big hips of a young woman.

"School out today?" asked Joe, casually.

"We ain't going today," said the girl without looking at him.

"Mama said we could stay home today," said one of the boys, unwrapping a gigantic Baby Ruth.

"Bus won't on time. Ain't our fault," said the other boy.

They stepped off the end of the porch and wandered up the road, candy wrappers and bottle caps floating away and hopping on the hot asphalt behind them. Joe watched them until they vanished around a distant bend, fat bottoms bobbing like balloons beneath the tails of their T-shirts. He knew he must have appeared like a freak to them in his black shirt and white clerical collar, as rare in these parts as a beefeater's uniform. He dropped his milk carton into a rusty garbage can on the porch beside him and decided it was time to move on. He started to get up. The screen door screeched open, and the thin woman from behind the counter, the one who had sold him the milk, stepped out.

"You a preacher?"

"I am a minister in a church."

"Well…can I ast you something?"

"Of course."

The door screeched again, and a tall young man came out and leaned against the wall in silence. His hair was pulled back tightly and tied in a pigtail, and even in the heat, he wore a long-sleeve thermal underwear top. He pretended not to see Joe.

"We got this sister of ours over in Coal Creek," said the woman. "She's got these two kids, teenagers, and a baby a year old, and she was getting child support, except the twins' father got put in prison for five years and now she ain't getting it and she's all full of cancer and the health department is helping her, but it ain't easy, you can imagine."

"That's terrible," said Joe.

"And she been good most of her life. All along, ever which one needed help, she was right there. Nursed Mama before she died. Worked till the baby come along by surprise. And I been wondering, we ain't real religious, but we do believe in God and all. Mama, she was a member of Coal Creek Baptist all her life. Buried with a church funeral and all. And what I was going to ast you was, Why is it when people pray to God for something, nothing ever happens? I don't mean to be sacrilegious and all, but a lot of people I know pray for things to God and it seem like God don't hear. God don't answer prayers."

She stopped talking and looked at Joe. The young man glanced at Joe quickly and looked away.

"Tell me about your prayers. How do you pray?"

"I pray to God for Lucinda, that she'll be cured from her cancer and all. I pray like, 'Dear God, make Lucinda's cancer go away and get Charlie out of prison and make the twins mind their mother and help us get enough money to get along and help Roy find a job and make the baby's pinkeye go away and let the welfare give Lucinda enough money and all. Amen.'"

"And?"

"She just gets worse. Everything goes along without no change."

"God hears your prayers," said Joe carefully. "Every word you say to God in prayer, God hears. Many believe that when they pray for something and don't get it, God has not heard, or that God has said no. Don't believe it. God hears. And God loves each one of us and God loves Lucinda. The mistake we, human beings, make is, we think God counts time like we do. You and I live in a world controlled by space and time. To you and me and Lucinda, life is divided into past, present, and future. God is not like that. God is not a part of the world. God made the world, so God stands outside the world and is not a part of it. Just as when you make a cake. You aren't part of the cake. God made the world. God is not part of the world. Since God is not part of the world, God is not controlled by space and time. With God, there is no past, present, and future. When God looks at the world, God sees it all at once. To you and me, it's what happened a thousand years ago, what is happening right now, and what will happen in the future. God sees it all and knows it all in a flash. Is this making any sense so far?"

"Go on," said the woman. "I'm listening."

"God does not measure time like you and I do. Time is relative. A great man named Einstein helped us understand that. God does not measure time like we do. We might think that God did not hear us or that God said no. What God is really saying to us is, 'Not yet. I know what is best. Trust Me. You are precious to me. I will respond to your prayers when I know it is right for you.'"

"Well, damn," said the woman, and immediately she apologized.

"You say Lucinda has twins, teenagers? When they were two years old, would she have given them a sharp knife to play with? No, they weren't ready to handle a sharp knife. Now, suppose they are fifteen and are helping fix dinner, peeling potatoes, say. And they ask for a sharp knife to peel the potatoes. Will she give them one? Yes, because she knows they are ready, they can handle it. It's the same with human beings and God. God knows what we can handle, and when, because God knows what is in our future, or what we call our future. God answers our prayers when it is right for us and in ways that are best for us. God loves us and knows what's best for us. So keep praying. Always, always pray. Not just asking for things, but also saying thank you for things. Never give up. Always keep in touch with God. God's time is not our time. God does hear you. You have to trust God."

She asked a lot of questions, and Joe went over it all again and again with different examples. Before he left, he prayed for Lucinda and the man leaning against the wall straightened up and came to attention as if he were in the Army and bowed his head. The woman thanked him and offered to make him a sandwich for the road, but he thanked her and said no, maybe next time.

Before driving on, he took off his collar and placed it on the seat beside him. It was cooler that way. He remembered the respect such a collar had caused in him and his friends as children. Times had changed. If people noticed it at all these days, it caused only momentary curiosity. Curiosity was not necessarily respect.

The collar made him think of Ted, the love of his life, who used to invite him to his middle school to have lunch with him and his friends. After some embarrassed indecision, Ted had asked Joe not to wear his collar to his school anymore. None of the other students knew what it was, and Ted did not want his friends to see his father as peculiar. Joe remembered well his own embarrassment when his own father arrived to pick him up from school or parties unshaven, smoking a gooseneck pipe, and dressed in an old Army jacket. For an awkward young man struggling to fit in with more affluent friends, trying to impress the girls, his awkward father's appearance had been a source of shame. Joe had obliged Ted and worn a shirt and tie to work on days when he visited Ted's school. At the rural middle school near Catoctin Springs, none of Ted's friends' fathers wore ties, and certainly not suits. So Joe began taking off his tie and jacket before going in to have lunch with his son. He could imagine the bishop's reaction, a lecture about how the collar in the cafeteria could become a "teaching moment," and himself struggling to explain, unsuccessfully as usual, that it was not always so simple, and the unfairness of turning precious social time with his twelve-year-old son into an exercise of church diplomacy. Now Ted was seventeen and providing plenty of signals that his father was still an embarrassment, leaving Joe to interpret the signs and try to understand why.

For the seventy-five miles between the roadside store and home, Joe thought about Ted. Would his son have faith? Would he grow up into a calm, well-adjusted man? Would courage and kindness mark his character? What would he do in life? What would he study in college? Where would he live? When would he marry? How many children would he have? He could hardly imagine it—Ted's children, Joe's grandchildren, Kate's grandchildren, their family. He prayed daily for love and decency and self-control for his son as he matured. He cross-examined himself rigorously—was he a good father, setting a good example, doing enough to lay the groundwork, encouraging these treasures, and helping Ted lay them up in heaven?

He could not be a good father unless he was a good husband. The two were inseparable. He had never been a husband to anyone before Kate, but he knew instinctively that he should be doing better. If he were a better husband, they would be happier. But what kind of husband was he? He was doing the best he could, but it was obviously not good enough. Why was he able to talk reasonably with other people about their marriages but felt himself so inept, making so many mistakes, in his own? There was no scorecard, and anyway, Kate changed the rules to suit herself. The bottomless pit of her needs confounded him. Or did the fault lay in his efforts to meet them? How would a better man handle it? How could he know what was right? He told himself he was not shifting the burden for their rocky relationship to her, only lamenting that it takes two to make a marriage work and that one cannot do it alone. One trying to flounder forward alone, guessing at the other's motivations, trying to read between the lines, leaves a wide margin for mistakes and misunderstandings.

When he asked himself how he could be a better husband, he thought back to his own father, whose sincere, often bumbling, efforts to do right by his wife and children had left upon Joe an indelible mark. Opinionated, poorly educated, uninformed, a repository of frustrated talents and unrealized dreams, his father had sacrificed everything gladly for his loved ones. After working his back off all day, his father returned home at night and, before anything else, kissed his wife long on the lips while Joe and his squalling siblings charged around. Then he changed his clothes and immediately began to bring in wood for the fireplaces, set the table, feed the latest baby, and stir this or mix up that to help Joe's mother prepare dinner. After everybody had eaten and talked around the table until it was time for homework, he put away the leftovers and washed the dishes as he listened to Howard Cosell's *Speaking of Sports*. He never bought anything for himself. He wore the same clothes for years without complaint so that his children would have what they needed. His every thought, every action, each decision was for his family.

His father's example inspired Joe to devote himself to keeping his own household alive. He gladly drove to a distant town for Al-Anon meetings week after week, year after year. He always stopped in the parking lot of a bowling alley to pull on one of the turtleneck sweaters he kept in the trunk of his car, so that nobody would see his clerical collar and associate his presence with Kate. He bought his clothing at Goodwill and, except for sharing news of an occasional good deal, never made an issue of it with anyone. He willingly cared for Catherine in her old age and ill health. Even when Kate ignored his efforts or was openly scornful, or when she stood by passively while her mother ridiculed Joe behind his back, he continued to do what he understood to be the duty of a husband and father. He wanted Ted to have everything he needed. He struggled to teach their son values and tried to do it cheerfully, even when it meant working through Kate's determination to buy anything and everything for which Ted expressed a desire.

Somewhere in the years of sarcasm and denial that had colored his marriage, his desire for Kate had withered. Neither dislike nor contempt had replaced it; there was no room in him for such terrors. Instead, there had grown up a habit of vigilance, an active caution, that had developed beyond his will like the growth of a tumor. Despite it all, he still loved Kate. He would have had a difficult time convincing anyone that his tumor was benign. He knew its presence alone was enough to substantiate anybody's doubt. But he cared for her still and wanted only health and happiness for her and for them all as a family. The fading of his desire was painful and made him feel excruciatingly guilty. It was only through a certain detachment that he preserved his own peace of mind. But the shame and guilt aroused in him by this loss in his marriage, and the maddening, affectionate, protective pity it caused him to feel for his wife, compelled him to see himself as a failure, a wretched impostor who would let his wife suffer.

And yet how does one keep loving a stranger? How does one stay the course with a copilot whose flight plan is inscrutably personal and subject to change without warning? How can one be a good father where the mother's cross-purposes are possessive and defensive? He was certain that others had handled such troubles better, with more care and dignity, and with greater success, then he. A better man would do a better job.

What could he do? This was his lot. He felt the presence of God in the world and in his ministry. He had once felt it in his marriage, and his faith told him the Spirit was still there. His inability to feel it still was his own fault, the shabby result of his own inadequacy and blindness. And while he strove for clarity, there was only one decent path to take. He would say his prayers and do his best with the gifts he had been given. It was the only loving way, and through it he prayed to raise his son decently and support his wife with kindness and attention. He knew his marriage, like all marriages, was sacred.

He was grateful for it, despite how it had turned out. But for his marriage, Ted would not be in the world. And he knew that of all God's blessings, there was none for which a human being would be so called upon to answer as the gift of a child.

In carrying out his good intentions, he found his church to be a source of profound strength and encouragement. He took comfort in her Bible-based moral theology and long tradition of human reason as a gift of God. On the whole, he found the bishops and clergy better educated and much less narrow-minded than those of other denominations. He was pleased with their willingness to take risks, think creatively, and bring to their roles a broad social consciousness. He longed to be like them, to see himself this way, for God to see him this way. And he was failing at being a good husband, his core responsibility.

Like many of his colleagues, Joe was sometimes humiliated by the shameless political business ethic that had replaced biblical faith in some of the more outspoken of the church's leaders. He consoled himself with the knowledge that God was firmly in control. Although even as a lawyer he did not know much about canon law, all evidence indicated it was as sound and reliable as most of the rest of his denomination's ministry. Serving God in the broken world was a lonely and frustrating way to live, but what he knew of other polities confirmed his faith in the dignity and integrity of his own part of Christ's body. As this was the way he was called to spend his life, he was glad to be doing so in this branch of the faith.

At least the interminable travel provided room to contemplate, meditate, and reflect—the cherished gifts longed for by all clergy everywhere. From these gracious interludes, he returned to his family and parish with refreshed determination and new ideas. In all the chances and changes of life in the broken world, he took it as a further sign that he was never alone.

As he drew near to his beloved home and family, he thought back to the woman on the porch and her sick sister and the millions of drifting people like them everywhere. As he drove up his driveway and came within the lights of his own house, he instinctively, unconsciously, began to give thanks.

Chapter Ten

MORRIS LABELLE WAS a tall thin man of about six-ty-eight with bushy white hair and a benign, downcast expression. Quietly efficient and soft-spoken, he moved forward as though already familiar with everything that came along. He was comforting and pastoral, and the people of his new charge welcomed him, confident that anybody who had been a bishop for twenty-odd years knew exactly what he was doing. He was quite unlike the short, intense, somewhat-harried bishop who had just retired. When Bishop LaBelle arrived for his first meeting with the administrative council, Joe found him oddly familiar. Only later that evening did he recall the chilly, stormy afternoon in London when he stood for an hour in the National Gallery before Rembrandt's *Portrait of Jacob Trip*, trying to copy the great master's broad handling of light and shadow, mood and character, on page after page of a cheap drawing pad. The rigid old arms merchant, uncompromising, just barely biblical, emerging from darkness in golden earth tones and arresting whites, glowed on the canvas like a bird of prey, sin-ister and mercifully distant. Joe remembered going from the gallery into the cold gray rain strangely depressed, the portrait's arctic gaze following him, as though he had just left an exhibit of Holocaust photographs.

It emerged that peculiar baggage accompanied the interim bishop. His previous posting had been in a very large urban parish recovering from a sex scandal, where he had been asked to serve for a year to calm everybody down. A young choir director had been convicted of molesting children. Apparently, everybody in that unfortunate mess—clergy, lay leaders, parishioners, law enforcement personnel, social workers, and especially, it seemed, lawyers—had succeeded in arousing Bishop LaBelle's wrath. In addition to a lengthy criminal prosecution that kept emotions boiling in the community, a dozen civil lawsuits were screeching through the courts, causing apoplexy among the church's insurance providers and national leadership. The prospect of young children having to take the stand at trial unnerved and enraged everybody. Fresh from this explosive experience, the aged bishop had arrived in his new rural interim assignment.

In Joe's personal experience, prosecutors and police investigators learned to manage the stress of sex offenses, especially where children had been abused, or seek other professions. With everybody else, such cases were as unnerving as most of life's other tragedies combined. Joe had seen sex cases stir up elemental fears and visceral disgust that even homicides failed to arouse. It was obvious that the bishop's previous assignment had been difficult for him, but Joe was surprised, given his years of service, by the degree of the bishop's lingering disquiet. LaBelle's introductory remarks to the administrative council had been about this recent experience, and he described in much detail, over many minutes, the anguish and difficulty it had caused. All this was addressed to diocesan leaders with whom he expected to work intimately in coming months. It seemed appropriate enough, a way of letting everyone know his recent responsibilities and background. Joe admired his candor and felt he understood his anxiety.

As weeks passed, however, and LaBelle's brooding preoccupation with the experience continued, Joe began to wonder if it had been his first serious legal matter or his only exposure to a sexual offense. Could he have spent a long career in leadership and somehow avoided dealing with such matters? Or perhaps serious wrongdoing and human fallibility were less his forte than, say, academic theology. Other clergy said that LaBelle began and ended every conversation with individuals or groups, professional or social, with lengthy discourses about this sex scandal. Perceiving that the bishop had a need to talk about it, nobody objected. People listened, and no one dared to change the subject. After some months, there grew up an understanding that the bishop was obsessed with the matter. People grew tired of hearing about it and began to work around it, as kindly and diplomatically as possible.

There was friction between LaBelle and the former diocesan bishop. Months after his arrival, the two still had not met, creating a strain of which everyone was increasingly aware. The new interim upset the former bishop's friends by criticizing some of his work and commenting upon how unpleasant it was trying to deal with him. This encouraged people who had been at odds with the former bishop to begin a fresh round of gossip and idle speculation. It turned up the heat beneath the natural discord always simmering below the surface of diocesan life, a sort of ecclesial counterpart to the political corruption and ineptitude that had for so long characterized the state.

Joe's colleague in the neighboring parish, the senior priest who had been on good terms with the retired bishop, after hearing some of LaBelle's remarks, had confronted him privately during a social gathering following a diocesan meeting. He reported to Joe that LaBelle had retreated to a distant corner of the room and remained moodily alone for a while before joining the rest of the group for dinner. His comments about the retired bishop soon ceased, although few knew why except Joe and his neighbor. Although LaBelle continued to be absorbed by the sex scandal, it was a relief for many to be rid of at least one issue that added friction to an already-troubled diocese.

Despite these vexations, Joe was relieved to have the advice of LaBelle, an older and wiser man who treated him with professional courtesy. Joe respected him. LaBelle seemed dedicated to serving the people. He was a stickler for proper parliamentary procedure and provided valuable advice as Joe conducted council meetings. He willingly met with Joe and the treasurer before each meeting, lengthy sessions in which they examined the tight budget and carried on the commendable financial stewardship of the retired bishop.

* * *

For almost ten years, Joe had lived with the Redeemer Congregation in joy and adversity, and they had come to know each other well. His old friends had heard him extol the good he had found in every community where he lived, the good people he had known in all of them. Their influence upon his life had been profound, frequently in ways he did not understand until he could look back upon them from a more mature perspective. He was grateful for all of it, and the people of Redeemer and Catoctin Springs were dear to his heart.

In the wider church, they talked about the 20 percent of people in every parish who accomplished 80 percent of the work. There was in the Redeemer congregation a solid core of decency and kindness that made all the troubles of ministry seem worthwhile. The parish leaders, the young people who had grown up and entered college before his eyes, the elderly who moved forward to new life, babies born and playing soccer before one turned around, new families and individuals moving in, older ones retiring to distant places, whose going was always touching and sentimental—in all the world, he believed there were no better people with whom to share the great journey.

One of the gifts Redeemer gave him was clarity in understanding that nobody can please everyone. The church assumes that every priest's common sense tells him this from the start. Emotionally, however, it is a lesson of ministry that must be learned the hard way. Joe counted it a blessing that the people who despised him were a mere handful in so large a congregation. Not only was their number small, but they had given his predecessor similar trouble, and some of them the man before him.

Most of those who would become Joe's detractors had been brought into the church years before by a charismatic, long-haired, handsome young priest, an independently wealthy activist whose railings against the establishment and war in Vietnam had dismayed the majority of the people. His radicalism and unconventional theology had endeared himself to a young and impressionable Lottie Bascomb and a few others. In their eyes, priests who followed this man's short tenure were doomed by comparison. Joe was mystified at first by their attachment to this man. They followed his career and rebellious exploits, made possible by the liberating independence of a private fortune, like fans of a rock star. Their comments about him in unguarded moments, however, mocking his mountainous ego and envying his enabling wealth, would have shocked their hero profoundly.

Redeemer helped Joe understand all this and much else. It brought clarity to his efforts to assess himself and his ministry in the eternal struggle of growth and maturity that must go on if one is to continue to serve. In the law, Joe had not been bothered much by the dislike of others, an occupational hazard in lawsuits, trials, and criminal prosecutions. It came, as they said, with the territory; it was part of the price one paid for going to the mat and lasting in the ring at all. The stakes and consequences of litigation confirmed a certain adversarial toughness in life in the broken world. Those who could stand up to it and meet its challenges with courage and decency grew stronger in the law regardless of who prevailed on the merits.

It was very different in the church, where emotions were more apparent and less controlled by rules, and the uncertainties of serving professionally, effectively, in a sea of volunteers challenged a priest's every gift and deficit. The closer people came to God, it seemed, the more delicate became the balance between self-sacrifice and anger. Sensitivities and sentiment churned into human relationships in the church a swirl of emotion that could, because the context was almost wholly volunteer, blaze up with little provocation or restraint. That the church was the household of the Spirit and the Spirit was at work within these human dilemmas made it that much more vital that clergy be grounded in prayer and keep their eyes on God. These were realities often impossible to explain to the faithful and one of the reasons ministry was such a lonely way to live.

Joe had ceased to worry as much about his detractors. He was saddened that Lottie Bascomb's temperament and nastiness had seeped into her children, who regarded Joe with a sullen contempt that everyone recognized. Only when he served as a counselor at the diocesan summer camp, when for a week they were away from Lottie and the comments she and her friends made about him routinely in her home, did her children appear to lose their contempt for him. By the end of a week of fun together and sharing the rustic spirituality of the camp, they were smiling at him and beginning to treat him as a friend. It was an attitude he prayed would carry over once they returned to Catoctin Springs. After a few weeks back at home, however, they had returned to their depression and rudeness.

Lottie's confidant and comrade was Nancy Dodd, a capable person subject to quick changes of attitude toward Joe. He had often wondered if she suffered from bipolar disorder. Periods of glee and enthusiastic kindness would alternate in her with weeks of fussy, opinionated, irritable complaining and an unerring instinct for the bitterest view of any situation. After some years, Joe succeeded in detaching himself from the personal seesaw of her emotions, learning to treat her evenly and kindly regardless of her moods. He was grateful to her for one thing, however. Apparently, she did not rail about him at home. Her children showed none of the contempt for him that occurred in families in which he was always criticized.

There was another opposed to him, an aged hippie whose favorite conclusion to letters was an underlined "Hugs," and whose peace-and-love exterior concealed a vast volcanic anger. She surprised Joe, who had welcomed her and her genial husband into the parish, introduced them to everybody, and done all he could to make them feel at home. It astonished him especially that the husbands of these critical women were all easygoing, friendly, somewhat-quiet men who had always related well to him. At first, he was cautious toward them. When they gave every indication of genuine friendliness, he had wondered if it was their way of making up for their wives' behavior. As time passed, he decided that he perceived their personalities accurately and that they were living their lives making accommodations where necessary. He liked and admired them all, and there grew up among them a sort of understanding that they would be friends with him despite what he knew they must have been hearing at home. Perhaps they were hearing it about others too. He didn't know, and certainly never asked.

Several more were in the picture, especially two heavy women whose children and husbands, too, shunned him. But they were continually leaving the parish over one thing or another, returning for a time until Joe created another indiscretion or something new irked them, when they would depart again in anger. Joe noted that all the people who despised him appeared to have made particular friends with nuns who had settled recently near Catoctin Springs. The four nuns had been polite to him and were very willing to have his help in settling in the community. He was glad that they could provide spiritual companionship to people whom he had been unable to reach. It could only be a blessing for the future of the whole community.

And how most of the people at Redeemer had helped him in all this! They paid him the highest personal tribute by seeking him out for discussion when stress or grief overwhelmed them, confiding in him, sometimes seeking his advice, sometimes wanting only to be listened to. To his continual astonishment, they thanked him for things he had said in sermons that he did not remember. In a thousand small ways, they let him know that his ministry had value in their lives. They did not take advantage of his eagerness to serve well and were generally as concerned about his health and rest as they were of their own blood relations. This was often a blessing for Joe, whose own experience at home was often lonely and disappointing.

For his part, Joe was faithful to them. He observed the necessary boundaries in relationships, striving not to cross lines while nourishing his own capacity for intimacy. He kept confidences, provided encouragement, loved the children, supported the elderly as they neared the great moment, and tried to conduct himself in the community with the dignity he knew his parishioners expected, and had a right to expect, in their parish priest.

Chapter Eleven

I S DESIRE LIKE certain personalities, withstanding life's trials and growing stronger and prevailing, or else becoming weaker and, in the end, breaking down? He had seen love go both ways in people around them. Who can account for the difference? Faith, upbringing, wealth, success, tragedy, culture—none of it seems determinative of whether one prevails or goes down. The resilient emerge from the quietest of lives, and some of the most dynamic go down. He knew instinctively that love must mature with a relationship, ripen in compassion and humor, and keep pace with the hope of life in an absurd world. He never knew what Kate thought. She reserved talk of such matters, if it occurred at all, for days of philosophizing with summer renters on the porches of Wicomico.

What had happened to them? Two average people living ordinary lives, making choices, seeking peace. When he thought about it, sadness overwhelmed him like a storm in the desert, driving the grit of loss into every crease and corner of him. Recalling the days of Kate's pregnancy, when she had been so beautiful, and Ted's birth, and the promises, and hope that had seemed to overcome so many trials, Joe grew unspeakably sad.

He asked himself how he had succeeded in parts of life where relationships and empathy had been so fundamental and yet failed in the most important relationship of all? In the classroom, law, and ministry, life had depended upon good personal bonds. Clarity in word and deed had been indispensable. There were friends in his life going back to the first grade. His former students, whom he had known for twenty-five years, called him in the night to talk. People from his days in the law and his first parishes were still in weekly touch with him. But he was failing in marriage. Kate was a good person. What had happened? He knew the answer was not wholly within her drinking and secrecy and denial. He had made his mistakes too, especially in the amount of time he had devoted to the law and ministry. He should have been at home more, spent more time with her, done more things with Ted, listened to them more, played with them more, not worried about money so much, or planning for the days ahead. It had seemed like life with an irresponsible teenage daughter, but perhaps the problem had been more his than hers. If he had approached it all in a different way, been more patient, kept his mouth shut about what he took to be lies, let Catherine have her way, allowed them both to drink as they had before he married into their family, it might have all been different. But thoughts of Ted, images of his shining face in every year of his growing up, precious recollections that overwhelmed his heart led Joe to ponder his bumbling attempts to protect his son from reckless harm and destructive truth.

He should have let Kate and her whole selfish family live the natural consequences of their own behavior, but he had never had the intelligence or the nerve to do it. How does a man take that kind of risk when his young child is part of it all, his wife's health is at issue, and their home and family life are the setting for the unknown results?

He knew in his bones that all along God's guidance had surrounded him. Had he misinterpreted it, doing busily what he told himself was right and missing the divine direction? Had he made of the gift of his own free will a mess that had drained the joy from the main relationship of his life? His love for Kate had been wider and deeper than any mere duty, but had he been right about it? Had he heard God right?

He had always believed God would guide him in the marriage God had led him to. One went with the other. Had he missed the directions? He must have done, because there had been so many problems over the years. Small things could have long-term significance.

When Ted was born, she had wanted to buy a movie camera. He had been against it because they needed a new car and were saving for a house. If he could only go back and have a second go at things, there was so much he would do differently, better. Over the years, he had interpreted the fading of her sarcasm, shouting, and tantrums as a sign that she loved him and was glad to be married to him. But while at first the surface had appeared to heal, he had become gradually aware of an internal rigidity that expanded and stiffened.

Was it all his fault, or was most of it? The support of his family counselor, spiritual director, and Al-Anon companions, who alone knew something of his feelings, never wavered. He knew God was speaking to him through them. Without this conviction, when he laid it all before God and listened for guidance, the silence would have been deafening. Life should go on moving forward as a stream through great obstacles, seeking new directions and outlets. The healing mystery of prayer despite the uncertain silence, the great pleasure of Ted's company, and the presence in life of so many friends were all blessings. He was grateful.

Neither Kate nor Ted still had any interest in Joe's vocation. They came to services at Redeemer when they could. There was always an excuse why they had to be at St. John's. Some of the St. John's students at Redeemer told him curiously how Kate was often in the liturgy at school services, wearing a robe much more complicated than his and marching in procession behind Hervey and the school chaplain. Kate had never mentioned it; Joe wondered if it contributed to her minimizing view of his work. In unintentional ways, she and Ted demonstrated they did not consider his to be a real profession, exactly, but rather like the shallow work of an event organizer or the social director of a cruise ship. Joe appeared little more than the head counselor of a year-round camp. Real work in life was being done elsewhere, in schools and factories and doctors' offices. Joe had a whole big parish full of people to help him and not very much to do really, a truth confirmed by the fact that he spent considerable time tending to the house, keeping up the lawn, paying the bills, and doing laundry. Why, even Kate, with all she had to do, could step in and conduct worship.

When he tried to talk with Kate and Ted about his work, they listened patiently, as though enduring a chapel homily, not wanting to be caught daydreaming. As soon as he stopped talking, they began a discussion within seconds of much more momentous issues, the roles of mother, son, teacher, student, adult, and youth blending with undefined abandon. A loud, wild girl, not at all the St. John's "type," had been expelled a month before and had nevertheless made a brazen forbidden appearance on the grounds to the glee of the students, irritating Father Hervey enormously. It was rumored the academic dean was furious with one teacher or another, and everybody could tell by the way they passed each other in the refectory without speaking. The football team was terrible. Somebody was "going" with someone new this week. A junior class trip was being planned next year to Mexico.

Joe understood Ted. He was a teenager, after all. Joe's vocation was dry and foreign compared to the exciting work that important men were doing in the world, insight into which was but an internet connection away. Often, when Ted was younger, he had asked Joe to tell him about the frightening criminal cases, some well-known in their day, that he had tried. He would listen and ask questions and always ask Joe again why he had left the life of a trial lawyer for the church. Much more exciting were the exploits of Tina, or Gina, who had vigorously defied Hervey's admonitions to wear a bra beneath her blouse or to keep her school blazer buttoned. Professional athletes. Rock stars. The fathers of his school friends, successful businessmen who took their families and children's friends to Aruba or Barbados for spring break. Politicians.

Joe understood. He was prepared to be patient. He reminded himself that the most spiritual and practical men and women he knew in the priesthood had come up through lives of action and responsibility. He would wait for his son to grow a little and understand him more.

But with Kate, an adult, he found this preference for schoolyard gossip alarming and unhealthy. It might have been helpful to Ted if Kate had shown some interest once in a while or encouraged Ted to pay more attention to his father and his career, assuring him that Joe's vocation had value for their family and others too. But there was no more of this than there was interest in current events or their home.

Kate could not bring herself to give away clothing she could no longer wear. She could not define NATO or identify the Taj Mahal. Behind every calamity in the world, she perceived the sinister hand of the American government. AIDS, concocted in a government laboratory in Maryland, was a CIA plot to control the world. And this was the reasoning of the primary influence upon Ted, the one with whom he talked on the way to school and on the way home at night. Joe perceived that his own efforts to make up for it often came across as pitiable, dry, irrelevant attempts to show off his naive understanding of life.

Ted was a good boy. He loved Joe, Joe told himself over and over. He was in the midst of those years when mothers dote on sons and sons on mothers, reinforcing unique bonds that sometimes seem to exclude fathers. Even as he assured himself, however, Joe had to admit that he did not know what he was talking about. Everywhere he turned, he could see exceptions, and he had recognized them all his life. No matter what kind of scoundrel the father was, there was always at least some love and grudging respect from his children. He had seen it in court for years, sons and daughters who had been neglected and abused by their parents and who, in the end, wanted one thing only—to be with those parents despite everything. But between Joe and his uninspiring, grown-up views of things and discussing with his mother the latest school doings that had set Father Hervey's intrusive nose twitching, his teenage son's priorities were predictable.

Joe remembered his own boyhood embarrassment at his father's ways. He had appeared bumbling and unsophisticated as he went about his earnest attempts to do right in life, so often mortifying his children in front of their friends. His mother would take them aside and kindly and patiently defend their father to them, explaining his idiosyncrasies and peculiarities lovingly and with compassion. She helped them distinguish character from mere composure, and honor from the stains of poverty and low self-confidence. Her manner and words helped them see their frustrated, overworked, strapped young father in a truer light. Such conversations nourished their respect for him and deepened love for both their parents. It was part of learning sympathy, empathy, and patience. Joe's father had done the same in urging them to help their mother, seek out ways to lighten her burden, anticipate her desires. It was from this background that Joe counseled Ted as a small child to do all he could to help Kate, obey her, and be patient with her. On the very rare occasions when she had steeled herself and disciplined Ted or denied him a toy, or a snack before mealtime, Joe tried to help Ted understand that limits mean love, that discipline is a way of caring. As he himself had always had to set the limits for Ted, he dearly hoped that Ted would learn to apply that understanding to him too. When Catherine's drinking grew unmanageable and she said terrible things about Joe or became sarcastic toward Kate, Joe would follow the example his mother had shown him as a child. He tried to explain to Ted that his granny was elderly, sick, and almost deaf and that she should be treated with kindness and respect however she behaved. He made a conscious choice to save for much later discussions with his son about alcohol, addiction, and denial. For years he believed his son was too young to comprehend.

Even when Ted was twelve and thirteen, Joe still hesitated. He knew that Ted would question Kate about whatever Joe said. He knew that Kate would minimize whatever Joe had said and deny to their son that her mother or anyone else in her family abused alcohol. And as between Kate and himself, he knew whom Ted would believe.

He remembered days when Ted was about three and Kate was teaching substance abuse in one of her high school science classes. It was about that time Joe had talked to her about her credit cards and offered to pay them off and she had begun contributing her paycheck to the family account. Her sarcasm and ridicule of Joe were constant, although it would be several more years before they reached their most destructive pinnacle. Her behavior was always worse after several big glasses of white wine. He recalled asking her how she could teach about the dangers of something she was covering up in her mother's behavior and her own. Even as a veteran of the trial court, he had found her outburst of rage and denial unnerving. There had been no peace for weeks. And although life had settled down eventually, he knew the fire still smoldered.

Ted helped little around the house. He was away all summer in Wicomico. Throughout middle school, he had played on a traveling soccer team that practiced from the end of classes until dark, when it was time to come home, eat dinner, and complete his homework. When he entered high school at St. John's, he embarked upon the routine of academics, athletics, and relentless afternoon and weekend activities by which private schools claimed a unique ability to educate the whole student. It seemed Ted was never at home. Family meals ceased. When he was there, Kate was with him too, and she never got around to enforcing the rules about his chores and other small responsibilities assigned during family "discussions." Reminders from Joe came as jarring interruptions.

The routines of homelife, which Joe had tried to establish for Ted—regular bedtime, avoiding certain shows on television, a weekly allowance from which Ted must deposit a bit in his savings account, emptying the wastebaskets, and picking up sticks and windfalls so Joe could rake or mow—often lasted only as long as Joe was around to reinforce them. Ted was good about caring for Cory when Joe traveled on diocesan business. But rules agreed to in family discussions were left behind when Kate took Ted to Wicomico, where she did not feel compelled to observe any other influence then her own. He could get his way with her with a minimum of wheedling. She accepted the role of co-conspirator as long as it endeared her to her son. Self-absorbed, irresponsible, and unwilling to acknowledge anything in herself that might warrant change or even close scrutiny, she enjoyed relating to Ted as a contemporary and saw no reason to do otherwise.

Joe missed Ted dreadfully when he began to board in his last year at St. John's. Ted and Kate had promised that Ted would return home on weekends. It happened rarely. Joe's work, with its long hours and travel, had increased with the departure of the bishop and his resulting new duties. It always seemed that Joe's presence was required at this or that weekend meeting on the rare times when Ted was home from St. John's. Joe was not blind to what he was missing. As he was doing what he believed God expected of him, he was certain that God would preserve rightness at home. Occasionally, during Ted's last summer at Wicomico before his senior year of boarding at St. John's, Joe allowed some teenaged neighbors, and occasionally their fathers, to come into the quiet house at night to use the computer. It had been set up in the living room for Ted's use for his studies during the previous school year. Joe was in the family room or upstairs in the big bedroom while they were using the computer. Hearing them talking and horsing around made him happy to have a joyful noise in the house again. It reminded him of Ted being at home, and Kate. After they had thanked him and left the house, he was always in a good mood.

Before Ted had even begun to think of applying to colleges, Joe was anticipating his going and dreading having him at a distance. The thought of Ted in college filled him with pride and happiness, but he knew his heart would break anyway. He could not imagine life without Ted around, and he used Ted's final boarding year at St. John's as a chance to prepare himself. He was so proud of Ted, his accomplishments and friendships, easygoing personality, and sweet nature that after meditating upon his son for a while, he found himself humming, and whatever trials the day had brought him became somehow more manageable. The world was a more decent place with Ted in it. Whatever his own faults and failures, Joe could always say that he had raised a fine son, a decent man, good-hearted and sincere.

* * *

For all its joy, Christmas had always been difficult. In Ted's last year of high school, it was especially so for Joe. He supposed that most people assumed it was the cheerful pinnacle of a priest's yearly round. Christmas. The tilting of the universe, the shifting of reality. How the world had misunderstood it, ignored it, turned it to every mercurial advantage, junked it up with reindeer and the inane crèche and other sanctimonious misinterpretations. The Maker of All Things translating from outside the universe to become a human being, and an infant human being, born in a barn, fragile, vulnera-

ble, relegating sin to its true disposition, triumphing over the ultimate horror, for the love of creatures whose abuse and ignorance
of their gifts and one another go on and on. It is so absurd that at
times Joe found it hard to believe it himself. Can we blame them? he
wondered. Human minds cannot comprehend the universe, let alone
the One who exists outside it, the One who made it, the One who
creates time and space and transcends them both. God has done a
good job of domesticating incarnation for us, reducing the miracle to
images we can comprehend, a baby, a loving mother, a decent father,
shepherds, wise men, a star. The high and lofty One who inhabits
eternity, coming from the high and holy place for children, street
people, prostitutes, the sick, the lonely—if it were not true, it would
be preposterous, almost hilarious.

What has the human heart made of it, the eye of the soul beholding ancient promises, coming again, different this time, to judge? It
was too much for failing intellect and brittle sinews, fragile heart jerking like an insect in a web, mystery. His head filled with wonder and
hope, struggling to overcome the shock, so vivid at this of all times of
year, Joe cruised the potholed streets and unmarked country roads of
his parish, tending to priestly duties in the oblivious world, striving
to serve as he had promised. It was always a complicated time, one
of those periods in which he especially lamented the impossibility of
an assistant. In addition to parish activities and responsibilities that
became doubly pressing, he took Holy Communion to every parishioner who was bedridden, confined to home, or institutionalized. He
did so every month of the year, but with the added seasonal responsibilities, it was more complicated getting around to everyone at
Christmas. He served in one of those dioceses where laypersons were
not allowed to take the consecrated elements of Holy Communion
to their disabled sisters and brothers, the bishop fearing the clergy
would become lazy and leave that sacred ministry wholly to laity. Joe
began in early December, making visits each day, driving hundreds
of miles with Communion and small Christmas gifts prepared by
the women of Redeemer. Keeping up, too, with all else that needed
attention, he often completed these trips on Christmas Eve or the
day before.

On this particular year, all things that could have grown more complex had done so vigorously, and Joe was wearing down. The parish budget had to be ready by the fifth of January. Long-range plans for the diocesan convention in Catoctin Springs in March had to be finalized. Three parishioners died in the first two weeks of December. The organizer of the Christmas pageant was felled by a virus. There was a crisis in the day care center where a teacher had shouted at an obnoxious parent. The ancient office printer had broken down again with half the seasonal bulletins unfinished, and Milly was in tears. Dozens of people were calling or coming in for assistance: parents unable to buy food and winter clothing for their children, transients trying to get home for the holidays, people without fuel who needed transportation to the doctor or a distant hospital, who had nothing to eat. There were sermons to write and packages to mail. One thing or another for home or vocation took up every minute of each day. He would go to bed exhausted each night.

Ted, and often one or two of his friends, had always accompanied Joe to cut a Christmas tree and bring it home and install it in the family room, a custom Joe had always looked forward to. As his school had recessed on the eighteenth and Ted was a young man now, taller than Joe, and had been driving for a year, Joe asked him to take charge of getting the Christmas tree this year. Ted very gladly agreed to cut a Christmas tree and have it at home on a certain night when Joe returned from work. They would trim it into shape, bring it indoors, and set it up in the family room together as they had done for years.

But this was not to be. A friend called suddenly and asked Ted to accompany her to the mall for the afternoon to shop for Christmas presents, an unanticipated invitation that Ted was eager to accept. With no thought of encouraging him to follow through with what his father had told him to do, or considering the time constraints of Joe's work, Kate told him to go shopping with his friend and not to worry about the tree. Neither she nor Ted, for vastly different reasons, could look beyond the moment or consider life outside their immediate desires. Kate herself also had been released from school and, as she had about the twentieth of December every year of her life since the first grade, was preoccupied with the anticipation of her two-week vacation.

Once classes had ended and Kate was "finally free," as she liked to say, she intended to enjoy every minute. She saw the time as a rightful cessation of responsibility of any sort, and all threats of infringement upon it were insensitive and unfair. No one had a right to make demands upon her. In her mind, this euphoric state extended to her son as well.

Joe agreed that teachers, of all people, needed time to rest. He did not begrudge Kate any vacation and was very glad to see her enjoying herself. He had said as much to her for years. But family life continued on during her vacations. It was Christmas. There were things to do, and he could not do them all alone. He had found it very difficult over the years to reason with her about this. When he pointed out other teachers who had three or four children at home and lived on a tighter budget than she and Joe did, she became sullen and sarcastic. When he reminded her she was a grown woman now and it was different from her days in grade school, she walked away in disgust. She had a different view of it. She had labored in the classroom since the Thanksgiving break, and now here was Christmas vacation, a holiday specifically designed for schoolteachers and students, and she deserved to enjoy it. "I have to work, Joe! I need a break!"

There were Christmas gifts to assemble and wrap, a Christmas tree to fetch and decorate, the house to see to, packages he should have mailed days previously, shopping, invitations to parties, and a dozen other seasonal matters needing attention. Much of it had to take place way ahead of Christmas Day and the week before it. And every year as the season grew near, the responsibilities of Joe's ministry increased at the same time. As with cleaning the house, sorting through the closets, handing on Ted's outgrown clothes, the yard, bills, and other domestic responsibilities, Joe found it necessary to push Kate to do anything during her Christmas vacation. She preferred to spend her days making the rounds of stores and malls, or in her nightgown, reading and watching television, and making her traditional plans for visiting some of the Wicomico summer people in the week between Christmas and New Year's Day.

During November or the first week of December, Joe arranged for the two of them to make a list and shop together for Christmas gifts. It was fun. Kate enjoyed searching for the right gifts for certain people, and they had lunch or dinner along the way. If she shopped alone, the checking account was soon depleted and she would leave it up to Joe to cope with monthly bills and pay taxes in the new year. And after some asking, she would relent and decorate the house if Joe brought up from the cellar the boxes he had packed away the year before. She would gladly buy Christmas gifts for Ted and others, and if Joe would shop for the necessary ingredients, she would make several dozen jars of her superb preserves, jellies, and spicy mustard to give to friends as Christmas gifts. Each year, in the first few days of December, he would purchase everything she needed so he was sure to find jars and ingredients before the stores sold out. Her cheerful small jars with their glowing contents, wrapped in colored tissue paper and tucked into bright gift bags, were a delight to give and to receive. Their friends were grateful, and eager requests for her recipes were included in thank-you notes received in January.

The days leading up to Christmas always required caution and diplomacy. Joe went about them never knowing if Kate would do her part gladly and without prompting or with petulance. During it all, he continued to be astonished at how she could appear to change in seconds, becoming bright and pleasant when Ted entered the room or if neighbors knocked on the door. Although he had endured her tantrums by the hundreds over the years, he still found himself, especially at Christmas, depressed and discouraged by them when they occurred so unexpectedly in an already-complicated time. On some Christmas Eves, they were still delivering gifts as Joe was on his way to Redeemer to conduct services. In years when she began to cook early, he felt great relief as she padded barefoot about the kitchen in her apron, considering him warily as he, wondering about her mood, came and went as if walking on eggshells. It brought him back to the early days after their marriage, when he was learning the secrets of her labile emotions. She had been lovely and lovable in Joe's eyes despite her temperament. When she took time in the kitchen to do anything, perhaps because she was so good at cooking, he could usually rouse her with a joke or a bit of ribald news. Her laughter was music to his ears.

Of all the family festivities that could and should have been a joy, the happy moment on Christmas morning when Ted opened his gifts had become a yearly occasion of deflation and disappointment for Joe. And each year it took him by surprise. He should have foreseen it from years of experience, but it was lost to him in the rushing to and fro of the season until the moment it occurred. By then it was too late to do anything about it for another year.

Each year, Joe and Kate would decide together on the gifts they would give to Ted, both individually and from Santa. In his childhood years, when great, expensive toys were popular, usually computer games or equipment, like most parents, they made choices together within their means, trying hard to balance what Ted wanted with what they could afford. And every year, Kate ignored their understanding. She kept the checkbook during her "free" days after classes ended and, while Joe was in his seasonal duties, proceeded to purchase all sorts of gifts for Ted, of which Joe had no knowledge.

Joe wanted Ted to be happy and to have everything his friends had. Thus, it was deeply troubling, after going to bed at 2:30 or 3:00 a.m. after the Christmas Eve services and getting up at 7:00 or 8:00 a.m. to open gifts with Ted and Kate, to find himself a spectator at a two-way conversation that excluded him year after year.

"All right, Mom! I didn't even know they had these around here."

"I saw it at the mall and figured you'd like it. Is it the color you like?"

"And this! Wait till the guys see this! Andrew has one of these."

"Well, I was talking to Andrew's mother when she was picking him up at school and saw one just like it in the back seat of her car and she said they had them at Connor & King, so I went right over there before they sold out. I didn't even stop to grade papers. I went right over."

"Thanks, Mom! And these! How did you find them? Maria said there weren't any of them left in the stores around here!"

"Not if you're quick like I am. I got them the Monday after Thanksgiving so they wouldn't be sold out like last year. Now, when you open that big one behind you, remember that I can always exchange it if you don't like it. Be careful and don't crush the box, and I can take it back and exchange it the minute the stores open tomorrow. And that one, the one with the green ribbon, I thought you could use when we go down to see the Chandlers day after tomorrow, something you can do in the car during the ride down there."

"Wow. Thanks, Mom. I mean, Santa." The three of them would chuckle.

"Anything for my boy!" Kate would say, brightly, without looking in Joe's direction.

She knew he would not express his hurt in front of Ted and spoil the moment. Or perhaps it never entered her mind how it made him feel. Or he thought in the following days and nights, perhaps she knew perfectly well how it made him feel and it did not matter to her. Whatever her feelings might have been, in his own fatigue and disappointment and anger at himself for failing to foresee this yearly dilemma and trying to resolve it ahead of time, and knowing that Ted thought that Joe had thoughtlessly not participated in these plans for his gifts, he knew he spoiled the moment for all three of them in his exasperated silence.

Christmas morning. His loved ones with him, the tree perfuming the cherished air with the pungency of cedar, the appealing holiday colors of paper and ribbon reflected on each glistening ornament, candles burning in their furrows of ground pine on the mantel, his good-natured son seated on the floor in front of him, happy and smiling, his wife happy, pleased—a joyful time. Time for coffee and a bit of breakfast with family, a rare treat, before going up to shave and dress and driving to the church for the 10:00 a.m. service. And small-minded bastard that he was, he could not rise above his disappointment in the midst of these blessings—and on the anniversary of the birth of the loveliest life ever lived, the one he tried to follow and honor. He hated the weakness within him that allowed his own selfish emotions to overwhelm what little of that striving he was able to manage.

I cannot see what flowers are at my feet, nor what soft incense hangs upon the boughs. Would Keats or anyone have understood? When Ted was young, Joe had chimed in, pretending not to be surprised at the unexpected choice of gifts, but suspecting he sounded like a weak player taking credit for someone else's goal. As Ted grew older, it became obvious that he understood his mother perfectly and that he knew Joe had nothing to do with most of the surprises waiting under the tree. In the excitement of the moment, his father was relegated to obscurity, eclipsed by the intimacy of his mother's knowledge of his preferences, likes, desires. Joe attempted to make the best of it when Ted was younger, with "Great, Ted, I'll bet you'll have fun with that," or "I'm glad you like that, honey, and it will look good on you," and "It's so nice of Mom to think of that." By Ted's early teens, nobody was fooling anybody. It had become a sort of Christmas tradition, giving way in Joe to wondering, year after year, why she just didn't take the time to mention it to him, let him know what she'd done, be open with him, be honest about things. It was petty, denigrating self-loathing for neglecting to anticipate what she would do and trying to discuss it with her, say, in mid-December. But with all else that came with the season, he spent no time trying to second-guess her. Later, in his more rested and less preoccupied moments, he seethed with shame for his self-centered preoccupations in the golden moments of Christmas morning.

And when on a gray January afternoon or frigid night, when she was already going into her winter doldrums, he blunderingly attempted to discuss it with her after the fact, she became dismissive and irritable with him for his tiresome insistence on bringing up such issues.

"Just get over it, Joe. It's over. Stop thinking about it."

"But I've talked with you about it year after year, and you've promised not to do it again, and to let me know what you've bought, and—"

"So I forgot this year! So what? I can't do anything about it now, so get over it."

"Kate, it ruins Christmas morning for—"

"Wait a minute! *I* ruin Christmas! Is that what you said? Give me a break. You're the one we have to call two or three times to get up. You're the one we have to wait for while you hold everything up. You're the one who stays out late Christmas Eve instead of being home with the family. You're the one who goes into church on Christmas Day and then sleeps on the couch in the afternoon while I have to sit here. You're the one in a bad mood. *I* ruin Christmas! Give me a break."

"But you turn it into a two-way thing between you and Ted, just like dinner table conversation when you talk only about—"

"Well, just get over it, Joe!"

"Why can't we talk about this, Kate, like other couples?"

"Because there's nothing to talk about, Joe. And don't start that stuff about counseling again. If there's any problem in this family, it's you. You're the one, Joe. Not me!"

She had told Ted to go shopping with the girl from school and not to worry about cutting a Christmas tree. The excursion to the mall had turned into an invitation to dinner and an overnight stay in the girl's parents' guest room. Joe had moved his plans around and cut corners and changed clothes in his office and gone out late in the day to cut a tree, arriving home after dark with a plump cedar from a tree farm in the neighboring county. By the light from the garage door, with Cory's tail thumping the driveway in approval with Joe's every move, he snipped away the webbing, trimmed some ungainly lower branches, sawed off a few more inches of trunk, and plunged the cedar quickly down into a bucket of water. He left it propped up in the corner of the garage so the limbs could settle down overnight. From the cellar he retrieved the box containing the green-and-red stand, the round felt skirt with its big border of prancing reindeer, and the roll of industrial plastic he spread out first every year to protect the carpet. All this he left in readiness for Kate, who promised to set it all up when Ted returned the following day. She was vexed when Joe reminded her for the second time how important it was to put the plastic sheet down first.

139

He returned the following night to find the tree, gloriously decorated, standing in the family room with majesty, with a surprising number of wrapped gifts nestled carefully around its base. It was a lovely sight, and Kate accepted his effusive praise gladly. She had not bothered to roll up a small oriental carpet, which protruded from beneath it all, but he was wise enough not to say anything. Only when he took the tree down in the week after New Year's Day did he discover she had not put down the plastic sheet as promised. Year after year, he had used it to protect the wall-to-wall carpet. Water had leaked from the stand and through the small red Bukhara rug onto the carpeting beneath, leaving a scarlet stain that had spread to the size of a card table. No amount of scrubbing would remove it, and Kate studiously refused to take notice or discuss it. He rearranged the furniture and another rug to hide it. *Yes,* he thought to himself, *it is not the end of the world. We can replace the carpeting whenever we sell the house. It is the sort of thing that…just happens.* He had spoken similar words a thousand times before.

And so it had gone in the Christmas of Ted's senior year.

Was it reasonable to be troubled by living life this way? Other men and women managed such things all the time. Were his anger and disappointment justified? He had learned the hard way long ago that reason and justice had nothing to do with it. In a world where millions of children grow up without parental affection, without attention, gifts, or even dental care and clean water, was it right for him to be distressed at the means by which his son's good things came to him? Should he, instead, have been glad that his wife was lavishing gifts upon him, regardless of how secretive she was about it? Had he any real right to find fault with the way she insisted on doing things?

How energetically he could listen to others speak on similar issues and, without offering any advice (he had none to offer), speak encouragingly with them until God granted direction, understanding, at times even wisdom. For himself, he could do nothing. All the meditative hikes along the river or in the mountains, conversations with therapists, listening in Al-Anon meetings, and time on his knees had led him only to getting up and trying again the next day. Should it have been enough? he would ask himself for the rest of his life.

There was another matter too. Because it involved a Christmas gift, Joe saw it, too, as a part of that particular Christmas. A compact disc player for Ted's car, a gift they had agreed upon, was to be selected and installed. Joe had promised to meet Kate and Ted at an auto shop to make the arrangements. This they did in early January, following Kate's and Ted's return from a New Year's trip to visit some Wicomico friends. In the shop, Kate, who had been in possession of the family checkbook since her return, handed it to Joe to pay for the installation. When he recorded the check, he saw that she had written a dozen checks in the preceding days, several of them for cash, totaling about four hundred dollars. As was her way, she had said nothing about it, given him no warning. He had intended to begin paying bills when he got home that night. After he would write the check for the player for Ted's car, there would be no more money until he was paid in the middle of the month.

He should have been used to it by now, but in his exasperation, he had asked her about it—What was there to ask?—hotly and loudly. She had become surprised, submissive, like a dejected servant scolded by a harsh master. He recognized the carefully calculated reaction she presented on the rare occasions when he challenged her in front of Ted. In the seconds it took to analyze what was happening, he knew he had already become more of a cad in his son's eyes. She had probably waited until Ted was standing by to give him the checkbook. After leaving the shop, they proceeded through the snow to their respective cars, and Kate was the first to pull out of the parking lot. Exasperated, Joe turned to Ted, who was unlocking his car door.

"Did you go along when she spent all that money?" he demanded, almost as though Ted had done something wrong. "What did she buy?"

"Calm down, Dad. What's the big deal? She needed some summer clothes for the beach this summer."

"I don't mind summer clothes. But I didn't know about it!" He was raising his voice, and it was strained, like a man being compelled to repeat the obvious for the ten thousandth time. "There are a lot of bills to pay."

"So what? Pay them next month," said his teenage son, sounding very much indeed like his mother. One of the shopkeepers locked the front door with a clatter, and the outside lights went out. It was beginning to snow again.

"Goddamn it! That's not the point." Joe was so angry his voice was cracking. What was it? Why was this impasse, a matter he had attempted a thousand times before to discuss with Kate, a topic he had explored calmly and rationally with his family counselor and spiritual adviser for years, so filling him with emotion now as he stood in a snowy parking lot in the night, facing his own son?

"Calm down, Dad! You act like you hate her."

"What are you talking about?"

"You always seem mad at her." As he said this, Ted was grinning, and later, Joe would wonder if his son had been trying to soften the impact of his words.

It should have been clear to Joe, clearer than anything in his life, that here was a moment that called for calm, careful, fatherly assessment of the facts, appreciation for how the moment was unfolding in his son's eyes, and for mature self-restraint and compassion. He should have calmed himself, apologized to Ted, driven him to a nearby diner for coffee, answered his questions, talked over with him the background, the realities. He could have turned the painful, shameful episode into something healing and constructive. Even if Ted had despised him, Joe could have *shown* him that he was a father who loved him, loved Kate, thought deeply about things, whose heart was kind, whose intentions were fair and honorable.

With a parishioner or parishioner's child, a client, a former student, a neighbor, or anyone of a hundred others who routinely sought him out to talk, Joe would have had the presence of mind to do all these things. He would have behaved with the best instincts of a loving father, in the most pastoral tradition of priestly vocation, the finest intellectual composure of a good lawyer, the most open and sensitive tradition of teaching. But in this critical moment, filled with raw anger and the bitterest, most inarticulate disappointment, to his lasting shame, he turned away from his son, the dearest person in his life, and jerked open the door of his car.

"You think I hate her? Is that what you think?" he roared, as years of coping flashed before his eyes and his son's antithetical words burned into his brain.

As he spun out of the snowy parking lot, enraged, tearful, his insides burning, leaving Ted staring after him, in the back of his burning mind, a voice hissed, *Yes, you miserable bastard. That's what he thinks!*

Chapter Twelve

SOMEWHERE IN HIS confused teenage years, in preparing for confirmation or a high school course or for some other reason long forgotten, Joe had read the Book of Job for the first time. It had changed, or rather had begun, something in him he did not recognize and was unable to articulate when later his awareness began to grow. But small gears he never knew had interlocked and quietly begun turning together, changing his course by a minute angle that would, in time, raise a new horizon. It was not unusual. The great book had altered many lives more complicated and pivotal than his. Joe had not at first understood his own encounter. It would take a long time before he knew anything of justice and cosmic responsibilities, of God's active role in human lives, or the mystery of faith in suffering. The new direction had been corrected over time and many re-readings and had become apparent to him, as with so many of life's profundities, only in retrospect.

From a conventional childhood and typical, ungainly adolescence had emerged a young man who tended quietly, sometimes embarrassingly, more toward introspection than his friends did. As he grew older he had an increasing itch to get to the point, to turn off the relentless radio blaring in the life's background, clear away the ubiquitous clutter that obscured essentials, and reveal the truth that waited to be identified. Everywhere about him, he perceived the rational evidence of a plan—planes, proportions, angles, spaces, sounds, and temporal relationships. He was confounded by a growing awareness that everything could be reduced to mathematical clarity. He perceived a unity whose nature remained elusive.

In the law, there was too much to retain too quickly to allow for breakthroughs. When a window opened, it was usually in recollecting the words of someone, a witness or another lawyer, who was trying to describe motives or how something had happened or what someone had been thinking. When he got to seminary and the study of systematic theology and world religions, he recognized some of the territory and knew he had been there before.

The desire for clarity and simplicity brought Joe a tangible benefit. When the craziness of the world or his own sinfulness felled him, he was increasingly able to focus upon the truth that God is good and good to *him*. This certainty purified existence like dregs settling out of wine, allowing the grace of life to glow and sparkle and confirming, wherever he turned, the dignity and order in creation. It helped him accept the unfinished nature of things and recognize that the divine plan is still unfolding.

Such insight as he was given sharpened the contrasts of life and forced things of value into a troubling focus that St. Paul would have recognized. Joe knew that his small individual existence was locked into the great forward movement like a speck of dust in a glacier and that he possessed no power in himself to help himself. But against reality stood the gift of his clear and simple conviction that the Creator God had made him, knew him, and though there was much, much more to preoccupy the divine mind, valued his existence. The knowledge was so absurd that he had trouble believing it himself at times, but he turned back to it again and again, instinctively, like a homing pigeon staying the course.

Clear vision and a reduction to fundamentals come with a cost as well as blessings, however. An ancient enigma, the great paradox prowling the fringes of faith like a cruising shark, becomes clearer too. God is good. God knows me and knows every other human being too. Why does God who loves me allow the innocent to suffer? He thought of the woman on the porch of the mountain store.

The eternal question becomes more practical, visceral, and persistent as comprehension grows. If even dim faith exists in a human being, awareness of one's own blessings compels a cautious look around once in a while. And Joe knew that they suffer by the hundreds of millions. Because they breathe, because they were born, they suffer routinely and casually. Because of what they believe or how they look or where they live or how they worship, they suffer. And yesterday and the day before were worse than a thousand years ago.

What was so special about Joe that God permitted him to live and even prosper while others suffered? Christ teaches us that God knows all God's children and when the innocent suffer God's is the first heart to break. Joe knew he was a sinner. It was imperfect knowledge; no human understanding is perfect, but Joe's was enough to know how blessed he was and how thick the darkness for so many others. Much better men than him had been brutalized by the millions. Or worse, they had survived to learn of the suffering of loved ones. His heart jerked as though electrocuted when he thought of the anguish of survivors mourning spouses, children, parents, friends, neighbors. Being shot or gassed must be merciful compared to knowing that one's child is adrift and alone, helpless, lost, victimized. Behind the eyes of every child in Theresienstadt, Nanking, and Armenia, wandering the roads of Africa and Russia, stuffed into Arab wells in Algeria or the soil of Cambodia, the pain of parents screams like fire alarms. Faces of the kidnapped and runaways in public places, shrines of anguish and hope, kindle a horrid fear of seeing our own children lost in a world more ravaged than we found it. What does a human being say in prayer to God? Even the psalmist's wail is inadequate. The only adequate prayer may be the silence of the attentive. A believer could go insane pondering it.

God had allowed *him* life in Christ, in a democratic land, in the legacy of Magna Carta, with family, friends, medical care, food, and clean water. God had blessed *him* with life in a church that valued compassion and reason in a world of theological ignorance and fanaticism. He knew it was a gift and that there was nothing random about it. How could one enjoy blessings without consciousness of the millions who lived so wretchedly? It was impossible not to be moved by it. He could have surrendered to despair or, worse, to the agnosticism that others saw as the only sane response to absurd reality.

Through no credit of his own, however, he never descended below loyal but profound perplexity.

Since beginning to read Job, he never had it in him to be a traitor.

He was not obsessed. But the sorrow within the human family is different, the intentional cruelty and blind indifference of one human being toward another, and it withered his heart.

He did not believe that God caused it. But why didn't God prevent it? Joe would never have allowed Ted to play with dynamite or razor blades. Nor can the suffering of the innocent be blamed so easily on evil people. He suspected that humanity would always have evil people. The answer, if anything can be said to be an answer, lies not in evil people but in the many good people who do nothing. It all unnerved him, made him woefully self-conscious and unspeakably sad.

When he was about twelve, he had known a camp counselor, a big high school bully, who had taken a liking to him and a couple of his friends but was cruel and unfair to the other campers. Joe and the other favorites feared him, enduring his attention nervously and wondering when he would turn on them too. Christ had shown that this would not happen with God. God is faithful and kind to the end. In his confusion, Joe examined himself—Was he irrational, mentally ill, or emotionally disturbed to be so plagued by what seemed not to concern others? Was he unnaturally morbid? Was the fault in him? In his own imperfect perception?

He knew a good man and woman who had been generous with their fortune and time. After many visits to a fertility clinic, they had conceived, to their great joy. The child was born profoundly retarded. They had spent fourteen years caring for him at home, and they were weary.

He kept in touch with a former client, an obese woman of eighty who suffered from sickle cell anemia and chronic hemorrhoids. She spent her sixties and seventies, when she should have enjoyed some peace and quiet, raising four of her great-grandchildren to young adulthood, on welfare. Joe had assisted her *pro bono* in obtaining legal guardianship and in a few other matters. For many years, he provided presents at Christmas and, in recent years, had referred her to defense lawyers as the four, one by one, broke the law and were incarcerated.

A decent, hardworking farm family near Catoctin Springs, roused in the night by smoke, watched as their house burned down before the volunteer fire company arrived. News from Central America tells of mudslides sweeping away whole villages of dirt-poor peasants. The Chinese deny the presence of AIDS in their land. He knew the history of the twenty-first century. All his life, for reasons he would never understand, people had poured out their hearts to him.

Why was *he* so blessed? Why *do* the innocent suffer? The universal questions—and he had studied the best answers faithful minds had managed to provide. He had read them, carefully marked what was there, and learned what he could. The result was an anguished, lifelong indigestion of mind, body, and spirit for which there seemed no remedy, no purging, even if he had vomited himself inside out.

And what of himself and all that was his in trust? Like a guilty man living next to a vast prison, hearing the cries of the incarcerated as he goes about his small life and aware of how little separates him from the terror next door, Joe wondered that the Author of grace did not allow the barrier to lift upon him too. And yet his heart and mind were sure that God is wholly good, and when humans suffer, especially the least of them, even the guilty, God's is the first heart to break.

There were moments when he felt the closeness of hope. They happened in the middle of the night and always followed the same pattern. Occasionally, he could even predict them. Something hurtful would occur in the family triangle during the course of an evening at home: his exclusion from dinner conversation between his wife and son, or Kate's persistent interruptions of his attempts to converse with Ted—small and usual losses of the sort he tried not to dwell on anymore. Ted would sense Joe's discouragement. The matter would pass. The three of them would proceed through homework, television, reading, or one of a dozen other evening routines. Then, in the middle of the night, Ted would enter his parents' bedroom silently and touch Joe on the shoulder. Joe, awakened the moment his son's door opened, at Ted's touch would move over against Kate so that Ted could lie down too. Ted would say nothing, lying on his side, facing away from Joe. Joe would cover him with a flap of quilt and pat him once or twice on the back, and Ted would fall asleep immediately. Occasionally, he would sleep there all night, but more often, he would get up after a few hours and return silently to his room.

In the center of the universe, between his sleeping wife and child, staring into the darkness, where the alarm clock's glow washed the ceiling in a ghostly blue, Joe contemplated existence. His mind bloomed like a summer day in Wicomico, gleaming with light from the sea and buffeted by breezes. Excitement filled him, and with it came a stupendous calm, like gaining a long view from some rocky crest in the Blue Ridge and beholding the azure grandeur spreading away in uplifting waves. Between the music of Kate's small snores on his right and Ted's quiet breathing on his left, Joe knew he was a blessed man, showered by grace in a thousand ways. Mystery and wonder led to a joy that woke him completely.

Like a high school sophomore growing in character and moral sensibility in spite of himself, Joe read and listened and meditated upon wisdom and simplicity, revelation and mystery, and the years went by. He was nourished unconsciously by life's small and unnoticed consecrations: words, smiles, gestures, renderings of compassionate attention, acts of forgiveness, the gift of a shoulder, the mere sitting down of someone next to another. The external circumstances always brought him around again to his kitchen table and the late-night self-examinations that caused him such guilt. He was alarmed and ashamed at his own reactions to Kate's behavior. He was discouraged by his own frustration at things he could not change and his unending search for the serenity to accept them. He regarded his own pride, hypocrisy, and impatience, and he was horrified. He saw his anger at her as a cruel self-indulgence, a dishonest reaction for a man so blessed and nurtured by God. Was he exploiting her by looking for change? Was it fair of him? He had learned that the only thing he could change was himself.

What was truth? Where were answers? In his life and in the world, what did suffering mean? He wanted understanding, comprehension, wisdom. Every week of his ministry, someone sought an answer from him. The human heart—who can understand it? He did not know. Yet when his son came and slept beside him, with his wife close on the other side, and his midnight contemplations focused upon the essentials, he thought he could almost see the light.

* * *

On the lovely Holy Saturday before Easter Sunday of Ted's senior year in high school, the world shuddered and came apart. In truth, Joe tore it apart in about sixty seconds, in ignorance and a failure of every good intention, destroying the most precious aspect of his life in a flash of anger. In one deplorable act, he ruined what he had nurtured and preserved for many patient years. That he could destroy so much that was precious in a few anguished moments would have been unimaginable to him even the day before. But he had seen the moving finger write many times, a word spoken without hope of recapture, a trigger pressed in an instant that shattered eternity, a failure of nerve, moments of neglect from which love would not recover.

He had not seen Ted in about ten days. He had tried to telephone him. The pay phone rang and rang at the end of his son's dormitory hall. Once, it was answered by a disinterested foreign student, who appeared not even to know Ted. Joe left messages, but they were not delivered. He knew if Ted had received them, he would have called back. When he asked Kate about Ted, she replied that she hadn't talked with him in days and had seen him only from a distance, in passing. He knew it was not true, because she stayed for dinner every night at the school, and on evenings when he had joined her, Ted had been seated at her table. Kate had told him again that her contract now required her to have dinner at the school every night. Joe listened but was not fooled. It had never been a requirement before but had suddenly become necessary when Ted became a boarder. As with so many matters over the years, her invisible contract had once again conformed to an emerging preference.

Joe missed Ted dreadfully. He needed to see him and hear his voice. The weeks leading up to Easter had been especially complicated this year with increased responsibilities at Redeemer and for the diocese, all requiring additional hours of travel. There were three parish families in crisis. As was often the case with very private situations, except for obvious illnesses or accidents, no one knew of these situations but Joe and Harry Campos, the incomparable senior warden. Joe visited each troubled family daily. Several elderly parishioners would be moving to nursing homes, two of them quite against their wills, and he spent time with them and their families too. Holy Communion must be taken to about fifteen people in their homes, nursing homes, or hospitals. The mostly indigent area families with children in the day care center had neglected their April payments, as usual, so as to prepare for Easter, and now a loan was needed to pay salaries. A local physician from another denomination had asked for Joe's assistance with an unchurched young couple grieving over their stillborn infant.

He had organized the food boxes for the ministerial association, and half the drivers had been in bed with a virus all week. A second grader in the parish had requested his presence at her birthday party. On his desk, there were two dozen calls to return. His Easter column for the newspaper waited, half-finished, on the word processor. There were Easter sermons to prepare, critical because they would be heard, he hoped, by members of the flock he might not see again in church until the following Christmas. Small matters, all of them, but to each was attached, justifiably or not, the needs or hopes or expectations of people who were depending upon him. As important as their concerns were and as negligible as his presence might be in the totality of their existence, he knew his duty and he knew who expected him to fulfill it.

In all the busy complications of this most glorious of seasons, he missed Ted terribly. To go to the school meant attempting to see him awkwardly between classes or while he was on the athletic field. A visit at dinner did not really help anymore. Ted would be preoccupied with his friends, and Joe would spend the time, barely touching the food, trying to talk with Kate at a table with a dozen teenagers. He always felt uncomfortable at the school, out of place, different, his collar strangely a barrier between him and the young people he would have enjoyed knowing. Kate became strangely reticent when he inquired about the students, as though he was daring to trespass upon some private territory of her own. The exceptions were several students from his own parish who had known him in Sunday school or as acolytes or members of his youth group, who had sought his advice over their growing up and who knew their parents valued him in their own lives. When they could sit with him, he did not feel so out of place. They seldom sat down at Kate's table, however, but waved at him across the dining room and made a point of speaking to him on their way out, after dinner. When he did get a chance to speak with Ted, he found his son less enthusiastic and communicative among his school friends. He saw it as only natural, given Ted's age. Joe had known hundreds of teenagers over the years, but he had never been the father of one before. Ted was not a little boy anymore, although his father could look at him at any moment and review unending images of every moment since his birth. He wanted to see Ted and hear his voice, a fundamental necessity in his life like oxygen and water.

Joe knew that Kate's need for Ted was just as strong as his own was. She doted on him, her only child, the love of her life. Joe understood. Her possessive and exclusive affection for their son was less troubling now. He accepted it as her inexplicable way, in the same way she kept her possessions separate from his, the fate of her summer home solely to herself, her personal documents and mementos squirreled away in separate drawers and closets. After years of marriage and raising their child together, Joe was still unable to tell whether she truly did not understand his need for Ted or whether she understood and found it less important than her own. He recalled a thousand images of her unannounced early departures, leading a compliant Ted away by the hand, from church, social occasions, family gatherings, even insisting that Ted go to bed on weekends at the same time she did.

She had assured him that Ted would be at home the previous weekend, but last-minute plans had intervened and Ted had joined some classmates in spending the night at a friend's house and going to some sort of traveling Russian circus at the county fairgrounds across the river. If the sudden change of plans, or Joe's disappointment at missing Ted yet again, touched Kate in any way, she gave no indication, not the smallest sign.

Hoping to spend time with Ted on the Saturday before Easter, Joe had worked night and day to finish everything so as to be at home. Except for his Easter sermon, which he would review again late Saturday evening before bed, he intended to spend the day with Ted, hopefully doing some much-needed work in the yard. He hoped the three of them could go out to dinner that night, and maybe to the movies.

A hundred things needed attention around the house. The old riding lawn mower, which Joe had nursed along for years, carefully repairing at the end of each winter and using with caution throughout the mowing season, needed cleaning, greasing, and a new belt and air filter. Before he could start mowing, there were windblown branches to be gathered and burned, casualties of the winter storms scattered everywhere about the rolling lawn. In the trees dead limbs creaked ominously in every breeze, squeaking to be cut down. There were chores in all directions, and to Joe, it was an invigorating time of year to be outdoors and doing them.

The crocus, at least those the squirrels had not eaten, had already bloomed in their jeweled clusters. Everyone liked them, especially Joe, who considered them the most optimistic of plants. He had found an early lavender variety the squirrels did not like and, in their first few years, had put in several hundred of them, hoping they would naturalize. Now the welcomed daffodils were emerging everywhere, coming up through drifts of dried leaves along the borders and beneath the trees, shaking their golden heads to a silent jaunty music. Together with lily of the valley, they were Kate's favorite flowers. He had planted several bushel baskets full the first year, hoping to make her happier about their new home. The great yellow blossoms of Dutch Master, King Alfred, and Unsurpassable had been

splendid and huge every year since he had put them in, working evening after evening that first October until it was too dark to see. And
the good whites, Mount Hood, Beersheba, and Silver, had drawn the
curious and appreciative from all over the neighborhood. The many
others whose names were slipping, Duke of Windsor, Pink Glory,
Daydream, and most of the rest, names now forgotten, had been a
yearly pleasure. Even Ted and his buddies had admired them, stopping and looking around and saying "Wow" before moving on. Kate
took bunches of them to school, where they adorned her classroom,
and to Wicomico on occasional spring trips, where they diffused a
sunny glory in the wintry old house.

The roses needed cleaning and other attention. Although they
were old roses, they required some treatment for their miserable
black spot and other diseases. Brazen groundhogs skulked about in
defiance of Cory's frisky presence. They would have to be run off
and their burrow beneath the front porch stuffed up with some bags
of dog hair. The cool nights and warm days had raised lush emerald
grass, which spread luxuriantly, shivering to be mowed. The flower-
ing crab apples and cherries would require pruning, and although
their lower limbs were easy to reach, the tall shoots that rose above
their crowns always gave him trouble. He had hoped to be able to
separate and replant the iris this year, but he knew little about them
and had no idea when to do it. In every winter storm, branches of
the great white pines on the north side of the house had tapped the
windows like cold creatures longing to come in. He would have to
trim them too. He had done it years before by climbing up into them
and had reached some of the limbs by leaning from the upstairs windows. A few years before, Ted had climbed up and sawed off a high
limb, but it was time to do it again. He was amazed at how quickly
they grew, these vast lovely pines that gave the neighborhood such a
pleasant air of privacy. And the troublesome stand of ailanthus tress,
which he had meant to destroy upon moving in, persisted in rejuve-
nating like bamboo. One of them, with a decayed trunk, felled by
a windstorm in late February, lay across the lawn now like a dead
python. He intended to borrow a chain saw and clean them out once

and for all. But the ailanthus was like the iris, the least of his concerns at the moment.

Kate came and went among these springtime chores, ignoring what few of them she recognized. Unless Joe went down in the spring and cleaned it up, her seaside lot in Wicomico remained littered all summer long with the previous winter's windblown trash. Lovely as it was, the old house and lot presented a contrast to the neighbors' places, which were all lovingly cleaned up every spring. The owners took pride in keeping their places presentable, just as they were with their town properties. Catherine had been that way. Kate was different. Whatever efforts she made upon arrival in early summer to make Ted clean up the yard, Kate abandoned after his first complaint. It was all such a contrast to her perfectly ordered classroom and tidy apartment at St. John's. Joe had given up trying to understand it or do anything about it.

And he had learned the consequences of insisting upon her help at home. She would eventually, reluctantly, come out and participate in yard work at his urging, but only on her own terms and in her own way. In the long run, it created more work for him. Although he had nursed the old mower along for years and learned how to cut the acres of grass in the fastest way, she would take silent umbrage at being told how to mow their lawn. Instead of picking up sticks, which needed to be done anyway before mowing, she would insist upon starting the small push mower and cutting some random swaths near the house. She had done so the previous spring and trimmed across the exposed roots of a big maple tree, knocking the blade askew and making it impossible to restart. Joe did not know how to repair it himself. Taking it to any small-engine mechanic that time of year meant he would not have it back until the middle of June. It was another consequence of her own behavior to which Kate turned the usual blind eye. He had learned that it was easier to do the work himself or try to get Ted's help.

So that Ted would be prepared ahead of time, Joe had called his dormitory and left a message: "Looking forward to seeing you. Need your help in the yard for a few hours." In anticipation of Ted's coming home on Friday night as promised, Joe also left the same message on the kitchen table before he went to bed. When he got up at seven, Ted's door was closed, the note had disappeared, and his blue Honda was parked in the drive. Joe went out and began to clean the rose beds.

Ted came out about ten o'clock and with no preliminaries, without even saying hello, explained that he had to go to a friend's house to paint a fence. Joe understood this. Ted and several friends were planning to drive out west following graduation. This particular friend's parents had generously offered to pay for the gasoline as a graduation present to all the boys. In turn, they had promised to tend to certain chores around the friend's house, and one of these was the garden fence, which needed painting. Joe understood, and his mind weighed quickly the small shifts that sometimes even the most mundane matters generate in family life. The springtime of his senior year was busy for Ted. It was a lovely day, and no rain was forecast for the coming week, a perfect time to paint the fence. The friend's parents deserved some help for their generosity. Evidently, the other boys could paint today. The sticks he had counted on Ted picking up and hauling to the burning pile would just have to wait, as well as mowing the lawn, which he had hoped to finish before dark. Ted promised he would return by early afternoon. He would help Joe then. Although he would have much preferred to have Ted's help then and there, Joe told him to go ahead and that they could work together when he returned. He asked him to give his regards to his friend's parents, good people whose company Joe enjoyed. There was about Ted an uncharacteristic mild sullenness that morning that Joe attributed to being a teenager. The moment Joe agreed, Ted walked to his car and drove away as though he had been all set for departure when he came out of the house.

Several times during the morning, Kate came out to explain to Joe all the latest school gossip and faculty intrigues. Although the ground was still cold, she was barefoot and dressed in summer shorts and T-shirt, inspired by the temperate day to dress for her eventual departure for the beach. Joe was glad to see her in such a good mood, and he listened as she rambled on. It would have been nice to have her help, but he was glad to accept her good mood instead.

When she returned to the house, he thought how strange it was to have her at home on a Saturday. She had presented no excuse for going to St. John's. Perhaps it was because Ted was at home for the weekend. Joe found it tiresome to hear the St. John's gossip, and the exploits of Father Hervey bored him. But at least she was at home and talking to him. It amused Joe that the teachers' conversations always drifted to Hervey eventually and to his provocative ways. He found it embarrassing too. He disliked hearing complaints about other clergy, because, no matter what their personalities were like, he knew something of what they were up against. He hoped others were as charitable toward him when Lottie and her few friends expounded upon his faults in public. He did not like being identified with Hervey but knew their clerical collars created in the eyes of the world a unity that transcended even the greatest differences of personality and lifestyle. Hervey's precious piety and dubious erudition always impressed ministers of other churches. Among clergy in his own denomination, however, Joe was familiar with the grin exchanged at the mention of Hervey's name. Before it subsided, someone always said, "Uh-oh! Hervey! What's he up to this time?"

Joe shook his head, as if warding off gnats, and returned his attention to the sheer enjoyment of working in the soil. He loved gardening and the way its pleasures came in the process as well as in the results. In planting, cleaning, and pruning were health and wholeness, sanity and spirituality. The process was as inspiring as the blue mason jars of summer filled with sprays of New Dawn or Westerland or stuffed with the glorious sunflowers that waited in the months ahead.

Growing things in the soil brought clarity and order out of chaos. In his next life, Joe wanted to be a farmer, or run a nursery, or at least build a greenhouse. For years he had hoped that growing and gardening would provide a common pastime with Kate. Except for her seasonal excitement at vases of daffodils or sprigs of lily of the valley, her interest had never strayed beyond the textbook and the laboratory. Still, in addition to its other blessings, horticulture was spiritual therapy, especially for children. For years he had tried to interest Ted, but with minimal success.

At about five o'clock, with no sign of Ted, no phone call that he knew of, Joe rolled the mowers into the garage, put away the tools, and went inside. It would be the following weekend before he could get to them again. He sat at the kitchen table and ate some fresh coconut cake with Kate. It was a great favorite of Joe's. One of his parishioners had baked it for him as an Easter gift, cracking and grating a coconut as Joe had done as a small boy with his grandmother. It amazed him that Kate had been at home all day. She was in a very good mood. While she returned to the television, he went down to his cellar room to complete his sermon.

He was tired after the past few weeks. His back hurt from bending in the yard. Unless the three of them could go out to dinner, he was determined to go to bed by ten o'clock to be alert and rested for the three services and several hundred people at Redeemer the following day. Only the 20 percent of a congregation at the core of life in any church understands something of a pastor's stress. Redeemer was much more sensitive to such issues than most, most of the people having grown very close to Joe. But many churchgoers are like people who live near a racetrack and know nothing about horses and believe that riding or racing is a simple matter, like sitting in a rocking chair, while the horse does all the rest. Joe had seen novices come out to the country for weekend trail rides, filled with equestrian knowledge acquired from years of reading Westerns or watching television. Appreciating the difference between a rocking chair and a sitting trot never took more than a hundred yards downhill, but nobody could have told them—like Kate and Catherine years before, turning from their television crime dramas to lecture him on courtroom procedure or crime scene investigation. "They only work on Sunday, and even then, what do they do? Preach a little sermon. Anybody could think up something to say in a pinch. Stand around and grin and pat everybody on the back." It hurt that his own wife behaved as though she believed it too. But she grew furious when anyone babbled the iniquitous old indignity that people who couldn't do anything else became teachers.

He stared at the screen of his word processor. Easter. The tilting of the universe, the blazing forth of glory, the broken and triumphant body of Christ wedging open for eternity the door between human beings and God. Describing the cosmic joy of it in words was barely possible. Even the language of Shakespeare and the King James Version, the stupendous ethereal music of the English language, most glorious of tongues, applied to the loveliest moment in the whole of benevolent creation, could not capture it. The resurrection, the ultimate certainty of love. Candles, flowers, the faces of children—the lovely secular images that crowd round the empty tomb may be the only language to convey it.

He heard the slam of the kitchen door, rattling everything on two floors with a soft combustion of air that penetrated to the basement, and above him Ted's rapid footsteps across to the family room, where Kate was watching television. It was five thirty. It was unlike Ted not to have called to say he would be late. There was silence above as he and Kate apparently conferred. Then Ted came bounding rapidly down the basement stairs. He came into the room and leaned on the worktable, opposite Joe, and said, "Well, Dad, I'll see you tomorrow afternoon."

Joe was confused. Tomorrow was Easter. Had Ted forgotten?

"Buddy," he said, "tomorrow is Easter."

"Well, I want to go over to the school and be with my friends overnight."

"But, Ted, you're scheduled to serve as crucifer tomorrow at the eleven o'clock service. You know that."

"But I don't want—"

"The orders of service have been printed. You are listed as crucifer. Everybody wants to see you. It's almost six. It's too late to try to find a replacement. And besides, this may be the last time that you and I can ser—"

"But I want to be with my friends!"

"Ted! You've known all week that you're scheduled to serve tomorrow."

"I have not! This is the first I've heard about it. Why do I have to go to *that* church, with *those* people? I want to go over to St. John's…"

Although Joe had never known Ted to behave this way—and he was aware continually of how blessed he was to have a son with such a good disposition over so many years—Ted's defiant and sarcastic manner was nonetheless depressingly familiar. It was suddenly clear to him why Kate had been at home all day. Biding her time until Ted returned from wherever he had been, she had been waiting to drive him over to St. John's. It was a familiar pattern now expanding to include something wholly unexpected. Suddenly, his son's immature comments about Redeemer and the contempt in his voice, and his wife's collusion in it, came as an excruciatingly painful surprise. The shock of Ted's words, sounding so much like his mother's, and the thought of Kate's deviousness in enabling their son's poor conduct, roused Joe to a peak of anger he had not known in his adult life. In an instant, he jumped up and reached for Ted, but only succeeded in catching the hood of a sweatshirt draped over his son's shoulder. Ted backed away, and in anger, Joe tried to swat him with the sweatshirt. He chased Ted around the basement for a few seconds and followed Ted as he sprinted up the stairs.

Joe was absolutely sure that Ted knew he was scheduled to serve as crucifer. The acolyte sponsor had called all the young people scheduled to serve, as she did before every high festival day, and had reported to Joe that everyone would be present. Unable to reach Ted at St. John's after several calls, she had telephoned their home and spoken to Kate. Kate had assured her quickly that Ted knew he was scheduled to serve but that she would remind him anyway.

"You know you're scheduled to serve as crucifer!" Joe shouted. "The sponsor called you. Mom told you!"

"She did not! She didn't tell me anything!" shouted Ted, wheeling around on the stairs to face his father.

"Yes. I. Did!" shouted Kate from the family room, entering the argument now that her own name had come up. To emphasize her point, she noisily descended the stairs a few steps.

"You didn't tell me anything!" Ted shouted.

"Yes, I did, too," said Kate, her voice rising and head wagging from side to side.

His mind reeling with exasperation, and so angry he could not see straight, Joe tried to grab Ted and succeeded only in walloping him again with the flailing sweatshirt. They both pushed past Kate as Joe pursued their son up the stairs. Kate followed close behind Joe, loudly declaring that she had never received a call from the acolyte sponsor even though a moment before she had sworn she had told Ted about it, and Joe, in his anger, turned and tapped her lightly on the cheek. Ted began to shout at him that one never struck a woman, that Joe himself had taught him that and now Joe was proving he was a liar.

"Where were you today?" Joe roared. "Where were you? You didn't call. You would have been out there picking up the damn sticks if you needed something from me!"

"Whoa! What's going on?" Ted shouted. He had never seen his father like this.

"Well, I could have done it instead, but you wouldn't ask *me*!" shouted Kate, inches from his face.

"What's going on?" Ted shouted again.

"You knew he was supposed to serve!" Joe yelled back at her. "You're an adult! You're supposed to help with this stuff, not ruin it—like Christmas."

"What the hell's going on?" said Ted.

"*I* ruined Christmas?" Kate replied, and even through his anger, Joe saw that she was about to say something sarcastic. For everybody's good, he turned instinctively and walked into the hall and climbed the stairs to the second floor. Halfway up, he turned and sat down, clutching the sides of his head with his hands like a man with a severe headache. He expected Kate, or both, to follow, shouting. Instead, after a few seconds, he heard the sound of the kitchen door clicking shut. A moment later, he heard Kate's van starting up. He raced down the steps and through the kitchen to call them back, but the big van was leaving the foot of the drive as he came out through the garage.

What have I done? he began thinking to himself over and over. He was trembling with anger and something else, too—a maddening, infuriating resignation. He had long ago abandoned any delusions of change in his wife. What he had heard and seen just now was the same behavior in their son. For a few frantic, chaotic moments, it had been like dealing with two Kates. He had totally lost his serenity. He couldn't stand it. His head ached, and his insides burned. He lay down in the cold grass and looked up into the gathering darkness. *What have I done?* The words kept spinning in his mind. *I've never gotten that mad before. Even when she came in and started shouting about Ted that night.* As thoughts of that night mingled with the memory of the past few minutes, it seemed the pain in his lower abdomen would boil up through his skin. Cory, sensing his anguish, came slowly over in a roundabout way and lay down beside him and put his head on his chest. His tail thumped on the cold grass, and he regarded Joe with sorrowful eyes. But no reproach of Cory's or any other living thing in God's creation could diminish the savage guilt and self-contempt that was beginning to churn inside Joe.

I know what I've done. What do I do now? he shouted inside himself in desperation. He decided it was best to stay away for a few hours and give everybody a chance to calm down. He was certain that Kate had taken Ted to St. John's, where he was determined to go. He well knew the rage he would face upon her return. Whether icy and sarcastic or hot and defiant, he knew he couldn't handle it just now, even with all his years of experience. He lay there for another ten minutes or so, allowing his mind and nerves to regain a frenzied composure. Anguish was already eating away at his gut like battery acid. Guilt was creating a stench in his own nostrils. The eve of Easter. What a sinner he was. What a wretched sinner.

He went inside and picked up his keys and billfold and pulled on the same sweatshirt with which he had chased Ted. He left the lights on and the door unlocked and drove away in his car, intending to sit for a while beside the dark river. On the way out of the subdivision, he passed Kate, returning home. For once, he decided not to try to talk with her. He knew himself well enough to know his uncharacteristic burst of anger was spent and there was no chance of him losing his composure again—probably for the rest of his miserable life. But he knew she was livid and her sarcasm and twisted reasoning would be at full throttle. He could not stand up to it at the moment, and the shame of his own behavior made him want to throw up. So he drove on by, and she did, too.

Chapter Thirteen

T HEY DID NOT come home. When he returned to the house, Kate had left again. He wandered around, each room screaming at him in a new quality of silence, its own interpretation of his terrible guilt. For the rest of the evening, he prepared mechanically for the following day, Easter, and their faces came and went in his mind, surfacing for a moment and soon lost again in the cold shadows. He went to the telephone a dozen times and bent over it, his hands resting on either side and his head down, as though he were praying over the elements before making his Communion. Even though he had never become so angry in his life, he knew exactly what to expect if he succeeded in reaching her: his sincere apology blurted out, his attempts to talk of what had happened, her complete silence and total disassociation. If she said anything, it would be petulant and resigned, or bristling and sarcastic, an acknowledgment of his apology and allowing the silence afterward to punish him, a mocking denial of all the issues they should be working on together. He considered the dry spring of his own patience and knew he could not cope right now with another dead end. He wasn't afraid of becoming angry again; he knew that had been unlike him, uncharacteristic and shameful. But he feared that enduring another episode of her denial right then would make him sick. The trouble he would experience trying to carry on the following day, with so many people depending upon him, was only a secondary factor. More powerful now was his need to deny Kate a chance to make him sick. For both their sakes, he refused to permit her an opening to worsen the damage he himself had already done.

Until he found a few fitful hours of sleep sometime after three o'clock, her face and Ted's moved in his mind, every glimpse stirring up the most profound guilt and sorrow. Ted. He had never been able to reach him on the dormitory phone. He was with his friends, or in Kate's apartment, listening to her rant about Joe and his endless faults. The son he so loved, the son he would die for, the son whom he had driven from the house on Holy Saturday, the greatest gift of his life, precious as his marriage. His marriage, the woman he still felt so protective of. Sick with grief, he stared into the dark, watching the familiar shadows as though answers might emerge from them like creatures of the night. When he slept, he woke every fifteen minutes from dreams in which he recalled only that they were all together. He got up at five, his usual time on Sundays, and showered and dressed in the most profound depression and anxiety. It was Easter. More than once, in waking in the night, he had considered driving over to St. John's and pouring out his apologies and bringing them home. But the better judgment of the earlier evening returned and, in any case, given where they were and the hour, it would be futile.

At his bedside upon arising and at the altar rail at Redeemer, he begged for forgiveness and the strength to carry on for the benefit of the worshippers, asking God to spare the innocent from the plague of his own turmoil. He conducted the services with a dignity that was wholly a gift to him for the people's welfare. In his years of speaking to juries in atrocious cases, enduring difficult behavior in students and the hateful anger of those who rejected him as a priest, his patience had matured. His faith in ultimate fairness and justice had strengthened his coping with a humble confidence. He had always told himself that in the century of Auschwitz, living in hope was not merely a means to an end but a victory in itself. On this Easter morning, he called forth all his reserves. He had always known that for all the difficulties in his life, others had it far, far worse. Thus, the profound sense of shame, closed within him like smoldering ruins, was invisible to others. Ted's name was printed in the order of service as crucifer, and many people asked if he was sick and told Joe to tell him "Happy Easter" for them. They were used to Kate's absence, but some of them sent regards to her too.

Joe was numb with fatigue. The good people of Redeemer were used to seeing him tired. During years of serving God together and sharing the most intimate moments of life, they had accorded Joe an honored position in their lives. He was their pastor and an outsider, but they let him know in a thousand ways that they regarded him as one of them. It was a blessed dual role born of their genuine kindness and his own capacity for caring and friendship, gifts to one another that gave light to their common journey. Twenty years of covering in an alcoholic marriage had taught Joe many lessons in masking grief, but whatever anguish he betrayed on this bright Easter morning was attributed generously by his flock to fatigue.

He preached well. Insincerity in sermons reveals itself quickly, and people who know their pastor well detect it like siblings in a big family. The present reliving of the passion in Holy Communion must be a credible moment of awareness in the celebrant, who speaks for all the faithful in the pews. It is not an exercise in acting, wholly unlike the image many have of reciting lines in a play. Worshippers recognize its mystery but can seldom define it. Some clergy probably never feel the graceful inward motions. If the truth is not evident in thought, word, and deed, its absence becomes as penetrating and conspicuous as a chill. On this Easter Sunday, Joe knew that his voice bloomed in present memory, a gift known only and intimately to him, for the benefit of people among whom he served. The ancient words of the triumphant liturgy soothed his screaming conscience and broken heart. He knew he was blessed. He knew that despite everything he had said and done, he was loved. He knew that his fervent desire to take it all back, to live the moment over again, and to do better this time was known and understood by God even though it was an impossibility. The assurance of being understood, of having the attention of someone who was forgiving and strengthening, was as contagious as it had ever been since his ordination, and it flowed through him without pause to others that needed it too. His clarity and good faith surprised even him, feeling as he did. In spite of his churning shame and remorse, the natural gratitude of one that knows he is loved echoed in his voice. The candor and kindness were gifts for the people, Easter presents from a merciful God to the needy faithful, who should not be made to suffer for his own bad conduct. Worshippers wanted to gather and talk. The reception in the parish hall was festive and lively. He was invited to a dozen homes. The girls, lovely in their Easter happiness and new dresses, wanted their picture taken with him. They would give him copies, as parishioners always did, to keep in his desk drawer. A group of middle school boys gave him a critique of the new action movie everyone was discussing and eagerly offered to go again if he wanted to see it with them. "And maybe Ted wants to see it too. Tell him to go with us. We can go this afternoon, if you want to!" If he could only have told them how happy that would make him, to go anywhere with Ted on that particular afternoon, to see him, hear his voice, explain how dreadfully sorry he was, how ashamed he was of getting angry.

On the drive home, he faced his relationship with Kate. After parking in the driveway, he sat at the wheel for an hour, staring ahead with the blindness of introspection.

Whatever love and respect Kate might have had for him in the beginning had disappeared long ago. He could not bring himself to believe that she hated him. It was not hatred that moved in her, but a selfish reaction to anything she perceived as a threat, no matter how reasonable or necessary it might be. The semblance of love that he had insisted on seeing in their working together as parents had vanished too. He had been unwilling to acknowledge it, perhaps in a way his own kind of denial. His own voice roared up inside him in dismay and alarm, even at this late hour. *No! She is my wife. I love her. We've been through so much together. We've worked out so many things. There have been good times too. She loves me. She does. She's just not made for intimacy and trust—it's not the way she grew up. She loves me. I love her.* But no, no, said the same voice in a gentle way. It was time now to wipe the mirror clean and take a careful look.

Kate's role as enabling best friend for Ted was clear, and he could do nothing about it. Attempting to reason with her, appealing to her sense of adult responsibility, had long ago ceased to mean anything. It was his own fault that he had not recognized it before. He had worn blinders of his own making, expecting the road to become straight and level beyond the next bend, over the next hill. Agreements with her lasted until her personal desires took precedence. If he had only been smart enough to understand it earlier. And Ted had learned to work his parents to his own ends. Joe could not bring himself to say that Ted had ever done so maliciously; he had none of that sort of thing in him. He was only a teenager learning to make his way in the world. His choices were no worse, and, in fact, a great deal better, than those of most other young men his age. He had a conscience. He was his son. Joe loved him.

How had it come to this? How could he have reacted that way? Neither Ted's selfish behavior of the previous evening nor Kate's sneaky collusion justified his losing his temper that way. The fault was his. He had lost it. Of the three of them, it was his behavior, his own reaction that could have made a difference. It was too late now.

He went in to see what message they had left on the answering machine. There was none. It was evident, however, that someone had been in the house since his departure that morning. Drawers were everywhere ajar. Closet doors stood open. The house had the look of a raid by those who had entered and left in a rush. There was no note.

What should he do? He must apologize. He could and would do that, sincerely and immediately. It was the right and decent way to start. He could handle that part. But what would happen next? He was burned-out with Kate and her issues. His coping skills were spent. Short of binding and gagging her and driving her bodily to someone who could help them sort out their relationship, he was powerless. She would say and do anything to protect herself. She had almost everything she desired: their child and a tidy apartment at her place of work, where she knew the players and exactly what she had to do to fit in, and where she did not have to bother with a husband. She lacked only financial independence. She did not earn enough to keep herself, Ted, and Wicomico going. She needed Joe for that, as much as she resented him.

What could he do? He recognized he could no longer manage it on his own. In truth, the healing nurture of his family psychologist, spiritual director, and twelve-step group had helped to save his marriage for years. It was strange that they worked so diligently together with him for his son's welfare and yet Ted had no idea of their existence. There was nobody left from Kate's past to whom he could appeal. She had seen to that. Her best friend and her closest relative were on her side reflexively, regardless of the equities. Ted was on her side. She could do no wrong in his eyes. Joe feared that Ted, too, had adopted his mother's eternal refrain: "I don't have any problems, Joe! If there's a problem in this marriage, it's you."

God had worked miracles in Joe's life through twelve-step members. Kate had reacted with silence to anything he had ever said about it. There was no way of putting value upon the calm, constructive guidance of his spiritual adviser. She knew Joe saw him several times each month, and after years of marriage to a clergyman, she, he knew, would assume that they talked about "Bible stuff and about how to do things around the church." Exploring how to live out one's vocation within the family and the world was beyond her imagination. There had been a number of licensed marriage counselors over the years, every one of them healing and energizing. God had blessed his life through all these channels of grace, granting him wisdom, increasing his patience, inspiring him with ideas and solutions, guiding him through his own ignorance and shortsightedness. However much they disdained him, she and her mother, and their summer home, had been the blind beneficiaries of the treasures that had come to him through all these good people.

In his fatigue and shame, he could still feel the upward inspiration of the Easter liturgy, the ancient words like honey on his tongue, moving in his mind like a soothing breath of wintergreen. He would apologize to both of them. He would pour out his heart in remorse. God would send him direction, as he always had before. God had given him his marriage. It was his duty to be faithful in it in sickness and health, for better or worse.

In his mind and heart, over and among his rational thoughts, like the winds of an oncoming storm, a turbulence of hope and shame roared and churned. Halfway up the stairs to their bedroom, he paused and winced. He closed his eyes and heard Ted singing in the bathroom as he did in the morning, or bounding down the stairs in his usual good mood. He changed into old clothes and lay down on their bed, his and Kate's. What was she doing now? It seemed he had spent half his life wondering what was going on inside her, even when she was next to him in bed, or seated on his lap. What was she doing *now*? It was about five o'clock. It would be dark soon. Was she drinking wine in her hideaway? Was she still spitting fire? If she was filled with anger, it could be no worse than his own twenty-four hours ago. He was a bastard.

He was deeply disappointed in Ted. Ted knew the significance of Easter, the importance of following through with commitments, the strain it created on Joe when people did not show up to serve as promised. But Ted was a teenager, after all, an immature person in the body of a young adult, still getting things straight in life. Joe should have handled it better, much better—as a father, husband, priest, adult, lawyer, everything. But he had failed.

He had spanked Ted two or three times in his whole life, and never in the past ten years. He had always tried to reason with him, encourage him in the right direction. Ted was a reasonable young man, fair, reliable. Joe had never been reluctant to tell him no when it was the right thing to do. Yes, he had his mother's habits around the house and in family life. He took no initiative. It was like having two teenagers at home. But Ted was not mean. He was good-natured, kind, and intelligent. Joe had always been proud of him, always admired him.

When Ted had reacted as Kate had done for so many years and Joe had heard Kate's words coming from Ted's mouth, and he realized she was waiting upstairs in collusion, that was when he had lost it. Not so much at Ted, although the thought of trying to explain the truth to Ted now was preposterous. He knew his anger had been directed toward Kate—for telling their son to forget about helping him with the Christmas tree, for planning with Ted to avoid serving on Easter Sunday, for refusing to follow through with counseling, for manipulating him and lying to him for years and years about everything.

Kate. His wife. In his mind and heart, he reached out and touched her face. Through the resistant smothering layers of denial that surrounded her like so many thick shells, he plunged and groped toward the soft down of her cheek, the person he had loved despite everything. Even if he had been capable of hating, if it had existed within him at all toward anyone, he could never have brought himself to feel that way toward her. He loved her. He did not like her very much at the moment, but she was his wife and he still had in him affection at the sound of her voice, in contemplating her welfare, and it emerged into the light with a natural strength of its own.

He got up from the bed and stood still, his head pounding. He went into the bathroom and took two aspirin, something he was not supposed to do, but the pain in his forehead and neck was severe. He went down to the kitchen and drank a glass of skim milk. He sat at the table and looked at the glass. He remembered the four years it had taken while Ted was in elementary school to get Kate's cooperation in buying skim milk for Ted and him. He went into the family room— were they a family, despite his efforts, his coping and hopes?—and lay down on the sofa. He covered his face with a pillow to block out the light. The darkness and quiet soothed his aching head. Despite the whirlwind in his mind, after a few minutes, he slept.

* * *

The jangling telephone woke him in the dark. He sat up and turned on the light and reached out. He was prepared to give Kate or Ted his sincere apologies, profoundly, abjectly.

"Joe?" said a determined voice. "This is Morris LaBelle. I'm sorry to have to make this call. I understand there was some trouble there last night."

"Bishop LaBelle?"

"Yes. Father Hervey called me."

"Yes, we had a big argument over—"

"That was what Father Hervey explained."

"I'm terribly sorry about it. For years I've been trying to cope with…" Joe paused. For the first time in his married life, he was on the point of admitting to someone other than a professional counselor the truth of his alcoholic marriage. It was a betrayal of Kate. If anyone was to know, she must be the one to tell. That had been his faith and reasoning until this moment. But his wife and son had left the house, and here on the phone was his boss, asking for an explanation. There was only one thing to do. "We've had a troubled relationship for years, Bishop. I lost it last night. My wife is an alcoholic. I usually handle it better, but last night we had—"

"You say she's an alcoholic?"

"Yes."

Silence, then, "But Father Hervey didn't say anything about that." For a moment, Joe was uncertain how to reply, and before he could say anything, LaBelle asked, "Would you be willing to get an evaluation?"

"Of course," said Joe. "I have been seeing a family counselor for years and am a longtime member of Al-Anon."

"You've been in counseling?"

"Yes."

The bishop was quiet for a moment and then said, "Well, thank you for discussing this with me. I'll call you at the church tomorrow morning, and we'll go from there."

"All right, Bishop. Thank you."

"Good night," said Bishop LaBelle. And he hung up.

Joe put down the receiver with a disquieting mixture of suspicion and relief. A dozen issues began to rattle about in his mind. Finally, for the first time in their married lives, some professional help would be brought to bear upon them together about their issues. An "evaluation." The truth would be uncovered. Kate would join him in counseling only to save face, but they would be there together. Professional counselors knew how to draw people in. At last, they would be able to work on their issues as husband and wife.

But what had Hervey to do with it? He had called LaBelle. Apparently, Kate had gone to him complaining about the way she had been treated. He could imagine the petulant disquisition of the travails she endured and Joe's unfairness in accusing her of things of which she was wholly innocent. In the early days of their marriage, she had blamed everything wrong in her life on her mother or coworkers or neighbors. In recent years, her problems had been largely Joe's fault, especially after Catherine's death, with Hervey and coworkers responsible for what could not be attributed to Joe. Now she was complaining about Joe to Hervey. Despite twenty years of contending with her Ferris wheel of denial, he was still surprised that she would talk about him to Hervey. The thought of it filled him with a distinct uneasiness. Hervey had never taken pains to conceal his contempt for Joe, and Kate was aware of it. She had commented on it when searching for cutting remarks to defend herself when Joe confronted her about her own behavior. How long had she been talking to Hervey? What lies had she told him? He knew about incidents where her disposition had gotten her into trouble at St. John's. He was certain there were matters he had never learned about. Had she defended herself to Hervey by complaining about Joe? Since her mother's death, he had been the only one to blame.

Chapter Fourteen

S INCE HIS YOUTH, the church had stood for hope and goodness. He had paid it scant attention as a child, when his young father limped about with his terrible battlefield injury and memories of World War II were fresh in everyone. Even then he was growing to see it as the place of truth and cleanliness in the midst of what human beings do to one another. Because his parents made him go to church, the worship services had begun to shape his character and personality long before he knew it. His friends had the same experience, but it would be many years before they were confident enough to discuss it with one another.

Joe opened his brokenness before the church's discretion with complete confidence. He heard Christ's voice in its assembly. He trusted the sincerity and competence of its leaders. He was thankful that so precious and intimate a matter as his family life could be entrusted to people of faith and reason. The house of the Holy Spirit, informed and directed in ways beyond human understanding, was as close to God as human community could get.

His experience with mental health professionals had been positive and affirming. He had witnessed God ministering through medicine to soothe and cure the broken world. As a teacher working with staff psychiatrists and psychologists, and in the law seeking insight into people and their actions, he had learned much about the world and himself from medicine and psychology. His ministry had been strengthened through contact with physicians, counselors, social workers, psychologists, and especially nurses. Some of the public health nurses he had known carried civilization with them on their rounds.

He had no reluctance about submitting himself and his family situation to his superiors in the church and whatever evaluators they might appoint. He had confidence in the process. In whatever scrutiny was coming, Kate's denial would become transparent. At last they could begin to work together and grow healthy. They would get help *together.* God was good.

The very thought of the church deepened his remorse for his anger on Easter Eve. Of the three involved, he was the one responsible, the one in whom maturity should have made a difference. Ted was just seventeen, a teenage boy who saw his mother as perfect. Kate was an adult child, in some ways less emotionally developed than Ted. Joe knew he could have made the difference and set an example of calm, well-adjusted, responsible behavior. How many hundreds of times had he fulfilled that duty in the past twenty years? There had been days when Ted was younger and Kate and Catherine were drunk and fighting when he had managed to calm them and restore balance and, at the same time, shield his son from them and them from the world. The following morning, neither his wife nor her mother even remembered. Or perhaps they had known but pretended not to remember. In all those times, he was never certain. Had he been a peacemaker or a fool? He had been a fool because he had been a peacemonger.

Others could certainly point out how much better he could have managed this or that. No doubt they were right. He did not begrudge others their keener perception; it would be about as constructive as resenting others' good looks or mathematical abilities. But he knew his own heart, something others could not know, and he was content with what was engraved there, because he had never been a traitor. He had been faithful to those whose lives touched his. The remorse that churned in him now was older than Easter Eve. It grew out of his high consciousness, despite his loyalty, of his own mistakes, of forever in life falling short in spite of believing he had done his best. He knew he was bound to err but wished he had gotten it right more often. He knew he was accepted and forgiven his many wrongs, but why had he lost it on Saturday night? After all the times he had gotten it right, or mostly right, or more right than wrong, why had he failed that Easter Eve? Ted had behaved like Kate. He pondered all this as he went about the home he loved, cleaning up, trying to put the mess in order. Sometime after midnight, when he tried to sleep, he knew he had never felt so sad.

Bishop LaBelle did not call the following day. Joe arrived at Redeemer before eight on the day most clergy stayed home after the busiest Sunday of the year. He stayed until early evening but heard nothing from him. He told Milly, who knew nothing of what had occurred, to interrupt him if someone called from the diocesan office. He scheduled appointments for the following day with his good friends the senior and junior wardens, and with Clyde Candler, his family counselor, so that he could report to them what had happened. He would attend his Al-Anon meeting on Wednesday and tell the participants what he had done. His spiritual director, Lou, had departed after his Easter services to visit his wife's family in New England and would not return until the weekend. Joe called anyway and left a message asking to see him when he returned. He called Amanda Leffler's office in Dorchester. It had been years since he had seen her, but she had been so much help and he knew she would remember him and his situation. The office receptionist remembered him and, after a minute of catching up, told him Dr. Leffler had retired three years before. During the day, he received about thirty calls, each time expecting to hear Kate's voice or LaBelle's, or hopefully even Ted's. But each call, in one way or another, concerned somebody else's problem.

He left his office after dark, anxiously anticipating messages from his family or the bishop on the answering machine at home. There were many messages as usual, friends of his or Ted's, his mother, one of his sisters, and several calls from people wanting to sell things. But from Kate or the bishop, nothing.

Every moment was filled with thoughts of them. He tried to focus on other matters, but the thoughts faded like dreams and his concentration returned to their faces, the sound of their voices, something they had said or done. Everywhere he turned, their clothes or shoes or books or games were the first things he saw. On each table, every chair and sofa, everywhere were reminders that made him sit down with his head in his hands. He spent the evening writing long letters to each of them, apologizing for getting angry and asking them to come home. He left the house at midnight and drove to the small rural post office in the crossroads called Candytown. It was here that someone from St. John's picked up the school mail each morning at ten, and by posting the letters here, he knew that Kate and Ted would receive them the following day. He returned home about a quarter to one and went to bed. Sleep, when it came from time to time, was fitful and chaotic.

Bishop LaBelle telephoned the next morning at his office and asked Joe to meet him the following evening at a big motel at an interstate exchange north of Catoctin Springs. He said he was coming that way anyway and it would be a good chance for the two of them to talk. Joe agreed to meet him at six in the motel dining room.

He kept his appointment that day with the wardens, Harry Campos and Tom Downes, meeting them in the late afternoon in a small restaurant and explaining to them in detail what he had done on Easter Eve. They listened intently, sipping their coffee and nodding, and agreed that the whole thing was unfortunate. They volunteered their opinions that he had been provoked but concurred in his admission that he had handled it poorly and should not have lost his temper.

Joe felt constrained to tell them about Kate's history with alcohol and his own failing role in trying to stop her drinking. Both Harry and Tom were surprised, although not nearly as much as Joe would have supposed. He explained how dreadfully afraid she was of exposure and how he had kept her secret, except from professional counselors, out of love for her. He expected some mild annoyance on their part for having kept from them a family issue that could have affected his ministry. He assured them that he would have confided in them if an emergency had arisen before now. They assured him that they would have behaved the same way in their own marriages and that they thought he had done the right thing, especially as he was acting with the advice of professional counselors.

Joe knew they were trying hard to be supportive. Each sensed how deeply remorseful he was, and they both seemed confident that the episode would be resolved soon. These blowups happened in every family, they said, and each had knowledge of some family's fight more raucous than what Joe had described. They expressed their belief that Kate would return home and that she was probably already there as they spoke. She would acknowledge her own role in things, and perhaps this disagreement, unfortunate as it was, would shake her loose a bit and encourage her to join him in family counseling. Half the families they knew included at least one person with a drinking problem. There was nothing for Kate to be so paranoid about. All this would turn out all right. Joe should be patient. They asked him to call them after his interview with LaBelle the following evening and give them a report. Tom Downes had known LaBelle slightly. He had been stationed in the Army many years before in Calvertville, and LaBelle had served the local church there at that time. He had baptized his son. He did not remember LaBelle very well, but he thought it must be the same man—surely, there were not two priests by that name.

They talked for a few minutes more, and then all three departed for home. Their meeting profoundly relieved Joe. He was immensely grateful for such friends, and he trusted their judgment and insight. Still, revealing Kate's addiction to alcohol had been hard for him. He had never done it before, except to health care professionals, and to Bishop LaBelle, and his indiscretion—for that was how he regarded it—troubled him. He had complete confidence in Harry and Tom, and it was not telling them that bothered him so. It was telling anyone outside a counseling relationship, because it constituted a betrayal of Kate. However right it might have been to do it at that moment, revealing a secret he had guarded for almost twenty years filled him with a new anguish. He thought that telling LaBelle on the telephone the night before would have made it a little easier, but it had not.

He thought back over the wardens' reassurances that the crisis would blow over and that Kate had probably already returned home.

His fears were based on more knowledge of Kate than they had. Kate. He recalled the nights he lay in their darkened bedroom, waiting for the burning in his intestines to subside, for this or that medication to take effect, with Kate behaving as though not a thing in the world was wrong. Occasionally, she would poke her head in at the door and ask if she could bring him anything. She never asked what was causing his suffering. It was as close as she ever came to discussing how he felt or what was wrong. Occasionally, she behaved as though he was in pain only to inconvenience her. He was not as certain as his friends were that Kate would relent and return. Not sure at all.

There were no telephone messages for him at home that night. He knew they had read his letters; he had apologized profusely and asked them to call so he could do so by phone as well. If he could get this far, he believed they would meet him and hear him out in person. He made a list of those who should be advised in addition to the wardens. His neighboring clergy in the next county, decent men whose advice he had always valued, deserved an explanation. He wanted them to hear it from him before they heard the gossip. He called them at home and asked them to be his guests for lunch on the following day. He cleaned up the house, picking up Ted's room and folding Kate's many blouses and slacks draped eternally over chairs. He changed the beds and put out fresh towels for their return. He tried to eat a peanut butter sandwich but threw it in the trash after a bite.

He spent a while with Cory, sitting in a folding chair in the light from the opened front door so that he could hear the telephone when they called. The silence of the house was deafening. He was used to both of them being away, but this silence was different, and Cory sensed it too. He sat with his head on Joe's knee, looking at him with alarmed, upturned eyes and watching as though he expected Joe to cry.

Walter Lewis and Andrew Campbell met him at a roadside restaurant near the big bend in the river the following day and listened patiently to all he said. How he admired them, one younger than himself and the other much older, both ordained for many years longer than he and each better skilled in ministry than he would ever be. He told them everything, exactly as he had told the wardens the afternoon before, except for the part about Kate's drinking. About this he said only that there was one factor in it all that he could not yet explain, out of respect for Kate. He knew it didn't help their understanding to have to wait for an additional component, but he felt bound by his marriage not to reveal it again, at least not yet. He hoped silently that such a time would never come, that she would meet him and talk things over and they would make a fresh start. So he said only that his time with family counselors over the years had been needed to cope with some "deep misunderstandings" with Kate. Both these two good clergymen accepted this explanation and assured him of their understanding and that they trusted his judgment. Each said he was always available to help in any way he could. They would stand by. They, too, predicted that all this would be worked out. They had seen enough of life, they said, to know.

Andy Campbell, who had served in the diocese longer than Walt and Joe combined, said something that disturbed Joe. He expressed alarm that Bishop LaBelle might be discussing Joe's situation with the executive committee. If this was occurring, it was probably not good. All three of them agreed that LaBelle was probably doing just that, because in the absence of a diocesan bishop, the executive committee was technically the authority in the diocese. Any trouble with one of the diocese's clergy would be a matter LaBelle would certainly bring up with the committee. Walt Lewis, too, saw this as a potential problem. The executive committee members were good people, but not at all suited to managing sensitive issues. Together, the three of them named all the members, writing them down on a napkin to be certain they left no one out. Joe knew a few of them, and Walt and Andy knew them all.

"If I were you, I'd go to your old diocese this afternoon and speak with Bishop Spencer. See if he can find a place for you before that executive committee gets ahold of you," said Walt. "They could be vicious."

Joe was startled by this, and also by the fact that Andy appeared not to disagree. Both shook their heads slightly and looked at each other and then at the tabletop. Joe's own assessment was different, and he told them so. Maintaining eye contact, they munched their club sandwiches while he described the executive committee members as mature people, adults, and longtime servants of the church. They would certainly be reasonable. They knew that mistakes occurred in every marriage and that people worked through them and often grew stronger. Bishop LaBelle was a mature man, a bishop for twenty years, and he would handle it with fairness and sensitivity too. He had even called Joe and planned to meet him for dinner that evening. Joe trusted all of them, he said, and had confidence that they would act with reason. He had already agreed to an evaluation. He had nothing to hide. He would be clear and forthcoming. He had lost it and admitted doing so, and it would never happen again. The executive committee would understand all that.

* * *

"The executive committee feels that it would be best for you to leave Redeemer for the time being."

"Leave Redeemer..."

Bishop LaBelle gulped down a mouthful of some sort of Cajun chicken and rice and took a long swig of his ice tea. "This is good! You should have ordered some of thi—"

"Leave Redeemer?"

"Yes. Their feeling is that it would be better for the parish, at least until we can get the results of your evaluation." He handed Joe a slip of paper. "Here's the name of the doctor who is going to do it. I'm sorry I don't have his number too. Call the diocese tomorrow and ask Judy Johnson. She'll give you the number."

"But why?"

"You agreed to have an evaluation."

"I don't mean that. What is this about my leaving the parish?"

"The executive committee feels that it would be best for a while, until we can get the results of your evaluation, and then we can go from there."

Joe waited, but it seemed that LaBelle, returning his attention to the food, was in no hurry to add anything.

"Bishop! This is a surprise. I have been in this parish almost ten years. We have a lot going on. What in the world could have made the executive members think that such a thing is necessary?"

"Well, their position is that it would be better right now and to see what the evaluation indicates."

"That could take months."

"Oh, no. It won't be that long. Sometimes these things can be done in a few weeks. But one thing I can say: I want to come to Redeemer and speak to the vestry myself. I want to try to see if we can make this a leave *with* pay."

Joe was shocked. He asked if he could speak to the chair of the committee. He had worked closely with her since the departure of the former bishop. LaBelle said it was up to Joe and that he felt that she would speak with him. Joe requested that all these plans be placed on hold until he could have that conversation. LaBelle agreed, as long as Joe talked to the chair before the following Monday, because that was the evening he would meet with the Redeemer vestry. LaBelle had called Harry Campos that day and asked him to call a special meeting. This, too, surprised Joe. He had not spoken to Harry or any other vestry member that day. There was no way he could have known it. A vague sense of something at work around him, feint but discernable from the beginning in LaBelle's presence, began to grow, making him exceedingly uncomfortable.

"Joe," said the elderly bishop, obviously trying to be kind but appearing to have little appreciation for the effect of his news, "let's not get worried." He paused and finished his tea. "Of course, I know you're worried, but don't get too worried now. Let's just see what the evaluation shows. And until then, just be patient."

The meal ended and they left the table. Joe had not touched his food after the first few bites. If LaBelle noticed it, he made no comment. They said goodbye and parted in the lobby. LaBelle's final words were, "I'm praying for you, Joe. And I mean that."

It was after nine, too late to try to reach Margaret Hughes, the executive committee chair. He knew from working with her during the previous months that she retired very early so as to get into her office before eight. Halfway home, he pulled into the parking lot of

181

a deserted gas station and sat for a half-hour in the dark. His mind was spinning. He had not seen his son and wife in three days. He had just been ordered to leave his job pending the return of a psychiatric evaluation. He had had little sleep and had eaten little since Saturday night. The people he trusted were...what? Making him take a leave of absence until he could be evaluated. As disturbing as it was, he knew it was not unreasonable. They knew nothing about his marriage. All they knew was...what? What Kate told Hervey, Hervey told LaBelle, and LaBelle told them? Or had LaBelle spoken directly to Kate? LaBelle had never said that, and of course it had not occurred to Joe to ask.

Something about the thought of Kate or Hervey talking to LaBelle was alarming enough to make him start the car and continue heading for home. He knew Hervey had called LaBelle from LaBelle's call to him on Easter evening. What had he said? "Father Hervey explained it all to me...Father Hervey told me what happened..." Long ago, the lawyer in Joe had learned to approach hearsay, even among the most reliable people, with caution. Regardless of who spoke to whom, the trail led to tonight's conversation in which LaBelle told him to leave the parish. He knew the original fault that had set the whole process in motion was his own. He had lost it, and that was where the unraveling had begun. It was his fault. After the events of the preceding three days, he thought it would be impossible to feel any worse than he felt at that moment. But he was wrong.

Chapter Fifteen

H IS HOME WAS a few miles from the motel, and normally he would have invited the bishop there for coffee or perhaps a drink now that Kate was not there. After their conversation, he only wanted to be alone. His mind heaved and churned like the sea at Wicomico in a northeast wind. His shock at being ordered out of the parish had disoriented him for a while. What was happening? He heard about family fights every week that sounded more severe than his own. A hundred questions occurred to him that he wished he had asked LaBelle. He considered calling him at his motel or going back to speak with him in person, but as he stood in his own home and looked around at the signs of the people he loved, the best instincts of the priesthood and the law settled in to support him. He sat down at the table and prayed, asking God for forgiveness, to protect his family, and to give him wisdom and courage in the days to come. Then he took from his briefcase a white legal pad and began to make some notes about what LaBelle had ordered him to do. He copied down the therapist's name and address and called directory assistance in Washington for the telephone number. He began to anticipate what might happen and what he would have to do in each case, like a chess player contemplating future moves.

As he organized his thoughts and made his notes, he grew less and less apprehensive. He was dealing with capable, honorable people. Whatever Hervey might have told LaBelle, the matter was now in competent hands. He could trust the church hierarchy explicitly.

The possibility that this whole mess was God's way of getting Kate into counseling with him formed in his mind like someone switching on a light. There was more here than he had been able to deal with. Her resistance was too deep, beyond a husband's capabilities, at least beyond his.

In the way things have of popping suddenly out of the past, he remembered Kate's words to him after the intervention years ago at the same kitchen table where he sat now. In chastising him for something, she had said to him, "That night you all talked to me? When the Gallaghers were here? They cried! *You* didn't even cry!" She was perfectly serious. Why he should think of it now, he didn't know, except that her words had been ridiculous, almost outrageous. Perhaps God was stepping in now in a new way.

The thought of her voice reminded him that he had not seen her and Ted for three days. Perhaps one might think that under the circumstances, he would not want to see her. But he did. He needed her presence and Ted's right then, at that very moment. Even their anger would have been preferable to what he was experiencing.

He had been given one week to conclude ongoing matters and depart the parish pending the results of a psychiatric evaluation. The evaluation itself did not trouble him in the least. In fact, he welcomed it—he would welcome anything that would bring out the truth. But separating himself from his parish while it was occurring was a bitter price to pay.

He had represented many people in crisis and been able to think and plan reasonably for all of them. Now that the crisis was his own, he knew he needed to approach everything from a slightly new perspective. It would be a test of his skills to remain objective and patient during an emotionally harrowing time. He got up and stood at the kitchen sink and gulped down the last of the skim milk. Beyond his own reflection in the dark window, his little dog sat looking back at him, twitching in alarm. He realized he had walked past Cory without a word. He went out through the garage to pat him, but the phone rang and he returned to the kitchen quickly, praying it was Kate.

It was his good friend Harry Campos, and he felt distress at the tinge of alarm in this decent man's voice. He had been talking with Tom Downes, and they had been calling Joe all evening. LaBelle had left a request for Harry to call a vestry meeting for the following Monday night, saying he wanted to discuss Joe's position at Redeemer and asking him to keep the meeting confidential. Joe told him about his own conversation with the bishop and about the executive committee's decision that he must take a leave of absence. Harry was astonished.

The following morning, he called his friend the executive committee chair. She was always glad to talk with him, she said, and she sounded as she always had in their months of working together. When he began to question the committee's decision that he leave Redeemer, her tone changed, and she replied plaintively, "Let's not get into it, Joe." He took his cue, thanked her politely for speaking with him, and said goodbye. She was a reasonable, responsible person, and he was alarmed by her reaction.

Within moments of arriving at his office, he was called by Harry. He had spoken with Bishop LaBelle and could not change his mind. LaBelle said the executive committee had strong feelings that Joe should take a leave from Redeemer. Harry explained how well Redeemer's mission and ministry were progressing, the community outreach taking place there or under Joe's leadership, and how attendance and giving were growing as never before. LaBelle said that none of that would change and that the diocese would assist Redeemer in finding someone to conduct services.

Harry's irritation was evident, and it saddened Joe. Harry did not like being told by this stranger not to worry about a crisis in the congregation he had served so faithfully for almost fifty years. The disappointment and sadness in his voice were significant in a man widely respected in politics and business throughout the state.

"I told him that these things happen in families. They're unfortunate, but people get over them and go on. I told him you just got pushed past your limit and that you'd been dealing with this situation for years and years. Everybody makes mistakes. It's human nature. It's

185

evident to all of us that you love her, I told him. Nobody's perfect. But he wouldn't change his mind."

"Thanks for trying," said Joe. He knew this good man's distress was his own fault. He expressed his profound sorrow and accepted responsibility for everything.

"Well, you just hold on, Joe. This isn't over yet. The parish has got to have some say in this. They can't just step in and take our priest away all of a sudden. LaBelle doesn't know Hervey's reputation around here. We are not giving up on this thing. You just wait. I've served this diocese all my life in every position they've got. Somebody is misjudging this thing. We are going to work this out."

He hung up and immediately began a letter to Kate, explaining what was happening and asking for her help in straightening it out. She had some affection for Redeemer. The people had always been good to her, and they loved Ted, and she knew it. Kate must surely realize she had pushed him too far. He knew she was furious with him, but she understood right and wrong. He apologized again for his ugly behavior. He accepted responsibility for everything he had done. He appealed to her not to let their personal problems cause trouble for the hundreds of people at Redeemer. He appealed to her sense of fairness.

Halfway through the letter, Bishop LaBelle called. He said he had been reviewing the canons before bed last night and he thought it might be useful to remind Joe that as a priest not actively serving a parish—his words, so casual and detached, cut into Joe's ear like a needle—Joe was not eligible to participate in the upcoming diocesan convention and, he regretted to say, Joe would be unable to vote in the election of the new bishop. "I'm sorry to be the bearer of bad tidings, but the new executive committee chair will probably contact you after the convention, and we'll go from there." He told Joe again to call his secretary and she would give him the number of the doctor he was to see.

The thought of this "doctor" again raised Joe's hopes. A professional, responsible person would be able to see the situation clearly. Joe had years of familiarity professionally and personally with the work of physicians and psychologists. He had confidence that an intelligent, skilled professional could get to the truth and reassure everybody that Joe was a sane, rational man.

The recommended professional was a Dr. Frank McMahon. His office was in suburban Maryland, and Joe wondered why the church had chosen a specialist so far away. McMahon had probably worked for the church on other matters. That was good, too, having someone familiar with ecclesiastical hierarchy and clergy life. He called and was connected to an answering machine. A voice said to leave a message and advised that messages were checked throughout the day. Joe explained he was calling at the direction of Bishop LaBelle and left his numbers.

He hung up, and Ted's face was before him immediately. He saw his son's face every time he closed his eyes. What was Ted thinking now? Was *he* all right? Joe had not seen him in several days. He was used to that. He was away a lot, all summer at the beach with Kate, at school all week at St. John's, and since moving into his midteens, he seemed always away with his friends, at somebody's house, at someone's party, at a school activity. When they all came to his house, he enjoyed them immensely, but it meant little personal time with Ted. And of course, Joe often was away from home too. The church, and especially this rural, fractious diocese, had a way of sucking up every moment of its servants' time. The church preached clergy wellness, but the reality was relentless demand and each priest had to achieve a healthy balance in his own particular circumstances. From time to time, Joe had considered how much of his life was spent on the road and how better it would be for single clergy, with no family responsibilities, to serve this diocese. The shortest of meetings meant hours of travel. And no meeting was ever short. The smallest matters could become the subject of passionate disagreement; it took forever to get anything done. Especially since the retirement of the former bishop, it seemed Joe was always going somewhere.

In all those travels, the faces of his wife and son filled his mind like music. Sometimes after a particularly trying spell with Kate, the music was angry rap more than Mozart. He could hear the addictive voice of a famous country singer; they were always on his mind. The chatter at the Third Base subsided a little when that song came on as everybody listened in melancholy preoccupation. He worried on those long drives: about the long, slow wearing away of their marriage and what he could do about it, Ted and his life and maturity, his relentless concern that his son grow up in a calm, reasonable, loving home with two parents, security, and spiritual nourishment. He thought about their future and planned for it consistently, saving for Ted's college years, saving for the day when he and Kate could retire, travel, have some time free of schools, church, drinking, everything, and longing for the day she would join with him in these plans and dreams.

His senses filled with these images, and his gaze shifted unknowingly. He had a habit of coming out of these reveries of his wife and son and finding himself staring at the cleanest, most beautiful thing in his surroundings. Now he found himself looking at a fistful of daffodils protruding happily from a blue mason jar on his desk. They were the short, ragged, hearty early blooms that appear in patches of sunlight before all the snow is gone, rearing up faithfully, naturalized in places where their grower's home collapsed or burned down ages ago, reminding the world of spring, of former times, of joy and the resilience of life. An elderly parishioner had brought them in the day before, a reclusive old man whose dilapidated farm, with its once-elegant boxwood gardens, burst forth in golden glory every spring. He looked at the yellow flowers and their emerald stems shining above the watery blue jar. They were in the broken world a glimpse of intrusive and heartening beauty, magical, mysterious, invigorating, like sea air or mountain vistas.

For oft, when on my couch I lie in vacant or in pensive mood, they flash upon that inward eye which is the bliss of solitude. Who had time anymore to lie upon a couch? There were plenty of pensive moods these days however, though not many vacant ones, but oh, how his inward eye had been ablaze with wondrous flashes since his childhood. Daffodils and lily of the valley, Kate's favorite flowers—how many dozens had he planted wherever they had lived? And English peas—she liked them too. And the gardens of these and other things he had tended, a past where he might lose himself in memory from his guilt and humiliation of the present moment. He looked at the golden flowers and drank them in, for a second or two imagining van Gogh imbibing the sunlit wheat fields of Arles and ingesting his great, crazy canary-mustard and lemon sunflowers. How good it would be to stand in the surf now, pulling in the big chopper blues on their northward run, or maybe even a big striped bass, and watching the clouds moving on the spring sea.

He turned to his word processor and recomposed the beginning of his letter to Kate. She would understand. He would drive it up to the Candytown post office after work, and she would read it the following day. She would help put all this right. She was being careful of what she said, surely, as he had taken care for years, rightly or wrongly, to preserve her confidence about her.

As soon as he arrived at his office, Milly opened the door and came briskly to his desk, saying, "There are three people here to see you about getting some help with electricity, and they're not together, so you'll have to see them one at a time I guess, and here are some calls"—she deposited a half-dozen pink slips onto his desk—"and remember sometime today, you and me are going over the list of last year's gifts for the memorials committee to double-check their figures, and they took Nell Waller's little girl to the emergency room this morning with something in her ear, but she's all right and back at school, and before you call anybody, call St. Ambrose and talk to Father Bazich about whatever it is you all are going to be doing for the Week of Prayer or whatever. He says you're organizing it this year on account of he thinks he did it last year. He's called twice, and he's got somewhere he's supposed to be at and he won't be there long, he says." The office phone began its unrelenting summons, and she turned and went quickly back to her desk.

* * *

The bishop postponed his meeting with the Redeemer vestry for one week, until after the diocesan convention. Redeemer's disconcerted delegates attended the convention without Joe. They found themselves surrounded uncomfortably by a gleeful commotion over their absent parish priest, in which everybody appeared to know more than they did. The convention, which everyone approached in hopes of spiritual refreshment, was for them awkward and embarrassing. Joe's dilemma was the topic of animated conversation everywhere, even among people who did not even know what he looked like, and nowhere more vigorous than among the diocesan clergy. It seemed there was no limit to the possible range of Joe's infractions. There was much excited discussion as his brothers and sisters in holy orders compared stories about what he had done, to whom, and exactly how. That his wife had fled their home raised all sorts of intriguing possibilities, each of which was discussed in imaginative detail. Was it two or three policemen who had responded? Joe had been put in jail. No, just taken in and fingerprinted like on TV. Poor Kate ("Was that her name?") was so distraught at the moment she could not even work. The congregation was calling for Joe to be fired. LaBelle ("What a saint!") was working overtime to straighten it all out. They were going to put Joe ("Poor thing, just imagine") in a hospital somewhere.

A bishop from the Midwest who had never met Joe, in the diocese for the first time in his life as the convention's keynote speaker, sauntered from group to group, inquiring what various people thought about what Joseph Stephenson had done. When confronted by one of Joe's clergy friends and a Redeemer delegate about the propriety of his questions, the bishop appeared to take some mild offense and walked away. Bishop LaBelle was questioned politely by a mature lady who had attended many conventions as a Redeemer delegate about how all this misinformation had come to be discussed on the floor of convention. LaBelle replied that he had no idea and quickly excused himself.

The Redeemer delegates returned highly disconcerted and understandably annoyed with Joe, for letting them go unprepared into such a trap. Joe was mortified. He knew these good people well. He had been with them in their most trying personal situations, and his concern for them was powerful. He let them know the degree of his own surprise that any such thing had happened. He had no idea who had spread the gossip or why his fellow clergy had chosen to discuss it so loosely, or exactly what they had been told, or were telling one another, or where it had all originated.

Because they knew him well and sensed his own surprise and pain, the Redeemer delegates overcame their hurt feelings and accepted Joe's assurances that he also was taken by surprise. Their discomfort added to his own grief over losing his temper at home with his family. He understood that all this trouble led directly back to him. Had he not lost it…had he controlled himself better, as he had so many times before for years and years…if he had tried to talk to Ted, reason with him. What difference did it make if he was acting like Kate? She was his mother, after all. He had always tried hard not to put on Ted the pressure other clergymen placed on their children, driving them away from the faith instead of bringing them closer. Why had Ted's serving on this Easter Sunday been so important? So what if it was their last time to serve together? Joe was to blame. He had set in motion all this trouble. He closed his eyes and pressed his fists to his forehead and wished he could blot out the world or blot himself out of the world.

And was this current guilt and grief bringing him nearer to accepting the truth? He had known it for years, hadn't he? His marriage was over. It had ended the night several years ago when he had slapped Kate in the kitchen, the night she thundered down the stairs in rage and began to talk about things Ted had said about him. He had known since then that his coping was no longer shielding either of them. He had handled it all wrong, probably from the beginning, and it had all culminated in a slap, Kate's astonished, wide-eyed expression that still burned on his heart like a sizzling brand, her incredulous anger, and her departure in the night for several hours.

It seemed to him that there had been a dozen times when he thought he must leave her for his own sanity and Ted's safety. But then would come a change in Kate's mood and temperament for a few days, perhaps a week, and her uneven emotions would seem to level out. He had always grasped at these transient shifts as though his prayers were being answered. It only made the later reality harsher. Separating would break Ted's heart. He could imagine nothing worse in himself, nothing more cowardly than risking a court awarding

Ted's custody to Kate. He well knew the official line that the old presumption in favor of the mother had been abrogated. His experience, however, especially in rural courts with female judges, was something altogether different.

Had any further convincing been necessary over the years, his heart would have been filled with the vows he had made as a husband and priest. It would have been easier to look at his vows in what passed these days for a more modern way, less serious, as though they were not pledges to God upon which he would one day be examined and judged, but loose agreements, relative and situational, drawing their meaning and validity from the changing world around him. It revolted him. Such an attitude was an offense against God and a betrayal of one's word. He had seen witnesses lie under oath in court for years. An oath might mean little nowadays, especially among the young and trendy, who hooted and smirked at *Schindler's List* or shot strangers for their jackets and wristwatches.

Following Kate along her erratic course, entangled in the complications of her anger, must come to an end now. Maybe the present crisis was God's way of turning them both in a new direction, toward health and a new wholeness. Perhaps he would not have to shore up his alcoholic marriage ever again. Could it be that what looked to be defeat was actually a chance for a new start?

He stared at his computer screen, where the words "Dear Kate" floated on the gray background. It occurred to him that she had done exactly what she told him she was going to do on that night years before, when the three of them were riding home after dark. She and Ted had moved to St. John's. And he was so dumb and blind that it had happened without his realizing it.

But no. He was beginning to feel a growing confidence that this crisis would turn into a blessing in disguise. Their relationship would grow stronger with marriage counseling. There were a thousand good times in the past on which to build. The future was bright. He wrote his letter to the wife whose behavior exasperated him but for whom he still had affection.

He waited a few days for a reply to his letters, but there was none. He wrote again, this time confining his apology to one paragraph and devoting another long paragraph to a proposal to sell the house. He knew she did not like it and that a new start in another home might help the healing. It was their only asset—Joe had no ownership rights in the Wicomico property—and he figured she would move herself to reply at least on this issue. The night after he deposited his letter at the post office near the school, he came home to find a message from her on the answering machine. It was the first time he had heard her voice in weeks.

"Joe, it's me. Got your letter about selling the house. Yes, good Lord, sell it so we can get the money. Call Jane Ellen and put it on the market as soon as possible and let me know if I have to come over there to file papers or anything. It's the best idea to sell it, and we ought to go ahead and put it on the market now. Okay? Let me know."

He replayed it several times. "Yes, good Lord, sell it" had clearly come out "*sell* it," as if she were referring to a chance to be rid of something dirty and burdensome. Their home. She had never liked it, or maybe she had never liked him being in it. Whichever it was, she had made her feelings clear in a hundred ways for years. And he, simple shit that he was, had continued to live as though her sullenness and argumentative opposition was a phase that would end the next week, the next month. This was the place where they had celebrated Christmases, birthdays, entertained Ted's friends and his— the obvious appeared to him now as he had not permitted it to do before—the place where they had cried together, visited with family, where Catherine had last lived before entering the nursing home. This was their home. They had lived together here as a family. It was part of them. He loved this place.

He played the recording one more time and then erased it.

* * *

What had Hervey said to the bishop to precipitate what was happening? Father Hervey himself was kind enough to supply and answer. A copy of a letter addressed to Bishop "Marvin" LaBelle supplied an answer.

Dear Bishop LaBelle:

This is to confirm our conversation over the telephone on Easter in which I reported to you an incident of domestic abuse by a priest of your diocese. As I reported, Ted Stephenson came to me at ten o'clock on Holy Saturday evening and reported to me that his father, the Reverend Joseph Stephenson, hit him with a clenched fist across his face and then about the head and then repeatedly with a zippered jacket, because he was infuriated when Ted told him that he would be returning to St. John's on Saturday evening and attending chapel at St. John's on Easter Sunday. Ted reported further that Father Stephenson slapped Mrs. Stephenson forcefully with an open hand across the face when she intervened on Ted's behalf. They then gathered some clothes and came immediately to campus. Ted boards at St. John's, and Mrs. Stephenson has been a member of our faculty for eight years. When I asked Mrs. Stephenson her account of what happened, she entirely agreed with Ted.

As I explained, Mrs. Stephenson came to me at Christmas two years ago with a similar account of abuse in which Father Stephenson had become very angry and hit her. At that time, she asked me to keep her confidence, which I agreed to do on the clear understanding that I would be immediately informed if it ever happened again. As this is now the second incident reported to me of a longstanding pattern of abuse, I see no recourse but to report this matter to you. I do this in the hope that you will address this matter forcefully and make sure that Father Stephenson receives the kind of counseling he obviously needs in order to establish a more appropriate relationship with his wife and son. Fortunately, Mrs. Stephenson has an apartment on campus and a secure future in our employ, so she and Ted can live safely away from him while this matter is addressed.

Yours faithfully,
Andrew Philip Arthur Hervey

cc: Mrs. Stephenson, Father Stephenson

Lest he miss it, Joe's name at the end was highlighted in a forceful yellow dash. With the school title and crest emblazoned across the top and Hervey's vast signature filling the lower quarter of the page, the letter had the look of a medieval document of much importance.

Chapter Sixteen

BISHOP LABELLE AND the executive committee determined that the people of Redeemer should hear their fate, and Joe's, directly from them. A parish meeting was arranged for Thursday night of the week following the diocesan convention. At Diocesan House, a team of specialists was assembled, people with whom Joe had worked closely for years. There was Kirby Porter, now chairman of the executive committee, and Mary Lake, the capable diocesan development officer. She was especially astute in women's issues and had once directed a shelter for abused women. A lawyer came, too, the assistant legal officer for the diocese. Joe did not know him well but had admired his competence the few times they had worked together. The team included a clinical psychologist from somewhere in New York. Under the former bishop, the diocese had begun to employ her for workshops on human relationships. Joe had participated in one of them and found her professional and competent

Bishop LaBelle ordered Joe not to attend this meeting. "It could be embarrassing for you, but also for the congregation. It might be easier on everybody discussing all this, ah, without you there." Joe thought the bishop's position made common sense, and whatever would help the situation was what he wanted to do. He would spare everyone having to speak on troubling issues, for which he was to blame, in his presence.

The meeting was to begin at seven thirty, and LaBelle had assured everyone it would be over by nine. Parishioners began to arrive quite early, coming directly from work and gathering in small groups throughout the building. Someone volunteered to stay in the nursery with small children so parents could focus on whatever was going to be said. Joe waited at home in the deepest distress, imagining the familiar people gathering in the church and knowing that whether they were angry, sad, or confused, he was to blame. He felt the same anxiety he had known when he feared Kate was driving drunk or worried at what risks she might take with Ted.

He wrote a letter to Kate and Ted about the parish meeting, although he was sure they already knew. He began his next newspaper column, about the rite of baptism and its origins in early Israel. He made some notes for his meeting with Jane Ellen Rush, a real estate agent, the following morning. He spent a while with Cory and paid a couple of bills. Throughout the evening, he found himself jerking awake from turbulent meditations like a man warding off sleep at the wheel. How could he have caused such turmoil? All the important people of his life were in distant places, doing something because of him, and here he was in exile, like them paying the price of his mistakes. In his innate faith in divine guidance, the assurance that had unfolded consistently within him since childhood, he knew the ultimate resolution would be right. But how could he have forced it all in this direction? How had he made such a mess of so many good things? When he went in to use the bathroom, he consciously avoided looking in the mirror.

The telephone was silent all evening until a few minutes before eleven, when it began to ring steadily and continued jangling each time he hung up until sometime after two the next morning.

The first caller was Harry Campos, speaking from his car phone in the parking lot across the street from the church. Joe was alarmed by the anger in his old friend's voice. After forty years in state and local government, Harry was no stranger to confrontation and turmoil, but it was clear he had just experienced something startling. Following his lengthy call, Joe heard from a half-dozen parishioners and nine more left outraged messages on his answering machine while he was talking to others. If LaBelle and the diocesan staff had set out to infuriate everybody, they had succeeded.

The vestry and over a hundred parishioners attended, sitting in the nave. The bishop and his team sat up in the chancel, taking turns speaking to everyone from the lectern microphone. The bishop spoke first, thanking everyone in a kind, pastoral manner for attending and expressing gratitude to his "team of experts" for interrupting their busy schedules on such short notice. Then, in an abrupt transition that created dismay, he compared Joe's family situation to the sex-abuse scandal he had been "forced to deal with" in his last assignment. He assured them all that Joe would be evaluated promptly and the church would then do what it had to for everybody's good. Domestic violence was a national dilemma. The church was appalled by it, and he certainly was, personally. He was sorry that "all this" had arisen in their midst. In the meantime, he said, the diocese would help Redeemer as much as possible. The first step would be to find someone to conduct services and tend to the pastoral needs of the congregation. He assured them that the parish and the Stephenson family were in his prayers.

When the bishop stopped talking, a swell of voices arose and several people in the rear got up and moved closer to the front. People leaned over the pews and spoke to one another across the aisle. A number of people stood or raised their hands to speak, but the bishop, momentarily startled, urged everybody to hold questions until all the visitors had spoken.

When the commotion subsided, the Reverend Mr. Porter jumped up and advanced to the microphone like a school principal determined to quell a noisy assembly. This formidable charge subsided to a patronizing intimacy as he began to speak. One elbow on the lectern and the other hand propped on his hip, he leaned toward the people like an informative neighbor over a garden fence. He lectured everybody on the responsibility of the executive committee to conduct the business of the diocese during this interim period, lofty matters of which the people were understandably unaware. One shoe poised vertically behind the other, he presented this revelation at length and backed it up with references to canon law, all of which the congregation endured with patience. He assured the people that the committee was doing only what it had to do, and Redeemer's responsibility was—and he hated to put it this way, but it was after all the position into which Joe had forced everybody—just to do what the committee directed. ("I wish you could have *seen* him!" said a half-dozen people in the same words to Joe in the days following.) He finally went stealthily back to his seat like someone trying not to wake the children, and the nave began to rumble like water starting to boil.

Mary Lake did not say anything, or if she did, nobody remembered what it was. The vice-chancellor did not speak, his contribution presumably having been covered eloquently by Porter. Then the psychologist spoke. She did not know the congregation or the denomination's structure, she admitted. She had met Joe once but did not actually know him, and she did not know many details of what he had done. Smiling warmly, she went on with a few more disclaimers, unaware of the irritation they roused in her listeners, who wondered why she was there at all. Then she became quite serious and, maintaining much professional detachment, outlined briskly the clinical stages of grief that a group should expect to go through when separated from its leader. They were not to worry, because in time they would come into an "acceptance stage," in which—so they would recognize it when they got there—they would resign themselves to doing what the diocesan leaders knew was best for them. She had begun confidently but concluded like a teacher who has brought the wrong lecture notes to class. As she sat down, she seemed to appreciate that the congregation's silence was an act of courtesy.

With a few exceptions, the people listened to all this with mounting irritation, interrupting and being told each time that speakers would answer questions after the "presentation." When that moment came, an eruption took place (as one caller told Joe, "You would have been proud of us! We didn't let them get away with anything!") that lasted long past the bishop's prediction of closing time.

Why, they wanted to know, was all this happening on the basis of a family fight in the privacy of a home? Trouble happened in every household, and was the diocese going to remove their minister on the basis of a family fight? Clergy families were like everybody else. It was clear Joe loved Kate and Ted. Whatever had happened, everybody makes mistakes. A number of people began to provide examples from their own lives, or those of their friends, but the bishop and Parks hastily refused to hear about them. Was it true that Hervey over at St. John's School was the one who complained? Did they know about Hervey? A lawyer stood up and asked how they knew that Kate Stephenson was telling the truth and, if it was true, that what was happening had grown out of something she had said to Hervey, who had conveyed it to LaBelle, who told it to the executive committee? When LaBelle replied that Joe had acknowledged "participating in a course of domestic violence," the congregation wanted to know what he had said, but the bishop advised guardedly that he was not in a position to say. A dozen parishioners attempted to give examples of Joe's ministry and pastoral skills, but Parks stood up each time and said that nobody was questioning that and so they didn't need to hear about it. Questions were raised about why the punishment did not fit the crime, why this severe reaction, why was the whole parish penalized for a private family argument? LaBelle replied sternly that there was no punishment in what was happening. Someone in the rear asked where Christian love was in all this. Wasn't Joe entitled to a mistake like everybody else? Parks replied by quoting some more canon law, which encouraged a dozen additional parishioners to have their say.

Everyone wanted to speak, except the occupants of the front pew. Here, Lottie Bascomb was seated stiffly with her following. They included Nancy Dodd, a vestry member who frowned and scribbled notes furiously each time anyone spoke. During the speeches by the bishop and Porter, she and Lottie exchanged looks and bobbed their heads vigorously. Between them sat a gaunt, scowling woman who had transferred from Redeemer to another denomination years before after divorcing her husband, who continued to attend Redeemer regularly. There was another woman whom nobody knew very well, whose former husband had joined the parish and become one of Joe's supporters. These two did not attend services and had never taken part in parish life. Jane Ellen Rush was with them, the real estate agent who had helped Joe and Kate find a house when they came to the parish. Joe had approached her before learning about Lottie and her friendship with Jane Ellen. Joe had always believed that the choice of Jane Ellen had turned out to be one of life's "good" errors, because he and Kate had grown very fond of Jane Ellen and her family, who had been helpful in softening Lottie's campaign against Joe. These people sat close together and exchanged comments, turning their heads to hear the parishioners but avoiding turning around and looking into their faces. In the next pew sat Frank Bascomb and Don Rush, staring in silence at the backs of their wives' heads and exchanging an occasional wave with friends.

Anger filled the room like prickly heat. The parishioners' outspoken defiance, so completely different from the wary civic reticence that characterized the state, clearly confounded the diocesan representatives. The parish was thriving, they were told. The children were engaged. Teenagers were bringing friends to church. New people were joining. Outreach was strong. Redeemer was once again the center of a vigorous community ministry. They had known Joe and his family for years. One speaker stated carefully and diplomatically that everyone knew Kate but, at the same time, nobody saw her enough to really know her well. Someone stood up and said that no one knew her personally. People all around spoke up in agreement. A teenage girl in the rear said in a choked voice that it was a mistake to remove Joe, both for him and for the congregation, on the basis of a private family matter. Why didn't they just come out and say what they thought he had done? said a man. An elderly woman wanted to know why they were accepting the word of Hervey, a man who raised many questions himself. The bishop interrupted her immediately, but she began to tell about an acquaintance deciding to take their sons out of St. John's. Clearly vexed, the bishop would not let her continue. Couldn't they just proceed with their investigation and let Joe continue to work? asked others.

Bishop LaBelle met all this with the look of a man used to being obeyed. Now he could not believe his eyes and ears. When he responded to comments, the people were respectfully quiet, but a swell of voices arose the moment he finished. Porter ratcheted up the tension each time he approached the microphone, while the rest of the diocesan team hung back in silence, looking very uncomfortable. At ten thirty, the bishop closed the meeting hastily, without the usual prayer.

LaBelle led his people and the Redeemer vestry into the parish library for a private talk, while dozens of parishioners lingered about the building, talking in the small groups in which the church placed such importance. The bishop asked the vestry to consider paying Joe's salary for the time being. "Until we can see what the next step will be." In making this request, he began to make another reference to the sex scandal that seemed to obsess him. Before he could finish, he was challenged vigorously by a vestry member, a retired military officer, on the inflammatory nature of such a comparison. LaBelle replied that he was acting in the church's best interests. Several vestry members assured the bishop that the vestry had no intention of cutting off Joe's salary. "How is he supposed to live?" they wanted to know. This point, so obvious to the Redeemer vestry, clearly took the team of experts by surprise. LaBelle, annoyed by now at many things, advised that Mary Lake would contact them about a supply priest and lapsed into pensive silence. Mary Lake smiled and said yes, she would be calling them in a few days. Nobody responded to this. Porter, having exercised stupendous discretion by saying nothing until that moment, suggested it might be time to end the meeting so everybody could go home.

"We told them that we would pay your salary—there was no need to even suggest that we wouldn't—that we wouldn't abandon you…we wouldn't even consider it," said Harry. "The whole thing was preposterous. They were condescending. They talked to us like they were talking to a damn bunch of kindergartners. I've never seen anything like it. And I've been in the church for fifty years!"

"I really think we surprised them, Joe," said another caller, a former delegate to the state legislature. "They came here to lecture us on what they were doing and how we had to accept it. They thought they would tell us and we would sit there meek as mice and take it." Joe recalled her bravery in moving for change on so many social issues, especially matters involving children that had been addressed in other jurisdictions decades before. They had discussed local legislation and how matters were being handled in other states dozens of times over the years when she returned home during legislative recesses. He had admired her poise and principles, and especially her courage in speaking up for change in a resistant environment. It was clear to him, even on the telephone, that she felt insulted and demeaned.

A local physician called. "They were arrogant. I suppose they thought they could just send you away—from us, the ones who know you." As this good man spoke, Joe recalled long discussions with him during the three years he and his family suffered through a baseless malpractice lawsuit and watching him age a decade before it was dismissed. "What does the church have to do with an argument you and your wife have at home? The bishop, Porter, that Hervey character, people like that, what do they know about life in the trenches? I told the bishop I'd been in this denomination my whole life but I might not die in it after what was going on."

"LaBelle is a buffoon," said a lawyer who had taken his son out of St. John's several years before and enrolled him in a private school in Virginia. "He and Hervey…how can they understand the domestic scene, family life, or how hard it is…I'm sorry, Joe. But the word now is that Kate might have an alcohol problem. You might as well know what people are saying. A lot of us are not totally surprised. They say you've been covering for her. I don't know what the story is on that, and I'm not asking. It's your personal family business. As one lawyer to another, I'm just saying that there is a hell of a lot of family problems that are nobody else's business."

"It's true, Andy. I don't mind talking to you about it. It has been a problem with her and her mother for years. But I have to tell you, too, that I lost it over something that happened, something I should have handled better, and I smacked her on the cheek with my open hand. I just lost it. And it happened once before, about three years ago. There's no two ways about it. I lost it. It was my fault. I told it all to LaBelle when he called. My guess is he's convinced himself that I'm some sort of a violent Jekyll-and-Hyde monster or something. The church has an obligation to parishes. And the church is paranoid about getting sued. Especially LaBelle, after what happened with his last position."

"Well," said his friend after a pause, "these things happen, as they say, in the best of families. Any good district court judge or marriage counselor hears this kind of situation every day. God knows, I'm not condoning you smacking her."

"I understand that," Joe said, quickly, quietly. "Thinking about it, I grieve like somebody died. I carry it around like a big icy rock inside. It's all my fault."

"But they're reacting like they've got a homicide on their hands. I don't think they know how to handle it. Did they consult an attorney for the diocese?"

"No. LaBelle is most likely working with people at headquarters in New York. Let's see how it goes, Andy," said Joe. "The evaluation will be a good thing, and I'm hoping it will encourage Kate once and for all to come out of hiding and get some alcohol counseling. I just hope…"

"What?"

"I just hope that finally getting her to do that…that my work as a priest is not the price we have to pay to get her…for her to…get on the road to health. I don't know."

His friend thought this over and said, after a long pause, "I just can't see the church, of all institutions, being like that."

"I can't either," Joe replied. "But this is all new to me."

* * *

Jane Ellen Rush arrived the next morning promptly at ten o'clock, came into the kitchen, and accepted a peck on the cheek from Joe and a cup of coffee. They sat down at the kitchen table. She was the first person in the parish whom Joe had met, and he had real affection for her. He accompanied her around the county before they moved to Redeemer as she showed him houses for sale. She and her husband had been their first guests after moving into their home. He recalled them coming by one evening and sitting around the same kitchen table with Kate and him, while Ted was playing in the family room with two new friends from the neighborhood. They stayed for an hour or so. It would have been pleasant and hospitable to offer them a drink or wine. He knew where several bottles of Montecillo Crianza were packed in an unopened box in the dining room, but he had not wanted to risk a bad start in this house. He knew that such elementary maneuvers did not curb addiction. Still, he could not bring himself to put temptation so plainly in the open. He remembered saying aloud how he would like to offer them something more than soft drinks, with some reference to having not yet unpacked, and how they were still looking for things. Kate sat by, initiating no conversation, suspicious of these new people without their knowing it, responding just enough to avoid attention, speaking in a light, happy way. Joe had learned that some people reacted to this by deciding that Kate was shy, which often led to a solicitous attitude toward her. In the following months, Jane Ellen would become a friend, the only one in the community Kate would telephone for a chat now and then. Joe trusted Jane Ellen and was grateful for her friendship.

In one respect, however, she mystified Joe. She had been close to Lottie Bascomb for years. Their husbands, very fine men whom Joe liked, were friends. Yet over the years, Jane Ellen had defended Joe against Lottie's acid tongue. From time to time, she and Don had even taken care to warn Joe in confidence about something Lottie was saying or doing. He had always found their advice accurate and constructive. How had someone like her become so close to the devious and chronically angry Lottie?

In the dark winter months, when Kate grew listless and irritated and took out her anger on Joe in small cutting ways, there had been women he could call in each community, without having to explain everything, who would call up and suggest to Kate a girls' night out. He would say little more than that he knew Kate would like to have a break and a new movie was playing at this or that theater, or that they might like to try the new restaurant that had opened across town. "Call Kate. She would love to hear from you. She has been so busy, and I'll bet if you called her, she would say yes." Such a break, which Kate would never arrange for herself, almost always lifted her mood. Once in a while, it backfired, seeming somehow to make her more resentful, but this had been rare. The other women had always appreciated the suggestion, telling Joe later that they wished their own husbands would take such initiatives. If they had children, Joe would babysit. Ted was glad to have other children around for the evening. These same friends followed up with calls of their own, inviting Kate and Joe to meet them and their husbands at restaurants or their own homes for dinner. Kate never initiated such evenings out, but she would agree to go if someone else took the lead. Jane Ellen had been one of two or three women Joe could call on in their years in Catoctin Springs, and usually the only one with whom he could convince Kate to go out and have an evening away from it all. He was grateful.

So when they sat down together to talk about selling the house, Joe felt it only right to explain that Kate was "away" for the time being and why. He did not know that Jane Ellen had attended the bishop's meeting the night before, and he said nothing about drinking. If Kate's only true friend in the community was going to hear about that, it would have to come from Kate. Even after the events of the past week, he could not bring himself to betray her. He told Jane Ellen that he had slapped her "because of something that happened." If he had decided to tell her, or anyone, of why it occurred, he could not have done it in a few minutes, or a few hours, anyway. How is one to relate the cumulative pain of twenty years in a difficult marriage? How does a person describe the slow death of desire, trust, and intimacy?

Behind Jane Ellen, hunched over her canvas carryall and piling printouts and brochures on the table, a chair glowed into focus draped with Ted's tracksuit, light winter jacket, and a bag of old gym shoes. The incidentals of home, family, companionship, everywhere he turned—evidence of the dearest blessings of his life, scattered everywhere, in every precious room, his wife's things, his son's things, and it made him want to cry. Ted's face at seven or eight. "Dad, Saturday morning, let's get up early and go out to Shoney's and have some pancakes and then go out and climb a mountain!" And at five, maybe. "Dad, my favorite animal is a robot dinosaur." And at fourteen. "Dad, thanks for the school trip. Australia was great. And New

Zealand. And except for the airport connections and getting on the right plane, I could have done it on my own." And…

He became aware of Jane Ellen's blank stare. She was waiting for an answer to something. She showed him a few neighborhood listings and what the houses had sold for and was saying something about a ninety-day listing or something. He smiled and cleared his throat and was about to apologize. Jane Ellen became quiet for a moment, glancing down at the tabletop, and then asked if it was all right to go over to St. John's to visit Kate. Joe encouraged her to do just that. He still anticipated Kate's return, at least by the coming weekend. It would do her good to see Jane Ellen. In the meantime, Jane Ellen would list their home and begin to show it as soon as possible. He would want to straighten up, she said, give it a good cleaning. And be sure to minimize clutter, because clutter discouraged buyers. They tended to remember the clutter instead of the house itself.

Clutter, he thought. *The story of my marriage, like trying to hold back the tide, wherever we've lived, extensions of the Wicomico house, stuff everywhere, nothing ever thrown away, clothes that haven't fit for years, and the complaining and procrastination if I dared to suggest taking things to Goodwill, or putting stuff out with the trash.* It had amused him in their early years together, this clinging to every single thing that came into life. But then it had begun to overwhelm them, control them.

He accompanied Jane Ellen out to her car, emphasizing again that they wanted to move to a smaller house and that Kate would be the one to decide which one. "Show her all your listings and take her to the ones she likes. I'll go along with her choice." Jane Ellen reminded him that if Kate preferred a house across the river, they would have to work with a different agent. Joe said he understood and hoped Kate saw something she liked around Catoctin Springs. He thanked her sincerely for her help and said again how much he knew Kate would enjoy seeing her. She sped off down the drive into the warming day.

Above the distant river, a bank of opalescent haze was dissipating into the cloudless sky. Everywhere, luscious shades of green, fresh and moist after the cool night, were blooming in a dozen savory tints across the brightening land. Songbirds foraged on the rough grass and fluttered in the trees. He thought he heard a robin. From beyond the great oaks that crowded along the edge of the lawn came a raucous conversation of crows. Cory raced over the winter stubble, scattering birds, leaving trails of dewy footprints each time he crossed the driveway.

Here and there among the drifting leaves, a few late spikes of crocus, purple and yellow, were still visible. They surprised him and made him smile despite the darkness within him. He patted Cory's wet back and thanked the happy dog for keeping the deer at bay. This year, he had wanted to plant some, what, *Crocus chrysanthus* or *Crocus speciosus*—no, that was a fall bloomer—whatever they were, the kind the deer wouldn't touch, which grew all over the seminary grounds, pale lavender, tough as railroad spikes, rucking up singly through the snow and leaves of February and early March, while the old oaks still howled aloft in the blasts of dying winter. The deer left this kind alone. He remembered driving Kate to the seminary during a particularly difficult March, when she and her mother were battling daily, filling the apartment with a mean winter of their own, to show her these carpets of hearty, dignified little blooms. There were hundreds of them cast among the great trees like amethysts in the snow. Kate had loved them, and he had planted crocus and daffodils every year after they moved to their first home following graduation from the seminary. He had planted them here, too, yellow and purple, and the deer had enjoyed them thoroughly until Cory assumed command of the yard. He also planted the lavender type grown at the seminary, which the deer wouldn't touch. These early bloomers always cheered him, appearing boldly year after year, looking up in patches of sunlight in the scrims of snow and icy wind, independent, responsible, sound. They made him feel good, so he lingered a while to watch these late holdovers.

No neighbor looking on from a distance could have imagined the misery inside him, so in contrast to the waking world, as he ambled about his springtime lawn.

Chapter Seventeen

April 12

Dear Kate,

I apologize to you again and beg you to please come home. You have my word of honor that it won't happen again. I have never lost it like that before, and it will never happen again. I am so sorry about it. I love you and Ted. You know I love you. I have done my best over the years to handle things well. You are my wife, and I love you. Please come home. You can live as you want to. I won't insist on anything— time, yard, house, counseling, AA, nothing.

If our marriage must end, let it not be this way. Let's do what has to be done together. For our sake and Ted's, for future relationships with everyone else in the family, let's go forward as friends. You can drink. I won't object. But please come home. Soon it will be time for Ted's graduation, and then you'll go to the beach for the summer. There are things we need to prepare for together, for Ted's sake and for so many other reasons. Please, let us spend the time preparing together for the future. You can live as you want to. But please, let us do what we need to do together, as friends. I have forgiven you so many times over the years. Can't you please forgive me this time?

Love,
Joe

* * *

April 12

Dear Ted,

I apologize again to you for getting so angry. Please forgive me. I am terribly sorry about it. I understand that you are furious with me. You have a right to be. I am sorry more than words can say. Please accept my apology. As I said in my last letter, there is a lot you don't know about. For years and years, I worked hard to shield you from it. It is too complicated to explain in letters, but I am ready and willing to apologize in person and explain it to you whenever you are ready to listen.

I hope you are well and studying hard. I am proud of you for your acceptance. You will love college, and everyone there will love you. I have started the paperwork process and will give you your part of the forms when they arrive. The financial assistance officer is a very nice lady who has been extremely helpful. We will soon be all set.

Ted, I hope you and Mom will come home this coming weekend. I miss you both, and I think of you all the time. It makes me sick to think that you won't even speak to me. Please call me after you read this. I will keep my promise and not come over until you tell me you will see me. But please believe me—there

is much you don't know. Maybe you will understand
if you will only talk with me.

Love,
Dad

* * *

ALL HIS LIFE, he had seen pain wring the enthusiasm from certain lives like twisting water from a wet towel, leaving people compressed, wrinkled, and knotted. Adversity and pain were especially ugly in innocent lives, where suffering was unearned and undeserved. In some of them, misfortune was a process and appeared to be without redemption. He knew this was not so. One had to be a realist. What mysteries lay beneath the surface of personality and genes, he might never know. But even in grade school, he sensed that people of faith accepted the pain of life in a different way. As a child, he began to believe that God is real. As he grew older and learned about human history, he came to believe that God is good. As we are made in God's image, he marveled at his own faith, that his increasing understanding of the evidence should convince him of divine goodness rather than divine cruelty and unfairness. Only later would he begin to comprehend grace and recognize gifts.

When he was young, his parents and their brood went to the Piggly Wiggly every Friday night to buy groceries for the following week. The big dilapidated store—small by the standards of modern superstores but the largest grocery store anyone in their town had ever seen—was like Disneyland to Joe and his siblings, a wonderland of mysteries whose very name evoked the happiness of Saturday-morning cartoons and where the shelves were laden with dozens of brands of exotic candy. The young Stephensons roamed the aisles, exploring the crowded store like adventurers in an Uncle Scrooge comic book. His young parents checked their list and searched the shelves for the best prices, adding up the costs on a small pad, lest they exceed the amount of cash they had. It would be mortifying to arrive at the cash register with insufficient funds. Before their cortege crowded into the narrow checkout aisle, the children were allowed to select one candy bar each, a highlight of the week. Each cost a nickel, a precious sum in the family economy in those days. From his father's paycheck to the bank to his mother's pocketbook to the waiting hand of the store cashier, within a few hours, the preceding week's toil had been converted into two wobbly shopping carts of food. They moved out into the dimly lit parking lot a single line behind his father and the heavier of the two carts. The week's provisions were stowed away in the rear of his parents' ancient Woody.

It was during one of these Friday-night shopping expeditions that Joe had his first taste of crime. From the store he pilfered a small glass jar containing about twenty-five silvery candy beads about the size of BBs, used to decorate cookies and cakes. The years had erased any memory of what he thought he would do with them, if, in fact, he ever had an intention. They probably just looked interesting. The bottle created a bulge in Joe's hip pocket, easy to distinguish in a short, skinny boy, and one of Joe's brothers saw it as they jostled about on the middle seat of the car. He wanted to know what it was. When Joe tried to ignore him, he became persistent, their parents' attention was attracted, and his father discovered what Joe had hidden in his shallow pocket. Leaning back toward him over the front seat, shouting, "Look at me!" and each holding him by a skinny arm, his parents told him what a terrible thing it was to steal. He was seven years old.

His father turned the car around and drove back to the store, everybody observing a silence that was more mortifying than anything they could have said. His young siblings scrunched together on the far end of the seat and looked fearfully out the window, turning now and then to glance at him. They parked in front of the entrance, and Joe's mother ordered him to go in alone and return the sprinkles to the manager. Humiliated beyond anything he could have imagined, Joe complied. The worst part was facing the manager, a kindly man who always spoke to him in a friendly way. When he handed him the bottle and said he was sorry, Joe began to cry. The manager was easier on him than his parents and said he knew Joe wouldn't do it again.

But he had done it again, almost a year later. This time, it was a tiny pearl, and the victim was his own grandmother. She strung pearls to supplement her income, lining them up carefully on a black velvet pad lined with narrow grooves, under a magnifying glass and a bright light. Each one had to fit in the right order so the strand would balance. It was tedious work for her, and it intrigued Joe, not unlike his father when he tied fish flies, or his father's habit of collecting pennies and arrowheads. From a little box beside the soft black pad, he took a pearl about the size of one of the pilfered sprinkles. In his seven-year-old imagination, it resembled a tiny orb of moonlight, a talisman like something from *Captain Video and his Video Rangers* or *Flash Gordon*. He was playing with it, rolling it around in his hand, while his parents and grandmother talked in the next room. When it was time to go, he went to the car with it and was playing with it in the back seat when his parents happened to notice it. They drove him back to his grandmother's apartment and made him go in alone. For the rest of his life, he would recall the dread of crossing the sidewalk and beginning to cry before he reached for the doorbell. His grandmother, together with his parents the loveliest treasure of his life, opened the door and wanted to know what in the world was the matter and led him into her small living room. He told her he "took something," and then "I took something from *you*"—by far the most horrendous part—and handed over the tiny pearl, sobbing at his own despicable behavior in a moment he would remember for the rest of his life. He could not look at her. It was worse than speaking to the merciful store manager. His grandmother was gentle, understanding, and gracious, as she had always been, and that made him feel even worse. She was so dear to him.

All of them—his parents, his grandmother, and the Piggly Wiggly manager—had taught him precious early lessons in truth and compassion. His parents' faces, when he dared to glance at them again when they had all returned home (they both had looked ahead silently through the windshield when he returned to the car each time), Kate's face, Ted's face, all of them over the years as they changed, made a constant music in his mind. The faces of friends, old girlfriends, children he used to teach, strangers, those glimpsed in passing—they rose to meet him in life like tropical birds arising from the surface of water. Movable exhilaration, a joy in his confused heart, he could see them anywhere he needed them, a comfort as he walked into the first day of homicide trials or entered the bedroom of the dying with the oil of unction. When he walked out under the stars at night, he could see them. As he had grown from child to man, he had only to pause and turn inward and not even close his eyes to see the faces of the people he loved, and the number swelled with the years. And how they had come to him in moments of temptation and error! They were there, glimpses of grace, when he would have erred or acted in ways that later would have burned up his insides with grief or regret or anguish.

It was the sight of his parents' faces floating in his heart that prevented him from dropping out of college. Kate's lovely face glowing in his mind in the early years of their marriage—when she was crashing forward into adulthood as much for him as for herself, because in those days, she loved him as he loved her—made his heart melt with tenderness and encouraged him to keep on trying every way in his power to understand her and forgive her as often as it took to make a marriage. In every year of Ted's life, every month, he knew his son's looks and expressions and the subtle changes in him as he matured, each forever grafted into his heart and held there in trust for as long as life lasted.

Joe's joy and satisfaction came in knowing that Kate and Ted were safe, happy, secure, fulfilled, free, protected. Planning for the future, saving for college and retirement, taking care with time and every other resource, staying close to home, making a place in life for Kate's mother, accommodating Kate's need to spend time at her summer home, making moves and choosing homes with Ted's stability and schooling in mind, praying for understanding and remaining open to it in the guidance of others—it had all felt right to him, the only decent and responsible way to live. It felt like justice.

He had known sleepless nights before, but he was learning now that he had known nothing, really, about sleeplessness and regret.

They had left their home. After the kind of family fight that most families suffer now and then, they had left and would not communicate with him. He stared into the sleepless night, the darkness softened only by the glow of his bedside clock, and saw Kate on the beach in Wicomico, Ted in his first soccer uniform, the two of them locked in conversation and mutual admiration at a thousand evening meals, their faces lightening up upon hearing a new joke or a funny story. Their voices hummed in his ears. He heard Ted singing in the bathroom as he prepared for school in the morning. He heard Kate at the kitchen window commenting on the little birds. "Just look at them on the feeders!" And her asking, "What's this one, Joe? Have we seen one of those before? And look! There's a nuthatch going head downward. And what's that one? Where's your book? A what? What? I've never heard of a pine siskin. You are making that up."

The remorse that filled his every waking second spilled into his dreams, too, flooding his sleep like a burst sewer line emptying its gruel into his unconscious imagination. And waking, or half-asleep, he pounded himself with his own guilt and failure like a primitive man driving in posts with a heavy rock. He was at fault and knew he deserved such punishment, even in his dreams. How could he have become angry like that? How could he have lost it so?

Why, after all the years of keeping his serenity and trying hard to accept the things he could not change, had he lost it then and there? Why had his own patience and self-control and reason failed then, when they had held securely for so long? If it were going to happen, there were so many other times when he could have imagined losing it. He had kept his composure each time she had abandoned counseling without a word to him. He had stilled his anger over all the unannounced withdrawals from their account, the half-truths and fabrications about plans and responsibilities at school, the refusal to take care of their home or engage in a social life with anyone outside her job. Their dwindling social life, constricted by a thousand school activities—he had complained, but he had accepted it. Even the hardest pain of all, the progressive want of intimacy and the sad death of trust, he had dealt with without allowing anything like hate to enter his heart. He had struggled to care for Catherine because she was Kate's mother, a person in need, an old woman sick with many ailments who had abused and lost all her friends over the years. His years of caring for Catherine had meant little to Kate and made not the slightest difference to her brother, and even in that, he had kept his composure. Except for her brother's failure to follow through with helping them pay for the nursing home, he had not complained.

Why had he lost it on Easter Eve? All night long, night after night, he tried to convince himself that it had been the shock of Ted behaving suddenly like Kate and Kate colluding with Ted to circumvent him. But no, that was no excuse. Nothing they could have done warranted his losing it. It was his fault. He was to blame. The mistake was his. He was a miserable bastard. No amount of trouble in the past could account for it. He was not a violent man. He had dealt successfully with much more provocation than had come his way on that awful evening. He had lost it for a minute or two, and now his wife and son were gone, and it was his fault. He could blame nobody but himself.

Chapter Eighteen

SOLEMNLY AND WITHOUT specifics, Bishop LaBelle had advised Joe that he was keeping the "facts" of Joe's situation confidential. He emphasized that neither he nor anyone else would make decisions about Joe. "Until we see what the psychiatric examination says," he said. These assurances were enough for Joe. His trust in God's church and her officers was uncomplicated. His experience with mental health professionals and his belief that God heals through the gift of medicine made him confident that the truth would emerge. Day and night, remorse gnawed at his heart like a famished rat, crippling his dreams and waiting to attack when he woke from a few hours of fitful sleep. He knew he deserved to suffer. The silence of the house was mocking. After all the years of care and patience, and of the enabling that filled him now with its own stinging regret, why could he not have managed it better on Easter Eve? His home, always a beloved refuge because of the treasures there, was silent and empty now of his own doing. The only comfort it held was in the hope that they would come back. He knew the same kinds of fights happened in most families. People got through these things, went on, and learned to behave better the next time.

He accepted the bishop's assurances. He had faith that the process would be fair. Once the truth was known, LaBelle would understand that his losing it on Easter Eve, no matter how wretched and unjustified, was not characteristic of him. LaBelle and the executive committee members would understand his remorse, and his reasons, if they could even be called that. He was not convinced that what was happening was God's will, but the very possibility encouraged him and made it easier to wait and hope. He had been surprised before. He was a hopeful man.

Yet the anguish of his long days and sleepless nights was withering; he could not get his mind off the many who were being affected. If God was acting in what was happening, why did wholeness in his own life require turmoil for Ted, the innocent people of Redeemer, his mother, brothers, sisters, and old friends? The anguish he felt on their account was overwhelming. As unfair and damaging as his outburst had been, he was still alarmed that the church was inserting itself into a family matter occurring in the privacy of a home. And it concerned him deeply that LaBelle, and whoever he had talked to, were taking action that troubled so many lives on the basis of hearsay.

Bishop LaBelle had sought the advice of Bishop Warren Jones about what to do in the situation. Bishop Warren Cabell Jones was an official of the national church. While he was still a parish priest, Joe had known him rather well and had assisted him in several matters when he joined Bishop Spenser's staff. He had always admired Warren Jones, and knowing that he had a role in what was happening was reassuring. Still, that Jones was involved and taking part in decisions about him came as another surprise. He was a good man, but what did he know of what had happened? In thinking it over, he concluded that there was nothing unusual about it; the church had its channels of authority like every other institution. It was only natural that officials should consult one another. Jones had always seemed a reliable man, dedicated and approachable. Bishop LaBelle had been a bishop for many years. The executive committee people were reasonable and honorable. As depressed as he was by so many things, he was convinced his "situation" was in good hands.

A few days following the evening meeting with the congregation, Bishop LaBelle called to inform him that the executive committee had decided that Joe should complete his work at Redeemer in one week and have no contact with the parishioners after leaving. He was not to go upon the property of the church and was not to converse with anybody at Redeemer in person or by telephone until the psychiatric evaluation was received and "certain decisions" made. Joe found these abrupt and extreme conditions shocking, and being uncertain at the moment of how to react, he asked LaBelle if he was sure that this was what the committee wanted. His question, which on reflection he recognized was unnecessary, must have annoyed the bishop. LaBelle betrayed some irritation and replied that Joe had heard him correctly. He reminded Joe quickly that they were all handling your situation pastorally, not legally. The implication was clear; Joe should be grateful. Carefully and diplomatically, Joe explained that the Redeemer people were important leaders and present all over the community and that it was not possible to go anywhere without seeing them. The bishop replied that the orders were clear and that it was up to Joe to comply with them. Joe wondered if the spirited defense of him by the Redeemer parishioners at the evening meeting could have roused Bishop LaBelle's anger.

Joe spent the next week in his office, trying to bring many matters to what he believed would be a temporary end. It was impossible to accomplish much during the day, because the office was full of concerned people wanting to talk, expressing condolences and outrage, and offering to help in any way. Many of them brought in folding chairs and sat around his office and in the adjoining library, talking with him and one another. Given what he had done to cause all this, and knowing he was not supposed to speak to them after the week's end, he did not have the heart to ask for some peace and quiet. The phone rang constantly. The editor of the local newspaper, a member of another denomination, called to express his alarm and proposed a story in which Joe could tell his side of things. Joe thanked him but declined. Clergy from other denominations came by for a while or called. Milly had made a list of dozens of issues to discuss with him, and they worked through it slowly in the middle of the general commotion. The wardens and members of the vestry came and went throughout each day, offering to bring him lunch, type letters, make telephone calls, anything. Several people told him cautiously to pay no attention to things being said about him, by which he understood that the network of Lottie and Nancy Dodd and their cohorts was already in operation. He ended up staying in the office until after midnight each evening, completing what had to be done while he had the place to himself. The only people who did not drop by were his fellow clergy in his own denomination.

The wardens, among the most decent people of his life, blushed and shook their heads when they told him he should leave his keys, cell phone, parish credit card, and discretionary fund checkbook on his desk when the last day arrived. They were mortified to have to remind him, and he knew they were doing only what they had been told to do. He apologized to them—it seemed he was always apologizing, every minute of every day—for putting them in the position of having to do such things. About midnight on the last evening, he assembled these tools of ministry in a neat configuration on his empty desk. He was not exactly surrendering his collar, but the sadness that came over him was like the distress he had known upon discovering that Kate had reneged on her promises again, following the last intervention.

* * *

The telephone rang all day long. Dozens of voices on the answering machine asked him to call. Friends left packages at the door, homemade bread and casseroles and cakes. The local gardens had not yet begun to come in, but he found that neighbors had left bags and bags of Southern produce from roadside stands whenever he returned home from distant towns. How word had gotten around to them in distant places, he did not know, but the daily mail began to swell with letters from people he had known in the law, parishioners from his former churches, children he had taught who were grown now with children of their own. Some of them were people he had not seen in years, and he was surprised that they even remembered him. Several clergy he had known well, who had left the diocese for other places, wrote long encouraging letters assuring him that he was a good priest and they had total confidence in him. He was grateful. Following his prayers each morning, he spent time writing notes to everyone who wrote to him, thanking them and assuring them that he was confident that all would be well.

He went to his hometown for several days to explain in person to his mother and younger sister what was occurring and what he had done to bring it on. Telling his family was painful, especially explaining it all to his mother, who had to hear for the first time after almost twenty years that Kate was an alcoholic. It seemed the whole world had known about Catherine's drinking, but he and Kate had been so careful about her own. His mother had loved Kate like a daughter. His brothers and sisters had loved her as their own. His family had doted on Ted all his life. Seeing his mother cry, answering her questions, and reassuring her made him grateful his father had not lived to see it all. In talking to his family, he found himself still protecting Kate. He found it easier explaining his own fit of anger than revealing the difficulty of her drinking. He did it as briefly as possible, without details, mindful of preserving her dignity and protecting the loving family relationships that he knew would survive these troubled days.

Of particular support was the attention suddenly galvanized among the old friends with whom he hunted and fished several times each year. He had known some of them since the second grade. Others he had met in college and graduate school, the law or his parishes. They were all one big gregarious group now, friends with one another for life. The spring and fall fishing trips to the islands south of Wicomico each year, and the canoe trip each summer through the mountain valleys of Virginia, had been his only breaks in the routine, at least since the days when going to Wicomico for vacations had ceased to be relaxing. One or another of his old friends telephoned every night or so, inquiring about his health, asking about Kate and Ted, wanting to know what the church authorities were doing now. Hearing their voices on the phone was reassuring in a thousand ways. They had all shared much in their lives together, accompanying one another through the death of spouses, divorces, troubled children, the loss of jobs, and every other difficulty and tragedy in which human life abounds. They understood one another, and their concern was genuine. One old friend especially, an experienced social work director, called several times each week and advised the others of any developments. He was another of the countless excellent people whose names were precious when Joe counted his blessings.

Diana Boyd, an old girlfriend, called every three days or so and joined him occasionally at Al-Anon meetings. She had always been easy to talk to, and her experience with her own mother gave her a better understanding than most of what it was like for him to live with the disease. Kate had never liked Diana or her family and refused to go to any of their parties. By the age of ten, Ted had begun asking provocative questions about her and other old friends of Joe's, especially those whom Kate considered to be rich. Joe knew where his son's curiosity was coming from, but there was no way of changing Kate's attitude and behavior. He wanted very much for Ted to know and like his old friends from childhood, his years of teaching and practicing law.

Once, when Ted was about fourteen, Joe took him to a summer party at Diana's house. On the way, he explained again how much she and her family had meant to him in the years in which he had taught school nearby. Ted said little, and what he did say was tinged with the hint of a familiar sarcasm. When they arrived, he was polite and friendly, speaking courteously to people on the lawn and following Joe around the porches, meeting more of his old friends. On the way home, he initiated no conversation. Joe tried to draw him out.

"I'm glad you came, Ted. Diana and everyone else were glad to see you. They hadn't seen you since you were about twelve."

"Yeah. It was very interesting, Dad," said Ted without interest or enthusiasm. He stared out the window and, after a few minutes, turned to Joe and said, "Are they really just spoiled little rich girls?"

"What?"

"Are Diana and her sister very rich?"

"They inherited some money. But why is that important?"

"I don't know."

"People can be your good friends no matter what they have."

"I know."

"You sound like you hold that against them."

"I don't."

"What made you ask about 'spoiled rich girls'? Where did you hear *that*?"

Ted glanced at him quickly, as though Joe had just said something preposterous. "I didn't hear it anywhere. Just forget it."

"Ted! You just said that one of my oldest friends and her sister were spoiled. You don't even know them. They have always been nice to you. They ask about you every time I talk to them. When you ask if they are spoiled, of course I want to know what you mean. You said it. I just want to know what you're talking about."

But Ted would say no more. And Joe knew exactly from where the idea had entered his son's head. The whole conversation was familiar to him. Ted even responded like Kate when challenged. Joe talked a while about how the Boyds were fine people, the good they had done in their part of the state, how well they were liked by everyone. It was not until he mentioned hunting on their farm years before and seeing a bear on a distant hillside that Ted brightened up and returned to his old self. He asked about the bear and hunting, and they discussed animals for a while. The rest of the ride home was quite pleasant.

When he questioned Kate later that night about what Ted had said, she looked away and said she had no idea what he had been talking about. Not even pointing out that she herself for years had referred to Diana and Cassie Boyd as "poor little rich girls," until after one of her particularly harsh harangues, he had demanded that she stop doing it. Nothing would make her discuss Ted's comments with him. A few cool looks from Ted in the following days assured Joe that Kate had reported their whole conversation to their son.

Diana's interest, and that of so many other old friends, made him somehow more remorseful, if that were possible. He went out at night after dark and walked for miles thinking about things, always beginning with Kate and Ted and moving on to family and friends, faces and voices filling his mind and deepening the grief over what he had done. He was a husband who had tried for years to be faithful in the face of destructive behavior, a man who had tried to be a loving father and a decent provider, a priest ordained in the church of God, a licensed lawyer and former public servant. In less than a minute, he had shattered the life God had given him. He could not sleep at night and lay awake until just before dawn, thinking of the people he loved.

Occasional visits to grocery stores, and to hardware stores and building suppliers for items to prepare the house for sale, and to Al-Anon meetings were his only reason now for leaving home. He had always attended Al-Anon in a distant town, an extra safeguard for Kate's protection. He shopped in towns outside his county so as to avoid running into parishioners from Redeemer. He wanted to see them desperately but knew it would compromise both them and him in the eyes of church leadership. Still, it seemed wherever he went, they waved to him from passing cars, called to say they had glimpsed him leaving this place or that, or that they thought they had seen him in one of a dozen places. When he did encounter them, they were gracious and kind, offering to be helpful in every way imaginable, the women often crying. Most of the men hugged him. He supposed that those who despised him were careful to go the other way if they saw him. For his part, he always kept his eyes down, a habit that seemed to suit him now, and was never on the lookout for anyone.

When he did meet parishioners, he apologized again and again and tried to make them understand the situation, assuring them of his belief that the trouble would be resolved soon. He had many friends in the community who were not members of Redeemer and who had never really known Kate. She was seldom with him at social events, a curiosity they had come to accept and no longer even afforded a source for comment. When they had met her, many of them remembered her chirping "I have to work!" in response to entirely unrelated greetings or questions. They were good people he had met in many civic organizations, in Ted's soccer games, and through his Redeemer parishioners.

His forced departure from Redeemer was a topic of consternation throughout the community, and these friends, too, maintained a link with him, inviting him weekly to their homes and leaving messages and news on his answering machine. Several families invited him to accompany them on their vacations, reasoning with him that they were not parishioners and he was unlikely to see anyone from

Redeemer at the beach or the lake or wherever they were going. They told him it would be good for him to get away. Their concern and hospitality touched him sincerely. He politely declined every invitation, explaining the need to remain at home for the psychiatric examination and repairing the house.

* * *

"Joe, this is Carmen Reynolds at the diocesan office. Bishop says for you to call Dr. Frank McMahon MD, M-c-m-a-h-o-n, at 410-477-7660 in Baltimore, Murland, 'cause he's gonna do your exam."

He had worked with her for years and found the unnecessary addition of her last name rather odd. She had hung up without saying goodbye. He knew that one of the other secretaries had recently had surgery, and he would have liked to know how she was getting along. In his contacts in the church, except for his parishioners who knew him well, he had begun to discern a coolness. Although only a few weeks had passed since Easter Eve, he was getting used to it.

He did wonder at what he thought he remembered as a change in the name of the examining psychiatrist. But he decided they knew what they were doing.

* * *

May 4

Dear Kate,

Please tell me how you and Ted are, your health, his grades, etc. I miss you both more than words can say, and I am so sorry for getting angry. Please come home. You can do as you like. I won't object to however you want to live. I need to see you and talk with you. And I need to know about Ted. How is he? How are his grades, his health, his emotional health? He is my son, and if our roles were reversed, I would want you to know about him and how he is getting along. Please let me know how he is. Please meet me somewhere and let us talk. We can meet anywhere you prefer. My only objection would be if you insisted upon Father Hervey's presence. I am working with Jane Ellen to find a buyer for the house, but it needs a lot of work and a great deal of cleaning up. Buyers are more impressed if there is a minimum of clutter. I don't want to remove any of your things without you knowing about it, but I have to do something very soon. If you all would come back, we can work on all this together, and you can decide what you want to keep. Please write back. We need to work together on these things. I expect to see the counselor for my evaluation in a week or so. I have called him but have not heard anything. Please let me know where we can meet and talk. And let me know about Ted.

Love,
Joe

* * *

May 4

Dear Ted,

Once again, I want to say how sorry I am for getting mad. It just took me so much by surprise, you're proposing to be absent from the service when you were scheduled. It would have been our last time serving together. I was just so surprised, and I was tired from the weeks leading up to Easter. But none of that is an excuse. I was wrong. I am terribly sorry, and I wish I could explain how terrible I feel. I know you are angry with me, and you have a right to be, but please, please forgive me. Please come home. I need you, and I need to talk with you. Disagreements and fights occur in all families. I have never gotten angry like that before. I am so sorry. I apologize. I was wrong. It was my fault. I should have handled it better. Please call me when you get this, and let's talk things over. I love you, and you are the light of my life.

Love,
Dad

* * *

May 15

Dear Joe,

By all means, sell the house. Do it as quickly as you can. Jane Ellen Rush will suit me fine as a realtor. I trust her, and she has been very helpful. Do not throw out anything of mine! Whatever it is, just stick it in a closet. You can put your stuff in storage and make extra room in the closets for mine. I don't want you to throw anything of mine out, and I mean it!

Kate

* * *

Early on a Monday morning in late May, the phone rang so incessantly and for so long that Joe took the risk of hearing a parishioner's voice and answered it. It was Amanda Rowland, the current senior warden, a perceptive, intelligent woman of great charm whose voice betrayed a vexation that Joe found immediately disturbing. The whole vestry had just concluded a 7:00 a.m. emergency meeting. For privacy, they had met in the conference room of Tom Ammon's law office, a block from the church. Amanda wanted to know if Joe had heard about Sunday yet. He had not.

Something quite regrettable had occurred. The Sunday school classes had met as usual, and several of the regular teachers had been away at college graduations of their own children or their friends' children. Jane Ellen Rush had substituted as teacher for the high school class. When the nine or ten young people had assembled, for what reason nobody could even guess, she had said to all of them with no preliminaries, "I hate to have to tell you all this, but Joe Stephenson is a chronic wife-beater who has abused Mrs. Stephenson and Ted for a long time." The young people had known Joe for almost ten years as priest, youth minister, chaperone in dozens of activities, and friend. Their reaction had been immediate, running up the stairs and throughout the church in search of their parents. None waited for Jane Ellen to finish her statement. The girls and one of the younger boys were crying as they sought out their parents around the building. An uproar had filled the whole place, and many people had taken their children home without attending the service. The vestry had met in a special session early the following morning and voted unanimously, with only Nancy Dodd refusing, that Jane Ellen Rush could no longer serve as a Sunday school teacher at Redeemer.

"This thing is becoming completely ridiculous, Joe. I can't wait for you to get this psychiatric exam over and get on back here. The whole situation is crazy! I'm ashamed of myself for talking this way, but I wonder if the bishop and his committee really know how to handle this. All the bad behavior that is coming out is deplorable."

"It's my fault, Amanda. I am so bloody sorry."

"Joe, none of us look at it that way. What happened in your house was a family fight, and it should have been resolved right there in your home. A lot of people over here are ready to…they just want nothing ever to do again with Father Hervey. And if Bishop LaBelle isn't careful, they'll feel the same way about him too."

The alarm in her voice was evident, and it cut into his heart. He apologized to her over and over. It was clear she had called him just to talk. The vestry had done all it could do. She needed to talk. So many people needed to talk. But the church had ruled that out.

Later that morning, Dr. McMahon called to arrange an appointment for later in the week.

Chapter Nineteen

D R. MCMAHON'S OFFICE was on an upper floor of an old five-story building in a neighborhood changing from residential to commercial. Major highways closed it in, and the noise of traffic on the overpasses clashed with the din of a street crew working on something underground. To arrive on time, Joe had set out very early for his appointment, and he still had a half-hour. Across the street from McMahon's building, a shiny new coffee shop, quasi art deco, bulged between two unoccupied high-rises with a mortarboard out front announcing a grand opening. He went in and sat at the counter and drank a cup of black coffee and glanced through an issue of the *Sun*. His mind was dark with the distracting shame he felt for the outburst that had brought him here and forced so many others into turmoil. About ten minutes to three, he walked across the street, crossing the deep excavation on a narrow board on which the Latino workers were going back and forth. They looked up at him in surprise.

In the drab foyer, a sign listed many small businesses and Frank McMahon, MD. Crammed into a small elevator with some loud teenagers, Joe rose to the third floor and got off a few doors away from McMahon's office. He went in expecting to find a nurse or receptionist but found instead a very small room with two chairs and a tiny table. The closed door on the left bore a sign reading, "Dr. F. McMahon," and on the door on the right was "Anita Faylor, PhD." He sat down on a rickety chair and waited. It was still a few minutes to three. He had never been in a sound chamber, or whatever they called those rooms, where the smallest outside noise never penetrated, but he suspected it would be like this closet-size waiting room. He sat, remorseful and humiliated, and waited for a door to open.

About a quarter past three, the door bearing Dr. McMahon's name was jerked open and a heavyset, balding man in shirtsleeves looked out and said, "Father Stephenson?" Joe shook hands and went in. The room was small and rectangular, with a desk and filing cabinets near the door and several chairs, a lamp, and a long narrow couch at the other end. The upholstered couch, without armrests or back, inclined upward into a cushioned backrest at one end, reminding Joe of dozens of cartoons over the years in *The New Yorker*. As badly as he felt, he could have smiled at seeing it but did not dare to do so. Besides, he saw that McMahon was clean-shaven, unlike the bearded psychiatrists dozing behind oblivious patients in the cartoons. A window at the far end provided light. The place was dingy and cheerless, as though it had not been cleaned in a while. Dr. McMahon gestured toward a chair near the window, and Joe sat down. He glanced at the long psychiatrist's couch and said, "I didn't realize these were still in use."

"Some of us use them," said Dr. McMahon. He looked at Joe without saying anything more and appeared to be waiting for Joe to say or do something.

"I did it," said Joe. "I'm guilty."

"Did what?" said the doctor, quietly.

Joe told him what had happened on the eve of Easter, sparing no details and taking responsibility for it. The doctor sat motionless and silent, his arms crossed and chin resting on one fist while Joe talked. Joe was prepared to answer all his questions, but he asked very few, only enough, it seemed, to keep Joe talking. When he had described the events of Easter Eve, Joe attempted to put them in context. He told McMahon about the ups and downs of his marriage and the issues for which he had sought help over the years. He named the various counselors and relative lengths of time he had seen them and spoke briefly of his years in Al-Anon.

McMahon then asked some general questions about his growing up, education, and what he had done in life. Joe rattled along,
trying to be thorough, providing what he hoped was enough detail.
He invited the doctor to contact any of the counselors whose help
he had sought, offering to call and leave their telephone numbers,
which he thought he could find. He said he thought that one of them
was deceased. He said he would sign releases so McMahon could
talk to the rest of them. He gave him his spiritual advisor's name
and telephone number and explained his role as spiritual director
and his familiarity with Joe's ministry and homelife. The only people McMahon would not be able to talk to were Al-Anon members,
whose last names Joe did not even know but whose identity he was
obliged to conceal anyway. McMahon said he understood.

The doctor made some brief notes on a legal pad and asked if
there was anything else Joe wanted to tell him. Joe asked what else
would be helpful to know and said he was willing to tell him anything. The doctor replied that within the next week, he would speak
with Kate and Ted and that he and Joe should meet again early in the
following week. Joe asked him how soon he would send his report
to Bishop LaBelle and the executive committee, and he said they
should have it in about three weeks. Throughout the time they were
together, the doctor was quiet and attentive, smiling occasionally,
and generally rather reserved. He seemed to be an indoor sort and,
Joe suspected, might be a good poker player. But he found him easy
to talk to. He left McMahon's office in relief at having spoken finally
to a professional who was familiar with family dynamics. He had
confidence that McMahon was capable and competent, because he
knew his church, advised by some of the best minds in the nation,
would send him only to a qualified examiner.

He was encouraged especially to know that McMahon would
interview Kate and Ted. He wondered if Kate would be truthful. After
thinking about it all the way home, he concluded that she would be
honest in these dire circumstances. Any affection left in her for him
was small, and her understanding of ministry almost as shallow as her
conception of the law had been. But she would realize that preserving
his vocation was to her personal financial advantage. Damaging him

through the old fabrications and deceit would mean a loss of income for her and Ted. She would be unwilling to risk such a calamity. Besides, judging by his own feelings, as though they were still an accurate gauge of reality in his marriage, he knew Kate had true affection for his family. They had always loved her as one of their own, a relationship he had struggled mightily to protect and preserve from the beginning. Surely, she would understand that damaging him would hurt his family as well.

Ted. Joe was in agony about him—he had not seen him now in weeks, his son, his only child, and the separation was excruciating. If only he could see him and talk with him.

The long drive home was mercifully uneventful and afforded him time to think. He stopped on the way at the small post office a few miles from St. John's School. In the last few weeks, he had begun to keep a box on the back seat with envelopes, paper, and stamps. He wrote a note to Kate and dropped it in the local box so she would have it the following morning.

Tuesday Night

Dear Kate,

I have just returned from seeing the examiner the church has chosen. I understand you and Ted are scheduled to see him. I found him easy to talk to, and I believe you will too. He said he will see you all separately, and I will be glad to drive Ted down to his office whenever his appointment is. If you need directions, I can give them to you. It is a little difficult to find, and the streets are torn up with construction. Please let me know. Please tell Ted I love him and miss him. You all are in my mind and heart night and day.

I need to know if Jane Ellen Rush is still coming over to see you. She caused serious trouble at Redeemer last Sunday by telling the teenage class that I have been "abusing" you and Ted for years.

It has upset everyone and caused a lot of pain. The parents and Sunday school teachers are extremely upset. I have gotten dozens of calls from parents and the teens, but I am not supposed to return them. The vestry won't let Jane Ellen teach anymore. The teens have been sending me cards. Kate, I cannot imagine that this came out of talks between her and you. You have to understand that anything you say in anger is likely to get out in the community and make my troubles with the diocese more severe. Think of the years and years I spent supporting you and your mother in spite of all the problems. I need to count on you not to tell Jane Ellen or anyone else things that are not true. Even as angry as you are with me—and you have a right to be—falsehoods are not fair. They will hurt not only me but you and Ted as well. For the sake of all our family relationships, I appeal to you. We both love Ted, and we don't want him affected by this sort of thing.

Kate, I have written to Ted, but he won't write back or talk with me on the telephone. I have to know how he is, his health, his grades, everything. He is my *son too. Please tell him to talk with me or at least let me know about him.*

Love,
Joe

* * *

Saturday

Dear Joe

I certainly have no idea how rumors got spread or what Jane Ellen said in Sunday school. I think it is

*very unfair of you, and I would never plan some-
thing like this with her. We do talk, because she
is a dear friend, especially since Easter, but I have
nothing to do with whom she talks to around Cat.
Springs. It seems to me you owe me an apology, Joe.
Hervey will take Ted down to see McMahon, so you
won't have to worry. He has been very helpful in
everything, and Ted feels very comfortable with him.*

Kate

* * *

A dozen times daily now, he came to his senses to find himself
sitting and staring. He could not at first recall what had been on his
mind. Cory was his only companion for days at a time. He still loved
his home, because it was where they had lived together, but it was
empty now and no longer the same. The phone rang constantly. He
had always received a lot of mail, but now the personal notes and
letters were so many that the postman, whom he had never met but
who turned out to be a faithful reader of his religion column in the
newspaper, came up to the house one day to inquire if he was all right
or if someone had died. All the notes and calls were comforting, and
he thanked God for them. He answered immediately all letters from
outside the community and from local people who were not members of Redeemer. He kept a list of all his parishioners who called or
wrote or left food or other gifts, so that he could thank each of them
in writing when he was allowed to contact them again.

Several days after his first appointment with Dr. McMahon,
Joe received word from a former legal associate in Jeffersonville that
Pete Conrad had died that morning. He was an old lawyer who had
befriended him when he opened his practice. Joe had called Pete's
widow immediately and listened for over an hour as she talked about
the illness and how kind people had been and how much Pete had
appreciated Joe's notes and calls. Depressed by what was unfolding
around him, Joe was turning increasingly to the solitude of home to

maintain a nonanxious balance. Even at home, he avoided glancing at mirrors and did not want to be seen by anyone. But the Conrads had been like family to him, and Agnes Conrad's grief poured out through the telephone touched him profoundly. He knew he must go to the funeral.

Pete was old even when Joe first came to Jeffersonville, and a popular legend of sorts throughout the state bar. Like many a gentleman lawyer, he preferred research and preparation to the courtroom, lamenting the want of civility and ability he perceived in lawyers from Washington, Baltimore, and such places who were appearing increasingly in local litigation. Whenever one of his cases seemed destined for trial, Pete associated Joe, young and new as he was, and Joe had never forgotten the honor. It was an informal partnership that, together with his nighttime tutoring of struggling students, kept Joe solvent in his early years. He had learned much from old Pete. Like many lawyers in general practice in the old days, Pete remained objective and fair amid life's chronic brokenness. He was not easily shocked and never cynical. In an age in which people increasingly saw themselves as victims, Pete could find humor in the most complicated and deplorable circumstances. Joe knew intuitively that God had taught him well in life through people of decency and dignity. Old Pete was surely one of them, and Joe would miss him.

Before the funeral, the local bar assembled in the old courtroom at the end of the square. The judges, clerks, and politicians were all there too, as were many of the older legal secretaries. Joe had not seen some of them since entering seminary. They asked him to say a prayer for Pete, and as he came forward to the familiar council table, perfect silence reigned among the lawyers in the old building for what might have been the first and last time anyone would remember. In a room in which justice had been sought for two hundred years, they all bowed their heads as Joe addressed the Author of justice itself, praying that their old comrade go forward now from strength to strength in a new life of service, in a place where stress and toil were no more.

Afterward, they walked together up the street to St. Paul's Church. The nave and narthex were already filled when the vast legal community arrived. Most of them had to stand along the walls during the service or in the ancient choir loft, where the slightest shifting of weight created curious, loud noises. As soon as the last verse of "The Church's One Foundation" was over, everyone advanced like a cavalry charge down the street to the Beverly Tavern for a reception in Pete's honor. Everyone had a war story to tell about Pete. There was a lot of laughter that, together with the food and drink, would have pleased the deceased honoree. After great quantities of crab cakes, ham biscuits, and bourbon, everyone drifted back to work to catch up before going home.

Seeing his old friends again was like a transfusion for Joe. People with whom he had battled at trial for years came up and greeted him with warmth and interest. His collar inspired much joking and the usual comments about a lawyer doing penance for his legal career. It felt good to be with them. He would have liked to join them in a drink as in the old days, but he had a long way to drive. Besides, it would be his first taste of alcohol in many years, and he knew it might not be safe.

After an hour or so of catching up with dozens of old friends and promises to return and visit overnight, he left the old tavern by the back entrance and walked a few blocks through the alleys to his car. Jeffersonville was several weeks ahead of Catoctin Springs, and the old town was redolent with the scent of roses in the backyards. Except for some prolific specimens of New Dawn, they were mostly old roses, hanging over fences and walls and filling the night with a grand fragrance. He remembered taking cuttings from many of these bushes, some of them quite rare. He and Kate were just married then. By the time Ted was born, most of the cuttings had taken root, and a few were blooming, as if in honor of their son's entry into the world. He thought about going by the house where they had lived, but something told him it would be better to go home. He drove north out of town.

His old friends and their talk of former times had filled him with longing. It was a craving for the relative freedom in which they existed, openness and frankness and directness required by the law itself. Life within the justice system had its flaws, but at least in former times it had been civil and erudite and others could be relied upon to observe every rule explicitly. The lawyers, judges, police officers, clerks, and investigators worked in a reasoned order where fairness was subject to continual scrutiny. Everyone knew his duty and was careful to fulfill it. Circumventing the truth was anathema, and transgressors were rightly marked forever. Juries tempered the rigidity of the law with a rough sense of justice. The legislature kept watch and made changes. A person's word was substantive, formative, and given and taken with appropriate gravity. The structure and the participants' oaths to work vigorously within it could mean a fair resolution of conflict. It was all a blessing in a world of greed and self-interest. The closest old Pete ever got to religion was when he spoke of Magna Carta and Anglo-American law as gifts from heaven. As Joe had explained to a mildly interested Ted over the years, one had only to look at Mexico, Iran, or Russia to appreciate what a gift we have in our system of justice.

There had been great tension, especially in trial practice. Joe knew that many of his old colleagues and dozens of others he had read about but not known had been felled by strokes and heart attacks in recent years. Each month, when his bar journal arrived, he read the "In Memoriam" column first before turning to the disciplinary decisions. He was saddened and surprised by the names of men and women he had known in practice or law school and astonished by how many were younger than he. Some of them had never known the dignity and clarity of people like old Pete, or the remarkable temperament they brought with them to the profession.

The few hours spent with old colleagues lifted Joe's spirits for a while. During the drive home, he thought about his years in practice, old friends, memorable cases, and situations. In their day, they had been the most important matters in the world, occupying the center of his life for weeks and months until others took their place, and then forgotten in the busyness of things. Now he had trouble even remembering the resolutions of some of his most important cases, so critical to him and others in their time. The world had changed around him, and he had changed within it, and reflecting upon it all was somehow quite humbling. Faces and names and situations emerged in his mind and were crowded out quickly by others, all of them important once, and they faded again and vanished, *like snow upon the desert's dusty face, lighting its little hour or two.* With memories of old Pete, his life in this world gone now, mortality and transience brooded over his thoughts like darkness over the land as he drove forward toward the night, toward home. The stars raced along overhead and, like the passing road signs, disappeared behind him.

From these reflections, quite against his will, rose a new uneasiness, a different sadness from what he had brought upon himself and innocent others. It was vague and general—there was so much on his mind—but his few hours with old friends had awakened a curious yearning.

The law had been a constructive, useful way to live in the broken world. He had felt a rightness in seeking justice, building up, and straightening out. The call to ministry had been clarified in many of these endeavors. His service now was in the highest court of creation, and its jurisdiction was human minds and hearts. But *The Federal Rules of Civil Procedure, Uniform Commercial Code,* and *Common Law Rule Against Perpetuities* were models of crystal clarity compared to the substance and procedure of faith. There had been a directness and transparency in the law and a kind of corresponding intelligibility in lawyers. He knew that people in general could not imagine it that way, and he had had trouble understanding it himself at times. But there had been lucidity and a manageable, unemotional precision that the law itself nourished. Even the most provocative interpretations were bound closely to principles. And yet ultimate explicitness is revealed only as one draws nearer to the Source, and the property of the Source is ultimate mystery. It is a paradox. It is utter absurdity, and believing it is a gift. And now that he was closer to it and in possession of the gift, a brief time with his old colleagues had made him look back and long for the clarity of the law.

The faith life was so difficult, so confusing, and so fraught with relentless tension. He understood that it is but a moment in time, a passing through things temporal, that fade and cease, on a brief journey that leads to eternity. And he knew the truth: love is here from the beginning, we are never alone, and our short rough journey is sacramental. It leads through a universe, however broken by human sin, that is itself wholly sacramental. The gift was his. He was grateful. It was all that mattered. Then why did the brokenness shake him so? Why did it confound his reason and his faith? How does one live in brokenness with integrity? "The Lord has told us what is right and what he demands: 'See that justice is done, let mercy be your first concern, and humbly obey your God.'" Sometimes it seemed so much more possible in the law than in the church. Ahead of him, the night spread out and the road disappeared, and his lights penetrated a little way into the darkness.

"The Scriptures say, 'Love the Lord your God with all your heart, soul, strength, and mind.' They also say, 'Love your neighbors as much as you love yourself.'"

"Jesus said, 'You have given the right answer. If you do this, you will have eternal life.'"

Lightning split the black distance, and he knew he would have to go through the mountains in a storm. He could take the long way around, but the narrow road through the mountains was faster. A storm would be a blessing; it had been so dry. He drove on, wondering.

Long ago, his experience and education had begun the progress of reason within him, the journey he shared with childhood friends who had found their own parallel ways. His years in the law had moved him along in ways he had always been too busy to ponder. He saw that now. He understood that the law had shaped and deepened his thinking into a means of arriving at sound conclusions through a mental process that was independent of his own experience. He could consider facts with less interference from emotion, and he could follow the natural and probable consequences of things to a set of likely and reasonable outcomes. He could separate himself emotionally from facts and make principled use of experimentation and observation. Somehow, he knew his early passion for drawing and painting had been a nourishing beginning for the growth of logical reasoning. He had to admit that reason could be an impediment in clerical councils, easily contributing to the tension that was so much more generalized in the church than in the law that it had become an institutionalized anxiety. Life with church leaders was blessed by nothing like the sustaining directness of the legal profession. He suspected the tension contributed to the suppressed anger he sensed in many clergy, although seminary had taught him that many of them had brought it with them to ministry. A wounded lot. He had learned to deal with the tension and even with the exceedingly more powerful loneliness, so different from the legal profession where all the leaders and practitioners observed similar principles. Sometimes he thought it was the emotion of the church against the essential democracy of the law that made so different what should have been so harmonious.

From his days in the law—and he had not realized how much until old Pete's death summoned him for a refresher course—he missed the frankness and openness. The counsels of the church filled him with a positive hunger for clarity in the same way he supposed worshippers listened to sermons. The excessive, paralyzing care to offend absolutely no one—difficult in a world broken by sin—and the mindless optimistic obsession with politics and cultural trends became wearying. The realities of grace and sin required soft, warm packaging to be marketable. They became liabilities if presented too bluntly and without a proper regard for policy.

He was a normal, average man and therefore familiar with the seductive ache of sadness. But Joe was a blessed man too, and he knew it. Why did "the tears of things" overwhelm him so? Had there been in him a predisposition toward them since birth? Did he perceive the world rightly? *Lacrimae rerum.* Did Virgil's perfect words reflect reality or merely have the shallow feel of it like an after-dinner nap or a dream? In almost everything, he felt the tears and heard the cry of innocence and outrage. Lost sheep were everywhere. In such a world of brokenness, broken relationships, broken hearts, might clarity not be a blessing at all? What value was vision if one could do nothing? Clarity comes with a cost.

It was growing darker, and he switched on his headlights, something he should have done earlier. The glow spread out ahead of him as he turned off the highway into the system of country roads that would lead eventually to his home. He loved country roads. Why? What did he perceive in them? Why did they make him feel good? It was not just the scenery or the quiet. It was a whole perception made up of those and other qualities—history, agriculture, rural life and values, poverty, flora and fauna, geology, time, the change of seasons, the whole experience with its feeling so much greater and different than any sum of its interrelated parts. As with other ordinary things, a drive down a country road had the power to structure his perception and open to him completely unrelated phenomena. Why? Or more to the point, how? "Don't ask how it happens," wailed from somewhere a chorus of old rabbis in varying tones of resigned impatience. "Ask this! What does it mean?" Could one apply the interpretation of miracles to all else in life? Wasn't everything, in its way, a miracle? The beauty or essence of everyday things—what had Freud said? *Unheimlich.* He cruised through the night.

He thought of painting and language and informed but subjective judgment. He thought of beauty, artists, the role of art in human self-perception, the viewer and the work, engagement and detachment. Contemplating the great works had rescued him again and again. The splendor of everyday things. Clarity. The perception of things in themselves, the apprehension of the infinite at any moment. Access to the nature of things. There was always a fineness, a beauty and wholeness welling up from essential character, revealing sacramental fingerprints through the tears, visions, whether intended or realized or understood or recognized or not. Christ in the Buddha, Gandhi, Jonas Salk, Barbara McClintock, in compassion itself. Because Christ was essential, people everywhere in their own measure perceived him in things, whether they recognized him or not. A few could translate perception into paint, words, stone. Vermeer, St. Augustine, Bernini, Wordsworth, Elie Wiesel, Rodin, Roman Vishniac, Hemingway, Li Po, Mozart, Flannery O'Connor, Henri Nouwen, Beethoven, Einstein, de Kooning, Kant, William Temple, Gershwin. They raced in elegant slow motion in his mind like vast horses through clouds. What a blessing to be a human being! To read Tolstoy and Dickens. To gaze at the work of Caravaggio, the landscapes of Monet, Cezanne, Claude Lorraine, Poussin. To comprehend something of *Four Quartets*. Of everything to ask, What is it in itself?

And what had these thoughts to do with anything, *anything*, as though his contemplation had sputtered like an old engine down to idle, coughing and about to expire. Had there been a thread connecting a desire for clarity and the confusion of the church and the sadness of the broken world and the salvific comfort of great art? Or were they the disconnected musings of a confused mind? Or did they help him, somehow, to conceive the meaning in his own ordinary life? "What does it mean?" croaked the old rabbis as he turned up the driveway toward his home. "First principles. What is it in itself?" counseled Marcus Aurelius. The rain continued to fall.

At the sight of his house and Cory dancing in ecstasy in the headlights, every thought in his head vanished and the two people in his heart, whom he longed for more than anything else in the world, came forward and took their places at the center of the universe.

* * *

For years, he had watched troubled students in classrooms and witnesses in interviews and on the stand, reading expression, posture and gesture, and attentive to choices of words. It is all communication, and for those who read the signs, much can be learned. Those whose success or livelihood depend upon an accurate reading are often very good at it. A person saying yes with her lips and no with everything else warrants a certain attention. There is no magic in such skill, merely an ability to pay attention, use common sense, and be open to intuition. He had observed such skill in infants, who appeared to lose it about the time they began to walk.

At his second psychiatric appointment, the door was opened lazily by someone very different from the Dr. McMahon he had met before. The frown, so slight that he had to observe it for a moment to be sure, the tightly wrapped posture, and the tinge of suspicion in the voice all presented quite a different effect than a few weeks earlier. It was all subtle and quite uncalculated; Dr. McMahon was, after all, a professional. He could have had a bad day or received some devastating news. He was too well qualified to dislike a patient, or at least to show it. Nevertheless, for ninety minutes, Joe faced a man who looked as though he was enduring a bad smell. What had before seemed attentive interest had turned into wary suspicion. Arms folded tightly across his paunch, without the slightest hint of a smile or any other sign of ease, the doctor listened to Joe for a bit and, at the first mention of drinking, looked away and said abruptly, as though correcting an undisciplined child, "No, no. She's not an alcoholic. And her mother wasn't either."

Joe, stunned, looked at him in silence for a moment and began to reply. McMahon glanced around the room and interrupted with a series of questions. Joe responded, but halfway through each answer, the doctor, as though testing him for something rather than seeking information, asked a further question. He wanted to know about Joe's relationship with his mother-in-law. Did Joe ever speak harshly to her? Had he ever forbidden her to hold Ted when he was a baby? Did Joe withhold money or the family checkbook from Kate? Did he perceive Kate's close relationship with Ted as a threat? Had he ever spoken negatively about Kate's boss? Did he get along with her boss? Did he think Kate's job had value? Why had he suddenly left the practice of law? Was it true that he kept pictures of the children in the parish in his desk at work? Why did he do the youth work himself? Why had he not assigned that to an assistant? Why had he decided to move from his previous parish? Had Kate wanted to stay there? How much time did he spend away from home? Had he ever taken Ted to a bar? Had he been opposed to Ted attending St. John's? When he invited people to the house, were any of them friends of Kate? Did he ever include her boss? On social occasions at their home, who did all the cooking? How would Joe describe his own use of alcohol? How much alcohol did Joe use daily, weekly?

"I had interesting talks with your wife and son. You were accurate about one thing. She admitted she had not helped keep the house clean."

Joe answered each question, aware of McMahon's direction and refuting his suggestions wherever they were wrong. The doctor, no longer appearing objective or neutral, seemed to expect Joe to correct what he had said in their first meeting. When it grew clear to him that Joe was prepared to argue his position and would not back

LOVERS IN A SMALL CAFÉ

down, the doctor remarked that Joe appeared to think everyone was an alcoholic. As he said this, he smiled for the first and only time during this appointment.

Joe thought quickly of the few times Kate had acknowledged her dependence: once in seminary with a classmate of Joe's who now lived somewhere in the Midwest, once with Dr. Amanda Leffler in Dorchester, and a few years back with the Gallaghers at the intervention. He offered to put McMahon in touch with all of them. He would pay for the conference calls. He would try to bring them to his office. But Dr. McMahon explained that he couldn't do that. "Because I don't know who they are."

Joe attempted to argue, suggesting ways he could assure himself of a priest's or a psychologist's professional standing and qualifications. Dave Gallagher was an editor of a well-known newspaper. His wife was a professional teacher. He would bring them here, to his office, so he could speak with them personally. But no, none of what they said could be verified, said Dr. McMahon. There would be no point in speaking with them. Joe pointed out that McMahon had spoken with his spiritual adviser, Dr. Lewis Batterton, and with his family counselor, Clyde Candler. What was the difference? The doctor replied he had not spoken with them but intended to do so within the coming week. He stood up to indicate their time was over.

Joe proceeded to gather up his notes and files. He was shocked by the doctor's attitude, which carried in its skepticism a thinly veiled contempt. He was dumbfounded by his contention that neither Kate nor her mother drank and that Joe had been lying. He was so astonished and angry that he hardly knew what more to say. McMahon acted like a man in control, someone who had gotten to the bottom of things and was certain of his next move. He walked to the door to show Joe out with no mention of another meeting, saying he would write his report soon and send it to the bishop.

He left McMahon's office and went to his car and sat there for an hour, writing notes about the interview and recording the doctor's questions and statements. He could not believe that Kate had told the man, in a critical conversation with a professional evaluating him concerning his career, that she had no alcohol problems. And her mother, who had been fired from two school districts for drinking, lost her license after a DUI conviction, alienated all her friends and ruined her health and family relationships because of bourbon and wine, she, too was not an alcoholic! Kate had told this to the doctor. And McMahon had believed her! He believed her!

Chapter Twenty

DEFENDING HIMSELF WOULD be different from representing clients. A surgeon operating on his daughter, a priest burying his father—they must struggle to remain objective and thorough, to focus on facts and avoid the distractions of emotion and anxiety. Defending himself would be complicated, stressful. The presence of his wife and son in the process would make it excruciatingly difficult.

He thought of Kate and Ted. The separation from them was like physical pain. His fear of Kate acting out of her denial and lying to shield herself, a quagmire he had struggled through all his married life, was pulling him down again like quicksand. This time, it was all made worse by the psychiatrist, who apparently believed her. It was astonishing to think that McMahon's brief talk with Kate could lead to professional disgrace, perhaps even to the end of his service in the church. And the initial fault was his; he alone had set the whole downward spiral in motion. And now losing his own case would mean trouble for many people and an indelible stain upon his character. He could foresee a bad psychiatric report, enshrined in his professional record, following him to the end of his vocation. Kate would never see the consequences ahead for him or for them as a family. Or maybe she could see the probable results of her lies and it made no difference to her. After all these years of marriage, he still was unable to tell. His confusion was either proof of the strength of her impenetrable shell or of his own stupidity in misunderstanding her.

The truth did not bother him, even when it was troubling or damaging. His reverence for it was no credit to him, nothing for which he could be proud, any more than a man should be admired for being subject to the laws of gravity. There was a fundamental rightness about truth that had always made him feel a part of the universal harmonies that signaled God's presence in life. Avoiding truth led to chaos, brokenness. How he had gotten that way was nothing for which he could claim any credit. It was a gift.

His years of coping, his faithfulness to Kate in the face of relentless problems, and the care he had taken to protect his son would dissolve in the false image of a bully. He had made as many mistakes as any man, probably more. But he was not a traitor to his family or his vocation. He had been overprotective of Kate, covered for her for too long, and in the end, bungled his tardy attempts to detach from her problems. But he was guilty of bad judgment and making a mistake, not of meanness and dishonesty. He wanted the record straight.

And the church herself gave him comfort. Regardless of how badly McMahon portrayed him, he was confident that Bishop LaBelle, and even Kirby Porter and his executive committee, would recognize the truth and handle his case decently. They were intelligent people, they had common sense, servants in the house of truth, and his faith in them and in the One they served was consoling and healing. They would not permit false evidence to lead to his family's rupture or his disgrace, poisoning memories and his reputation for the rest of his life. In criminal and civil cases, he had seen such mistakes go on damaging the innocent, and even the absolved, long after those who could refute them were gone or forgotten. He had made a mistake and confessed. He had confidence that the church would see that the record was accurate.

The message light was blinking in the dark when he returned home. He found a legal pad and a manila file and shuffled together the notes he had made in the car after his appointment. He called McMahon's office and left a recorded message asking for one more appointment. In an old address book in his filing cabinet, he found the number of the clinic where he had visited Dr. Leffler years before. He called it knowing the office would be closed. The generic recording directed callers in crisis to the Dorchester Hospital Emergency Room and provided the clinic's business hours for the following day.

He left a message on Clyde Candler's recorder requesting an immediate appointment. He knew his old friends the Gallaghers stayed awake reading until midnight, and he called them and made plans to see them the following evening. He left a message at Harry Campos's office asking him to call. He recorded the time and telephone number of each contact in his new file.

He went into the family room and sat down and stared for a long time into the shadows of the cold fireplace. Two brass colonial soldiers, reflecting a dull glow, marched in frozen stride across the sooty background. With no logs to constrain, they stood their watch anyway. He dropped his gaze to the floor, where Ted had played video games for years in front of the television. He had seldom joined him, having absolutely no interest in video games or the other electronic gadgets so popular with young people. Now he would trade everything he had to play a video game with his son. He sat for a long time bent over, with his head in his hands. He had to face it. It was time.

He called James Edelman's office and left word in his message box that he needed a referral and would appreciate a call the following morning. He was careful to say he did not intend to discuss parish business. Jim and Carol Edelman were Redeemer parishioners, and he knew that contacting Jim violated the executive committee's order. But a simple referral to another lawyer, outside the parish, was all he wanted. He thought it would do no harm. He made a note of this too.

He fed Cory. He was hungry himself, but his side had begun to ache as he sat in his car after leaving McMahon's office. Eating anything would make it worse. He mixed up some Gatorade in a plastic pitcher and poured out a glass and began to take small sips. He turned out the lights and went upstairs. Several of Kate's drawers were ajar, and some of her sweaters had toppled from a shelf and lay sprawled on the closet floor. In Ted's room, the closet door was open. His two top bureau drawers protruded slightly and were empty. They had known he would be away at his appointment. Bishop LaBelle, or maybe McMahon, had told Kate. He went back down to the kitchen, praying that he had missed a note, an invitation to call, anything. There was nothing. He sat down at the kitchen table, the site of so many discussions in the past and so many attempted discussions with Kate. He and Ted had assembled the table together one evening to surprise Kate when she returned from a faculty meeting. He spread out his hands on the tabletop and closed his eyes like a psychic trying to sense information. Had they sat here, even for a few minutes, when they came to the house hours earlier? Had Ted come with Kate? He sat in the silence for a long time.

After a while, he began to pray. His words flowed out in the old rhythmic patterns familiar to him since childhood. In every darkness of life, their shapes and cadences and colors had opened to the light. *"Almighty and most merciful Father, we have erred and strayed from thy ways like lost sheep, we have followed too much the devices and desires of our own hearts, we have offended against thy holy laws...."* Praying, like death, was a bridge. He had tried substituting *I* for *we* in the gracious common prayers to make the confession more personal, but the original words had always had more urgency, more power. He could not improve upon them. *"It will flame out, like shining from shook foil.... Oh, morning, at the brown brink eastward, springs—because the Holy Ghost over the bent World broods with warm breast and with ah! bright wings."* In the most threatening and ordinary situations, prayer had sanctified places and circumstances for him, revealing at street corners and junk lots glimpses of glory like Chartres and Hagia Sophia.

He prayed for Kate and Ted, his mother and sisters and brothers and their children, the people of Redeemer, and the whole worldwide church. He prayed for his old friends, too many to name individually, so most of them got in as a group. Then he prayed for himself. He explained to God, because he knew God already understood, that he was not at all happy about it but he would walk the path before him and was confident and grateful for Christ's companionship on the way. He prayed that God would open his eyes to Christ at work in the world around him. *"The salmon-falls, the mackerel-crowded seas..."* He asked forgiveness for saying so, but he believed he could not go forward on the present path and deal with his inner sickness at the same time.

As he said it, the face—as he imagined him—of St. Paul, pleading his case over his thorn, whatever it was, hovered into view and bobbed rhythmically on an invisible sea. Between the receding hairline and hooked nose, a pair of red-rimmed eyes grimaced with irritation. *I am not Paul,* he silently said to God, *but I'll do my best. But I cannot manage this pain and fatigue at the same time. I need some relief. I beg you.*

* * *

"I've been trying to call you. How soon can you get over here?"

For a moment, Joe wondered if he had done something wrong.

"I can come right now," he said, "as soon as I shave and put on some clothes."

"Just get dressed and come over. We can talk before my first appointment gets here." Clyde Candler hung up.

Joe left the house immediately and drove to his office. From the moment they sat down together, it was evident that something had happened. The well-known and respected family counselor looked at his notes and smiled and shook his head.

He had taken a call from Dr. McMahon the previous Friday and, although he was much too professional to be any more precise, had found the psychiatrist arrogant and rude. Clyde had counseled Joe for several years, and McMahon had met Joe once. Yet the psychiatrist had lectured Candler on Joe and his problems and made it quite clear that, between the two of them, his diagnosis alone was accurate. McMahon did not say so exactly, but it was clear he expected Candler to defer to his superior qualifications and training.

Joe listened with empathy and regret. He had known many good therapists in special education and the law and in his personal life. He had found Candler intelligent, insightful, and immensely helpful in understanding himself and those he loved. He knew he could have helped Kate too, and the two of them together, if only she had been willing. Candler had been bold and "confrontive" with

Joe, helping him understand his own enabling and codependence and teaching him how to change himself. Joe knew that after similar confrontation, Kate would have refused to return. But Candler would have handled it well and would have known how to keep her involved. If only he and Kate could have seen him together. Now he listened with alarm as Candler spoke about his talk with McMahon. The implications were severe for the report that would soon be in the bishop's hands.

McMahon had inquired about a brief period when Joe had discontinued counseling, suggesting that Joe had dropped out because Candler was bringing him "closer to the truth." He suggested that Joe projected his own problems onto his wife and that Joe had been dealing with great anger for years. "I'll bet he had a real problem in court controlling his anger," he had told Candler. He asked about evidence that Joe had a drinking problem. When Candler objected and said he had found no evidence of any of these suggestions, McMahon said wearily that it was too bad, implying that Candler had missed the obvious. The psychiatrist made a categorical statement that all clergy were "suffering servants who project their issues onto other people." Apparently, McMahon had not remembered Joe telling him that Clyde Candler was ordained in the Lutheran Church. Again, Candler tried to disagree. McMahon informed him that it was obvious that Joe searched for someone to blame when his own problems got out of control. He raised the issue of Joe's involvement in the community, suggesting that it was evidence of a desire to appear important in the eyes of others. It seemed to Candler that McMahon, despite his role as an examiner for the church, actually knew little about parish ministry.

McMahon had gone on questioning and lecturing Candler, raising one point that had particularly surprised the family therapist. He noted that Joe chaperoned youth activities in his parish and had admitted to having school pictures of the parish children in his office. He wanted to know what evidence of pedophilia the counselor had discovered. Candler's rejection of this suggestion at that time, vigorous as it was, was mild compared to Joe's astonishment upon hearing it. Given the mood of the times, McMahon could have suggested Joe was a serial rapist without raising the horrific turmoil that surrounded the sin of victimizing children. Later, when he had calmed down and reflected upon it, Joe supposed it was possible that McMahon raised this query about any clergy he evaluated. The church had chosen him to examine Joe, so probably he had evaluated other clergy, although Joe hoped not.

This psychiatrist had little insight into the vocation of ministry. Could he not understand that most clergy view youth ministry as a critical part of their vocation? He thought of the special training the seminary required to help clergy relate better to children. Could the church's own examiner not understand this? On the other hand, everyone who watched the evening news or read the newspapers knew the tragic stories of Roman priests molesting choirboys. Perhaps the issue, raised between professionals, was understandable. Even so, any such suggestion in his evaluation, especially in the eyes of the church's insurance providers, would end his ministry without further ado. It was shocking. How had it all come to this?

He thanked Dr. Candler sincerely for his confidence and warnings and left. His counseling had helped Joe, and helped Kate and Ted too, a blessing of which they were unaware. He regretted that someone representing his church had talked down to such a skilled and dedicated man. Candler was a good man, a professional. He could handle it. Still, it was a shame.

He received another shock when he reached Dr. Amanda Leffler. She was retired now and living with her family in North Carolina while her youngest son finished college. To his great relief, she remembered him after a little conversation, and she began to recall the few times Kate had come with him to appointments. Her memory surprised him, and yes, she maintained her old files, although it would take her a while to find Joe's because they were in storage. After hearing about Joe's circumstances, she suggested something he had not anticipated. In going to evaluators or to church authorities, she said it would be helpful to take along someone who could speak clinically about alcoholism. It was a subject everyone claimed to know about. Everybody knew somebody who drank. Actually, she said, very few people understood it and almost nobody could comprehend the denial that accompanied it. Joe thought that might be accurate for people in general, but certainly not for mental health professionals and for the higher authorities of the church. Intelligent people knew enough about addiction to make sound decisions. But Dr. Leffler was the expert, and he thanked her and said he would try to do so. They would talk again after she had found her file.

Jim Edelman called late in the morning. He had attended the evening meeting with Bishop LaBelle and members of the executive committee and was still getting over his surprise and disappointment. He gave Joe the name of a younger attorney who was gaining a good reputation in domestic relations law. He reminded Joe that the whole parish was standing by if he needed anything. Edelman also urged him plainly not to worry about the handful who evidently were in touch with Kate. Edelman was professional, calm, and perceptive in the quiet way of the lawyers who Joe had most admired. Edelman had always been easy to talk to. He and Carol were raising five children, four of whom were teenagers. All this, together with the objectivity with which many lawyers can discuss difficult matters, and the alarm Joe still felt after hearing about McMahon's cross-examination of Clyde Candler, led easily to some discussion. Jim Edelman's concern was evident as they discussed the situation with McMahon and speculated upon his report to the diocese. They agreed to speak again by telephone after Joe's final visit with the psychiatrist.

* * *

Sunday Evening

Dear Kate,

Please ask Ted to talk to me. I need to see him and hear his voice. How is he? How are his classes going? I have completed my part of his application for financial assistance and will mail it to you tomorrow after Milly notarizes my signature. I'll enclose a stamped envelope, so please send it to the finan-

cial aid office as soon as possible. The financial aid people are efficient and friendly. When you contact them, ask for Angie. She is the one I have been working with. I like the college and know it is the right place for Ted. Please tell him to talk with me.

I have found another realtor, because it would be hard to work with Jane Ellen after what she said to the teens in Sunday school. His name is Carl Casey, and he will call you this coming week so you can meet with him. Harry Campos recommended him, so I think you'll approve. I am working hard getting the house ready for showing. Please come home and take your clothes in the closet and the stuff on top of your dresser. It is very cluttered and dusty, and Lula, the new cleaning lady, doesn't want to rearrange anything, or your piles of stuff in the dining room, until you go through it first. Carl warned me when he went through the house that it will show better if there is no clutter and stuff in corners. I really need your help on this.

I am so sorry for getting angry. I hope you will be able to forgive me. I am willing to talk with you at any time and place. I will gladly meet you at a restaurant near St. John's if you like, if you don't want to talk here.

Love,
Joe

* * *

Friday Afternoon

Joe,

Do not move any of my stuff from where it is. My things are not clutter. What about all those shelves of books of yours downstairs? Leave my stuff alone and tell the cleaning woman to leave it alone. There is no reason that she can't just dust around it. Carlton F. Casey, broker/manager, came by Wednesday but I was supervising a table and could not talk with him, so he left me his card. He didn't seem to understand that I have to work. Just go ahead with him. Jane Ellen would have suited me fine, but you won't work with her. She told me everything that happened, and she did not say what the teenagers said she said.

Kate

* * *

May 18

Dear Dr. McMahon,

When my husband and I moved to Dorchester, Joe and Kate Stephenson were among our first friends. We were new families together in the church where Joe worked. Over the next few years until they had to move away, they became quite good friends. We spent several vacations with them and helped Kate open and close her beach house in Wicomico.

When they moved to Catoctin Springs, we stayed in touch and visited when we could. On our last visit to them in their new home, it became apparent early in our visit that Kate was not her-self. When we asked Joe what was wrong, he looked puzzled and asked what we meant. Kate's speech was slurred and incoherent; she had alcohol on her breath. In any social situation we had been in together, Kate did not drink and, in fact, insisted she never drank. Therefore, her behavior demanded our attention. Kate went to bed earlier than us and we sat up talking to Joe. He explained to us that Kate had a drinking problem. The three of us agreed that we needed to confront Kate about this the next day.

The next day, we all sat in the kitchen and asked Kate about her drinking. We surrounded our discussions with expressions of love for her. She vehemently denied that she drank and insisted she had no problem. She remained very controlled in her denial. We recounted the events of the night before, and finally, with all three of us as witnesses, she admitted she had a problem with alcohol abuse. Joe had found hiding places where her wine was kept, and she said it was hers. She agreed to enter coun-seling to deal with her problem. She reported to us regularly over the ensuing months that she was in counseling and that it was going well. Whenever we talked to Joe, he expressed his pleasure that she was in counseling. Joe himself was attending Al-Anon. Since that time, our contact with the Stephensons has been sporadic, both families having teenagers who required us to be at home on weekends. We have had infrequent visits, cards, and emails.

This past week, Joe called and asked to speak with both of us. He explained the current situation and separation. He asked that we write to you to verify the intervention we had with Kate at their

*home. This letter is as accurate as our memories
serve but is true in the essence of what happened.*

*Yours sincerely,
Tonette Gallagher*

After reading the Gallaghers' letter, Dr. McMahon handed it
back to Joe and said he was sorry but he could not consider it because
he did not know the people who wrote it. No, he would not speak
with them in person if Joe brought them to his office. He had no
way of telling who they were. Yes, he *had* spoken to several other
people, but they had all been recommended by Bishop LaBelle, so
he knew they were reliable. Yes, he had spoken with Father Hervey
when he brought Ted to his office. Joe shouldn't worry, however,
because he had spoken to people on his behalf too: "the family counselor Candler" and Joe's spiritual adviser, "the Reverend Batterson."
When Joe asked if the Gallaghers' letter would make any difference
if he *could* consider it, the doctor explained that, yes, it certainly
would, but he couldn't take it into account. Kate was no alcoholic.
There had been problems in the marriage and she had tried hard to
resolve them. There was no alcoholism in her family, and her mother
was not an alcoholic either, he said, setting Joe straight once and for
all. He had all the information he needed to write his report to the
diocese, and Bishop LaBelle should have it within a week or so. He
found Joe to be a troubled person in need of intensive psychotherapy and would recommend that it begin immediately. He seemed
mildly amused at the degree of Joe's concern about his conclusions
and made no secret of his desire for Joe to get out of the office.

In all the difficulties of his life, Joe had never felt so depressed
as during the drive home from this final visit with the church's psychiatrist. He was devastated by McMahon's words. Not only were
they wrong, but they would now enter an official medical report that
would go into the hands of his superiors. He knew it would be very
hard to refute McMahon's findings. He had never felt so depressed
in his life.

He had not seen Ted in over a month. Kate would not speak with him. She replied only to selected parts of his letters. Whatever the diocese did with McMahon's report, it would mean further difficulty for the people of Redeemer. He was working daily to prepare the house for sale. There were repairs to be made, and some of them he could not accomplish himself. He was paying all the family expenses from his salary alone, as Kate's check now went directly to her, and he was running out of money. Soon he must resort to their savings account, money he had been building up for Ted's college years. The grass needed mowing constantly. He had let the garden go; there was no time for it now. He needed to discuss McMahon's intentions with someone, anyone who could guide him, but with whom? He did not want to take advantage of Jim Edelman's kindness. Jim was his firm's lead trial attorney and was always busy. The vestry was continuing to pay his salary and, at the same time, was paying for retired priests from nearby dioceses to conduct services on Sundays. He was ashamed to accept his paycheck and knew he could not go on doing so. Redeemer was not an affluent parish. No parish in the diocese was affluent. But how would he get along, pay the bills, prepare the house for sale? He would have to take another job. But what? Where? And suppose McMahon had been bluffing, trying to frighten him as punishment for getting angry with his family. What if he did not write the negative report he had described?

He drove west as the night behind him grew darker and the light faded faster over the distant hills ahead. Stars were visible in the moonless blue-black void, the same stars at which he had marveled in good times and favorite places—the beach and dunes in Wicomico, the Appalachian Trail, the rivers of the great western valley, the gentle rolling sweep of the lawn at his beloved home. In his distraction, he saw nothing but the hypnotic road with its white and yellow broken lines racing backward beneath his car, and an occasional possum or cat crushed in a sticky black pool.

He was out of his mind with worry. He must have stopped somewhere for coffee, for he was sipping the last of it as he headed over the last big bridge toward home. It was cold, so maybe it had been in the car for days. He knew the great river was below him, but he could not see it.

A few hundred yards after reaching the far bank, he turned off the highway to the right and doubled down and back on a gravel track that led to a public boat landing under the bridge. He pulled to a halt in the crunchy gravel facing the bank, and his headlights spread a hazy luster over the moving water. Within seconds, two nearby cars started up in the darkness—teenagers having sex, he supposed. They wheeled around and sped up the lane toward the highway, one with a taillight out, their headlights coming on halfway up the hill. He waited for the dust to settle, turned off the car and the headlights, and got out and stood in the dark beside the big noisy river. An occasional car or truck rumbled along the bridge far above him. It was after midnight. He was lonely. On the far side, a few miles inland, Kate was sleeping in her apartment at the school. Ted was in his dormitory.

Chapter Twenty-One

B ISHOP LABELLE AND Kirby Porter received Dr. McMahon's report and summoned Joe to a late-afternoon meeting at the diocesan office the following day. He drove the six hours there in great anxiety, spent a half-hour with them, and returned to Catoctin Springs shortly before midnight.

They directed him to enter psychoanalysis immediately, twice weekly for a year, at his own expense. He was ordered to disassociate himself from the Church of the Redeemer and every member of the congregation. He was to contact a psychoanalyst: Dr. Alderman. After one year, Dr. McMahon would re-evaluate him and determine whether more psychoanalysis was required. At that time, the executive committee would determine the next step in his rehabilitation. They smiled and wished him well and assured him that he and his family were in their prayers. They explained that they felt it necessary to write a letter to diocesan leaders, explaining what was taking place. Then they moved forward in their chairs as though to rise, a signal to Joe that the meeting was over and that they had said all that needed to be said.

Joe sat calmly through their short presentation, writing notes on a yellow legal pad while these dour leaders of the church of God pronounced his fate. As they talked, he mentally reviewed some logical consequences and probabilities of their directions, and he allowed his face to show an appropriate concern. He asked to see McMahon's report. This was refused, the bishop and executive committee chair claiming the committee had not authorized them to allow this. Then he requested a meeting with the executive committee. Taken aback, they replied that the committee was busily preparing for the coming of a new bishop and there was no time for such a meeting. Kirby Porter reminded him helpfully that he was under the authority of the committee and that he and Bishop LaBelle were following the committee's orders as well. Joe suggested quietly that the executive committee should consider certain information in addition to Dr. McMahon's report, whatever it said, before making such a drastic decision about a priest's life and career. The bishop glanced at Porter and then reminded Joe that he had, after all, acknowledged slapping his wife. The decision as to what to do about it had been made, and now it was Joe's duty to do as they had decided. This was all an effort to save his ministry. If he had any question about it, he could consult canon law. Joe replied calmly that he would do so and stated his intention of making a formal request to meet with the committee. At this, LaBelle and Porter, clearly surprised, stood and said goodbye. They watched him warily as he rose and left the room, as though fearing he might turn suddenly and leap in their direction.

Two days later, together with fourteen letters and notes from old friends, bills for monthly payments on Kate's and Ted's cars, and a quarterly bill for homeowner's insurance, Joe received his instructions again, in writing.

Dear Joe:

At its recent meeting, the executive committee issued a Pastoral Directive (title IV, canon 15) directing you to receive psychological testing from a person designated by the executive committee and you must enter intensive psychotherapy twice a week for a period of one year at your own expense with a psychoanalyst to be recommended by the executive committee, during which time you are to completely disassociate from the Church of the Redeemer, Catoctin Springs. You may perform no pastoral or liturgical functions, and at the end of the one-year period, you will be re-evaluated. This pastoral directive is issued following the evaluation and recommendation of Dr. Frank McMahon.

Faithfully in Christ,

Morris G. LaBelle
Assisting Bishop

The Rev. Kirby Porter
President, Executive Committee

When his friend Jim Edelman heard about the meeting at Diocesan House and read the letter received two days later, he conferred with several other lawyers in the Redeemer congregation. They were surprised to learn that the church was requiring their priest to see a psychoanalyst. After consulting with Joe, Jim Edelman called the diocese's lawyer and proposed obtaining a second opinion. After a lengthy delay, during which several people apparently read and re-read McMahon's report on Joe, the diocesan authorities agreed. Jim had known many mental health professionals in his trial practice. He had sought their advice in significant cases over the years and cross-examined many and knew the field fairly well. He insisted on Joe's behalf that Joe have a say this time in who would perform the evaluation. He recommended a very well-known psychologist, Dr. Marjorie Williams, and after a brief delay, the diocese agreed. Joe thought he remembered Dr. Williams's reputation from his own trial career.

Dr. Williams's private clinic was in the same part of the metropolitan area as Dr. McMahon's. Joe felt much acute anxiety as he cruised the same congested streets, not knowing what to expect and hoping that it would differ from his first experience with a church examiner. There was comfort in knowing that this time he was seeing someone whose qualifications and track record were widely recognized. But McMahon's report, whatever it said and as unfair and inaccurate as he suspected it was, was not the source of the present troubles. Joe was. He was the culprit who had lost his temper with his wife and set in motion the ugly events now unfolding around him. It was his own fault. He woke every day in the deepest remorse. What snatches of sleep he got at night always ended in waking to this terrible reality. As much as he regretted his life ever touching LaBelle, Porter, the executive committee members, or McMahon, he knew he had only himself to blame.

He parked in a small lot beside Dr. Williams's office, an impressive white brick mansion that still reminded passersby of the affluent, leafy neighborhood the area once had been. After a few moments of prayer, he got out of the car and went in. The cordial receptionist offered him coffee, which he declined. People were going busily to and fro. The long bright reception area was furnished comfortably. He took his seat with four other people, all scrutinizing magazines held tightly before their faces. When he was called in to meet Dr. Williams, who interviewed him for over an hour, she confirmed that his evaluation would require about three days. He had nothing else to do, but if he had, he would have changed heaven and earth to be here. He prayed that this time an accurate picture of him would be revealed.

Dr. Williams was a small dark woman of about fifty, with beautiful eyes and an open and impressive professional manner. He answered all her questions. At her request, he gave her Kate's telephone number at St. John's School. She also required the names and telephone numbers of several old friends and former therapists. He promised to bring these with him the following day.

After this interview, he was given time to go to lunch in the neighborhood and asked to return at one o'clock. He spent the rest of the afternoon at a conference table in a quiet room where one of Dr. Williams's assistants administered a series of tests. He was allowed several short breaks. In the following two days, and during part of an afternoon in the following week, he answered hundreds of written questions and was given additional tests by Dr. Williams and her assistants. At the end of the final afternoon, Dr. Williams interviewed him again and advised she would contact him in a few weeks to tell him if she required anything more. Her report would be completed shortly after that.

In his office in Catoctin Springs, Jim Edelman was approaching Joe's situation with the care he accorded every case. He decided yet another medical opinion was needed. He and the other attorneys who knew Joe recommended an evaluation by a credible psychiatrist completely unconnected to the church. Dr. Williams was an excellent, widely known psychologist. They were completely confident of her abilities and objectivity. What they were discovering about Dr. McMahon, however, was causing much surprise and concern. He was a psychoanalyst and not professionally qualified to administer tests or draw conclusions from results in developmental neuropsychological or forensic evaluations. Psychoanalysis was regarded as the dinosaur of the mental health field, and American insurance companies would not approve coverage for a psychoanalyst's services. Joe supposed this was the reason the church had ordered him to receive therapy from McMahon and his appointee at his own expense.

To confirm their suspicions, Jim Edelman consulted one of the diocese's own psychologists. Dr. Timothy Marshall was in local practice and with his wife, Cindy, and their children had been members of Redeemer for many years. He was routinely called upon by the diocese to evaluate prospective applicants for the ministry, part of the process Joe remembered well from his own early days before seminary. In over thirty years of practice, Tim Marshall knew no one who had been through the long process of psychoanalysis, which often required many years. He was clearly surprised that the church had sent Joe to a practitioner not skilled or legally qualified in current mainstream practices and techniques of therapy.

* * *

Dear sisters and brothers in Christ,

We are writing to inform the clergy of the diocese of a situation that involves the Reverend Joe Stephenson and to request your prayers. The executive commit-

265

tee considers all incidents of domestic violence as very serious. There have been two specific incidents involving the Reverend Mr. Stephenson alleged to be of such a nature.

The executive committee has issued a pastoral directive to the Reverend Mr. Stephenson. This direction requires him to enter into counseling for a year and to disassociate himself from his parish during this time. He is to do no pastoral or liturgical work during this time.

Due to the gravity of the situation, the executive committee has decided to call on the church attorney to investigate these incidents as potentially chargeable as conduct unbecoming a member of the clergy. We take this action to clarify to all concerned that there are serious issues to which the Reverend Mr. Stephenson and the committee must respond.

We would ask your prayers for Joe and his family. We would ask your prayers for the people of Redeemer Church and the members of the vestry. Our extended diocesan family can be a source of strength and support in difficult times. Your prayers and support are much desired for Joe and for all concerned.

Faithfully yours,

Morris G. LaBelle
Assisting Bishop

The Rev. Kirby Porter
President, Executive Committee

Although every member of the diocesan clergy and other church leaders received this letter, the executive committee did not go to the trouble of sending a copy to Joe. The Reverend Andrew

Campbell, an older priest whom Joe had come to admire over the years, sent Joe his own copy after reading it. It was in this way that Joe learned what everybody knew before he did: he was now being investigated to determine whether he should be tried for an offense under canon law. Over the weeks, he had received a half-dozen kind notes from clergy colleagues telling him they were thinking of him and praying for him. They did not come to see him, nor did any of them telephone his home—although it seemed that everybody else in the world was calling. After the letter from LaBelle and Porter, however, no more clergy contacted him. Alone among them, Andy Campbell continued to call every few weeks, urging him to be brave and reminding him that ordination had always led to a lonely and troubled life. Campbell was almost seventy years old, of a different generation than most of the other clergy, and, until recent years, had worked in other dioceses.

"Thank heaven the seminarians never see this side of it before they're in it with both feet," said Campbell wearily on the phone.

"I suppose so."

"We're all thinking of you, Joseph."

"I suppose. I haven't heard from anybody since that damned letter everybody got. Except me."

"They're scared. Don't you know that?"

"What do you mean?"

"If this could happen to you, it could happen to any of us. Nobody wants to risk anything. The letter makes you sound like a psycho. They don't know the facts, so they keep their distance. And probably imagine the worst."

Joe was silent for a while. When Campbell inquired if he was still there, Joe said, "What's happened to fairness? When I asked LaBelle why this private family matter was being handled in public, he promised me that he intended to handle it pastorally."

"Come on, Joe. He has the final word regardless of what he told you. Bishops can fairly much do what they want."

"But as a lawyer, I'm used to the whole truth, or as much of it as possible, being on the table before—"

267

"You're not a lawyer anymore. You're a priest in the church of God. The church is not a democratic institution. LaBelle has power over you more than any judge ever had. Nobody is going to buck him. He's a bishop. Get used to it. And you know what Porter wants. Don't blame us if we can't do anything to help you."

"Andy, some of those people on the executive committee are my friends. We've worked together for years. They know me."

"So?"

Joe knew he was right. Their personal experience of him was not what mattered now. With some of the clergy and executive committee members, he had sat up half the night at conferences and retreats, hearing them out on the troubles in their lives. In confidence and compassion, he had listened to them for years unload their most intimate woes. He was a good listener. He would have discussed his own marital problems with a few of them except that he had always reserved that issue for professional therapists, out of loyalty to Kate. Knowledge of him, or anybody's former trust in him, made no difference now.

But he was gaining insight into LaBelle's devious ways and Porter's nasty personality. Who would ever have thought that people of responsibility in the church hierarchy would act with such feeble regard for fairness? Who would have thought that persons in the national church would have had the atrocious judgment to send a priest to an unqualified examiner for a life assessment to determine whether he could continue to serve God?

* * *

"I was asked to perform a psychiatric evaluation on Reverend Joseph Stephenson," began Dr. McMahon's report, "after he had struck his wife and teenaged son. Two years ago, he had also struck his wife. I was asked to evaluate Father Stephenson's ability to perform his priestly duties and to recommend whatever steps should be taken to help him. I spent six hours interviewing him, one hour interviewing his wife and his son. I have also spent over two hours on the phone talking with Reverend Lewis Batterton, Father Stephenson's spiritual director; Dr. Clyde Candler, his former counselor; a parishioner to whom Bishop LaBelle had referred me as a man who liked Father Stephenson and could give me a fair and balanced description of his work; and with Father Andrew Hervey, headmaster of the school where Ted Stephenson attends and where Kate Stephenson teaches. The histories elicited from Father Stephenson and from his wife and son differ substantially. It is impossible to sort out what is truth in many regards, and I have not set that as a goal of this evaluation. From the data collected, I believe I can give an accurate evaluation."

Bishop LaBelle, with barely concealed irritation, had at length consented to provide Joe with a copy of his own evaluation. Through the diocesan attorney, the bishop made it clear that he felt no obligation to do so. The diocese had paid Dr. McMahon's fee and was therefore, according to LaBelle, sole owner of his assessment. Giving Joe a copy was an act of kindness, and Joe could express his appreciation by complying with the church's directions.

The community believed that the bishop's giving a copy to Joe had less to do with kindness than with Jim Edelman's personal conversations with the diocese's attorney, a lawyer he had known professionally for many years.

According to Dr. McMahon, Joe suffered from a "deeply ingrained disturbance" and an "inordinate need to be in control." "Prior to the two incidents that led to this evaluation, his family reported that he would shake them physically and push his wife when angry at them. He proceeded to tell me how disturbed his wife was, how she refused to get help, and that he stayed with her for Ted's sake and for his Christian duty. Each example he made against her was met by a similar example and reproach against Father Stephenson by his wife and his son, with the exception that no one said that Father Stephenson was an alcoholic as he claimed his wife was. Of all the people I talked to, none who knew Mrs. Stephenson thought she was an alcoholic."

Had Kate and Ted really told this man that Joe shoved them and shook them? And besides Ted and Hervey, whom had McMahon spoken to who claimed to know Kate well enough to determine she was not an alcoholic? He could imagine Candler and Batterton stating that they had not met her and had therefore never seen her drink alcohol but that Joe had spoken of it to them. But who were these people who knew her so well that McMahon would rely upon their word? And who was the parishioner whom LaBelle had recommended that McMahon interview? LaBelle had only known Joe a few months, and he knew no one at Redeemer.

Dr. McMahon reported that Joe showed limited insight into his own personality despite having been in therapy. He saw "his own problems in other people and was blind to them in himself." His "enmeshed relationship" with Kate certainly demonstrated his poor personal psychological boundaries as who was doing/feeling/thinking what." "Such a condition makes true empathy difficult to achieve, as other people are not seen as truly separate. He seems to have inflated or devalued opinions of himself and of others that probably change over time, rendering his appraisal and understanding of others unreliable. He would have trouble functioning as a counselor and identifying the problems his parishioners bring to him. He would have more difficulty working with youth, marital problems, and with healthier and more independently minded parishioners. I am concerned that with his marriage coming apart, Father Stephenson may become increasingly anxious, frustrated, and angry and act out in ways that could be a danger to himself or to others around him. He needs skilled, intensive psychotherapy twice a week for an indefinite period of time (I am willing to provide the names of therapists who can do the type of work needed). The therapy he has had to date has not been useful in changing his underlying difficulties. At the end of a year of therapy, and at further periods of time thereafter, Father Stephenson should be re-evaluated by a psychoanalyst who is not treating him, in order to access progress. I would be glad to do this, since I know the baseline from which he is starting. It would be useful to have psychological testing done to give a second opinion and to lessen any doubts about this report. (Matthew Jasden, PhD, is a skilled tester who could do the psychological testing. You can reach him at…)." Then Dr. McMahon signed his name.

Joe was stunned. It was as unfair and outrageous as he had anticipated, but he was still shocked. Seeing his life and personality portrayed in such ways was demeaning in itself, but that it should happen at the hands of the church's own examiner was disgracefully unfair. In three double-spaced pages, his years of faithfulness, coping, attention to duty, and striving for balance were excoriated and denounced as worthless. And he was dangerous. He could be a dangerous man to himself and others. Who was being described here? Who shook and shoved his wife and son, had difficulty dealing with healthy and independent people, and would have "problems" working with youth?

A deep sadness spread through him like a disease. He read the report again and again as though he might have misinterpreted something, some disclaimer, a small sign that it was all a joke or a bad dream. He refolded the report and left it on the kitchen table and went out and sat in a lawn chair and stroked Cory's golden head. The perceptive dog regarded him with mournful eyes and leaned into his hand as Joe scratched the side of his face.

He was churning with anguish and humiliation. His lowest points in life—his father's death, accepting the hopelessness of Kate's recovery, the evening before Easter when his burst of anger drove Kate and Ted away—had been painful as this was painful now. If only he could talk to Kate and Ted, show them what McMahon had written, apologize again as he had done so many times over the weeks, and ask them if this was what they had said. It was astounding. The people he wanted most in the world beside him apparently had contributed to McMahon's destructive report. Was their anger against him still so hot? How had it come to this? He was a fool and a scoundrel. "There is no health in us" and "Miserable offenders" echoed in his mind with the sound of ice cracking on frozen rivers. All the self-doubt of his life seemed to come back to him in a rush. An awareness of his own shocking inadequacy and ignorance tumbled up inside him like a log jamb.

He sat under a tree, gazing out over the lawn for a long time. Cory kept him company through the twilight. As the darkness came on, his inner sadness turned gradually to anger. It was outrageously unfair. McMahon's description of him was inaccurate and dishonest. He was an average man who had made his mistakes in life, but he did not deserve to be judged on the abominable lies folded inside on his kitchen table. He had bent over backward to be a good husband, coping alone, trying to prevent Kate from going the way of her mother, and urging her over the years to accept treatment. He had been a decent father to his son, whom he loved dearly. He still had affection for Kate, he wanted her to have a good life, and if the years of her emotional abuse and lies had killed his desire for her, they had also strengthened his resolve to remain patient and wait for better times. He would not desert her. It had been lonely and difficult, but he had been faithful. And he had worked his back off for Christ and the church. He had made his share of mistakes in life, but being a traitor was not one of them. He had fulfilled his vows.

In the past, when clients brought confused and troubling situations to him for legal resolution, or when law enforcement or social workers presented him with tragedies and brutalities, he had begun immediately to work toward justice. No matter how confounding or gruesome the facts, Christ had shown him that justice, in some measure at least, was always somewhere to be achieved. It was never perfect; perfection must wait for the world to come. And attaining it required determination, organization, and a certain passion for seeing fairness prevail. His experience had taught him that the best tools for going forward were a cool head and an open mind, and they were even better in most cases than the keenest forensic skills. Anger could jumpstart righteous motivation, but once the wheels were rolling, anger was like driving with the breaks on. It made difficult situations worse. And he was not about to allow the present situation to get worse. His heart and mind told him that his dilemma was not God's intention for someone who had tried so hard. That he had not been successful in each of his struggles made no difference to the Lord. Christ does not require us to be successful but to be faithful. It was what was written on the heart that mattered. However awkwardly his heart bore his scribbled convictions, he knew that however lonely life became, he was never alone. There would be a companion.

* * *

His old friend Diana Boyd called the next morning at seven o'clock, the price one paid for having once loved a farmer. She got up with the chickens, she liked to say, although no one had kept chickens on her place for fifty years. She knew about what was happening; she had called early because she knew Kate was living at her school. She was concerned, as were all his old friends, and scolded him kindly for not responding to her many messages. What could she do? she wanted to know. "Just talk to me," he said. And they did, for over an hour.

No one could know the pain in his heart over Kate and Ted. And he knew that no one could understand his fear of being deposed from the priesthood. It was like expecting someone to comprehend his anguish if he was in danger of being disbarred. Only another priest or lawyer could know such nauseating dread. But everything Diana said reminded him of better days, and he was surprised to hear that many of their mutual friends were writing to his diocese in support of him.

The moment he hung up, Jim Edelman called. He was always in his office by eight o'clock. He was glad to know that Joe had been talking with an old friend. He was sure, he said, that Joe knew about Abe Casselman. Joe did. Anyone who followed the big legal cases in the *Post* or the *Sun*, or occasionally the *Times*, knew about Casselman. His testimony had been critical in some of the most difficult trials of the past twenty years, including the attempt to assassinate the president. Jim Edelman knew him personally and had used his expert testimony in several of his own cases. Jim wanted Joe to submit to an evaluation by Casselman, and he would try to arrange an initial appointment as soon as he hung up.

Joe thanked him—there were no words adequate to express how grateful he was for Edelman's time and friendship—and explained carefully what he knew Jim must already know. Dr. Abraham Casselman's fee, surely one of the most substantial in his field, was entirely beyond Joe's ability to pay. Even if he were to qualify for a loan, which was doubtful in his present circumstances, he could not pay for such an evaluation. Of all psychiatric evaluations, he knew Casselman's would carry great weight. But it was beyond his ability. Jim had thought of that. Joe was not to worry. The people at Redeemer had already chipped in, and the fee was as good as paid. Joe thanked him profusely but said he could not allow this. Edelman assured him that the congregation was becoming increasingly angry. The parishioners needed a positive, constructive way to help. They wanted an end to all this for Joe and for themselves, and they wanted him back as their pastor. They all wanted to do something to make it happen. And they did not expect any thanks. After many expressions of gratitude, Joe hung up to await Jim's call later in the morning.

The phone rang constantly. When he saw the caller was a parishioner, he left it unanswered and allowed the message machine to record their words. People he had known so well—they had shared each other's lives for years. How he would have loved to speak with them, to know the latest news on their many situations. He loved these people. He had to be careful to moderate his thinking of them, almost like the hours he could have spent daydreaming about Kate and Ted. Too much of it would drive him crazy, cripple him with loss and self-loathing for what he had done to cause all this anguish. While the sound of the telephone filled the house, he typed a letter to Bishop Spencer, the bishop of his former diocese, who had ordained him and who had known him for many years, saying he needed pastoral guidance and asking for a brief meeting.

He wrote a letter to his mother. They spoke on the telephone every few days, but he had always harbored an old-fashioned appreciation for the consoling power of letters. He wrote to her with the same assurances he provided over the telephone. She was depressed by his situation, and she pined for Kate and Ted. A letter was tangible, tactile, and permanent. It could be carried around and read and re-read and shared with other members of the family. He wanted her to have something to hold on to. He wrote notes to his sisters, too, and his brothers. They were all suffering, having trouble sleeping, fearing the worst for him in a bad situation. They were on his mind constantly. He wrote another letter to Ted. He wrote to Kate. He would go out and mail them following Jim's second call.

He went nowhere now other than the post office, Jim Edelman's office, and distant places for the necessary evaluations. On Sundays he worshipped in nearby dioceses. His own diocese had been silent since agreeing to Dr. Marjorie Williams's evaluation, and he was taking the risk of assuming that LaBelle and the committee were at least willing to await her findings before expecting him to start counseling with McMahon's protégé. He had a great deal of time to himself, something he had craved in the busyness of life over the years. Now that he had it for entirely wrong and unfortunate reasons, it weighed him down like a wet mattress. As calm and clear as he strove to be, he found himself lapsing into blind stares a dozen times a day—wondering, processing, anticipating, planning, speculating—and always with Kate and Ted on his mind. He found his greatest comfort in prolonged and silent prayer.

* * *

The diocese's attorney advised Jim Edelman that LaBelle and Porter would agree to look at an evaluation from another psychiatrist, but they really believed they had all they needed in Dr. McMahon's report. They vigorously refused to pay for another evaluation, however. They expected to receive Dr. Williams's recommendations any day, and although they had agreed to it, they viewed her report as an additional and unnecessary expenditure of diocesan funds. They did not know who Dr. Casselman was, although the church's lawyer had heard of him. Nor did they understand, the diocese's lawyer was obliged to concede, the difference between a psychoanalyst and a mainstream psychiatrist. They knew only that McMahon had been recommended by a Dr. Bird, some sort of expert for the national church, who advised bishops and executive committees when the deplorable conduct of clergy had to be dealt with. A psychiatrist was a psychiatrist, said LaBelle and Porter. This Dr. Bird had recommended McMahon to Bishop Warren Jones, Joe's friend and colleague from his former diocese, who had passed the name on to LaBelle, thus determining what should be done with Joe. That was all they needed to know, and they were irked by all the fuss Joe was making over this. Besides, any recommendation coming down from the national church, from the likes of Bird through Bishop Jones to LaBelle himself, was plainly bound to be sacrosanct.

Once again, Joe drove into the metropolitan area to be evaluated, this time to downtown Baltimore. Dr. Casselman's clinic occupied two lower floors of a professional building at a busy intersection near the Inner Harbor. Joe had to wait a long time to see him; the receptionist advised that the doctor had been held up by something at the hospital but would be along shortly. He accepted a cup of coffee and took a seat in a crowded waiting room with people who seemed to be shielding themselves from one another in various ways.

Across from him, an attractive woman of about fifty pretended to read a paperback book. She was dressed immaculately, and he found it interesting that she wore a stylish hat. Beside her sat someone he supposed was her teenage daughter. There was a strong facial resemblance, but the similarity ended there. The girl was overweight and dressed in soiled, baggy sweats, and her head was tilted back against the wall with her eyes closed and her mouth open. Joe knew she was not asleep. Greasy hair drooped around her head and spread out upon her fat shoulders. He might not have noticed the girl if he passed her on the street or in the Food Lion. Sitting across from her now and seeing her mother's lovely face and anguished eyes, he wondered about them, the blend of volatility and tenderness they seemed to share.

In a nearby chair, a man coughed and coughed, bending over with his hands folded, staring at the floor. An obese black couple filled every inch of a small sofa and stared straight ahead, scowling and blinking. At the far end of the room, a silent blond woman watched two towheaded boys jump and wrestle noisily in a play cubicle. There were a half-dozen others too. Except for the two children, nobody spoke. He imagined Dickens or Tolstoy writing the story of their lives, all converging here now, a common denominator seen and unseen, so much done and left undone. He thought of himself, of the trouble he had caused for so many good people, and a new wave of shame swept over him like a chill.

An approaching nurse, rousing him from his daydream, asked to copy his insurance card. She brought it back in a few minutes, saying they did not need it after all. "Since everything's all set."

When he was finally called in, he found Dr. Casselman to be severe and not a little impatient, as though he was having a bad day. Extremely businesslike and with a great deal of focus, he looked carefully at Joe and asked many questions. He scrutinized some documents in a file, looking up from time to time to ask further questions. He said he was still waiting for Joe's bishop to send him copies of the evaluations by Dr. McMahon and Dr. Williams. He should have them by the following day, he said. In the meantime, Joe could expect to spend two to three days at his office, being interviewed and tested by his associates, and he himself would interview Joe again later in the process. He asked a few further questions, made some notes on a pad, and went to the door and called for someone in an adjoining room. A young man in a white laboratory coat came in and led Joe to a conference room and asked him to provide written answers to a list of questions. After several hours of this, he was advised to go out for lunch and return by two fifteen.

He spent till early evening working with a chipper young woman with an English accent who administered many tests. A man came in twice to observe, sitting quietly to one side and making notations in a file. In the early evening, they scheduled more work for the following day and advised him that on the day after that, he would work at home, or in some quiet place, completing a long series of answers to written questions. It would be necessary to return early in the following week to meet Dr. Casselman again. The young English girl told him cheerfully of a distinct advantage to working till early evening: they would miss the worst part of rush hour.

He drove home weary and desperate for sleep. He wondered if he would be able to sleep through the night. The light was fading as he left the busy expressways and drove west on the quieter interstate. The big road plunged relentlessly on through the countryside, spanning lowlands and cutting through hilltops as though eons of geology had never mattered. The big highway paralleled the big river, which flowed seaward a few miles to the south, the two of them split-ting the yet lovely countryside into two great east-west worlds.

He could not stop thinking about the people he had seen in the waiting room. It was an old habit, an ardent, insatiable curiosity about people that was connected somehow with the inner question-ing and self-doubt that had always kept his mind alert. The thin old man with the military crew cut, bent forward in his chair facing the floor, coughing, seemed the embodiment of, what? Resignation? Sadness? What had he done in life? Did he have a family? The well-dressed woman with the slovenly daughter—he was sure she was her daughter—reminded him of something he had read years ago by Flannery O'Connor. And the black couple, so overweight, look-ing so angry. Black and young, how could they not be angry? And the dreadlocks they wore with such pride. They were their own worst enemies, he supposed. The silent woman with the hyperactive boys—he wondered where the father was. If Ted had needed the ser-vices of a doctor, any doctor, Joe would have swum the Atlantic to be with him and Kate at the appointment. But it might have been the mother who was the patient. All these people—what were their lives like? Did they believe in God? Did they know love in their lives? What did they do all day? Were they generous? Forgiving? Had they found forgiveness in life? Peace?

Sometimes he sat in the Third Base, in the rare moments when no one was talking to him, and looked around at the people and wondered about the same things. Or as he walked through stores or shopping malls or passed vacationers on his beloved long walks along the beach in Wicomico—the people raised in him a profound and affectionate interest. Every person was a story worthy of telling, a novel in themselves. Every face a portrait, a Sully or Sargent. At one time, he would have checked himself and stopped such ruminations. People, after all, would think he was crazy. But he was getting better, less concerned about being thought a lunatic, giving his mind a loose reign and letting it plunge forward through open country and over obstacles. It did not mean he liked all people or valued them all. He didn't, although he realized it was what they did, or didn't do, that appalled him more than themselves as persons. If God loved them all, who was he to hate any of them? Even the worst, the Nazis and Communists and butchers of Sierra Leone, the violent Muslims, the ones who destroyed justice and decency, probably longed for some sort of peace in their lives.

Many people talked about peace, especially the idealistic clergy fresh from seminary. There had never been peace on earth, and human beings were incapable of bringing it about on their own. Yet they all talked about it as though if everyone would just calm down and be reasonable, peace would naturally follow. Or maybe they were afraid, without realizing it, that ceasing to talk about peace as a human possibility would make the world that much worse. He supposed that everyone in that waiting room, including him, was there seeking some sort of peace. They were all in it together. In the eternal sense, there was no difference between any of them. They were all the same, troubled human beings resembling him, in a troubled world. Seeking some kind of peace.

It occurred to him he had never met anyone who seemed satisfied with life. Most of them had every reason to feel that way, buffeted about in an unfair world like the fractious occupants of an overloaded lifeboat, struggling for space, dreaming of dry land. The wealthiest people he knew, who gave the appearance of wanting for nothing, yearned and coveted as much as the rest of them. He had his own troubles, God knew. But God had been good to him. He knew he was blessed in a thousand ways. Compared to the man in the waiting room who coughed and kept his head down, Joe could probably be considered, anxious as he was, to be riding high. It was all so confusing, so sad.

What would happen now? He knew himself, for what that was worth, and he had confidence that if Dr. Williams and Dr. Casselman portrayed him accurately, the diocese would cease and desist. The bishop would chew him out for having caused all this trouble in the first place. He deserved that. And although the chances were slim, he thought it might still be possible to reconcile with Kate. He would accept her as she was. She could live as she liked, so long as it did no harm to Ted. He hit the steering wheel with the heel of his hand, causing the horn to beep and himself to remember suddenly to turn on the headlights. Who was he kidding? Why would she come back to him? She had what she had always wanted—her son, her job, and her complete independence. She no longer had to answer to anyone for anything.

He drove on into the darkness, wondering how long it would take to resolve all this. He missed his wife and son and the people of Redeemer. He wanted to apologize in person for what he had put them through. Did LaBelle and Porter have any idea how the church was being damaged by their public reaction to his private wrong? If the church authorities reacted this way to every domestic problem in clergy households, the church would long ago have been bankrupt and depleted of clergy. LaBelle was old, strange, and had retired as bishop twenty years before. He was right to be alarmed by domestic violence. But there was no telling what Kate had told him. She was a woman, Joe was a cad who had acknowledged slapping her, and nothing else mattered. In the eyes of the church in this secular and highly political age, there was no mitigation.

Kirby Porter should be able to approach his case with reason, but here again Joe had to force himself to be a realist. Nobody among the clergy considered Porter a close friend. Few liked him. He was known as ferociously ambitious, someone who would step on his own grandmother to advance himself. The clergy accorded him a brisk deference. He was a native of the state, and the former bishop, before he knew him well, had made him a dean of one of the four diocesan regions, one of the four who served as the bishop's special advisers. Porter was head of a small parish in those days, before Joe came to the diocese, and had plenty of time to devote to this special role. Then a clergyman retired at a very large church on the other side of the diocese, and the congregation began to search for a new pastor. It was a historic church in a formerly wealthy community and retained some trappings of its former prestige. Porter submitted his name immediately. The former bishop advised him against going there. Porter was still a very young man, and the bishop feared he would, in time, grow tired of the place and find himself stuck with no further room for advancement. But Porter agitated so passionately for the position that the bishop finally relented. Moving to the new church meant leaving the part of the diocese he had served as dean. In his determination to move upward, as he saw it, Porter had not considered losing his position as dean. He asked the bishop to redraw the deanery lines, shifting them around so he could continue as one of the favored four. The bishop refused, appointing another person to replace him as dean. So began Porter's thinly disguised animosity toward the former bishop that persisted and simmered until the former bishop's recent retirement. Now Porter was looking ahead to the arrival of a new bishop and, according to many clergy who seemed to know, determined on fresh advancement of some sort in the new episcopacy. Joe feared that his own case afforded Porter a chance to show himself as a tough, no-nonsense leader. He was plainly bucking to become the next bishop's canon.

Looking back upon his naivety when he entered the church, Joe was surprised at his own gullibility. Growing up and knowing the clergymen at his small-town Southern church, he had grown to expect a sort of pervasive goodness among ordained people. The ministers of his youth, never, ever referred to as priests, were scholarly men of patient disposition and trustworthy character. He had grown older believing that all clergy were like that. After years in teaching and in the law, where he had met his share of bad actors and should have known better, he had entered holy orders unprepared for the same reality in the clergy. He had been profoundly disappointed by the likes of LaBelle, Porter, Hervey, and a few others he had bumped into along the way. It was not that they were necessarily bad men or women. They were merely like everyone else: self-centered, defensive, opinionated, often with something to hide and frequently highly ambitious. And none of them, he knew, liked or respected him.

Yet, he still believed in an overriding goodness in ordained men and women. He was convinced that God's power worked in them. The faults and wickedness in a few delinquents did not invalidate the power they had received at ordination. The clergy he had known and served among were imminently decent and spiritual people. Perhaps that was why the traits of the occasional rascals loomed so large in comparison. He wondered if the laity saw it this way too, or if the truth was apparent only to clergy.

We are a wounded lot, he thought to himself, looking into the darkness ahead. *And I am ashamed of making it all so much more tragic.* Clergy, he knew, might be climbers at the expense of all around them, or living double lives with contempt for the truth, or totally lacking in humility or understanding. None of it mattered. Much of it actually enabled one to blend seamlessly into the broken world. And all of it could be forgiven. What mattered was the sort of thing he had done. He had lost his temper and slapped his wife. In this day and age, no explanation, excuse, or remorse could wipe away that indelible stain on his ministry in the eyes of the church.

Chapter Twenty-Two

A FAMILY FIGHT IN the privacy of home had been transformed by the church's leadership into a raucous public *cause célèbre*, no enormity being too heinous to attribute to Joe. Fresh, nasty details emerged every day like the trashy sequels of bad movies, all of them cheaper and more bizarre than yesterday's. He could no longer recognize himself in the gossip. He sat alone at home, banished from his community, as the lies and rumors swirled about like dust devils. Details of his lurid life, news to him and his old friends alike, circulated routinely through an eager network so the whole community could share the excitement.

His guilt had become an engaging summer obsession for the small Redeemer group arrayed against him, and all the evidence showed that they were in daily touch with Kate and people at Diocesan House. Most mornings found them gathered at Lottie's home, a mutual support group processing the whole ugly matter relentlessly and examining every possible extrapolation into Joe's character. After some weeks, it repelled even the Bascomb children, sullen and suspicious around Joe from his first day in the community, who complained to their friends about hearing nothing else at home but how evil Joe was. They were not taking up for him but grumbling about how boring it had all become. Good people consulted one another in alarm.

Joe knew that Lottie and Jane Ellen were capable of inventing such things, yet there was no way to counter their rumors in his banishment. He had to rely upon what people already knew of him to guide them. Everybody knew that Lottie's small group had never liked him. People in other denominations found it curious that several of them were immersed in diocesan affairs, doting on church politics the way some people thrive on soap operas and film stars. They were always rushing off to something or other at the seminary or a conference on the other side of the state, where they maneuvered the small levers of church power with touchy gravitas. At times he had found it hard to carry out his own diocesan duties when several members of his own congregation were so negative about him. He admired the great majority of employees and volunteers who worked in his diocese and for the national church. They were faithful, good-hearted, the sort one would want for neighbors. But among them was a small class of angry people, devoted to their social or political causes or particular lifestyle issues, who saw in the church a pathway to power. They were pleasant and good-hearted too, until someone dared to buck their personal agendas. They could be vicious.

Still, the visceral contempt of his own small opposition had surprised him. He knew he was not perfect, that he made as many mistakes as anyone did, and that he himself was bound to be part of the problem. There were two sides of everything. But he was no serial rapist, just a lone parish priest in a small town in rural Appalachia. He was not running for political office or bishop or canon or anything else. He had no ambitions and was content to carry on that way to retirement. He would have stayed in the law if climbing had been his goal. Their spouses had always seemed to like him. He had tried hard to become friends with their children. Perhaps that was their point, getting him out of a place in which he seemed content to stay and where people liked him. Whatever motivated them, they had all the advantages now and the gossip was degrading. People were hearing that he had abused Ted for years. He had pushed poor Kate down flights of stairs. He was forever throwing things at her, refusing to give her money and had never allowed her to leave the house except to go to work. That was why she stayed away all the time at St. John's. Joe might be good with his ministry—although that, too, was subject to much criticism—but he was a tyrant at home, cruel, unreasonable, and negligent. And now he could only sit in that home and pray.

How had it come to this? It was the sort of sleazy, destructive gossip that no one believed, except the poisonous few. He could not help believing that even they knew that what they were saying were lies. And the network of gossips worked well. The people at Diocesan House knew what the vestry was doing, and his detractors were saying it before the Redeemer congregation found out. Matters that should have been known to the bishop and executive committee alone were suddenly in the rumor mill and acquiring sensational details, like the talk that went round at the diocesan convention. In his professional and personal life, Joe had always deplored trashy hearsay and sneaky behavior. In other circumstances, he would have wasted no time with it, the sort of stuff that festered in certain types of angry people. He avoided the chronically angry, the conspiracy nuts, America bashers, and rap music for the same reasons. He remembered interviewing managers in a half-dozen porn shops in an old homicide case years before. The places had made him feel dirty, and the terrible situation around him now was like that. It made him feel dirty, as though he had spent a while with the Ku Klux Klan or some other pack of racists or homophobes.

How had his own character and career come to this? And although the people in his adopted community knew him well and rejected the ugly gossip, he knew that the terrible insinuations would have their cumulative effect when good people looked back over the years. He had seen it happen, honest men and women damaged by sleaze, their reputations colored forever by the sheer weight and ugly quality of false accusations.

It had been going on since the Easter weekend, when he had slapped Kate, but he thought it had peaked on the floor of the diocesan convention. He knew that people would shake their heads and smile and slap him on the shoulder and tell him not to worry, that it was all a vicious overreaction and nobody believed it. The truth would come out. He would see. "Keep things in perspective, Joe," they would say. A nobody clergyman in a nowhere place? And it was not the crime of the century, after all. His picture wouldn't appear on the world news anytime soon. Steady now. It would turn out all right. Yes, it was a shameful spectacle, but the church had bigger problems than Joe losing it with his wife. It was all a temporary tempest in, let's face it, Joe, the smallest of teapots, really. "And they would be right, probably," he said to himself. Except that damage done here, overreaction now, a reputation ruined in the current charged atmosphere, would stain his name forever, wherever he went.

Then one night, he received a call from Amanda, the new warden of the parish. A vestry meeting had just ended. He could hear the tension in Amanda's cultured voice as she told him that Milly, the parish secretary, had unknowingly in the meeting made a series of brief remarks that caused everyone to pause. Her contract required her to be present and record such meetings, a custom in the parish for many years, which Joe had not liked but had learned to live with.

"All around the table, people looked at one another and realized at the same moment that she was the one. We had all wondered for weeks and weeks how the people at Diocesan House and Lottie and Jane Ellen and that bunch knew what we were doing by the morning after we met. It was Milly the whole time. It may have been Nancy Dodd, too, but she always denied it and we didn't want to question what she said." As angry as they were, the vestry members decided against firing Milly, who had worked in the office for years. The parish was in enough turmoil without having to break in a new secretary while the rector was being kept away. The members waited around after the meeting and conferred, after Milly and Nancy Dodd had left the building. They decided to guard their discussions at future meetings and save anything critical, and anything about Joe, for separate times and places. For the time being, they decided to say nothing to Milly, who apparently did not realize she had revealed herself.

Joe reacted to this news with an anguish that few would understand. It was like a kick to the head of a man asleep on the ground. He had worked shoulder to shoulder with Milly for years. Lottie Bascomb had recommended her for the job of parish secretary a few years before Joe came to Redeemer. She had always had a sort of loyalty to Lottie, but Joe had seen it lessen over time as she had come to know him better. In recent years, Milly had even warned him about

286

things Lottie was saying about him. He had been grateful. He had done all he could to assist Milly in her personal life, where troubles seemed to abound. In his absence, she must have returned to her old loyalties. He thanked Amanda for telling him, and after asking about her family, he thanked her a second time and hung up. He went outside and sat with Cory in the dark, thinking of many things and feeling sick to his stomach. Of all the people and possibilities, he had not expected Milly. When he did go in, a little after midnight, he did not sleep at all and finally got up again and went down to the kitchen when it was light.

And there was more. He was getting used to the punches, shaking his head to clear his vision and keeping up his guard like a boxer. A few days later, he received several urgent calls from parishioners, who demanded he call them back immediately. They must speak to him now, they said. It was urgent. One of them, Cindy Marshall, had attended a weekend party where she overheard Jane Ellen and Don Rush tell several people that the reason Joe chaperoned church youth activities was that he was sexually attracted to children. Cindy was horrified. After finding out that her husband, a psychologist, had heard them say the same thing, they called Jim Edelman. As much as she hated to put more pressure on Joe, considering everything that was happening, the Marshalls and Jim Edelman felt Joe should know about it immediately. In rapid succession, he received a call from Jim Edelman asking him to come to his office, and another call from Stuart and Jane Holloway, who had decided not to wait for him to call back. It was evident the Holloways were deeply alarmed and conflicted, and they wanted Joe to tell them what to do now. At a weekend gathering, they had overheard Lottie Bascomb tell a woman they did not recognize, probably someone's weekend guest, that Joe had "touched" some of the girls in the parish. Standing by was Nancy Dodd, nodding gravely in agreement. As Stuart Holloway and Carl Dodd were both physicians, they knew each other fairly well. The Holloways had held off confronting Nancy until they talked with Joe. Probably fearing becoming targets of her acid tongue, no one, as usual, said anything about confronting Lottie.

He had thought his despair upon leaving McMahon's office for the final time had been the worst he would experience, next to slapping Kate and her anger. But this was something new. Years before, an imprudent young lawyer in her first criminal trial had told the court that Joe had failed to provide her certain evidence under the rules of discovery. She gave notice of an intention to file an ethics complaint against Joe. The court set a hearing and soon determined that Joe had provided the evidence in a timely way. He knew he had done so. Even so, the days leading up to the hearing had been terribly anxious, and he still remembered them. A violation of legal ethics might mean little to many people, but attorneys approach such matters with profound concern. Even when they are false, certain people will remember the accusations long after the truth is known and the record cleared. And the prospect of having to clear his name in the church was, if anything, even more alarming. The process in the church was ambiguous, adapted from a code of military procedure and managed by people with a stake in the outcome. He knew the dangers. He had served for years as president of his diocese's ecclesiastic court and prayed daily not to have to preside at a trial of any member of the clergy. Defending himself seemed to become more and more difficult with every day.

The same issues that worried Joe were on Jim Edelman's mind too. He was as outraged as others were at what was happening. The vestry members and congregation, and people in the community outside Redeemer, were appalled. Anyone could see that the lies being spread about Joe, together with the letter LaBelle and Porter had mailed to hundreds of people throughout the diocese, had set up a deplorable situation. Given the diocese's unambiguous suggestion that Joe was guilty of something truly heinous, some people might be willing to listen to the Rushes, Lottie, Nancy Dodd, and their several cohorts. Damage had been done by what they had said already, but it was important to stop any further lies immediately. So Edelman sent Joe to an attorney in the nearby town of Petersfield, a good lawyer with no connections to Redeemer and who had never lived in Catoctin Springs. After a consultation with Joe and satisfying herself that grounds for action existed, she wrote letters to Jane Ellen and Don Rush and Lottie Bascomb advising that they would face a lawsuit if they continued to talk about Joe.

Joe decided against having the letter sent to Nancy Dodd. She was a follower and probably not smart enough on her own to concoct such atrocious lies. She would be effectively silenced by the receipt of the letter by her friend Lottie. But more important was Joe's respect for Carl Dodd, a likeable man who, like John Bascomb, had always been friendly and fair with him. Receiving a warning letter from an attorney would cause a paroxysm in Nancy that everyone would learn about. Joe was reluctant to put that strain upon Carl Dodd. He had been a respected member of the medical community over the years, and Joe would do nothing to damage his practice. Lottie, on the other hand, was known to hide whatever suited her from her husband. John Bascomb was innocently oblivious of the way Lottie was regarded in the community. She would receive the letter and never mention it to anyone, especially her husband.

Andrew Hervey very likely contributed to the gossip too, not with the others, but on his own. They had no witness who had heard him, however, so he was excluded too.

At the beginning of his ministry, Joe would never have imagined taking legal action against a parishioner, especially people who had served on diocesan committees or were well-known across the diocese. He drove back from the lawyer's office in Petersfield depressed and despondent, questioning God about the reason for the whole terrible mess and filled with anger at those who would tell such vicious lies about him. How had it come to this?

Because you slapped your wife, said a calm, reasonable voice in his head. *You violated a social prohibition, and nothing, no amount of provocation, can explain or justify what you did.*

"I know," he said. "I know. I know."

And you cannot take it back, nor can you offer anything in mitigation, and none of the circumstances make any difference.

"I understand," he said.

And you, a priest in the church of God…

He pulled quickly across the oncoming lane into the parking area of an overlook and got out of the car. Before him, the mountains receded into the early summer evening like gentle waves. The river glistened in the distance, a silver ribbon forming its great oxbows. From the trees below came the flutelike voice of a wood thrush, singing ahead of the sunset the way birds do in the late afternoon. It was all so radiant, alluring. It needed Albert Bierstadt or Frederick Church for the distances, Asher Durand for the foreground. But such thoughts sailed away like the lone buzzard overhead, wings straight out to its sides, descending gracefully against the blue and soaring along the remote mountainside until lost in the distance. Not even these glories could relieve the pain that filled his mind. He thought of Kate and Ted, and the tears came in a rush. He was glad he had the overlook to himself. He was not embarrassed to cry. He had urged other men to do so often enough, reminding them that tears were God's way of cleansing, expressing sorrow, giving thanks. He had sat with many people over the years while they cried. He remembered the times Kate had cried, pressing her face into his neck, when she had waited until an hour before going out to announce that she had nothing to wear. He went through her closet with her, telling her how nice this or that outfit looked on her, exasperated once again that she had waited until now, knowing she was preparing herself not to enjoy the evening. He could see her face, smell the fragrance of her hair and the scent of the sweet powder she liked. Even with the denial and manipulation, he would have taken her back.

And now, of all the hateful lies that could be told in society about another human being, the people against him were spreading some of the worst. Such garbage had only to reach the ears of LaBelle, Porter, and the executive committee for them to abandon all restraint in their condemnation of him. In all his life, he had never faced a situation so nasty. He began to understand that his reputation might not recover even if the church authorities relented tomorrow.

* * *

For reasons never made clear, the executive committee finally changed its position and agreed to grant Joe a hearing. Whether in response to his formal letters of request, or the conversations between the diocese's lawyer and Jim Edelman, or because of the volume of mail the diocese was receiving daily in support of Joe, or for some other reason, a meeting was scheduled for early July. He would be allowed to explain himself. They would meet him in a small motel conference center in Minewoods, a dreary crossroads in the center of the state used by the diocese for meetings.

The Redeemer vestry members began hearing rumors of this meeting, potentially so crucial to the parish and to Joe's vocation, days before the executive committee notified Jim Edelman or anyone else. Several even heard the place and date discussed by people in the community who were not Redeemer members. It was evident to everybody that a channel existed between the diocesan authorities and someone in Catoctin Springs. Milly talked to Lottie and her group, but certainly not to anyone at Diocesan House. Who was it there, and who was it on the Catoctin Springs end? Suspicion fell upon Nancy Dodd, who spent hours at Lottie's house every day discussing the latest revelations of Joe's despicable personality. Whoever it was seemed to know the most intimate matters taken up in vestry meetings, the executive committee, and in the interim bishop's presence.

In preparation for the meeting, the vestry and congregation of Redeemer formally petitioned the executive committee to change its course and return Joe to their parish without any more delay. The petition expressed this belief by the whole Redeemer community: "The process used and the measure of your actions so far, without involving any of us, may be open to question in respect to fundamental fairness to the congregation, our parish leaders, and to our rector." Over a hundred people came to the parish office to sign during two days before the petition was sent overnight to Diocesan House. Every vestry member signed it except Nancy Dodd. Amanda, the capable warden of the vestry, inspected the packet personally before Milly sealed it, and took it to the post office herself.

"Although we believe domestic violence is serious and unacceptable, it does occur in various degrees. We believe that any response should be measured in relation to the nature of the events and what corrective steps have been taken by the individuals involved. It is our concern that the process be fair and not unduly influenced by persons not directly involved or any person who may have an unfair bias. The decision, to date, appears to be an overly harsh judgment of a man well respected by his congregation, who is entitled to fundamental fairness. Our vestry is responsible and responsive and should be consulted in all important matters relative to this congregation. We very respectfully ask for your prompt reconsideration of your actions suspending our rector for the reasons stated at the congregational meeting."

Kirby Porter advised Jim Edelman that the committee would give Joe one hour with them and went to some trouble to emphasize that nobody else "would be allowed to come in the room." Permitting Jim to accompany Joe was an unexpected grant of leniency. Jim's personal acquaintanceship with the diocese's lawyer had probably helped. Joe's mind would have been focused like a laser had he been representing a client. In the emotionally charged work of defending himself, however, he knew Jim's calming presence and overview of the issues would be blessings.

Jim began immediately the meticulous labor of assembling the evidence. He intended to show that in slapping Kate, Joe's conduct had been out of character, that he had tried conscientiously for many years to reason with Kate, that he should be allowed to continue his ministry and the Stephenson family permitted to deal with their marital affairs without further interference. As their marital difficulties had been disclosed to the whole diocese, and given that the bishop had chosen to proceed publicly, adequate punishment had already been exacted. Fairness demanded that Joe be allowed to return to his ministry.

To make the most of their hour with the committee, Jim Edelman assembled the reams of documents into thick notebooks, intending to mail a copy to each committee member before the meeting. Each one could read and be familiar with the evidence before the meeting. Each packet was bound in a blue jacket and marked PERSONAL AND CONFIDENTIAL. Each began with a table of contents. Numbered paper tabs separated the various categories of information. A brief chronology of events came first. This was followed by medical reports, copies of all three—the reports of Dr. Williams and Dr. Casselman were expected within days and would be added before mailing.

Dr. Timothy Marshall wrote a lengthy letter based on his personal knowledge of Joe and taking exception to Dr. McMahon's "recommendation that Reverend Stephenson be removed from his role as minister and participate in 'skilled, intensive psychotherapy twice a week for an indefinite period.'" He further added, "In my thirty years as a psychologist, I have never seen, or even heard of, any individual treatment plan that goes to this extreme."

Clyde Candler, Joe's counselor in Catoctin Springs, wrote a report about his years of counseling Joe and detailing Joe's chronic concern for Ted's welfare, his faithfulness in counseling, and Kate's refusal to take part. He emphasized his advice to Joe not to tell Ted anything about counseling, "as Ted would be likely to see this as a strike against his mother."

There followed a series of letters and statements by professional men and women who had worked with Joe over the years. The director of the special education school where Joe taught for six years, David Kane, now a family friend for many years, submitted a statement describing how "over fifteen years in confidence, Joe brought up the issue of his wife's struggle with alcohol and what to do in a situation where the spouse was in denial and would not consider treatment, counseling, or attendance at a support group. This was a subject of great pain and soul searching, and always about what he could do to make the relationship work better while dealing with this issue. In all this, he was extremely concerned about the welfare of his son." In addition, he wrote that he and his wife had "personal knowledge from observation that Mrs. Stephenson's mother was alcoholic. During twenty years of renting rooms in her cottage in Wicomico, Mrs. Stephenson's mother began drinking at breakfast and continued to do so throughout the day. When Joe's mother-in-law lived in the Stephensons' home in recent years, keeping alcohol away from her, and obtaining his wife's support for this, was a major problem."

Dr. Leffler, his counselor in Dorchester, had reviewed her file of years before and written to the committee about Joe's "concerns about intimacy, communication, and concern about his wife's alleged alcoholism. He was concerned about the marriage in general, his wife's outbursts, and the role that alcohol played in her life and the impact that it had on the family."

A copy of the letter of Dave and Tonette Gallagher, which Dr. McMahon had refused to consider, was included.

Over one hundred other people had written to Bishop LaBelle and the executive committee: parishioners, former parishioners, neighbors in various communities, Joe's professional colleagues in the law, judges, doctors, children he had known and taught, parents of Ted's friends, and others from all over the East Coast and elsewhere. Of those letters and statements of which Jim and Joe had copies, a representative fifteen were included in the binders. Among them were letters from the mayor of Catoctin Springs, wives of clergymen—now deceased—who had worked with Joe, and clergy from his former diocese. If any clergy from his own diocese had written in support, Joe was not aware of it.

There followed copies of all correspondence between Jim, Joe, and the executive committee, Bishop LaBelle, Kirby Porter, the Redeemer vestry, and the diocese's lawyer.

It took hours to make photocopies of hundreds of pages and assemble them all into a dozen folders. Joe and Jim Edelman worked together after hours in Jim's busy office suite, laboring past midnight for four days while many of the firm's younger lawyers toiled away in their cramped offices. From time to time, going from the copy room to the conference room, where they were assembling the documents, Joe glanced in at these young attorneys. He recalled the weary nights of his own first years of practice, preparing wills and deeds and trial notes between tutoring sessions with the young students who were helping him make ends meet. It seemed so long ago, in another century. As tired as he was, recalling those days made him wearier still. He knew these young lawyers would have to get up in a few hours and see their children off to school, then rush out to court or meetings with clients, alert, focused, and attentive to details to which few others would attach significance.

They assembled their mound of special evidence, and his mind reeled at the absurdity of what they were having to do: defend his uninspiring life and damaged reputation against the denunciation of his church. The church had already determined him guilty on his own admission. He could understand that, but the draconian punishment demanded of him was unreasonable and unfair both to him and his congregation. Once interrupted by McMahon's "skilled, intensive psychotherapy twice a week for an indefinite period," with McMahon determining its length, his life and ministry would be difficult, perhaps impossible, to recover. Surely, he and Jim could be plainspoken and direct with the executive committee members. They were clergy and laypeople he had worked with for years. When they finally understood the whole story, they would relent and bring this nightmare to an end.

Weeks of sleepless nights and loneliness had made him a quieter person than he had ever been. Day and night, he had to struggle intentionally against depression, rescuing himself by many means. At too much thought of Ted, or recalling slapping Kate, his tears came easily and quietly. He listened to the voices of friends on his answering machine and read the dozen letters that arrived each day. His old friend Diana called every few days, and he knew her door was always open to him. His fishing and hunting companions called, some of them every bit as faithful and concerned as his own family. His mother, brothers, and sisters were devastated by Kate's and Ted's departure and sick about the danger to his ministry. As with everyone else, he had told them exactly what he had done and taken responsibility for everything. That Kate had lied and manipulated and provoked him throughout their marriage was no excuse for losing his temper, and he knew it. If she should accept some blame because of her own behavior, it was not for him to suggest it. He had disqualified himself, perhaps forever, from blaming anything on her denial.

Cut off from his own community, he accepted some of the constant invitations from distant friends, including those from people on the far side of the river living within an easy drive of St. John's School. Several of them had been associated with the school in the past and were appalled by what was happening, and particularly by Father Hervey's role in it.

But the most effective way of dealing with his own sadness was in his sure and certain knowledge that the One on the other end of his prayers, whose understanding was limitless and compassionate, knew what he was going through. The One who heard him knew personally the unfairness and suffering that comes with being a human being in the broken world. His listener knew the strengths and weaknesses Joe brought to this, his own unique measure of life's brokenness. The tears of things had to be experienced to be understood, if they could be understood, and Joe had the shoulder of One, who had that experience in its cruelest manifestation. In his own daily anxiety and sleepless foreboding, he knew his suffering was little compared to others.

And he was conscious that many eyes were upon him. He knew from the moment he first put on his collar that everything he did and said from that moment forward would reveal not only him but also the One he served. He was aware he stood for something, or someone, beyond himself. In his life, there was more at stake than his personal interests. How could he preach it if he did not live it? And nowhere could a man or woman live it more faithfully than as the waters were closing round. And if he despaired at the world's brokenness, what kind of faith was he demonstrating to those who watched? What sort of example? What kind of ambassador was he if he showed himself a turncoat who did not believe in his own credentials?

As troubling as it all was, and growing more complicated every day, he knew he would ache with distraction until the results of the two recent evaluations were in hand. With neither Dr. Williams nor Dr. Casselman, or their colleagues, had he felt any of the contempt and bias exuded by McMahon. He had sat in their offices and in their meeting rooms for three and one-half days, taking test after test. Even after McMahon had presented his scathing report, Joe found himself still confused by the man's disdain and arrogance. He was a professional bound by professional ethics and guided by medical morality. He had taken an oath to do no harm. Even after he learned that McMahon was a psychoanalyst, legally unqualified to administer objective psychological tests, operating in a highly subjective field where preliminary diagnoses were neither made nor used, Joe would have still viewed an objective opinion from him with great seriousness. Even if he had known that the church was sending him to its hired gun, arranged by somebody in its omnipotent hierarchy, he would have gone anyway because he believed that God had called him into ministry and was at work in the church process.

But McMahon had missed some obvious issues. His report seemed tailor-made to keep Joe from his vocation. Suppose Williams and Casselman produced damaging reports too? He did not expect that, but just suppose. He believed he knew himself as much as a man could. He was open and honest. He had dedicated himself to the truth. He was a sinner certainly, but not a monster. But suppose their reports were like McMahon's? He felt he would have no choice but to accept them as God's signal that he was no longer fit for ministry.

But Joe put these thoughts aside and tried not to speculate too heavily. His circumstances were demoralizing enough without making things worse by feeling sorry for himself or imagining things that might never occur. He had never been that type. And God had been good to him. As bad as his circumstances were, he had the support of decent, honest, compassionate people. And for an example of the best that humans can be, he need look no further than Jim Edelman. He was fast coming to understand why everyone had always admired him. And as for the two medical reports, he had to wait only a few more days for a denouement.

Dr. Williams telephoned him at home. It was her practice to speak with clients before their reports were issued; she believed it was only fair to call him, as well as Bishop LaBelle, as she had been chosen by both Joe and the diocese. She provided a brief overview of her findings, answered all his questions, and advised that Jim Edelman would receive a copy of her report within a few days. Her candor impressed him, and he was grateful for her information, and he told her so. She wished him well and said goodbye, leaving him with a faint impression that there was more she would like to say. Her nine-page report arrived a few days later, and Jim Edelman's secretary called to say he could come over and read it.

"The results of the evaluation find Reverend Stephenson to be a highly intelligent individual whose approach to problem-solving both interpersonally and professionally is extremely clinical and unemotional but who clearly expresses compassion and concern for others. He is a highly controlled individual who seeks always to stay within the bounds of accepted behavior and whose self-control is only likely to break down under conditions of extreme provocation. It is clear that Reverend Stephenson is not an individual who is prone to aggressive behavior except under conditions of extreme provocation. There is nothing in the testing or the comments received from others, including Mrs. Stephenson, that would suggest that interpersonal difficulties or marital problems have ever interfered with the performance of his duties."

The nine-page report ended with recommendations: Joe should engage in counseling about his divorce. "However, I do not believe that it needs to be as intensive as that recommended by Dr. McMahon, nor does he need to complete the counseling before the resumption of his duties. It would be important for his therapist to help him understand his own role in the dissolution of the marriage." She suggested the consideration of "medication to relieve his anxiety and depression brought on by his current situation." She concluded with a concern for Joe's "potential for effectiveness, not in general, but with his present congregation, before whom all the familial 'dirty laundry' has been laundered." The report continued, "It would certainly be important for this issue to be thoroughly discussed and analyzed before he returns to service with this congregation, although it should be noted that there are many in the congregation who support him and who feel that he was inappropriately dismissed. If this congregation is not appropriate, there is no reason not to offer him a different one."

The following day, Jim received the lengthy report of Dr. Casselman and his associates. Joe was asked to come immediately and read it, which turned out to take considerable time. "As a general and forensic psychiatrist, I evaluated him to determine whether he had any diagnosable mental illness and/or underlying psychopathology that would impair his ability to perform his duties and responsibilities. A comprehensive history of Reverend Stephenson, as well as a detailed mental status examination, failed to show any past or present history of any diagnosable mental illness or psychopathology. The evaluation suggests that the two incidents in which Reverend Stephenson slapped his wife were isolated ones, aberrational and in the context of heated arguments, and not an indication of a pattern of spousal abuse or representative of an individual who uses bullying and intimidation to get his way."

Joe was delighted to find that he did not have "a clinical condition or diagnosable mental illness" and that he did not have "a diagnosable personality disorder."

The incidents of which Joe was so ashamed were "aberrational, not part of a pattern of behavior and not indicative of an individual with any mental illness or psychopathology." Dr. Casselman's report then went on, "In my opinion, there are no mental or emotional symptoms or any condition that is impairing his ability to perform his duties and responsibilities."

It finished with, "In my opinion, Reverend Stephenson is not in need of psychotherapy, intensive or not, particularly since there is no mental or emotional condition that necessitates treatment."

* * *

Friday Night

Dear Kate,

Please read this carefully and try to understand. I would like to speak with you face-to-face. I will come to any place you select. I would prefer to speak with you privately, but if you will talk to me only with someone else present, I will agree to that. I cannot speak in Father Hervey's presence under any circumstances.

Kate, I need to speak with Ted. He won't answer my letters and won't take my calls, but we both know he will do so if you tell him to. I need to know about him, his health, his grades, what he is doing and thinking. I ask you to please, please, please communicate with me about him and tell him to speak with me. He is my son too.

A lot of trouble has occurred because there seems to have been an open pipeline of information from Catoctin Springs to St. John's to diocesan leaders. It is causing a great deal of trouble. If you know anything about it, please do the right thing and help to stop it. It is very destructive and generating all sorts of ugly gossip.

There is still one last chance for you to help yourself, Ted, and me in this mess. It will hurt us all if I am no longer able to serve in the church or in the legal field. The executive committee has finally agreed to give me a hearing to see if we can resolve my suspension from ministry. They have McMahon's report. He is the designated church psychiatric examiner, chosen by someone at the national headquarters, and the committee will rely heavily upon his conclusions. It is extremely damaging toward me, and unless some issues are set right, the reaction of the committee toward me could be the same. What they do will affect my ability to work in the future. Positions in the law require background checks, and McMahon's report and conclusions will be discoverable in such a check. He finds me to be a liar when I say that contending with your use of alcohol over the years has led to a breakdown of trust and intimacy between us. He doesn't believe me when I explain that I lost it when Ted was talking to me with the same attitude. With the things you, Ted, Hervey, and others have said about me, he describes me as a seriously disturbed person.

The president of the executive committee is the Reverend Kirby Porter (address and phone number at end of page). If you will write him a brief letter, in an envelope marked "Personal and Confidential," so no one will see it but him, and tell him simply that you have abused alcohol during our marriage, that it is genetic, because your mother and siblings had it, that it has affected our relationship, and that I have always been deeply concerned that Ted would inherit it, I think it would make a difference in how the committee treats me. I am asking you only to tell the truth, briefly, without details, in a short letter, and advise that you intend it for the executive committee only, and not for any other person. The committee members will keep your letter in confidence. They are decent, honorable people who want to do the correct thing. On the basis of what McMahon has said about me, they will probably see their options as few and severe.

Love,
Joe

* * *

Dear Joe,

I have to work tonight chaperoning a big group to a dance, so I don't have much time.

There has not been a channel of information coming from St. John's. The stories about you began spreading after the diocesan convention, and Bishop LaBelle told me who had been talking and to whom they talked. He was very upset and very sorry and apologized to me for it, but it happened. I have had calls from the diocesan office, and I, too, think it is disgraceful and deplorable. This is a family matter and should be private. No one at diocesan convention knew anything we have said here at St. John's, and no one from here knew except Father Hervey, and he says he has shared the information with no one! I have talked again with Dr. McMahon and have written a letter to Mr. Porter at the direction of the diocesan office. I do not care to deal with any of them anymore. Look here for your leaks.

Kate

So she has "written a letter to Mr. Porter," he thought. A big grin spread across his face. He felt like a lost spelunker finally seeing light up ahead. She was going to help him. He knew he could count on her. Her letter, together with Williams's and Casselman's reports, and the testimony of so many people who had known him so well, and some of them for longer than Kate had—going before the committee with all this would surely move them to bring this tragedy to a close. He could try again with Kate, finally see Ted again, return to his parish, and he could sleep again, finally, and begin eating too. He felt euphoria unlike anything he had known since their wedding, or since the night Ted was born. His supporters would be satisfied, and the other people would understand he was not as bad as they thought. If not exactly like a man just released from jail, at least he felt like a prisoner to whom the judge has said, "Be patient. We are going to set you free."

For months the thought of being removed from ministry by his church had kept him close to vomiting. The prospect of the stain spreading to his place in the legal community had been hideous. It would all be resolved. He would be able to put right the harm he had caused.

Chapter Twenty-Three

THE DRIVE TO Minewoods took four hours. They arrived an hour early for the 1:30 p.m. meeting to have lunch and be waiting at the proper place ten minutes early. They could easily imagine Kirby Porter jerking open a door and informing them hastily that they were late and their time would be shortened accordingly.

They entered the cafeteria of the conference center and found the whole executive committee and Porter and Bishop LaBelle crowded around an immense round table, eating lunch. They were enjoying themselves and could be heard throughout the big room. Joe and Jim took a small table at the opposite end and ordered sandwiches. They were the only other customers in the cafeteria, and it was obvious they had been seen when they came in. They waved discreetly and smiled in the committee's direction. Most of them glanced over, and a few smiled back, without interrupting their conversation. None of them looked over again, and Joe and Jim began to go over their presentation one more time. Joe had noticed that two committee members were not at the big table. He considered them both fair and reasonable people, and he hoped they would arrive before one thirty.

At 1:10 p.m., they paid their bill and walked down a long carpeted hall toward the conference meeting rooms. When they entered the big foyer, they found thirty-five members of the Redeemer congregation standing in a group beside a grand piano and some potted fig trees. At the sight of them, the whole group began to applaud and move in their direction. Joe had known all of them for almost ten years, and he had not seen them for three months. He was astonished. They had come to express the parish's support and to make sure the executive committee was aware of it. As Joe greeted each one of them and hugged the children, the diocesan leaders began to stream through the foyer. They were silent and pretended not to notice these representatives of the fourth largest congregation in the diocese. Despite his official banishment, Joe thanked each of them personally for making the long drive and pulled away reluctantly. He followed the committee and Jim down another long hall and into a cramped conference room. LaBelle and Porter had already taken chairs in the far corners. The committee members were settling down at a long table that almost filled the room. Several members were finishing conversations with neighbors, and the long table began to fill up with pocketbooks, shopping bags, and somebody's briefcase. Two of the twelve blue folders, which Jim and Joe had spent nights preparing for the committee, were placed on the table too. The other eight members present appeared to have left theirs at home or in their cars. Joe spoke to each of them who made eye contact and introduced Jim Edelman to everyone in the room. Then he sat down beside Jim at the end of the table, but both of them had to get up again immediately and hold their chairs aside so they could close the door. Kirby Porter glanced quickly at his watch and rose halfway from his chair and announced that the meeting was in session. He thanked everyone for coming "at such short notice" and looked at Joe and Jim and made a motion toward them with his upturned hands as though shoving something in their direction. Then he dropped back into his chair.

Joe asked about the two missing members. Porter said quickly that one of them "could not make it" and that they hadn't heard from the other one but they should go ahead and get started because it was time.

Joe placed their presentation plan on the table between him and Jim where they could both see it. Jim began by thanking them all for agreeing to the meeting as he and Joe took out their bound blue folders. Seeing that they would apparently refer to them in their presentation, one more member produced hers. Joe could tell that Jim was surprised. He inquired politely if everyone had received a copy. Several people nodded, but those who had neglected to bring them offered no explanation.

Joe spoke next, thanking the committee for agreeing to meet with him. He began by saying how ashamed and dreadfully sorry he was for the whole thing. He explained briefly what he had done and then explained the reasons he had acted that way. He emphasized that he was not trying to absolve himself from blame but that he believed the committee would want to know what had led him to do such a thing as slapping his wife. He said he loved Kate and was deeply remorseful for slapping her. Then, for about ten minutes, he gave a chronology of his marriage relationship, the counseling and Al-Anon membership by which he had tried to cope with it, and the specific events that had led up to his losing his temper on the Saturday before Easter.

Jim spoke next, reminding the committee that Joe had nothing to hide and had readily agreed to a psychiatric evaluation. He explained that the church had responded by sending him to a psychoanalyst, a person not qualified to administer the many psychological tests that are a standard part of such an evaluation. Then, carefully referring to pages of the evidentiary file and giving those who were following a chance to find the places, he explained what a psychoanalyst is, how psychoanalysis differs from mainstream psychiatry, and how a psychoanalyst's training, treatment, and wholly subjective methods differ from those of objective, forensic specialists like Williams and Casselman. He gave a synopsis of Dr. McMahon's scathing report, referring to the full copy that each committee member had received and pointing out the open-ended nature of the intense therapy McMahon was recommending. He explained that American insurance companies would not pay for therapy by McMahon or other practitioners like him. He reviewed the vast expense involved and the unfairness to Joe of having to participate in such unnecessary treatment, so far from home, for an unspecified duration, and somehow work at the same time and earn enough to pay for the treatment and other living expenses.

Then he reviewed the many procedures and tests by which Williams and Casselman had come to their independent conclusions that there was nothing wrong with Joe. He referred to the concurring reports of the diocese's own psychologist, Dr. Marshall, and the Reverend Clyde Candler. He referred to the other professionals, too, reading brief passages from their supporting letters, and drew everyone's attention to the dozens of statements from people who had known Joe in all his fields of work. He reiterated Joe's remorse, the number of years through which he had dealt conscientiously with his marital issues, his many accomplishments for the diocese, and his good reputation over the years. He pointed out that Williams and Casselman had submitted reports that recommended Joe be returned to work immediately. He concluded by trying to help the committee understand the difficulties that lay ahead for Joe, his family, and his ministry if he would be forced to comply with Dr. McMahon's extreme recommendations. He thanked them again for their time and concluded his presentation at ten minutes before the conclusion of their hour. Then they offered to answer any questions the committee wished to ask.

No one spoke. The committee members toyed with whatever was on the table in front of them, and the few with blue folders began to flip randomly through the pages. Overhead, a neon light buzzed like a nest of hornets. Joe was shocked at their silence and unwillingness to make eye contact. Years in court and civic meetings had taught him how to control the outward signs of his anxiety. He sat placidly with his hands folded on the table before him, with a slight smile on his face, trying to appear open to questions and conversation as he attempted to read the expressions around the table. Finally, one of the members, whom Joe had never met, one of the two who had brought his folder to the meeting, cleared his throat and looked at Jim.

"Now, that petition you all mentioned? The one his church sent to us? From the Redeemer congregation? Where was that, now, in the blue folder?"

Jim directed him to the table of contents and then to the place in his packet where he found a copy of the petition and its accompanying cover letter.

"Is it true," he asked, "that some vestry members had signed it?"

Jim pointed out patiently the places where the vestry members had signed and the word *vestry* printed after each name. He stated again what he had said in his presentation: every member of the vestry had signed except one. Jim eased his own folder across the table to a woman who had not brought hers and who was carefully avoiding looking at Joe. Joe passed his folder, opened to the petition, to a man seated on his left. Both members bent forward slightly and scrutinized the petition without comment or expression. None of the members went to the trouble of opening the other folders on the table. In the rear of the room, LaBelle, who had stopped making notes as soon as Joe had finished speaking, beheld all this in silence. Kirby Porter stood up and, with a distressed look, pretended to stretch his legs.

As they began their long drive home, Joe and Jim would admit to each other that as they talked, watched the faces, and awaited the anticipated questions, they had felt the same troubling foreboding. Like many lawyers, they could tell when listeners had wandered away. Experience had taught them to identify opposition, boredom, and disbelief in the same way good teachers learn to read their students. Politicians and new preachers who mean to be taken seriously often learn it too. The person who is paying no attention from the beginning, the one whose attention soon lapses, those who fall asleep for a moment, wandering eyes, glances exchanged, posture, frowns— it all speaks powerfully to one with ears to hear. Like students who show up without books or homework, or people who develop a sudden interest in the bulletin during sermons, the committee members were disarmingly candid. They did not shake their watches, but that would have been next. And both speakers got the message.

In the far corners, the bishop and Porter had scribbled notes whenever Joe spoke and exchanged glances during Jim's presentation. Half the committee never made eye contact. One member nodded throughout and quite clearly went to sleep for a minute. Other than the one question about the vestry signatures, no one was curious about anything. They clearly wanted to get on the road toward home. The absent members did not show up, although one called to say he could not come because of "car trouble." Of all times, thought Joe. He had counted on this man's understanding.

Breaking the numbing silence, Jim Edelman had presented a request from Harry Campos to allow Joe to officiate at his small private wedding in the Redeemer chapel. Only family would attend, about ten people, and they lived away and went to other churches. Kirby Porter acknowledged receiving written requests several months before and promised the committee would discuss the matter at its next regular meeting. Joe reminded him politely that the committee would not meet again until late in the following month and that the wedding was scheduled for the coming weekend. Porter was silent for a moment, and the bishop spoke up and said they would have an answer after this meeting ended.

The bishop had not spoken throughout the meeting, although his head had jerked reflexively and he had rolled his eyes several times during Joe's presentation. Now he rose from his chair, Porter leaped to his feet, and at that, everyone began to get up and collect belongings. Joe thanked them all for their attention and consideration, raising his voice to be heard above the conversation and shifting chairs. Then Porter asked them all to sit down again and explained to Joe and Jim that the committee had some private business to consider and thanked the guests for coming. As Jim and Joe reassembled their documents and notes, the small talk interrupted by the meeting recommenced quickly. Several members filed past them on either side and into the hall without speaking, bound for the restrooms. Avoiding each other's eyes and saying nothing, Jim and Joe left the room and walked up the hall to the foyer.

The congregational group, seated in clusters around the foyer, stood up immediately and came over to meet them. Someone rushed to the cafeteria to alert those who were seated there. They hugged and patted Joe and Jim and apparently anticipated some good news. Jim carefully explained that the committee had heard them on all their points, but did not elaborate. They hoped to have an answer soon. No, it would probably not be today. Yes, they had been treated politely. No, the members did not ask a lot of questions.

As he was talking, the committee members emerged single file from the narrow hall and headed toward the main entrance without speaking. The Redeemer group waved to them and called out their thanks for allowing the meeting to take place. Everyone smiled back. The large Redeemer group then drifted from the foyer out onto the wide deserted parking lot and clustered around Joe. He tried to express his gratitude to each one of them for coming to support him, concentrating on being upbeat and reassuring and expressing his confidence that the committee would act "soon." He had no idea what "soon" was but kept his fears to himself. Behind his faithful group, he saw the bishop and Porter come out of the conference building and confer for a moment on the porch. Then they, too, headed for their cars. Jim followed Porter toward his car. Joe approached Bishop LaBelle. At Joe's approach, the bishop's long pale face turned the color of a pickled beet.

"Well, I hope you're satisfied. You've had your meeting."

"Bishop," Joe began, "if this keeps on, my ministry will be—"

"We're trying to *save* your ministry!"

"Then why not accept the opinion of the experts? Why keep this suspension going, this banishment? You have the power—"

"I don't have any power," the bishop almost shouted. Joe could feel a spray of spittle on his face and was alarmed by the man's demeanor. He realized he had made a mistake in approaching him and turned to go away.

"She's no alcoholic!" said the bishop, raising his voice, every lofty inch of him beginning to quiver with anger. "If she *had* been one, you would have taken Ted and left!"

Alarmed, Joe spoke deferentially, maintaining eye contact. "I made vows to her when we married, for better or worse. It's a disease. It runs in her family. People have got it on my side too. Would you leave your wife if she had tuberculosis?" He knew instantly it was a tragic comparison for a man who would never marry, who was gay. Trying to steer beyond it, he said, "And I took vows at ordination—"

"I know what ordination vows are. Did you ever push her down the stairs?"

"What? No!"

"Did you ever say Redeemer was a 'priest killer'?"

"No. Bishop McClenning used those words to *me*!" said Joe, confused and startled. And he had, as a former rector of Redeemer, soon after Joe had gone there to serve. He had met the affable bishop once, at a conference. Had he repeated the bishop's warning to Kate? He could not remember. He could feel his own anger rising and drew upon all his professional tact to remain composed.

"Has the executive committee received a letter from Kate?" he asked.

"I. Certainly. Have! And it would curl the hairs on your head. How could you have treated her—"

"What?"

"Her letter says it all!"

"Bishop, I asked her to write that letter…to tell the truth, hoping it would help you all bring all this to an en—"

"You asked her to?"

"What did she say? May I read it?"

"No!" And the bishop walked off rapidly across the parking lot toward Kirby Porter. From the sight of the two of them talking and the color of the bishop's face and the vigor of his gestures, Joe knew there was trouble, much more trouble, than he had anticipated. He leaned against Jim Edelman's car, clutching his files and notes across his chest and looking at the ground before him. They had come to this meeting with such high hopes. This was supposed to be his chance to clarify things.

The people from Redeemer had gotten into their cars and left, no one wanting to interrupt his conversation with Bishop LaBelle. Later, they would explain to Jim that they feared they had pushed Joe's banishment order too far by showing up and exchanging words with him. They wanted to part company while the bishop and Porter were still able to see them leave without speaking to Joe.

Jim Edelman approached the car with his briefcase in one hand and an armload of files and documents cradled in the other, and he was not happy. He set his files on the hood of the car while he dug into his pocket for his keys. With his elbow, Joe prevented the files from sliding off the car.

"Well, we'll have to tell Harry that the answer is no. You can't do his wedding. Porter would have driven away if I hadn't caught up with him. It's just meanness. They are clearly aware that Harry Campos supports you, with everybody else." Then he thought a moment, shook his head, and said, "*Almost* everybody."

Chapter Twenty-Four

J OE RECEIVED KIRBY Porter's letter on the third day after the meeting in Minewoods. Between his leaving the meeting room and the solemn procession of the committee through the lobby moments later, his word had been weighed and dismissed, the posture of his ministry evaluated, and his character, as far as the church was concerned, weighed and found wanting.

> Dear Joe,
>
> I am writing to you on behalf of the executive committee. The committee has decided to reaffirm its pastoral direction to you. The direction is for you to enter intensive psychotherapy with a therapist of the executive committee's choosing. Dr. McMahon will send us the name, address, and phone number, and we will forward it to you within a week.
>
> We want to reiterate to you the direction's prohibition from pastoral or liturgical functioning by you without the bishop's permission. We also remind you that you are to have no contact with members of the Redeemer congregation. We are concerned that you understand that the pastoral direction is no longer open to debate. You are open to charges if you do not obey it.

The committee takes very seriously all incidents of domestic violence. There have been two specific incidents involving you brought to the attention of the executive committee alleged to be of such a nature. The committee has decided therefore to call on the church attorney to investigate these incidents as potentially chargeable as conduct unbecoming a member of the clergy. We do so to clarify to you and everyone involved that there is a legitimate issue of concern that must be addressed by you and us. This step may lead to a presentment being issued against you and a trial being conducted on this charge.

Porter's letter went on to advise of the appointment under canon law of a "consultant" for Joe, a member of the senior clergy who could advise him on procedure and matters related to the forthcoming investigation. Apparently, someone at their meeting was listening when Jim explained the great costs of psychoanalysis and the refusal of insurance companies to get involved with it, because the committee expressed a desire to be in conversation with you "about the cost of the therapy that has been ordered," in order to assist you financially.

It was clear now where the church was heading. LaBelle and the committee had all the evidence any investigation would uncover: Joe's confession and demonstrated remorse, the testimony of people who had known Kate and him for twenty years, the advice of licensed professionals, and the observations of his parish. People living around Catoctin Springs and in every other place in which Joe had made his home, and his friends going back to the first grade, looked on with dismay at the church's handling of his indiscretion. None of them denied the seriousness of domestic violence, especially Joe. He had spent years prosecuting criminals who had beaten spouses or children senseless, cut them with knives, or inflicted injury and even death with all manner of weapons. It was a hideous plague in society, abhorred by civilized persons everywhere, an offense against the heart of God. Joe knew all this. He was shamed and disgusted by his own part in it, and he had said so plainly. However, it was evident now that an attempt to defend himself or explain anything only incited the anger of the church authorities. But what was a man to do?

No amount of remorse, apologies, or evidence offered in mitigation, professional opinions, or personal testimonies made any difference to LaBelle or Porter or the executive committee under their charge. The opinion and desires of the congregation were discounted. As astonishing as it seemed, Jim and Joe had both concluded that LaBelle, Porter, and the executive committee members either did not understand the meaning of the word *mitigation* or understood it but did not believe that anything could atone for the abomination Joe had committed. It was too early to be certain of such an extreme outcome, but if current actions and attitudes were reliable guides, it was easy to see that the inevitable end would be an ecclesiastical trial. He knew he would be found guilty on his own admission of conduct unbecoming a member of the clergy. His service to God in the church would end, and his integrity would be questioned forever. And apparently, this could be the result even if he submitted himself to McMahon's open-ended plan. After conviction, even if the possibility of continuing on in the church was possible, he knew he would not do so. He would be bound to accept a conviction as God's judgment upon him and his ministry. He would have to begin life again at his age in another profession. It was as possible to serve God in other work as it was in the church. He would find a way. He could teach, perhaps, or manage a homeless shelter.

The actions of the bishop and executive committee left him depressed. The quick decision by Porter and LaBelle in the foyer of the Minewoods center to prevent him from officiating at his friend Harry Campos's marriage filled him with rage. That the church would deny Campos's request after years serving as warden and supporting the diocese in a thousand ways was mean-spirited and cruel, an attack on one of the most decent men Joe would ever know.

McMahon's damned open-ended treatment plan, which the church had accepted with such enthusiasm—that no reasonable person would agree to such a thing, especially with McMahon deciding year by year whether or not enough had been achieved—appeared not to have occurred to the church authorities. They expected obedience to whatever they said, without questions or the need for explanations. Threatened by the slightest sign of resistance, they became angry and vengeful. The fate of an accused cleric, regardless of his record or the circumstances, was unimportant. Provided the offender was not a bishop, discipline and punishment were all that mattered. The canonical legal process and available evidence could be selectively managed and interpreted toward that end, secretly, privately, and in confidence among various authorities. Critical decisions depended upon personality and individual integrity. If a conscientious and objective bishop or executive committee was involved, the system might result in justice. If not, the accused was certain to go down. Joe's downward spiral had begun with the recommendation of some so-called expert at the national church office, a Dr. Bird or Eagle or something, who had advised Bishop Warren Jones to give McMahon's name to Bishop LaBelle, who was now only too happy to do what McMahon said was necessary. Who were these people who so casually proposed to determine his fate, whose knowledge and experience of him were so thorough and correct that they knew what was good for him and his family? What did they know of him or care? McMahon was probably Bird's sister's brother-in-law or played golf with Jones' cousin. How could the church accept Kate's side so readily, without question? Didn't his word, his veracity, mean anything? Why didn't the opinions of so many others count for something?

And what was the right thing to do? He had taken an oath to follow the directions of his superiors. LaBelle was his bishop at this point in his life, and what authority he lacked as an interim was invested in the executive committee. Together they were in ecclesiastical authority over him, and it was his duty to obey them. But what was one to do when all signs pointed to an absence of understanding in them and their determination to accept the directions of a marginally qualified examiner? What was one to make of their apparent dismissal of the conclusions of other experts, their clear reliance on lies and misinformation, and their excessive secrecy in denying him a look at the evidence against him? If he obeyed them and submitted to their plan, he would live the rest of his days with a stain of dishonesty. It would color his integrity. He was glad his father had not lived to see all this. How would he face his mother and sisters and brothers and old friends? How would he ever redeem himself with his son, his beloved son, who now despised him so much that he was in derision, showing his personal letters—according to one of Joe's friends with a daughter at St. John's—to his school friends?

And if he persisted in defending himself against the bishop and committee, he would be condemned anyway. Already they interpreted his efforts to defend himself as impertinence. He would hear over the months how the committee members were bored and annoyed by his insistence on a meeting, his presentation of so much material, his arguments intended to sway them. It was all "nitpicking," they would say, presented in a "cavalier" attitude. Psychiatrist, psychoanalyst, psychologist, psychotherapy, psychoanalysis—what difference did it make? They were all the same, they would tell others. It made no difference at all. He had slapped his wife, an absolutely heinous crime, and now he was trying to get out of it.

* * *

Jim was professional and severe with Joe in demanding that he stop communicating with Kate. Her letter to LaBelle or Porter, which Joe hoped would put his wrongdoing in context for the committee, had done enormous damage. Whatever she had told LaBelle or the committee had confirmed their worst image of Joe. He was unfit for ministry, and his word was no good. It was dangerous to give her anything more to use against him.

This was also the advice of Franklin Ball, the lawyer whom Jim had recommended to represent Joe in his divorce. This very capable young advocate, after his first telephone conversation with Kate's attorney, called Joe immediately and advised him not to contact her again or give her any information to use against him about anything. When Joe brought up the sale of their house, Frank Ball urged him to work through Carl Casey, the realtor, and to communicate with Kate only when absolutely necessary to make decisions in preparation for the sale.

With each new development, Joe's sadness deepened. It was never more painful than when he discovered the defection of friends. In his infinite wisdom Bishop LaBelle had appointed Mary Lake, the diocese's program director, to serve as an adviser for Kate. It was she who had urged Kate to write her poisoned letter to the bishop and committee rather than the truth Joe had pleaded for. LaBelle had asked him if he had pushed Kate down a flight of stairs or thrown things at her. That execrable accusation must have come from her letter, or from a telephone conference, and there was no telling what other hateful false accusations she had made against him. When Kate wrote to Joe that she had written to the bishop after speaking again with McMahon and "on the advice of the diocesan office," it was Mary Lake she was referring to.

Joe had worked closely with Mary Lake for years and had admired her immensely. They could always speak in confidence, and he valued her judgment. She had once run a shelter for abandoned women. She would have served as a good adviser for any other woman, but why had she accepted Labelle's appointment to advise Joe's own wife? And why had LaBelle appointed her, an employee of the diocese who worked in the office next to his and reported to him daily? Where did these people get their ethics? It made him feel almost as bad as Milly's betrayal. He had some insight now into the conversations between "someone" at the diocesan office and the small group at Redeemer who hated him. Mary's feminist position on most issues was well-known. The kind of work she had done, and done so well, in her former career was much admired by Joe and everyone who knew her. She had been his friend and coworker for years, or so it had seemed, and he had felt he could discuss anything with her. He had always thought she viewed him the same way. Was his own judgment so completely faulty? Had her background made her accept Kate's accusations without question, despite her years of knowing him?

There were many people working out their personal agendas in the church. There seemed to be more of them all the time, especially after seminary graduations. The church went to great pains to make room for them and to grant special latitude to the angriest and most radical. In Joe's experience, they did not always become effective parish priests. They sought other types of service after a few years of congregational conflict. The church continued to lose members. It was as much a cultural phenomenon as a crisis of theology and faith. A certain social style, not Christ, had seemed to have determined the complexion of his church's polity for generations.

In his younger days, he was certain that the Holy Spirit acted in the choice of church leaders, moving in hearts and minds, councils and conventions, guiding the body toward truth and right decisions. He still believed it, but his common sense—in which the Spirit could operate as in all other realms—increasingly convinced him it was the exception, not the rule. Those seeking jobs in the church, standing for election as bishop, admitted to seminary, or ordained in most dioceses had to have the sort of political credentials Mary Lake had brought with her. The whole church was moving steadily in a certain direction, jettisoning as it went those whose experience of God was different. He was convinced of the goodness and sincerity of those who dominated the drift, even in their exclusive agendas. He believed they wanted an end to injustice in the world and the establishment of peace. But they were convinced that Christ's will was reflected in their own tactics and timeline and that their vision alone was right for everyone. The form of their determination troubled him more than its content. Once in control, postmodern leaders took every advantage of their latitude in the hierarchical church, manipulating the levers of power to accomplish their agendas while the pews grew increasingly empty and the people did not know the difference between the Hebrew Bible and the New Testament. Leadership had acquired a certain cultural style.

In it all, he had always looked for objective common ground with everyone. Daily consciousness of God's presence, a personal reverent fear and mutual apprehension of the unseen, a belief in Christ's personal companionship on the way had kept the dwindling faithful together more or less, regardless of personality and politics. But the divine seriousness of discipleship had long ago begun to ebb. The fear of God is going, disappearing in an increasingly secular Western worldview, the sort of post-Christian society that flourishes languidly in Western Europe. Faith in God is increasingly a tradition, an old custom rolled out into the light at convenient times to encourage unity and confidence in certain broad moral directions. God is less and less a part of the daily life of individuals. Children grow up with no understanding of the communion of saints, the forgiveness of sins, or the resurrection to eternal life.

He observed it all from his small chaotic corner of existence and wondered, Can the world build on the foundations of the Christian West while no longer honoring Christ in individual lives? Is it not an abandonment of Western civilization's very birthright? Chartres. Cologne. Canterbury. Kazan. Empty. Unreal. And he had had a lifetime of sleepless nights in which to ponder it all.

He wrote to Bishop Warren Jones, asking to speak with him in person. He had known Warren Jones since before ordination and had worked on several projects for him when Jones served as an officer in his former diocese. As Joe saw it, next to his own offense, the emerging issue in his ugly little situation was the use of power in the church hierarchy. Although canon law had a process for clergy discipline, it had been loosely adapted from a code of military justice. In their original setting, such proceedings involved lawyers bound by a code of ethics and professional conduct. Few such safeguards had been adopted with the procedure. Responsibility for decisions made behind closed doors by people with personal stakes in the outcome could be shifted conveniently from one officer to another. "Defendants" in the church might never know who was doing what or whose personal agenda was being advanced. Evidence against a man could be withheld so that offering defenses and explanations became very difficult. Bishops and executive committee chairs and members could change their minds overnight, nullifying promises and assurances without having to account to anyone, as LaBelle had done with Joe and his parishioners at the Redeemer congregational meeting. Joe knew that if he questioned LaBelle on that point, he would be told that the executive committee had decided to open the legal investigation. A query to the committee, especially to Porter, would result in being told the decision lay with the bishop. Both would then tell him no further discussion was possible. And no matter how honorable and fair an investigating lawyer's report might be—and it would be a lawyer, someone licensed to practice law—the decision of how to proceed on it would be returned to the very people who were opposed to him now. He knew all this from his own years as president of the diocesan church court. Such issues had troubled him in those days. When he raised them from time to time, he learned quickly that they were of no interest to anyone else. Nobody claimed to understand what he was talking about. It was like the executive committee when he dared to defend himself, or LaBelle's seeing no inconsistency in refusing to allow him to know the "evidence" against him.

In a telephone call, he appealed for understanding to an executive committee member, a parish priest who had been absent from the Minewoods meeting. This man had talked to him over the years about problems in his own family. Joe had listened patiently each time, called to inquire about him over the months, and kept him continually in his prayers. When Joe called to express concern about how the executive committee was proceeding in his own case, this friend and colleague was not prepared to talk.

"It's better to just let due process take its course, Joe."

"But, Phil! If you all proceed this way, it will lead to—"

"Joe," said his old colleague, interrupting calmly as though they were discussing nothing weightier than weather or a television show, "in this world, I can live next door to someone else for ten years without ever really knowing them. I think we'll just let due process handle it."

There was a pause, during which Joe thought of many things he might have said to this "friend," but he knew he would not be understood. So he thanked him and ended the call. He went to the kitchen window and looked out for a long time, his mind a mess of anguish and anxiety. He was so worried he would not have noticed an elephant romping across the lawn. Due process. His "friend" considered it to be some kind of automatic remedy, a solution with a life of its own, which was grinding into action and was bound to produce justice. Joe knew it to be a series of subjective decisions by people who operate in secret and without constraints. Bishops and executive committees maneuver toward a desired outcome.

He knew from others about how vicious life in the church could become for those who cross, or appear to cross, certain boundaries. He had never believed it, convincing himself that the church functioned with the same integrity and impartiality as the legal system. People of the same quality and honor served in both. And even superior to the law in certain ways, the church was the house of compassion and mercy as well as justice. But he was witnessing the development of something different now, and as reluctant as he was to admit it, his awareness of it was entirely selfish. Because he was threatened with professional and vocational disgrace, he was more inclined to take seriously now what he had formerly resigned himself to leave to others.

It was all this that he longed to discuss with his friend Bishop Jones. But Jones replied in writing that he would not see him until he explained in writing his reason for requesting a visit. He knew this meant that Jones knew he was in trouble and wanted to avoid him. Jones was part of it, after all. Joe knew that he must be truthful in writing to Jones about his desire to see him and that Jones would not see him when he knew the truth. He folded Jones' letter and placed it in his file cabinet.

He telephoned Bishop Spencer's secretary in his former diocese and requested a meeting based on his previous letter. She told him she would call him back with an answer in a day or two.

He met his realtor, and together they went over the house, discussing preparing it for sale.

After talking it over with Jim Edelman, Joe wrote to Dr. McMahon and demanded copies of all notes and other documents created by him during his evaluation. Dr. McMahon did not respond. Joe wrote to him a second time. He was used to this. Several months before, he had to write to McMahon several times to make him release copies of his notes and report to Dr. Williams and Dr. Casselman. Finally, Dr. McMahon left a message for him advising he had discussed the matter with Bishop LaBelle and he and the bishop had determined that the notes were rightfully the property of the diocese, as the diocese had paid for the evaluation. Joe had heard this argument before. He replied to McMahon in writing, with a copy to Jim and Frank Ball, citing appropriate sections of Federal and state law and reminding the doctor that failure to provide such records within twenty-one days of request would subject him to liability for actual damages.

He began to work on the house in hopes of an early sale, following his realtor's advice and checking off the jobs, small and large, on his list over the weeks. It was not a large house, but a very nice one. They had been able to afford it because the costs of housing had turned out to be two-thirds of what it was in other states. He had loved this house and, over the years, had come to know its every corner and peculiarity. He could read its night noises and predict its needs, and he knew every bush and blade of grass that surrounded it. It had been their home, the place where they had celebrated Christmas—the thought of the thoughtless Christmas morning routine made him wince—and birthdays, tended Ted when he was sick, entertained friends occasionally, and laughed, cried, and dreamed. He would have loved most anywhere the three of them had lived together. The lawn was much too large, but the price had been right and the school district a good placement for Ted. A former owner had spent a few years and a fortune planting rhododendrons, forsythia, and hedges and then moved away, leaving the upkeep to somebody else.

Joe cleaned and trimmed a small patio and fountain behind the house. He and Kate had never wanted to use it, and over the years, it had become a small jungle. He trimmed out all the dead limbs in a dozen trees around the lawn and spent a day clipping the hedges and boxwoods. It was work he had been unable to find time for since the previous year, and he had just gotten to it when he lost his temper and lost his family on the day before Easter. He weeded carefully all around the house and the various planted islands scattered about the property. His back hurt for days.

Indoors, he did his best with the clutter, carefully saving every article of Kate's and placing them in closets and drawers and boxes in as much order as possible. This alone required days of attention. He cleaned and straightened Ted's room, experiencing the most unspeakable depression as he arranged his shoes and clothing in his closet, dusted his desk and shelf, and changed his bed. He cleaned all the bathrooms and washed the floors. He washed, ironed, and replaced the curtains throughout the house. Kate had made some of them herself, and he had to stop and work outside for a while in order to continue. Cory, always happily attentive, was especially solicitous at such times, as though he knew Joe was grieving.

There were some jobs he could not do himself. He arranged for a carpenter to replace the lower plinths on either side of the front door that, despite Cory's presence, the groundhogs had managed to gnaw like lions at a kill. As the repairman, when he finally appeared, saw to the woodwork, Joe sealed the latest groundhog hole beneath the front porch, stuffing bags of dog hair clippings deep into the burrow with a hoe handle and shoveling in rocks and soil on top of it. He did not like to use poison with Cory nosing around. Another repairman was needed to replace the garage door opener, which had ceased working several years before. He had always intended to get around to it, like so many other things.

He painted, trimmed, straightened, cleaned, polished, and for the thousandth time, put the garage in order. It was easier this time, since Kate had not been around for months to rearrange everything, searching in irritation as she did at intervals for things they had discarded years before. Yet he would have gladly straightened it up every day if she would only come back. And there was always grass to mow, several acres of it, and it grew luxuriantly during the warm months in rainstorms that followed along the river.

Preparing the place for sale was expensive. For four months, he had been paying all the household expenses, car payments, insurance, quarterly taxes, and now two hundred dollars per month as temporary spousal support, and all from his salary alone. Kate kept her salary to herself and occasionally requested money for this or that in writing, usually for something Ted needed. He always sent it. But his salary alone now was inadequate to cover all these expenses, and he had to resort to their savings account and to a small amount they had invested in treasury bonds. There would have been more of a

financial cushion if the past had been different. Running two households and being unable to work together toward a financial future
had left them with what he was managing now.

Each time he wrote a check to pay a bill, he felt worse and
worse that Redeemer was still providing him a salary. The vestry was
also paying retired clergymen to conduct services on Sundays. The
parish would not even consider cutting off his salary or benefits, a
lifesaving blessing in his current circumstances. It made him sick to
take the checks and depressed him to deposit them, but he had no
choice. With his career on hold and expenses mounting, he would
have been bankrupt in weeks had the good people of Redeemer not
supported him. So he gave thanks for them each morning and night
and resolved solemnly to do all in his power to bring the whole tragedy to a close as soon as possible for everyone.

Occasionally, he wrote to Kate about the house, scrupulously
careful not to say anything more except to ask about Ted. Kate
responded occasionally, sometimes answering his questions about the
sale of the house or certain bills and expenses. She would give him no
information about Ted.

He proposed to Kate that they meet and discuss the contents of
the house in order to divide them. He contacted several good friends,
husbands and wives whom Kate had always seemed to like, and got
their permission to meet in their homes with them present. Kate
would not reply to such suggestions. At last he drew a plan in black
ink of both floors of the house, carefully sketching in every piece of
furniture. Then he wrote Kate's name in red pencil over everything
she had brought into the marriage or had particularly liked when
they had acquired it together. He did the same with his name, in
green ink. He tried to be fair, giving her the kitchen Hoosier, living
room furniture, and dining room furniture, and assigning to himself
the dining room table, den sofas, and the oriental rugs, which she
had never liked. He divided the beds. At the foot of one of the pages,
he explained that he would divide the pictures on the walls too, giving her the ones she had ever mentioned liking and keeping for himself the hunt and wildlife prints that had never interested her. When
the plans were complete, he mailed the big sheets of paper to her,

asking whether she agreed with the distribution and inviting her to change what she wanted to change. He knew he might not receive a response and began to resign himself to the dreadful process of dividing their possessions through their attorneys. To his astonishment, she returned the plans ten days later, thanking him and saying the division suited her. She carefully noted the single item he had failed to mark, an inexpensive deacon's bench that stood against the dining room wall, and said that she wanted it. He wrote back and agreed.

He received a letter from Kirby Porter stating that he was "directed immediately to enter intensive psychotherapy"—how Porter relished that phrase! "With Dr. John Zander, the therapist with whom we are directing you to do the therapy previously ordered," and it provided Dr. Zander's address and telephone number. It came as no surprise to either him or Jim Edelman that Dr. Zander's profile appeared on the same web page as McMahon's or that his qualifications were similar. They considered approaching LaBelle and the executive committee again, reminding them that standard professional procedure called for presenting several names as referrals, allowing the patient to make a choice. But they knew that the response would be swift and harsh and their raising the issue seen as "nitpicking" and a further effort to avoid following orders. He anticipated that the bishop and committee members, who did not understand the difference between a psychoanalyst and a psychologist and disliked anyone trying to explain it to them, were equally unlikely to understand standard professional procedures. So Joe called Dr. Zander and left a brief message, explaining who he was and why he was calling and providing his telephone number.

Had Joe been asked to recall the worst days in his life, several would have come quickly to mind. He recalled the night his father died and the deaths of his grandmothers while he was still quite young. There was his failure in law school to pass his constitutional law course by a quarter of a grade point and the resulting loss of his vital scholarship, the time he believed he had failed to pass the state bar examination, and encountering Kate's rage for the first time after their marriage. He would have described the day he had to take Ted out of an intoxicated Kate's car on the drive back from Wicomico and the day he discovered she had been lying to him for months and had never attended counseling. Because she would not discuss these events and others almost as disturbing to him, he had felt beaten down by them, sick with anxiety and doubt, disoriented in his anguish and loss as to what to do next. He felt useless and hopeless before the monolithic wall of her denial. Each time he had prayed for guidance and prayed that their life together would become saner, healthier. But bad days continued to happen. At times it seemed there would never be an end to them. So he had some preparation in his background when early one evening he came in from the mailbox with the thick brown envelope bearing the return address of Dr. McMahon. He sat down at the same kitchen table where so many important occasions had transpired and calmly, professionally began an objective review of the written record of the church's expert.

He began to read the barely legible copies of the doctor's notes, scribbled in difficult longhand on legal pads. Kate had told McMahon she was not an alcoholic. She said her mother was not an alcoholic. Neither of them drank alcohol and had been brought up as good Baptists and were naturally opposed to it. According to Kate, Joe thought that everybody is an alcoholic. He had no empathy with her and was forever trying to control the things she did. Joe would never discuss anything with her. He was controlling with all his family members. McMahon must have mentioned the intervention with the Gallaghers to her after all, because Kate denied it had ever happened. Joe was making it all up. Kate told him at one point she had gone to a counselor for a year trying to learn how to deal with Joe. Joe would never give her any money. He was hard on her and Ted, and especially on her defenseless mother, whom she had always tried to protect. She had pleaded with Joe to allow Catherine to live in the house with them. Joe had always been unwilling to support her in caring for the house in Wicomico, the place she loved.

According to McMahon's notes, Ted had said, "Don't trust him." Ted claimed he would not ask his friends to come to the house because they did not like Joe. Joe was always acting, never genuine. On one occasion, Joe had made him watch a movie or movies—the handwriting was not clear, and he could not be sure—that made Ted

LOVERS IN A SMALL CAFÉ

feel "uncomfortable." Ted told him that Joe ignored him, would not listen to him, and that on the day before Easter, Joe hit him with his fist, not with a sweatshirt. Ted complained that Joe would invite people to the house for dinner. "And Mom would have to cook all the food." While Ted was in middle school, Joe had "gone to Europe with a bunch of priests"—Joe figured Ted must be referring to his precious ten-day sabbatical—and left Kate and him at home to fend for themselves. On youth group outings, Joe paid more attention to the girls than boys, and when he took the young people swimming in indoor pools during the winter, he actually got into the pool and played with them. Joe kept the checkbook with him and would not leave it where Kate could find it, and at times, his mother had to ask for it. Sometimes Joe's old girlfriends called the house, and it upset Kate. One of them invited his parents to parties and his mother did not want to go. She had to work. Joe was insincere; he would never spend the summers with them in Wicomico, making Kate do all the work there. Instead of sitting with Kate and the other mothers at his soccer games, Joe waked along the sidelines, watching him, making him feel self-conscious. His mother worked all day teaching school and worked harder than Joe did. Joe didn't do much and he had a lot of free time, and Kate didn't.

And each of them had given other examples of his worthlessness and unfairness, with Ted's comments sounding strangely like his mother's, even with the same familiar phrasing in some cases. It was all he could do to read them.

Father Hervey had advised that Joe was not a big part of Ted's life. Joe refused to attend his faculty parties and ignored him when they encountered each other at athletic events, refusing to speak to him. Joe preferred to walk around the sidelines rather than keep Kate company at Ted's games. According to the Reverend Dr. Hervey, Joe constituted a danger to Kate and Ted. He had even gone with her to the police on one occasion.

There were some brief notes of conversations with Clyde Candler, his marriage counselor, and his spiritual adviser, Lewis Batterton, but with none of the sickening content of what had gone before.

He was stunned to find that McMahon had interviewed Tom Downes, the former second warden in the parish. Downes must have been the one described by McMahon in his report as someone "to whom Bishop LaBelle had referred as a man who liked Father Stephenson and who could give a fair and balanced description of his work in the parish." Downes advised McMahon that half the Redeemer congregation liked Joe and the other half did not, that Joe favored sick and troubled parishioners over healthy people, and girls over boys. Many people had left the parish in anger at him. According to Downes, Joe was good with "people in crisis" and ignored "regular, healthy people." He told McMahon that Joe failed to keep appointments and that when he got busy with emergencies or other "crisis situations," Joe "just let everything else go." Downes related that someone had even told him that Joe had referred to an ill parishioner as "an old drunk."

To Joe's amazement, McMahon's notes included a copy of a religion column Joe had written for the local newspaper the previous year about horrific suffering among people of the Nuba Mountains in Sudan and how the international community was refusing to intervene out of respect for the Sudanese authorities. The column about this humanitarian crisis had been sent to the church's examiner by Downes apparently to illustrate Joe's gloomy personality. Across the top of the clipping was written "This seems really dark and grim. Thought it might interest you. T. D." Having been the recipient over the years of dozens of anxious notes from Downes, Joe recognized the handwriting without difficulty.

From what he could discern from McMahon's poorly reproduced, handwritten, sketchy notes and the brief marginal notations on a few of the pages, their contents had been related to LaBelle by telephone on several occasions. Their conversations together had not been recorded, neither were LaBelle's responses to what McMahon told him, but it was clear that they had conferred. A copy of the scathing final report was also included with the notes, but Joe felt he could not re-read it again, at least at this moment.

He stood up abruptly and walked to the front door and out onto the lawn in the warm summer night. The lights of his neighbors' houses gleamed in the twilight through their enclosures of ornamental trees and the screens of white pines that crisscrossed the neighborhood. He could see or hear no one, and there were no evening dog-walkers or vehicles on the distant street. Satisfied as much as he had time to be, he bent over, with his right hand on the trunk of a dogwood tree and the other hand braced on his left knee, and regurgitated mightily onto the grass. His innards lurched upward and forward in spasms, and he vomited again and again and he continued until not even spittle would come. He remained bent over, his eyes watering and his nose running, and he kept spitting, trying to rid himself of the sharp, sour taste in his mouth. He remained in that position for a while. Then he let go of the dogwood and drew a white handkerchief from his hip pocket and wiped his face and blew his nose. He straightened up and folded the soiled handkerchief into a wad and rammed it absently into his pants pocket. He became conscious of a noise behind him and turned halfway around. He walked a few steps to where Cory lay on the grass, whimpering. When he bent down, the alarmed dog emitted a weak yelp and turned his round stomach upward. Joe patted him and tried to say something, and Cory twisted about so he could lick his hand. After a few minutes, Joe led him around the house to the faucet near the garage door and ran fresh water into his bowl. He drank copiously from the hose while Cory lapped up his own cool water. Joe filled his bowl again and then filled a white plastic utility bucket he used on fishing trips. Together they returned to the scene of the sickness, and Joe splashed the lawn, where whitish patches were visible in the darkness, until the big bucket was empty.

He went inside and returned in a moment with a cigar, a cutter, and a box of kitchen matches. Seeing what he had, Cory led the way around the house to their sheltered place beneath a massive white pine where the ground was an inch deep in brown needles. Under the majestic tree, a rickety folding chair and small wooden bench faced out over the rolling lawn. On the bench glistened a chipped crystal ashtray, which Kate had used for scented potpourri and which Joe had recently returned to its original function. He sat down and placed the cigar and matches on the bench and forgot about them immediately.

He had been patient and faithful with Kate and stuck by her through chaos that would have driven other men away, but as between the two of them, he was the one who could have changed. He had tried, God knew, but he had not changed enough. He had loved them both and struggled daily to keep their family healthy and happy, tending to necessary matters that were beyond Kate's experience and which Ted had been too young to understand. But it had made no difference, and he had failed. He had allowed the church to jerk him around in the same way many attorneys relieve the anxiety of practice by devoting more and more time to the law, like a man trying to satisfy an increasingly demanding mistress. He had neglected his beloved son. He should have known better. It had been very hard shepherding a parish as large as Redeemer, one of the largest in the diocese, without an assistant. The clergy of other such parishes had assistants. He had done his best to avoid the role of peacemonger and had never, ever believed in peace at any price. But his time and energy had been poorly apportioned, and he saw now that Ted had suffered.

He should have left the church years before and taken a job as a teacher or run a business maybe. God would have been the first to understand. He made his vows to Kate before making them to the church. It would have given him more time with his wife and son, weekends to go places and do things. But he had hung in, and now his loved ones were gone.

He should have let Kate have her way and do what she wanted to do with her salary, and managed family needs on his own. Broken promises and broken trust and temper tantrums should have made no difference to him. He should have been more patient, kinder, less cautious about what she might do, or worried about what she had done. He should have been more forgiving, more willing to try again and forgive each and every disappointment. He had tried to live that way, but he had succeeded only a little.

He knew now where she had been all those hours, the night she thundered down the stairs and began to talk about Ted and what

Ted thought of him and he had slapped her. She had gone to Hervey, and together they had gone to the police. He knew the procedure. The police had taken her statement—he could imagine what she had said—and probably photographed her. He began to consider her relationship with Hervey. He knew from what she had told him over the years, and the one time she showed him the letter of reprimand, that her temper and tongue had gotten her into trouble at St. John's. She had deflected blame and explained her behavior by blaming it on him and how difficult he made life for her at home. Whom had she talked to? Hervey, certainly, and the chaplain and the academic dean, whom she disliked so. Was this the reason she would never invite them or others to the house for dinner?

But no, it was nobody else's fault. He was the one. Not the deceitful LaBelle, not Porter with his merciless ambition and pride, not the naive, self-absorbed Hervey, not even the mean-spirited Lottie Bascomb and her coterie. None of this had originated with the thoughtless sheep of the executive committee. None of them or anybody else had set the present troubles in motion, none of them had done what he had done, and not one of them was responsible. He had unleashed it all with a slap, an indiscretion that originated in years of failure to get things right. If he had handled it better, been wiser and easier, none of it would have happened. He had only himself to blame, and no unfortunate aspect of anybody else's personality had caused it. He was at fault.

It was not the guilt and remorse churning within that had made him physically ill, or his treatment by anyone aligned against him, however misguided or unjustified. At this moment, none of it powered the chaos roaring in his head. His nausea came of knowing what his wife and son thought of him. They had presented a disgraceful image of a man and stamped it with his name. And more terrible than *what* they said was *that* they had said it at all, those terrible things, his own wife and son, the people for whom he had lived his life. The thought of it made his insides churn once more, and he bent forward in his chair and faced the earth again. But his heaving brought only tears. There was nothing else left.

He stood up in the dark and felt like screaming. He thought briefly of loading his shotgun and eating it, splattering his foul, god-damned brains across the wretched ground. An image of his mother's face emerged from his grief, and he instantly rejected such a cowardly course. When he closed his eyes, he saw Ted at two, five, ten—the light of his life, age after age, the one he sought to protect. The one who spent so much time with Kate. Kate. He saw her laughing, cry-ing, sleeping, sunning herself at Wicomico, nursing Ted as a baby, and the tears flowed again. She was his wife. He had loved her. He knew there had been love in her for him, too, along the way. He was sure of it. It must have been true.

Kate. Since the early dreadful years of their marriage, before Ted was born, he had been presented with weekly, sometimes daily, evidence that lying was part of her personality, a defense mechanism with which she deflected criticism and avoided responsibility, a shield that routinely prevented her from having to live the consequences of her own behavior. He had never wanted to believe it and had rejected the evidence for years, telling himself he was wrong, that he mis-interpreted her, he didn't remember correctly, he was confused. He ignored the evidence and spoke to her about her "selective honesty." And now the most extreme example of it had kicked him in the stomach. "She lies! Oh! She lies all the time!" he recalled Kate saying a hundred times about Catherine, whose path and personality she was following in life, although she would never comprehend it. How could she do it? She would do anything, say anything, manipulate anybody to prevent the world from seeing that she was not perfect. And this determination extended to destroying her husband's repu-tation and ruining his career.

He had long ago learned to release himself from feeling responsi-ble for her behavior. And as Ted had grown more mature and learned to take care of himself, Joe had stopped worrying that Kate would injure him in an automobile accident or some other tipsy catastro-phe. The older Ted grew, the more careful Kate became in hiding certain things from him. Physical harm can be cured. The bending of a personality is harder to cure. He had left Ted in her company, and her influence had shown itself increasingly in his life. He had never imagined it would result in this. Ted. Yes, he was young, he did not know the truth, and he was completely devoted to Kate, and had been so since infancy. He had loved Joe, but his regard for Kate had always been powerful, and almost everyone who knew them could tell. And Joe had left him with Kate summer after summer in Wicomico, and time after time all year round as he traveled for the church to meeting after faraway meeting—where nothing of enduring value was accomplished and no one recalled six months later what was said or done. Ted's soccer games away from home always occurred on Saturdays and Sundays, so that Joe could not go with them. He had raised money for Ted's teams, negotiated the use of practice fields for them, and worked with the coaches in a dozen executive ways. But Kate had been the one to drop him off at practice and pick him up, chaperone the weekend trips, and drive him here and there. And when he became a student at St. John's, he rode to school with her every day and back home again. And the growth of it all in Ted's personality was clear to him now, as it should have been on the night before Easter Sunday, when suddenly he sounded exactly like his mother.

But how could Ted say such things? What hateful thing had Joe done to him? Or to Kate? Joe knew himself to be a sinner. He had made his mistakes in life and was not perfect or especially intelligent or gifted, only an average man trying to do right. But the things they had said about him cut to the heart of his character: he was insincere, "Don't trust him," and over and over by implication, he was a liar. His wife and son.

He stared into the darkness. Had it been light, he could have seen little for his tears. They were slow and idle, coming from an unknown place too deep for sobbing, something to do with his mind and heart, cleansing out what remained of dignity and stamina. Something had happened within, and the tears fell in silence. His anguish was overwhelming. Informed by his own mysterious perception, in the darkness, Cory sensed his friend's despair and silently inched toward him until he could rest his chin on the top of Joe's shoe.

Joe would never be the same again, although he was too distracted to know it.

He sat down and, for a long time, repeated the Jesus Prayer over and over. He had used it since learning it in college, throughout his teaching, his years of legal practice, and now throughout his ordained years, twenty, fifty, a hundred times a day. *Jesus Christ, Son of God, have mercy on me, a sinner.* Repeated over and over, calming the surface of his mind and soothing its depths, it called down upon him the divine cosmic attention and claimed the truth of what he was before its awful majesty, while he still had time.

Chapter Twenty-Five

H
E SAT UNDER the great tree all night, poring over his married life like a searcher picking up shells on a stormy beach. He slept for a few minutes every hour or so, jerking awake each time as another scene began, another conversation or argument, another incident or milestone in Ted's childhood, something, anything, everything he had said and done. Cory slept at his feet, waking occasionally to look over his shoulder at him and sigh. When day began and the first silent jogger appeared in the blue light on the road, he got up and peed under a moist rhododendron. As he was zipping up his fly, his knowledge of God matured in a single perceptive flash, and he froze. In an inexplicable flashback, he could hear his fourth-grade teacher saying, "God will come to us when we least expect Him." Instantly, the voices of his young parents followed, reminding him that "a smart person learns something new every day."

A few months before, as the reaction to his mistake began to churn, he had prayed to God about the recurrent pain in his side. He could not manage everything at once, he had told Christ. He had pleaded for relief, hoping he did not sound like Kate demanding that someone, or life in general, give her a break. Maybe relieving himself had made him consider relief in general. Whatever the connection might be, if there was one at all, he understood suddenly that his prayer had been answered. For some time now, he was not certain for how long, he had been free of the internal pain that had plagued his life for years. He realized he could not remember the pain since he and Jim had begun to prepare to meet the executive committee. He had not had to lie down in the dark or get by on a liquid diet or fill his standard prescription for pain pills. His behavior had stirred up so many terrible things, all of them so distracting, that his attacks had subsided, and he had not noticed until now. Like a man in a lifeboat with a broken leg, he had focused his whole attention upon the sharks. His ulcerative colitis had ceased, and he had not even noticed it.

He sat down again and stared across the brightening lawn. Cory ran off into the grass and soon returned with wet paws and tail feathers, twisting about and smiling, as though he, too, understood. Joe put his hands over his eyes and pondered the miracle that had slipped by him—after all the years of dealing with the pain. Like an attentive nurse in the night, the Holy Spirit had come to him with healing when he needed it most, whether he realized it or not. How could it have happened, after so many years of trouble, without his knowing it instantly?

He put his hand tentatively to his side and pressed but felt no inner burning. What was going on? But he knew what was happening. God had answered his prayer, eased him off a chronic trouble as his life was falling apart, giving him strength to face what was happening. As weary as he was, drained of mental energy and filled with sorrow from the preceding night, he stood up in the gathering light with a smile and stretched vigorously. Now, of all times in his trivial existence, he looked like a man who had just been handed a fabulous, unexpected gift.

He went inside and began to celebrate by making coffee. He did not drink it on an empty stomach, and he put some whole wheat bread into the toaster oven. In the pantry, he found a jar of damson preserves his mother had given him before Easter. He paused every few minutes to press his side, in case it had been his imagination and not God after all. Each time he felt no pain, and his mood lifted even more. As water began to stir in the kettle, he set out his old French press and took the Café Du Monde and skim milk from the refrigerator. He thought briefly how good it would be to share the news with Kate, who was always at her most cheerful and easygoing in the early morning. It was the stirring of the part of him that had always wanted to try again, but instantly there came an image of her and Hervey hurrying into the police station to report him. After all the years of faithfulness and effort with her, she had gone to the police. The time for talking had ended then, although he had not known it at that time.

The phone rang for the first time that day. The calls were down to about a dozen per day, about half of what they were when everything began. With thoughts of Kate fresh on his mind and in the excited wonder of his miracle, he answered reflexively, remembering the executive committee as soon as he said hello.

He heard the lively, encouraging voice of Harry Campos calling to check on him and to see if he needed anything. If the Lord himself had called him, it would not have made him happier than speaking now with this decent, honorable, universally admired man. He told Harry his good news, old news, but new to him within the past hour, and they talked it over for a while. In all his years as the state's chief pharmacist and faithful steward for the church, Harry had never expected such a thing. He was moved by what Joe told him, and Joe could hear it in his voice. They talked on about many things, spending a while on the Redskins, Cowboys, and Seahawks. Harry had met Joe Namath at a party in the metro area, and they reminisced about him and the Jets for a few minutes. They traded a few jokes. Before he hung up, Harry reminded him that he had been neglecting his friends at the Third Base.

"Rita was in here to fill a prescription yesterday, and she said everybody misses you. They know you're going through a hard time. I told her you were all tied up like the rest of us in trying to straighten this thing out. She wanted to know if there was anything that she and everybody could do. She says they talk about you all the time. Everybody wants to know the latest. She says they all have certain interesting ideas about how you can deal with the diocese on this thing."

"I would really like to hear those conversations. How do you know Rita?" Harry knew everybody.

"Known her all my life. We grew up together on Faulkner Street. She lived down on the corner, where Pennsylvania Avenue crosses. Nine children. We all played ball together. She told me to tell you your Third Base buddies miss you and to come by and see them. Hell, you won't run into any parishioners in the Third Base, Joe. Not the damn executive committee either. You got to get out sometime, talk to somebody. Raymond says everything for you is on the house from now on. You ought to go on in there and let him fix you a big drink."

"Things are bad enough, Harry, without having certain people report to the executive committee that I'm hanging out at a local bar."

"Private club, we like to say," said Harry.

"I can hear LaBelle and Porter and that bunch now."

"Aw, go on in to see them, Joe. They're the people that keep the county running—working on the farms, keeping the sewers going and the snow plowed and all. It would do Porter and his little committee good to meet some real people like that. You got to be a human being."

"Well…"

"Well, nothing. You go on by. Don't neglect your friends. They miss you. Rita says they've saved up all their religious questions till you come back. And I guess you won't need a refill on that pain medicine. You know, these miracles are hard on us pharmacists."

They said goodbye and hung up. He filled his coffee cup and poured the rest of the coffee into an old thermos bottle and twisted on the top. He sat down at his place at the table. Miracles. He was a blessed man. And it was not only his medical condition. At the time he needed help most sorely, Jim Edelman had stepped in. He hadn't asked him, and he couldn't pay him, and he knew Jim would have refused payment anyway. He was leading Joe's defense because he loved the church and he respected Joe, but basically because he was an honorable man who was appalled by what was happening. Jim was another answer to his prayers. And so, too, were Harry Campos, Amanda, and the good people on the vestry, and the great majority of parishioners who called and wrote to him and left food at his door. It was the same with his old friends from everywhere he had ever lived and every professional position he had held.

They all knew what was going on and were in touch with him, encouraging him and comforting him in a hundred ways. Many of them had written the diocese in protest. A few of his neighbors were avoiding him, but many of the people in his neighborhood were coming by regularly to see what they could do to help. People who recognized him from the small photograph that accompanied his newspaper columns came up to him in the grocery stores and gas stations and told him how sorry they were and asked when he would begin to write again. He was a blessed man, and he had almost always known it, and he expressed his thanks for it daily and simply. However this crisis might end, he was prepared to thank all the good people through whom God was showing his love.

God's care continued to come in unexpected ways, including through the church. Although most of the clergy would not come near him, one of the colleagues he most wanted to see was suddenly appointed by the interim bishop to serve as his "adviser." LaBelle's motives and sincerity might have been questioned in his appointment of Kate's adviser, but his appointment of Bill Saunders to work with Joe could not have been more welcomed. The Reverend William Nance Saunders was about Joe's age but had been continuously in the diocese longer than any other priest. He was much more experienced than Joe and had been at the center of diocesan leadership throughout his career. His wife was a teacher, and their son the same age as Ted. Joe had respected Saunders since their first meeting when he was new at Redeemer, and he valued his judgment. It was Saunders who began to talk with Jim and Joe immediately about the coming of the new bishop.

During the past three months, Joe's faith in the interim bishop and executive committee had bottomed out. They were obviously people who did not know what they were doing. He had been raised to respect authority, an attitude reinforced in his church, public schools, and native society. The concept of authority had been constructive in his maturity, and of it he had a view that it was benign and generally fair. He had found that most adults fit this pattern, and often the older they were, the more they dispensed authority with good judgment and common sense. There were bullies around throughout his growing up, but they were exceptions, largely older boys and one or two girls, who made the teachers and clergy and neighbors seem especially better by contrast. He had respected his professors, judges, other lawyers, police officers, clergy, and the rest of them, not with servility and disdain, but with as much understanding as he could muster up. So he had regarded the diocesan authorities over him in the same way. But there was another reason too.

McMahon's evaluation of him had been a massive surprise to everyone except, perhaps, Kate, who knew or should have known how her lies would affect the final evaluation of him. Joe understood the diocesan authorities' confusion and concern, but he had believed that the reports of Marjorie Williams, Jacob Casselman, Timothy Marshall, Clyde Candler, Lou Batterton, and Amanda Leffler would clarify for them that he was a sane, responsible man who had lost his temper after years of marital trouble.

Joe's expectations were based, however, upon the models of evidence and common sense brought to problem-solving in the law. That these models prevailed in much of society in a democracy, he was very willing to believe. It was becoming clear to him that they did not prevail in the current leadership of his diocese, and perhaps throughout the whole church. Something operating in the structure caused them all to grow more severe with each effort he made to defend himself. There were many enmeshed relationships and secret lines of communication and so many people privy to information and second-guessing him and his good friend Jim that order and reason were slipping away.

There was no judge to maintain the situation on an even course, no one to temper law with justice and common sense. Rules existed, but they were unsatisfactory. The truth disappeared quickly in decisions made in secret by people who talked to one another casually and traded opinions and hearsay. Joe was obstinate and rebellious when he tried to defend himself. It appeared that the bishop and Porter were determined to have a trial and settle it all that way, and their committee was glad to go along. The damage had already been done to Joe's credibility and professional standing, and except for his parishioners and friends, nobody seemed to care.

The congregation at Redeemer was incensed and suffering. His mother and siblings were sunk in depression over his broken marriage and the danger to his vocation. He was running out of money and trying to cover all expenses on his modest salary alone. And all the time the nasty accusations and gloating raced from Catoctin Springs to St. John's School to the diocesan office and back again. Hopefully, his civil lawyer's strong letter had chilled the behavior of Lottie Bascomb and her circle, although it was too early to tell.

He recognized that he saw the whole sorry mess in a unique way. His view was shared by Jim and Harry Campos and some of the other professional people in his parish and the professionals among his friends. He was still capable of evaluating the future with the realism and discrimination of a trial attorney. He had managed difficult situations and people for years, and his experience supported him now as he assessed his own troubles. Perhaps the ordeals of the past had been more of God's gifts to him, preparing him for the loss of Kate, Ted, his friends, his home, and his job all at once. The experiences of his past, whatever their nature, and his diversified education allowed him to predict a range of likely outcomes in the present tragedy.

Now that the bishop and executive committee were opening an investigation toward charging him, he knew a trial was a certainty. Regardless of what an investigation showed or what a legal investigator recommended, the diocese had made its intentions clear. These same authorities would decide in the end whether to put him on trial. Since Joe and Jim had already given them all the information an investigation would uncover, and based upon it they were nevertheless opening an official investigation, he could see what lay ahead. A trial would be conducted by members of the same extended "family" of diocesan leaders who were now determined to investigate him. He could imagine the odds that the bookies at Bowie and Saratoga would offer on a conviction.

He believed that in other dioceses, the bishops would have called him in, together with Kate, talked sternly to him, and urged them both to see a marriage counselor in hopes that reconciliation was possible. This might have been possible in his situation early on, before McMahon. A private argument or family fight between spouses in the sanctuary of their own home would never be raised to the level of diocesan inquiry in other dioceses. But LaBelle was not that kind of bishop. And Kate's boss, who had never been married or served as a parish priest and who worked as a businessman, had doomed any possibility of reconciliation from the start. Knowing Hervey was an artless, unworldly man in many ways, Joe was shocked by his actions but it came as no surprise to the wider community. Everyone speculated whether Hervey would have scurried to the police and the bishop if the culprit had been somebody other than Joe, a school board member perhaps, or a wealthy parent. In most other dioceses, a climber like Porter would have risen to the presidency of the executive committee but the members themselves might not have been so willing to damage a priest's credibility for the rest of time. He wondered whether, in other denominations, the national leadership would have sent him to a psychoanalyst, or gone along with an indeterminate scheme of treatment, or left his fate to the sole discretion of people who did not know what they were doing. However all these people behaved, and whatever their motivation turned out to be, the bitterest realization of all was the knowledge that his own behavior had brought it all about.

To have on his record a conviction for conduct unbecoming a clergyman would be abominable. To an average reasonable man and woman, it implied dishonesty, a failure of integrity, an abandonment of a man's vows. He had served the church decently and humbly, without ambition and with integrity. He knew he had committed a deplorable act in slapping Kate, but it had been a mistake, out of character, and wholly unlike the years of faithfulness he had maintained in the face of relentless domestic difficulty. He did not deserve the ruin of his reputation.

When Bill Saunders began to talk about the new bishop, Joe listened with care.

* * *

The church's investigating attorney was a member of another denomination and had no connection with the diocese. He was retained for the specific purpose of investigating Joe and submitting a report to the bishop and executive committee. Jim Edelman, who knew him professionally, held him in high esteem. They were encouraged by the introduction of a neutral, honest presence in the debacle that was occurring. His name was Henry Biller, and his colleagues in the law called him Hank. He interviewed Joe and several other people in a conference room at Jim's law building on a beautiful, breezy day in late summer. Joe and the other witnesses waited in the ground-floor reception room until they were called in.

In addition to Jim and Jeff Saunders and Joe, several others were present, at the request of either Hank Biller or Jim. David Gallagher came all the way from Dorchester to tell about the intervention with Kate several years before. The vestry, acting with the abstention of Nancy Dodd, chose two members to speak for them. Three parents of Redeemer children who had grown up during Joe's tenure had asked to speak, and Biller had agreed. Harry and Amanda were present as past and present wardens of the parish. The interviews began at nine thirty in the morning.

Dave Gallagher spoke to Biller first so he could begin the long drive back home. The others went in one at a time, except for the wardens, who spoke to Biller together. Bill, Jeff Saunders, and Joe went in last. Joe had prayed that this encounter would be different from the last time he met in conference with diocesan representatives. Unlike that dispiriting gathering, this time across the table sat an interested, attentive professional who gave every impression of listening without prejudice.

After a few preliminaries, Biller asked Joe to tell him what had happened. Joe explained what he had done, the same admission he had made to LaBelle, the Redeemer wardens, Jim, the standing committee, McMahon, Williams, Casselman, his spiritual director, Al-Anon companions, family counselor, family, and old friends. At the conclusion of his confession, Hank Biller looked at him, and then at Jim and Bill Saunders, and said, "That is exactly the same thing Kate Stephenson told me yesterday afternoon."

If Biller had questioned Kate about alcohol and other habits that had created such stress over the years, he did not say so, and no one asked him. If he had, Joe guessed that Kate had lied to him to protect herself, as she had with McMahon and everyone else. He doubted she would have broken a lifetime of denial with the diocese's lawyer when she had never been open even with her family doctor or gynecologist. But it amazed Joe that she had told the truth about his slapping her. She would never have admitted failing to remind Ted that he must serve as crucifer on Easter Sunday, and she would not have acknowledged conspiring to drive him over to St. John's. However, none of this would have surprised Joe. But apparently, she had told Biller the truth about Joe slapping her, and apparently without embellishment. This surprised him. Later, he would understand that she perceived no threat to herself in being truthful about it, because the truth, after all, portrayed her as victim and Joe as aggressor. But sitting in Jim Edelman's conference room, he was surprised.

In a curious way that he would have despaired trying to explain, Joe was ashamed of his surprise over Kate's honesty. He had been married to her for almost twenty years. Even in what was crashing down around him now, or their years of marital difficulty, she was still his wife. The quality of truth that he had been raised and conditioned to hold sacred was precious in any human being. And here he sat, amazed that his own wife actually had told the truth on a certain point, and in spite of everything, he felt shamed by his own surprise. He would have died to save her from harm. He could not hate anyone, whatever the record, and certainly not Kate. The turmoil within him issued not in pain now, or any other physical symptom, but was a sadness that was worse than pain. *"I felt a Funeral, in my Brain, and Mourners to and fro kept treading—treading..."*

He became aware of the ringing silence. They were all looking at him. He straightened up. This was his first introduction to Biller, and he wanted to be himself. As depressed as he was by all that had brought them together, he felt a sense of confidence in Biller by the way he conducted the interview. Like a good investigating attorney, he asked many questions. Joe responded, noting quietly that Biller did not come around again to points in different ways. Additional questions were designed to understand details and context and not, it seemed, to test Joe's veracity or consistency. He asked Joe if he had ever shaken Kate, as apparently she or Ted had claimed that he had. Joe said that he had not. He explained that over the years, in trying to discuss issues with her, she turned away and avoided him, as was her habit. He recalled sometimes putting his hands on her shoulders to speak directly to her, but she had pulled away and closed him off. Bill Saunders wondered aloud whether the shaking in Joe's hands, his familial tremor, might somehow have led to the accusation of shaking. They did not dwell long on that slim possibility. They talked about the years Joe had spent with marriage counselors, whose reports, with all other evidence from both sides, had already been turned over to Biller. Joe explained that it had not been possible for him to bring an Al-Anon member to these interviews because participants were sworn to confidentiality and anonymity. To approach someone would be like asking him or her to betray the trust of the whole group. Biller said he understood and that the presence of such a person would not have been necessary anyway.

Then, in a sudden refocusing that touched Joe's deepest anxiety, Bill Saunders, ordained for thirty years and having served both diocese and national church, spoke up. As far as Joe's reputation and career were concerned, "The damage is already done," he said. From now on, bishops and deployment officers would have an additional component to weigh in deciding whether Joe could work anywhere. His record would show that he had been removed from his parish and ordered into "intensive psychotherapy" and that his bishop and standing committee had ordered an investigation of his conduct.

Joe knew what he meant. He had seen it in the law. Once painted with a certain brush, an attorney never again shook off the subtle hint of dishonesty, unprofessional conduct, shady dealings, or whatever else might follow him around, regardless of the circumstances or even a finding of innocence. It was true everywhere. Law enforcement. Medicine. Teaching. The ministry. A high school teacher investigated for molesting students and found innocent is forever changed in the memories of educators. A treasurer found not guilty of mishandling funds raises caution in seeking a job ten years later.

"Oh, yeah! Stephenson. Didn't they have him up on charges a while back for beating his wife or something? Whatever happened with that?"

"I don't know. Too bad, really. They say he was a good parish priest. You never know about people. Did they find him guilty?"

"I can't quite recall. Must have, though, 'cause didn't the bishop remove him from his parish? Executive committee made him go all the way to Baltimore to get treatment. Wife left him. Daughter—or was it a son—won't have anything to do with him. A shame, really. Did he drink? Was he mentally off? Seems like a decent sort, but you never know. Too bad, really. Too bad."

"It's a little like that treasurer they caught in New Jersey that embezzled all that money at that cathedral."

"Or that jerk in Massachusetts that was fooling around with those choirboys, or acolytes, or whatever, a while back. No, wait! That was one of those Catholic priests. Hell, I can't keep it all straight anymore. Remember the days when everybody behaved?"

It was human nature. It was how the world worked. A man could do right his whole life and…

He looked up. The silence again. They were staring at him. Hank Biller was grinning.

Bill Saunders was looking at him and saying, "I was saying how hard it is to clean up a record once the disciplinary process starts. It is not like being sick or having an accident. You can get over pneumonia. What attaches with this sort of thing stays with you. I was saying you and I have talked about this part of it several times since I was appointed."

"Yes, we have," Joe said, quietly.

Hank Biller said he was driving down to see Ted after lunch, and Joe gave him directions to help him find his son. Jim reminded Biller that they were all at his service if he had any further questions. Bill wrote his home telephone number on his business card and handed it to Biller, telling him to call day or night. Jim reminded Hank that he could always reach him here at his office, and to call him at home anytime. Jeff said again, as he had several times during the interview, that he would do anything to help Joe. They all shook hands, and the meeting ended.

When he walked out to the waiting room, he was surprised to find every one of his witnesses still there, including Dave Gallagher, waiting in case they were needed again by Biller. Joe thanked them all. One of the mothers was crying, and another was close to tears. Jim Edelman walked up behind them, and Joe thanked him again, feeling completely powerless to express his gratitude to this good man who was doing so much for him out of kindness and decency. While Jim and Hank Biller continued to talk in the waiting room, Joe walked with Bill Saunders out to his car in the parking lot. He wanted to take him to lunch, but Bill had a long, long drive ahead of him, all the way across the state, and thought it best to get started. Continuing to be cheerful and positive, Joe thanked this good friend for coming so far and for everything he was doing. In parting, he asked about several friends, clergy colleagues who served near Bill's parish.

"They are doing well," said Bill, buckling his seat belt.

"Haven't heard from them for months."

"It's no wonder. They're scared, like everybody else. If this can happen to you, it could happen to any of them. They're keeping quiet, you know."

"I understand," said Joe, smiling. "Give them my best."

* * *

Like the practice of law and medicine, the priesthood requires keeping many things to oneself. Society considers the structure and practice of the professions largely applicable to the ministry. The nature and depth of spiritual vocation is different, however. Although the clergy is expected to adhere to practices and standards comparable to a lawyer's or doctor's, the internal structure of ministry is vastly more abstract, theoretical, and intangible than the professions. Rules exist for conduct, expectations, and standards, but within them, the day-to-day service of God is less specified, and profoundly lonelier, than other ways of living in the world. The support structure is weaker for priests, colleagues cannot always help, and much is routinely left to the ethics of the individual.

In the beginning, Joe expected a real collegiality and sense of support among clergy, and this had proved to be true of certain people. But the longer he served, the more he came to realize that they had been exceptions. In most communities, there was somebody, usually an older man who had seen it all and took his role less seriously because of it, and with an easier sense of humor. Joe had always gravitated toward these veteran men and women, because with their experience had come a capacity for intimacy with any of their colleagues who needed it. But mostly the clergy existed in isolation, going at it alone and dealing with a thousand expectations and demands the best way they knew how.

Tom Downes had served in various roles at Redeemer long before Joe came along. He was a retired Air Force officer, well educated and friendly, and early on, Joe became fond of him and his family. But Joe gradually came to see that much in Tom was hidden carefully from others. Affable, mild-mannered Tom Downes was filled with troubles that Joe did not understand fully but that Tom vented in spells of alarming anger. In the congregation, there were one or two others who became ferociously angry at times, people who drank or had been disappointed in life, but they were known and recognized. Tom Downes's rigid emotional control, however, channeled his outbursts straight to Joe six or eight times each year, dreadful tantrums carefully orchestrated for Joe alone and hidden from everybody else. Joe suspected that his family members suffered too and that Tom's behavior accounted for their odd personalities.

Early in their relationship, Joe tried to talk with Tom Downes about his behavior. The conversations would have taken all day if Joe had allowed it. Tom's were issues too deep for Joe's comprehension, and after three long sessions with him, in which little was accomplished, Joe advised Tom that church guidelines would not allow him to continue their counseling and offered to help Tom find a good therapist. But Tom would not hear of it. He had no problems. He took offense at Joe's suggestions and refusal to counsel with him further. Although Joe was not at first aware of it, Tom began to withdraw from him. But he continued to grow angry with Joe, expressing his outrage privately and occasionally in letters.

Joe,

I am angry, hurt, concerned, and frustrated about my relationship with you. The particulars: I called almost forty-eight hours ago with a message "Call me as soon as possible." I couldn't reach you, Harry C was out of town, and Dan Buford was desperately trying to find a priest for Mrs. Adams. He called me for help. I was calling Walt Lewis when Dan said he finally heard from you. We need to fix this! This is unsat! The office answering machine sucks. Bell Catoctin is much higher quality and reliability. Why do you want to keep the old service? The light over the lectern has been fixed. In the future, tell me when you see something that needs fixing. Delegate, godammit! We can go no further in updating the computer system till you give me the serial number of your laptop. The ball is in your court. Do not complain to anybody about it! We do not need to buy new lighting for the nave until we get the new lighting design. However, if you want to spend $ needlessly, I'll do it. Enclosed is a proposed new job description for the sexton. Read it and call me, dammit.

Tom Downes

It was a mild communication compared to others. Joe had saved it because it included something about a lighting plan for the nave and a new telephone service provider, issues he had heard nothing

349

about from anyone. He found it now at home. Tom had referred to a lighting plan and telephone equipment as if Joe knew what he was talking about. He searched his memory but could recall no discussion with anybody about new lights in the nave or new telephones. The letter seemed to have been sparked by Tom's inability to reach Joe in an emergency concerning Angel Adams. She was a nice lady, a friend of Joe's. Everybody in town knew her. She was a lifelong member of a big church in a different denomination on the other side of town. There were eight ministers of her denomination in Catoctin Springs alone, and another twenty or more in the surrounding county. He couldn't imagine that Tom thought she was a member of Redeemer. Dan Buford told him later that Mrs. Adams wanted to speak with Joe about differences in worship practice between her church and Redeemer. When all this came up, Joe had been at the hospital for hours with a parishioner's child who had been involved in a minor fender bender. Her parents were employed out of town; they had called Joe.

He had explained all this calmly to Tom when they finally talked. He had continued to be polite to Tom and work with him as best he could. He kept Tom's confidence and did not discuss his behavior with anybody. If others were to find out about it, they would have to discover it through their own experience.

It turned out that Tom had known Bishop LaBelle slightly many years before, while stationed in LaBelle's former diocese. He had visited LaBelle recently several times to discuss studying for ordination as a perpetual deacon. LaBelle, glad that Tom had remembered him over the years, had been impressed with Tom and his background and had encouraged him in his plans. And so it was that LaBelle had put Tom Downes in contact with Dr. McMahon as a reliable person who liked Joe, a person who could give an accurate account of his ministry.

* * *

The day after Christmas of the preceding year, a young man employed by a construction company in Baltimore met a girl with a green card from somewhere in the Caribbean. Five days later, they celebrated New Year's Eve together at a house party in Atlantic City with a half-dozen of his friends and their dates. The young man's retired, bewildered parents had come from New Mexico in late summer seeking to buy a house, to be near their baby boy, when his island girl gave birth to their grandchild, a girl. Carl Casey showed them the Stephensons' house. It was larger than they wanted. When it appeared that their son and his significant other, whose demanding employers had let them go, would need to move in with them with their new baby, the retired couple looked at Joe's house again and decided to buy it. The son and his girlfriend, about to be evicted from his one-room apartment because of some vexing dispute over rent, would need a place rather soon.

So it was that Joe began to pack his things, following scrupulously the distribution in the hand-drawn floor plan upon which he and Kate had agreed. He contracted with a mover to move his things and place them in storage until he had a place to go. He had no idea what the future would bring.

He called Dr. Zander again, McMahon's designated colleague, and listened to the same recording. Once again, he left his name and telephone number, explaining more fully why he was calling. He wrote a letter to Kirby Porter and the executive committee informing them that he had contacted Dr. Zander and that he had not yet responded to two telephone calls. He was worried that Porter and LaBelle, angered that he was not yet in "intensive psychotherapy with a psychoanalyst," might use it as an excuse to go to the next step, while the investigation was being conducted, and issue a Godly Admonition against him. It amounted to a severe warning of impending dire sanctions more punitive than he had dealt with thus far. Under canon law, LaBelle could do so without having to explain himself to anyone. Nobody could or would question him or speak up in Joe's defense.

He telephoned Kate and left word that buyers had been found and that they needed to move in soon. The finances had been arranged, and Carl Casey thought it would all go through rather quickly. Joe had not practiced domestic relations law for many years and only belatedly remembered that the proceeds of sale would have to be placed in escrow until their property settlement was finalized and a final decree of divorce entered. He followed up his telephone message to Kate with a letter, explaining the buyers' urgency and the need to put the money into an escrow account at the time of sale. Although he had heard nothing from her after his call, she replied to his letter within two days. He was trying to trick her, she wrote, and advised she would not sign anything for the sale unless she could get her money instantly. He contacted Carl Casey, who called her and tried to explain the law and procedure of sales during divorces. Whatever she had said to him—"Don't ask!" was all Carl said to Joe, shaking his head—had caused him to ask the settlement attorney to contact her. Eventually, this lawyer appealed to Kate's divorce lawyer, who, in due course, explained the matter to Kate and called Joe's attorney. Once again, Franklin Ball, Joe's divorce lawyer, advised that the lawyers handle all communications, even on the most routine matters.

The moving company would charge almost twice as much for packing Joe's belongings in addition to moving and storing them. He packed it all himself, driving to every grocery store and supermarket within fifty miles, gathering cardboard boxes and using newspapers he had been saving for wrapping up the fragile things he was taking. He was amazed at what the three of them had accumulated in ten years in that house. On several evenings, he drove to the closest Goodwill store with clothing that was too small for him or that he had not worn in a while, books that he no longer read, and the gardening tools that had served him so well. For several days, he worked day and night so as to be out in time for Kate and Ted to have ample time for their own packing. He did not dare accept offers from the dozen Redeemer parishioners who wanted to help him. They reasoned it would be no violation of the diocese's shunning order if Joe took a few days off and visited distant friends while they packed for him. As much as he appreciated their plan, it was too much to ask anybody to do and, in many respects, was something he had to supervise. He was not certain what would happen in the future, where he would live, and whether his possessions would be in storage for a few months or a few years. He had to set aside winter clothing and personal items and pack and label the rest so he could open certain boxes when they were needed in the future. Diane Boyd drove up to help him for an afternoon, and several old friends came from Dorchester and Jeffersonville too. When he was alone, he finished the outside repairs during daylight hours, staying awake until two and three in the morning packing his things, and getting up at seven to start again.

In every room, with everything he touched, a memory or an image bloomed in his mind, making him stop and close his eyes for moments at a time. There were so many memories, flashbacks, and recollections of words and incidents, good and bad. They came upon him one after another and slowed him down. He feared he would never finish and began to work through them, letting them fade or secreting them away to ponder later on. He found old photographs of Ted's birthdays and recalled Kate chatting happily on the telephone with his mother. He could see Ted's many friends and remembered weekends they had spent at the house. Memories of Ted and him bringing in the Christmas tree, the great snowstorm when the three of them shoveled out the drive, and the happy times of his parents' visits moved through his mind like slow summer clouds. Catherine's end-of-life days and memories of humorous things she said came back to him, and the worry he endured over her drinking. He never figured out all the ways in which she acquired alcohol. It was still a mystery. He supposed he would never find out now, unless Kate knew something about it. If she did, he still might never know. Scenes, good memories, came to him of the three or four of them watching video movies together, Ted's video games, the meals they once ate together. Some memories were splendid and warm. Others churned up in him regret or remorse, things done and left undone, said and unsaid. A thousand ways in which he could have handled it all better passed through his mind, each leaving its small stain of sorrow in him. He shook his head and wrapped things carefully in newspaper and put them into boxes. He had never imagined...

When she walked out, he figured she would take Ted to the school and return. When he left the house to clear his head, he had left the lights on and doors open for her. Now he was preparing to go too. He lay down on the floor of their bedroom and stared at the ceiling.

And while he lay there, the new bishop elect decided to call.

* * *

Donald Earl Solenburger was short, overweight, balding, and dressed in black. He wore wide glasses with thin dark frames. He was five or six years younger than Joe. He asked Joe to meet him in Catoctin Springs the following day and wondered where they might get together. Joe gave him the name of a good restaurant, easy to find by its gigantic sign visible a half-mile up and down the interstate. It was in this restaurant that he and Bishop LaBelle had met months before, and he had not wanted to go there since then. Besides, he risked seeing his parishioners there and violating the diocese's shunning order. But he decided on the place anyway, because it would be easy for the bishop-elect to find. He would have preferred the truck stop about eight miles north, where the food was just as good, but he did not know Solenburger and did not want to risk offending him.

His house looked much like a bargain basement open-crate sale as he put on a collar for the first time since meeting the executive committee. Dressed in his best suit, he departed his home and arrived at the restaurant fifteen minutes early.

He drank coffee and tried to read the *New York Times* while he waited in a booth, chosen so the bishop-elect would see him easily upon entering. He began to read an article about astonishing signs of thawing in the arctic permafrost, but he could not concentrate, nor did he really want the coffee. Every time the door opened, he wondered if it would be someone from Redeemer, and after years of using his French press, he found all other coffee weak and tasteless. From behind the counter the voice of Hank Williams drifted from a radio turned way down. He thought he could hear "I went to a dance and I wore out my shoes…" Somebody played it each time he stopped in at the Third Base, and he had memorized it unconsciously, he supposed. He recalled Harry Campos telling him weeks ago to go back there and see the people he had met, but the mere thought of confessing his bad behavior again to another person made his heart ache.

"Father Stephenson? Father Solenburger. Glad we could meet. Tell me about your situation." The bishop-elect had squeezed his hand and sat down opposite him before Joe knew he was there. Joe thanked him for his telephone call and decision to meet him. He congratulated him on his election and asked if he and his family had moved into the diocese yet. Solenburger talked briefly about his wife and daughters having to settle down in a new place, how hard it was, and how bravely they were managing it.

The bishop-elect ordered hot tea and asked Joe again about his "situation." Joe gave him a report, all matters of which he well knew Solenburger had heard already from diocesan leaders. He confessed to him what he had done, how terribly sorry he was, and how he had tried to apologize to Kate and make amends. He took responsibility for everything. He talked about the pain of being separated from Ted and how much he missed his parishioners. He spoke about his efforts over the years to protect Ted and change himself. He described his efforts since Easter to help diocesan authorities see that he was not a violent person. He talked about how the Redeemer congregation was suffering from the turmoil. He paused twice to ask whether he was giving Solenburger too much detail and to be sure he was responding to his question. Each time, the bishop-elect shook his head slowly from side to side and continued to look at him in silence like a man determined to fulfill a noxious duty.

Joe said that he had prayed daily for forgiveness and that his offense against Kate had been a betrayal of God's trust in him. He expressed his belief that God would act to bring wholeness out of what he had broken.

"Doesn't He always?" asked Solenburger.

Across a widening gulf, Joe asked if it would help for him to elaborate on anything. Solenburger tapped his fingers lightly on the tabletop and looked away in silence toward the long lunch counter. He frowned slightly. People were getting down from the swivel stools and fishing in their pockets for tip money, and others were taking their places and ordering food. A waitress wiping the counter swept a newspaper to the floor, and a small crowd gathered to pick it up.

Without replying to Joe's question or commenting on anything he had said, Solenburger said, "About a month ago, I discussed your case with a substitute juvenile court judge out in Iowa. We talked your situation over for a good half an hour, and I understand it now. Have you ever heard of ESGA?" The bishop-elect pronounced it like *Fresca*.

Joe replied that he had not. Solenburger explained patiently that Emotional Support Groups of America was a twelve-step program for people who were trying to learn to control their anger. He asked if Joe would be willing to look around and find the nearest chapter. He asked if Joe knew anything about twelve-step programs. Joe explained again about his many years in Al-Anon and his efforts to encourage Kate to enter AA. The bishop-elect looked at him again without speaking. Joe waited an interminable thirty seconds and, realizing the bishop-elect was waiting for something, said that he would certainly look for an ESGA group and promised to contact the bishop-elect when he had attended a meeting. Solenburger slapped the tabletop lightly with his pudgy hand and nodded, as though Joe had answered correctly. His expression did not change. He got up immediately, his task accomplished, shook hands, and thanked Joe again for arranging to meet him. He said he really had to get back on the road and asked where he could find the restroom.

Joe sat at the table and finished his awful coffee while Solenburger was in the men's room. About ten minutes later, he came out and walked briskly to the exit. Joe waved and smiled, but Solenberger did not look in Joe's direction. Through the window he watched him disappear among the crowded vehicles and, a few moments later, saw what he supposed was his new car leaving the parking lot.

"Out of what was broken God would bring wholeness," he heard himself saying, and the bishop-elect replying, "Doesn't He always?"

"Well...," he began to say to himself, staring in perplexity at the uneven tabletop. He closed his eyes for a moment while Jewish resistance fighters were pulled blinking into the daylight from a sewer in the Warsaw Ghetto by Nazi soldiers. He saw the poverty of a thousand hollows throughout his diocese (the outdoor privies poised picturesquely above the rushing streams), and a hydrocephalic child he had visited once who would wiggle her fingers in response to words bawled in her ear. The view from the Hotel Milles Collines. Katyn. Homeless youth on the roads of Africa. The Cultural Revolution. All these scenes crossed his mind as he thought of the words of the bishop-elect.

* * *

Joe placed his belongings in storage, reserving only winter clothing and personal items that would fit into his car. If Kate would now see to her own things and have it all out by a certain date, he could return to the house and clean it in time for the closing. Kate had known for over a month about the timing. Joe had moved out in time to give her three weeks for what she had to do. He had written to her about their moving out, the sale, the closing, the required cleaning, and all the other details. When she responded with her brief notes, she made no reference to the schedule, confirmed that she understood it, or promised to comply with it. He worried that she would suddenly claim ignorance of everything and hold up the closing. But she had signed the documents, and she knew the date, and he felt she would cooperate because it was so obviously to her financial advantage. On the day the movers drove away with his possessions, he received a note from her.

Joe,

> *I will begin to pack my things this weekend so that hopefully I will be out before the closing. I was not given much time in which to accomplish this task, considering my heavy work schedule, but I will do my best to be out by then. I will let you know when I am totally out so that you can organize the cleanup.*

This is only fair, since you are the one that has been living in there for the past six months.

Kate

Even with his life breaking down, he found the anxiety of depending on her for cooperation did not trouble him now as it had in their years together. There was some relief in knowing that she had a lawyer whose word carried more weight with her than his ever had. Her lawyer could explain the nature of escrow accounts and the division of property without encountering sarcasm and suspicion. In matters requiring cooperation in their current situation, it would have been dreadful to have to negotiate with her in writing. And for his part, the reprieve from his own inner distress held firm, day by day, allowing him a freedom from pain and worry he had not known in many years. He spoke to no one about it except his general practitioner and his dumfounded internal specialist, choosing to limit his own meddling with an extraordinary gift to unabashed gratitude in his daily prayers.

By the day of the closing, Joe and Kate had signed every document, and Carl Casey and the closing attorney had in hand everything they needed for sale. As he had done for Kate with the house and its contents, Joe had drawn a map of the property for the new owners and marked each of the rose buses and their names and outlined the places where flowers bloomed each year. He had planned to leave them on the kitchen counter with the owner's manual for the large mower, which was to convey with the house. Carl suggested he go with him to the attorney's office and give it to the buyers himself. Jane Ellen Rush, still smarting from Joe's discharging her as their realtor and stung by the vestry's dismissing her as a church school-teacher, discovered that Joe would attend the closing after all. She reported immediately to Kate, who called Carl Casey in a fit of anger, demanding to know why Joe was going to be present, obviously perceiving a conspiracy taking shape. When Carl, confused and surprised, asked her why she was upset, she said she had discussed the whole thing with Jane Ellen and knew that unless she was present at the closing, Joe would "get all the money." Carl explained patiently for the third or fourth time that legally the money must be given to an attorney to hold in escrow until the division of property was final and the court had entered a final decree. When she hung up, it was clear to him that she was still suspicious and might come to the closing anyway, lest Joe climb out a window with a bagful of her money over his shoulder. With Joe dreading the confusion that would ensue if she burst in, the closing proceeded, the manual and homemade map were handed over, and arrangements made for the transfer of proceeds into escrow.

The days before closing were hectic and tiring. At least he did not have to stop everything on short notice and leave home for a morning or afternoon so Carl could show the house to a buyer, interludes with which he had lived for several months. And he could keep everything clean and organized with only himself to pick up after. Every room of the house, each step, corner, and shelf poured out their memories like soap bubbles, clear and illuminated and fragile. As he went about packing his things, a memory appeared at every turn, and he could easily grow emotional in visualizing Kate and Ted. He could hear their voices, see them moving about, recall incidents funny and sad. And soon he would never stand in these rooms again. The place where they lived would be lost forever. He sat down from time to time and closed his eyes. Occasionally literary references crowded forward from the back of his mind, the unbidden connections that had always animated his interior life. He shook his head. As lovely as some of the memories were, he grew increasingly sad. He knew his friends would understand, although many were unlikely to say so. He was blessed, and he knew it, but he was a human being and he struggled to hold his heart together in what was happening.

Days away from going he knew not where, he telephoned every inexpensive motel for fifty miles around and inquired about rates. He found several of them where he could afford to stay for a few weeks. He thought it might be possible to negotiate a better rate at a couple of them in person.

He went about the maudlin affairs of his life, shoring up order and imagining dignity in small matters grown large, a fly buzzing about a train wreck. The assurance that he was never alone dogged him like a shadow, shifting behind him when he dared to confront it, a figment of peripheral vision he could neither quite believe nor deny. A misplaced kindness, an undeserved attention, worried his conscience like a messenger tapping at the wrong door. The world was full of brokenness. The innocent suffered at every turn. There must be some mistake, some routing error, a small miscalculation of a few degrees grown to a vector that crossed his mishandled existence.

A couple at Redeemer whom he missed terribly in his ostracism had long planned a lengthy trip abroad. Generous and well-mannered people who were old enough to be his parents, they had been faithful supporters of the parish for decades. Albert Henley had served in the legislature and was known all over the state. The Henleys were pain-fully aware of his dilemma. They found his treatment by the diocese outrageous, and they had appealed in vain to people throughout the national church trying to correct it. They invited Joe to live in their home while they were away. It was best to have their large house occupied for the seven weeks they would be traveling, and it was a blessing for Joe not to have to pay for lodging somewhere. He could come in following their departure and depart early on the day they returned and remain in compliance with the church's orders to stay away from his parishioners. It was immensely helpful to be able to cook, use a telephone, and not have to decipher messages scribbled in haste by a Pakistani innkeeper. It was further relief he knew he did not deserve.

* * *

For almost twenty years, he had sat down about the fifth of every month and paid the bills. Their paychecks were deposited by then. He paid everything and balanced their account and placed what seemed reasonable into savings. Sometimes thoughts of Ted's college years—he began to miss him already when he became a teen-ager—and some time at last to travel with Kate and have some fun together after retirement lent joy to the tedium of opening bills and punching the calculator. He had been attentive and careful over the years, and it had been lonely duty. Family finances was another bat-tlefield of mutuality and control in Kate's view of things, abandoned by her rather than learning the ways of cooperation and compromise that matured in good marriages. Joe's going at it alone had resulted in excellent credit ratings and the regular cooperation of financial per-sonnel in every place they had lived. Years into marriage, with a teen-age son, she gave every sign of continuing to believe she should be able to do exactly what she wanted with her paycheck without having to answer to anybody. So Joe had tended to their family finances at the beginning of every month. He contented himself that he had won the battle, in their second year of marriage, of her depositing her monthly paycheck into their family account when he had promised to pay off her credit cards. Thus month after month for years, he tended to the bills, calling up the stairs to her to ask about various checks and bills while she watched television and graded papers. A few times over the years—at the time of his prostate surgery and during his short sabbatical—she had paid the bills, paying several he had paid in the previous month, making a number of mysterious withdrawals of cash, and failing to balance the account.

He was in his temporary home, sitting at the Henleys' kitchen table, making a list of people to contact about returning to the legal profession, when the manager of his branch bank called to let him know the family account was overdrawn. A check had bounced. Although the bank manager did not say so, she was aware like every-one else of what was happening in his life and alerting him so that he could come in immediately and make it good. He thanked her and went out immediately. By the time he arrived, she had two more to show him: the previous month's utility check and another paid to the carpenter who had repaired the groundhog damage to the front door.

He had not nearly enough cash to cover these overdrafts, but he gave the manager what he had. It had been many years since he had miscalculated a balance that way. Embarrassed, he apologized several times, and the manager agreed to hold everything while he drove to their savings bank and withdraw what was needed. He went out to his car and sat for a moment in thought.

When Kate had left home, she had in her pocketbook a blank check to buy gasoline on Easter Monday. On Tuesday, she had cashed that check, withdrawing $2,500 from their family checking account. The following day, she had gone to their savings bank and withdrawn $4,300, approximately the amount they had anticipated spending to replace the roof on her summer cottage. Apparently so distraught that she could not speak to him by telephone, she had recovered rapidly enough to evaluate her personal financial posture, even thinking ahead to a bill—most unlike her—that would not be payable until early summer. He had continued to run the house and pay the bills for all of them on his salary and what remained in savings and in their checking account.

He got out of the car and returned to the bank with the enthusiasm of a man approaching a traffic accident. He inquired about recent withdrawals and was told that on the fifth of the month, a withdrawal had been made by cashier's check, leaving in the account about a quarter of what had been there before. He and the manager both understood that this would mean the return of almost all the checks he had written a few days earlier. He confessed to the manager that he had not known about the withdrawal. They knew each other well enough for her to venture that she had dealt with similar surprises in other divorces. He closed his eyes for a moment. Kate had seen him pay bills at the same time every month of their marriage.

He went to the savings bank and withdrew what was left in that account and closed it. It would not begin to cover the total amount of the monthly bills that had already started to bounce, even when added to what Kate had left in the checking account. He drove back to the bank and deposited everything he had with the branch manager. She advised him to close the checking account once the checks had cleared and open another in his name alone. He thanked the manager again and went out to his car. He was a lawyer. He was supposed to anticipate such things. But with his own wife, even after years of opposition and deceit, such betrayal had never entered his mind. Was he too trusting, or simply a fool? Either way, he should have been more careful.

He returned to the Henleys' house and carried to the dining room table the plastic file box in which he kept the family financial records. A quarterly family automobile insurance premium, several medical bills, and his insurance company's mail-order pharmacy bills were due the following month. He knew there would be others, but at the moment, he could not anticipate what they would be. He would no longer have to pay the mortgage, a thought that caused him to grow still for a moment. Perhaps there would be enough to cover everything. He got out his calculator and set to work.

After a few minutes, he got up suddenly and went outside. He walked down the long grassy hill behind the house to the small stream that divided his friends' property from the neighboring farm. A mill had stood here from the year before the Revolution, until burned by federal raiders during the War between the States. The much-diminished millrace was still discernable in the stream flowing sluggishly through the marsh grass. He watched some yellow walnut leaves drifting on the surface of the dark water. Runaway clumps of black-eyed Susan were growing in places, and he spied a checkered rattlesnake plantain still in bloom. He walked up the stream bottom a few hundred yards and found some unattractive stems of autumn coral root waving their tiny purplish flowers like grain-o-wheat lights. Nearby stood the bole of a massive dead hemlock, its top and brittle branches forming a lattice of crazy angles where they had crashed into the stream. The closest hemlocks he knew of were miles to the west, near the mountains. This one was the last survivor of an outpost colony, a sign of earlier times, a cooler climate, and a less-complicated era.

Why did he notice such things, dwell on them, find any importance in them? And why give thought to them now, when so much trouble was crowding in? He didn't know. And it did not make any difference anyway.

It was his own fault. He should have closed both accounts, but such a thing had never even occurred to him. When they left in anger, he would have bet his life on their coming home a few hours later, listening to his apology, and talking things over with Ted. He had not had enough presence of mind to remember that it was not like

Kate to talk anything over and that, in this case, Ted would follow her example. He could not foresee then what was coming, and how long it would drag on, and the reactions of people he trusted. Once again, he had misjudged everything. He was a fool. The torment of his self-loathing and remorse welled up inside him like a stream in flood stage, and his despair over Kate was so bitter that it made his eyes ache. But his side and intestines remained calm.

The following week, he received a note.

Joe,

I wanted to let you know some things that have taken place of which you need to be aware. Under the direction of my attorney, I visited the offices of our savings bank and we ascertained the total in the savings account as of the day months ago you made me leave our house. Taking one-half of this amount, and adding to it the amount we had previously agreed to pay the roofer on my house, this left a difference that amounted to my half of the account. Following a similar visit to our checking account bank in Catoctin Springs, we figured the account balance total as of the day you made me leave months ago, one-half of which amounts to my half of the account. The total of my share of our accounts as of that day came to $8,863.35. This amount was deducted from our family account and sent to me in a cashier's check. I wanted to let you know so that you could balance your accounts.

Kate

Chapter Twenty-Six

H E COULDN'T COUNT the number of people who had confessed to him over the years. It had begun in his teens, others telling him their secrets and him listening in a confidence they both knew he would never break. There had always been people—in every school he attended, each neighborhood where he lived, every job he had ever had. He never sought it out, but when it happened, he listened. Whenever he wondered about it—how it continued to happen, how often it occurred—he thought of all the people who had listened to him over the years. It felt right to give something back. He knew he could not fix anything. Except for those who pressed for his thoughts, he never had much to say. By the time he began to serve in the church, it was a familiar part of his life, although he had a limited idea of how unusual it was because he never discussed anything with anyone. He could understand why a collar kept it happening, but he had never understood how it had begun in the first place. He had known a few people who attracted cats. A couple of his students suffered beestings when nobody else had seen a bee all day. With him, he figured it had been people and their hidden troubles.

The disclosures were seldom sensational or dramatic. There were sometimes tears, even sobbing. As far as he could tell, confession allowed some cleansing and provided a safe place to take a risk, to treat old wounds, feel the movement of healing. As good as he hoped it was for those who did the talking, however, he knew that the real blessing was for him.

He hoped that confession for others had been different from what he was experiencing now. He had confessed to Kate and Ted and felt within him movement in a new direction. He had felt rightness in confessing to his family counselor and spiritual director. They had been careful not to comfort him, but both were supportive of his disclosure and determination to learn from what he had done. The cleanliness he had begun to feel had heightened his remorse toward his family. It had continued to draw no response from Kate, but confession and remorse was the only right thing to do, regardless of how she received it. Ted's silence made him feel dead inside.

Confessing to the women of his Al-Anon group had made the biggest difference. In their separate ways, they had all been pushed over the edge, known the twisted grief and self-doubt of losing the good things that helped them cope with life. In his sorrow and confusion, he did not try to define what they did for him, but they helped him feel cleaner inside. And like a young recruit learning from seasoned veterans, he was grateful.

In the church so far, each confession had brought an increasingly oppressive darkness, shutting out the light except for what beamed so kindly in his parishioners. The two neighboring clergy to whom he had confessed immediately were exceptions. But with his confessions to the interim bishop, bishop-elect, executive committee members and his attempts to speak to other authorities, his "situation," as Solenburger and his consulting judge had called it, had grown more threatening. Perhaps this was part of the punishment he knew he deserved, a process meant to chastise him and prolong his shame. God's wrath burned, and the church's officers were its willing conduits, letting it through to him with Vesuvian power.

When he perceived his ministry and reputation going down, he thought at first it was God's will. He knew he deserved punishment. But a voice kept assuring him that he was a reasonable man of some experience and that reason and experience were also God's blessings. And however warranted the punishment had been in the beginning, he understood now that the church's response had become vengeful and corrupt. When the subsequent supportive medical reports were dismissed and ignored, he perceived the witch hunt. He was still willing to believe that the church authorities simply did not know what they were doing and that ignorance and pride motivated them rather than malice. But their eagerness to ignore the truth was hardening, and the canonical legal process seemed designed to be manipulated by those in power. The church provided no corrective. Where was the cherished pastoral church in which he had been raised? Business, politics, and the social sciences had superseded it. Compassion and mercy, although assumed, were not in the job descriptions of modern church authorities, and their want rarely even warranted comment. If he wanted integrity and wisdom, he would have to find them on his own.

Confessing to Bishop Carrington Spencer was the most humiliating experience of Joe's life. In showing him Dr. McMahon's report, he felt he would die of shame. Before the man who had admitted him to holy orders and taught him much about clerical dignity and duty, he suffered more than before all his own diocesan leaders combined.

Bishop Spencer conducted their meeting professionally and respectfully, but he grew quieter after reading McMahon's report. The other professional reports were much longer, and he read only their conclusions. He returned to McMahon's report for a second look, shaking his head so slightly, almost a trembling, that Joe felt the bishop was not even aware of it.

After explaining what was taking place, Joe had asked the question that was confounding his heart and mind. "Is all this God's way of telling me that I should leave the ministry?"

Bishop Spencer paused and appeared momentarily shocked. "No," he said, as though dismissing something abjectly preposterous in their discussion. "Absolutely not."

Joe told him in more detail the direction his own diocese was taking. The bishop responded by saying that he knew clergy who had been deposed from holy orders and subsequently restored. "Who are doing good ministry and serving in good ways."

Joe knew that Spencer was trying to be reassuring, and he was careful not to betray the depth of his own anxiety. The thought of suspension was painful enough. At the mention of deposition, he could have easily thrown up.

They talked for another fifteen minutes, the bishop assuring him of his concern and giving him examples of how various matters had been addressed in the past. Bishop Spencer was extremely careful to say nothing that would appear to encroach upon the authority of any other person, never even mentioning LaBelle's or Solenburger's names. He did ask, rather soon, after the meeting started, who was president of Joe's diocesan executive committee. Joe could detect no reaction from the bishop to Kirby Porter's name.

At the end of their meeting, they prayed together, something no one else had done with him. The two of them bent forward in their chairs and joined hands while the bishop thanked God for making him a priest in the church. The bishop asked God's blessing on him as he went from strength to strength in his present troubles. He prayed for Kate and Ted and for all in authority over Joe, asking that God's will be done now on earth as it is in heaven. They prayed the Lord's Prayer together. Joe thanked him and left.

On the long drive home, he thought over every word of their conversation, pulling off the road a half-dozen times to scribble notes in his file. Together with the words of his parishioners and old friends, Bishop Spencer's advice had been more helpful than anything in many months. Spencer's sincerity and compassion would have come through to a two-year-old. Joe knew his interest was honest, without condemnation or vengeance. And yet against all his reluctance to consider it, he wondered if even Spencer, in all his integrity, realized any longer the profound anguish and destruction that a suspension from ministry created in the life of the garden-variety parish priest.

* * *

Discipline was saving him. He arose early every day, said his prayers, recorded his dreams, made notes in his files, consulted with Jim Edelman, tended to his dwindling affairs, answered letters, looked after the Henleys' house and animals, and listened to the messages on the answering machine. He ran at night on the country roads.

He visited people he knew in nearby towns, none of them members of Redeemer, and felt a peace and security with them and their children that was soothing and troubling at the same time. One couple included him routinely in their Friday-evening family dinners. The time spent with the Pattersons, their friends, and their children, sitting at the table and talking as people do after dinner, restored his sanity week after week and soothed the loss of his parish family and community. They were kind people, good parents, well-known throughout their state and civically conscious. Evenings spent with them were a healthy contrast to the insanity of life in his crippled diocese. They also made him long for his own family and for the parish family he had served for so long.

Kate's raid on their checking and saving accounts had cost dearly in overdraft fees and his ability to keep up with their bills. There was no longer a mortgage to pay, but also no savings on which to draw. Nothing quickened the glacial pace with which she and her lawyer accomplished their part of the routine steps that were leading to their divorce. He paid her several hundred dollars of spousal support twice each month when his paycheck arrived, as ordered by the court on her lawyer's motion. His lawyer reluctantly conceded that what she had taken from the accounts amounted to half their value on the day she left the house, regardless of what had been expended on her behalf since then, or the way she went about the withdrawals. It seemed to matter to no one that she had no living expenses in her apartment at the school, was receiving her salary, and that he was paying three family car payments and all the other bills. After all, he had slapped her.

With every necessary document, agreement, or legal maneuver, he and his divorce lawyer acted swiftly to bring the divorce to a conclusion in no more time than state law required. In every instance, Kate and her attorney acted at the last possible moment, moving the court twice over the months for extra time. Her attorney was known to the local bar—other lawyers rolled their eyes when he told them who was representing her—and Joe was warned that "he would be just as nasty as she wanted him to be." Frenzied, last-minute activity, exasperating to Joe in its predictability and meanness, had been the way with Kate long before her lawyer appeared in their lives. The two of them together made a memorable pair. He had dealt with other lawyers like that in his practice and knew that little could be done about it.

He had followed up immediately on the bishop-elect's advice to go to Emotional Support Groups of America. He found two ESGA twelve-step groups in the region, the closest about a two hour's drive away. Nobody answered at either telephone number. He called the community health departments in each locality and learned that one group met in the basement of a civic center in a small town and the other at a big Lutheran church in the metro area. While he waited on the line, one of the civic center employees went down to the meeting room door, read the notice of meeting times, and reported back to him. Nobody seemed to know whom to contact for any further information. At the metro area church, they told him the meeting date and time and gave him the telephone number of someone named Doris. He called. A laconic man answered and said that Doris was out and gave him meeting times and directions.

He drove to the distant civic center meeting, arrived a half-hour early, and waited. Fifteen minutes after the meeting should have started, a timid elderly lady appeared "to see if anybody showed up." They went into a dreary room and sat at a table, where she explained to him that the "chapter" was being disbanded for lack of membership. Apparently, everyone in those parts was emotionally stable. The only other regular member was somebody named John, and she was sure he and his wife would be along any minute. She gave him some brochures, some cards with their soon-to-be-discontinued schedule, and a folder with national hotline numbers. He listened with patience as she told him her troubles. They parted amicably before the hour was over. John never showed up.

The other meeting, in the metro area church, took almost two hours to reach and was very different. A dozen people were bustling about, making coffee and unfolding chairs when he arrived, fifteen minutes early. Several of them welcomed him warmly, saying their first names and offering him coffee. The room began to fill up until about thirty people were present. There were women of all ages and about five youngish men. The women chattered away to one another, while the men, carefully separating themselves from one another, leaned against the wall in silence, sipping coffee and glancing furtively around. At eight, o'clock everyone sat down in a large circle and the meeting began. It proceeded in the orderly, reasonable way of twelve-step meetings. A short obese woman presented her story. Discussion followed. Joe was given literature, some of which the civic center lady had given him. Browsing through it confirmed that this was the meeting closest to Catoctin Springs, now that the rural group was closing. He left about nine thirty, thinking all the way home about the people he had met and the story the speaker had told.

The following day, he wrote a detailed letter to bishop-elect Solenburger, describing what he had found at each meeting and enclosing a few brochures. He explained the great distance to the metro group meeting and stated his belief that the Al-Anon meeting he attended in a nearby town provided very similar support. He asked whether Solenburger would allow him to continue with that group instead of attending ESGA, which would eliminate some four hours of driving.

Dr. Zander finally called, leaving his apologies on the Henleys' answering machine. He and his family had been on vacation. The physician covering for him—Joe supposed it was his colleague McMahon—had left prospective new patients for Zander to contact personally upon his return. He regretted to say he was unable to accept new patients at the moment, although he thought it might be possible by the following spring. He would be glad to refer Joe to someone else if Joe would call him back. Joe reported all this to Kirby Porter in a letter.

He spoke to Bill Saunders several times over the weeks, conversations that left him increasingly perplexed. He was still the same old Bill whom Joe had so admired, but it seemed his enthusiasm on Joe's behalf was less than it had been. No, he had not spoken again to Hank Biller. He had met the bishops' assistants from several other dioceses at a meeting to discuss changes in the national disciplinary canons, and he had talked with them briefly about Joe's case. They were appalled, he said. They could not imagine why such a thing had been taken to such lengths and expressed regret for Joe. Bill related all this in a matter-of-fact way that made Joe wonder if he agreed with them. Yes, he had met with the bishop-elect several times on a number of diocesan matters, but they did not "get into" Joe's problem. When Joe asked, as diplomatically as possible, why he had not approached Solenburger about his circumstances, Saunders replied, "What makes you think I have any influence?" Joe found it a curious answer from his official adviser, the longest continually serving priest in the diocese. He did not know what had changed in Saunders, but his intuition warned him not to press further.

He spoke to Jim Edelman about his talk with Saunders and found that Jim and Saunders had exchanged some heated words in the preceding week. Jim concluded that Bill's interpretation of his own role as "adviser" did not include "advocate," a distinction that made a great deal of difference to him and to Joe. As lawyers, they were used to advocating for one position or another. They had thought this was Bill's view of his role in Joe's case. Joe recalled Bill's comforting words when LaBelle had first appointed him, "I'll do everything I can to help Joe Stephenson." Jim no longer felt as much confidence in Bill Saunders as before. Joe was uncertain what to think about his old friend's change of attitude, but the additional anxiety that it brought hurt more than he admitted to anyone.

The anticipation of Hank Biller's report and the executive committee's next move clouded his mind like a winter front moving in. He awoke each morning wondering if this would be the day. He trusted Biller's integrity but had no confidence in anyone else on the diocese's side. Even if Biller counseled a reprieve for Joe, the closed-door maneuvering and backroom decision-making did not bode well. Everyone recognized that LaBelle and Porter had made up their minds about him. He did not trust them anyway. Would the new bishop present more of the same? Everyone wondered.

An expedition was organized to go to the diocesan office and meet personally with Solenburger, who was gradually taking over leadership from Bishop LaBelle. Harry Campos and Amanda Rowland would go, as well as Jim Edelman and Dennis Hughes, a vestry member and well-known local businessman. They would all meet another parishioner at the diocesan office. This was Sally Kennedy, a distinguished delegate in the state legislature who would have served the state admirably in Congress.

After a six-hour drive, the group arrived at Diocesan House, where they went in and joined Sally Kennedy in the small foyer. A receptionist suggested that Joe go in and inform the bishop-elect that everyone had arrived. Through the open door, he could see Solenburger and Bill Saunders in conversation at a conference table. He entered and approached them, and they both glanced at him and continued talking to each other. For a few minutes, he stood by and waited for them to conclude their talk. He decided it would be better to leave until they called him in, and he was turning to go when they stood up suddenly and shook hands with each other. In the few minutes Joe had stood by, Bill Saunders had addressed the bishop-elect four times as "coach."

They turned to look at him, and Bill Saunders smiled and shook hands. The bishop-elect told him to call his group in to the conference table, and Joe turned and stepped into the foyer. They all came in, affable and polite, most of them meeting their new bishop-elect for the first time and very glad to do so. Solenburger shook hands all around and sat down at the head of the long table, and everyone else began to sit down too. As they took their seats and made room for one another, Joe heard Harry Campos say to the bishop-elect, in a chatty, courteous way, that the Redeemer people hoped he would help them bring the present difficulties to an end.

"We believe Mr. Stephenson is one of the finest rectors we've ever had, and I've been in the parish all my life, and all of us—"

Solenburger interrupted and said, "If Father Stephenson touched his wife again, we would be dealing with a felony."

On the ride home, they all discussed this remark, which Joe had heard clearly, all his professional instincts electrified by the use of the word *felony*. Harry Campos, to whom it had been directed, had heard it too. The others, in the act of pulling back chairs and settling into them, could not say that they had heard it. On hearing Harry Campos and Joe describe it, the others grew equally shocked.

Was this the attitude Solenburger brought to the table, using a word reserved for the most heinous offenses of the criminal law? Did he have any idea of the import of such a term? Did he believe such a remark had a place in what they were preparing to discuss? When he heard it, Joe was as outraged as he had been by Lottie Bascomb's vicious insinuations over the years. Had he been meeting with Solenburger alone, he would have challenged him immediately for saying such a thing. Years of trial practice had prepared him to see immediately, however, that the remark had passed unnoticed as everyone was settling down, except for Harry Campos, who, after one glance at Joe, had lapsed into silence. Joe decided to hold his peace, acting as though he had not heard what Solenburger had said, and waiting to see what would happen now.

The meeting proceeded for about forty minutes, with everyone speaking except Bill Saunders. The points in Joe's behalf, already made before the interim bishop and executive committee, in the medical reports of everyone but McMahon, and in the many dozens of other communications to the diocese, were presented to Solenburger in matter-of-fact, unemotional pleas. Sally Kennedy and Jim Edelman spoke persuasively of the legal aspects and the public interest. Harry Campos spoke in a personal way about the suffering within the parish. Dennis Hughes told about the loss of respect for the diocese within the state and how people were mystified by the extreme reaction, which seemed wholly out of proportion to the offense. Amanda Rowland also spoke about the parish and asked Solenburger pointedly why the church was ignoring all the other evaluations that came to opposite conclusions from McMahon's. Sally Kennedy informed the bishop-elect that some members of the legislature had asked her about the situation and that the church was gaining a sour reputation by the way the case was being handled. She urged him to understand that nobody approved of Joe slapping his wife—at which all heads around the table bobbed vigorously, and none more so than Joe's—but that common sense called for the punishment to fit the offense. Joe repeated the apology he had made so often, speaking of his remorse and the pain he knew he had caused.

The bishop-elect listened to everyone quietly, showing no emotion and asking no questions. He spoke up once during Joe's remarks, inquiring when he would be divorced. When they had all said what they had come to say, he thanked them and stood up. The meeting was over. He had said almost nothing. As he shook hands, as though perceiving the sense of something unfinished in the room, Solenburger said loudly that they would all have to wait for the report and recommendations of the church attorney, which he hoped would not take much longer.

A few went to the restrooms, and the others drifted outside with Joe to the parking lot. Bill Saunders smiled and clapped Joe on the shoulder and asked him if it was possible for him to go back to practicing law. Joe replied that it was always possible. Everyone else was silent. Joe asked Saunders why he had been silent in the meeting, and Saunders replied cheerfully that everyone else had said everything there was to say.

No one spoke until Harry's Cadillac merged onto the interstate highway a few blocks from Diocesan House, a turn that seemed to free them from whatever they were leaving behind. After a few minutes, it was clear that everyone felt the same foreboding, disappointment, and apprehension that had long disturbed Joe's every moment. So strong was the mood that possibilities were soon being raised to counter what they all felt. The bishop-elect was young, younger than any of them. He was from a different part of the country. He was said to be wealthy, which alone might keep him from understanding his diocese. He had spent all his adult life as a clergyman and had no experience outside the hierarchy. He was new in the diocese and new to his soon-to-be role of bishop. He would, of course, feel an urge to follow the example of LaBelle, who had been a bishop when Genesis was being written. As a new bishop, he wanted to start out strong, establish his authority, set a no-nonsense example. After all, Joe's sin fell into the sensitive domain of domestic violence, where there were no gray areas, and no excuses or mitigating circumstances could be allowed to influence leaders. There was only one correct way to approach such matters these days when the victim and perpetrator were ordinary people, and Solenburger would certainly want to be safe and correct in the eyes of everybody. In addition, they all agreed that Porter had gotten to him. As president of the executive committee, he would have naturally spent much time with the new diocesan leader. Some had heard that Porter was bucking for the position of the bishop's assistant. Someone opined again that new officers in every organization want to "start tough" and establish their authority.

They discussed these points and many others during the first fifty miles. None of it succeeded in making anyone feel better. Joe and Jim Edelman stared through windows on opposite sides of the car, each feeling the return of an icy feeling they had known following their appearance before the executive committee. There was less and less conversation after the first hour, and the final three hours were spent in silence as the darkening countryside sped by.

Joe watched the racing mountaintops and bumpy dirt roads that disappeared into dark hollows and thought about his life. Inconsequential and boring, a trifling drama poorly produced, it made no difference in the world. The great weight he felt descending was deeply disturbing to him, and significant for those who loved him, but it was no more than dust to an oblivious world. Others had it far worse. And soon he knew he must bear it alone. His friends, disturbed by the unfairness of it all, were doing all they could. His gratitude knew no bounds; the people in the car with him were God's servants. He had the most profound respect for them and for the many like them. But soon they would be able to do no more, and it would be up to him. His life revolted him. Where was his son? His mother and family members were depressed. So many were suffering because he had lost his temper and made such a mess of things. As far as the church was concerned, one could not be a parish priest and human at the same time. He understood. Clergy should be held to a higher standard. He loathed himself and his life. That God loved him and was standing by him was a miracle. He knew that God understood. That should have been enough, but he had to struggle to remind himself.

* * *

He thought about Ted day and night. His telephone calls were not returned. His letters drew no response. Good people who knew the St. John's community warned him to stop writing to Ted because he was showing the letters to his friends and their contents had become a source of derision. Joe could not bring himself to believe it, and he continued to write to him. Kate would tell him nothing about Ted in her occasional cryptic notes, written when she perceived that some interest of her own warranted contact.

He had been warned by the lawyer in his civil negotiations to have no contact with Hervey, who might still be named in a defamation suit, so he had not attended Ted's final day at St. John's. Missing his only son's high school graduation was a shameful neglect for which he knew he would feel bad for the rest of his days. At that time, he thought he was doing the right thing. His mother and sister came all the way from home to see Ted graduate, and their presence relieved some of Joe's guilt for a while. But legal advice notwithstanding, he sickened himself by not attending. After months of Ted's refusing to speak to him, Joe had accepted that he did not want any contact. He figured that his presence would spoil this important day in his son's life. So many things were possible, but none of them mattered. He should have been there, as he should have been at Ted's distant soccer games, chaperoning his dances or waiting at home for him night after night. Instead, he was laboring away for a parish that had grown so large under his watch that it easily required the presence of two clergy, and serving a far-flung diocese that had now turned on him like a poisonous snake.

The look of surprise and anger on Kate's face when he slapped her would affect him for as long as he lived, and he knew it. This was true despite all her years of denial, lies, subterfuge, and negligence. He should have been able to handle it better. But driving away his son, regardless of what Kate had been telling Ted over the years, was his most abominable failing. If he had been a good father, Ted would not have believed cruel things said about him, even from the mother on whom he doted. If he had been a good father, Ted would have talked with him, listened to his apology, accepted his remorse, told himself that this was the man who had always loved him, taught him to ride a bicycle and shave, cherished the ground he walked on. He knew Kate would say anything, concoct the most shameful, atrocious lies, to shield herself from threat or exposure. To defend herself, she had long been willing to cut Joe down. But Joe had always believed his love for Ted would overcome such dangers. He was certain Ted respected him. He was certain Ted knew that he loved him. He would have died for Ted.

The thought of dying for his son, or dying of remorse, or for any of his sins at this point in his life, set his thoughts drifting uncontrollably and, he thought, naturally and harmlessly of a pair of Walther pistols. His own PPK and his father's PPK/S nestled in their square clean cases beneath a box containing his suspenders, cummerbund, and black bow tie, at the bottom of a small suitcase that he kept beneath the colonial poster bed he occupied in the Henleys' guest room. In an accompanying box were holsters, a small cordovan sidearm clip-on and a black custom-made shoulder holster he had purchased long ago, preferring them to the government-issue models in the days when the courts authorized him to carry concealed weapons. Apart from their functional uses—unlike other clergy, Joe was not a pacifist and, in an emergency, would have defended his loved ones or their home by any means—he admired these renowned small firearms as works of art, elegant as the flintlock dueling pistols with mahogany grips and brass fittings that he had admired in museums and private collections over the years.

He had been to the scene of suicides in his law practice and ministry. One of his friends, a hale, irreverent sort with whom he had hunted for years, depressed by loss of function following a stroke, had killed himself with a shotgun. An elderly physician he had known had shot himself on Valentine's Day after mailing cards to all his friends. And there had been others, strong people, good people, pushed over the edge of despair by life in the broken world.

He had thought about it once or twice in recent months. In the dreadful loss of his family, the threat to his vocation, the separation from his parishioners, the reaction of the church he loved, and the calculated absence of his clergy friends, thoughts of suicide had percolated upward from his deepest sorrow. And if all that were not enough, plunging his mother and siblings into depression had created in him the bitterest self-loathing. The thoughts of shooting himself were fleeting, the sort he supposed afflicted most sane people in their worst trials, and they were gone as soon as they emerged. All that was needed to dispel them was to close his eyes and watch the faces emerge: the faces of his son, his parents and brothers and sisters, his nieces and nephews, people in a half-dozen parishes, countless friends, especially old girlfriends, and floating always in the foreground, the face of his own wife. Some of her images were from their early years together. In a recurrent one, he saw her face as he handed Ted to her in the delivery room, one of the loveliest moments of their lives. He knew now that even then she was masking whatever demons were there but unarticulated in the carefully guarded inner life she had lived. At each face, a cry arose within him like the howl of a dog.

He could think briefly about shooting himself. But his knowing that he was no coward and he had never been a traitor precluded anything more than a thought from time to time when his despair was deepest. He could never do such a thing—the ultimate act of selfishness and hatred—to the ones he loved or to the ones who loved him. He did not have it in him. He had no right. Free will determined nothing in the end, because he knew his life was not his own. Christ had given it to him in trust.

The faces within him, even in his grief, created a rush of gratitude that roared in his brain like wind, joyful as applause, stimulating as symphonies. Christianity is about relationships, he told himself, and he had been blessed with so many of them. Like rubies, emeralds, and sapphires cascading down upon a crystal plain, priceless and alluring, the people he loved poured down about him in wondrous light and drove him back from every cowardly thought of ending his life. He was left high on a sunlit upland to contemplate his blessings. His depression did not vanish, but thoughts of harming himself vanished like snow in the desert.

* * *

The great oaks on the Henleys' lawn turned rich hues of oxblood and claret, and Joe watched them from the windows and walked out beneath them in the early morning. Canada geese were in the air and strutting up and down the millrace, beautiful, raucous, and miserably messy. At night he could hear the beat of their big soft wings past the corner of the house where he slept, or where he tried to sleep. He lay awake reciting in his mind "The Wild Swans at Coole" until he got it right. Occasionally, recitation would help him sleep. From the house on Friday nights he could hear the faint boom of the marching band from the high school football games. He would have liked to go but knew he would meet parishioners there, among them the Bascomb children, leading to more trouble with the diocese.

Local people who were not members of the Redeemer congregation continued to invite him to dinner and to parties. As the weather turned chilly, he found he had to force himself to go. He treasured their friendships and was grateful for their concern, but he would just as well have stayed alone at the Henleys'. He knew he was depressed and that it was not good to be alone so much. He never felt completely alone, but still...

Friends in distant places had issued standing invitations to come and stay for as long as he wanted to. He visited a few of them for a day or two. He spent a few days now and then with Diana Boyd. But being away from Catoctin Springs made him apprehensive, as though something might happen, and he could perhaps make it less onerous by being there. He knew this was a false anxiety, but it was the way he felt.

His prayers were no longer the discursive petitions of so many recent months. God knew precisely what was happening, and what would happen, and however much Joe might have been tempted to doubt it in his saddest moments, he knew that God had it all in hand. Because he was human, his faith in God's control wavered now and then. In his better moments, he knew the truth: it was not possible for God to forget or neglect him. It is the nature and character of God to love. In God's gift of free will to us, God will allow those who are determined to turn away to do so. But God cannot abandon even them. If and when they turn and search for him, he is there. They will bump into him when they turn. For those who cling to God, as Joe was clinging now, God can no more turn away from us than a parent can from a child. God will not abandon us, because God cannot deny God's own nature. The Holy Spirit was in Joe's life, not directing events and changing people's minds, but present about him and acting within him, shoring up his courage, maintaining a good disposition, calming him, inspiring his sense of humor, cleaning out the destructive tendencies toward self-reliance, moving with cleanliness in his heart, making him in spite of himself an example of faith for others.

Among his family and many of his friends, the anxiety for him was overwhelming. He telephoned his mother and a few others every few days with calm reassurances, counseling patience, and confidence, hoping that the sound of faith in his own voice would ease their apprehension. They could hear in his voice that he remained dreadfully sorry to have brought all this about. Now that it had happened, however, he was determined to do all in his power to soothe the pain it had created for everybody. It was the only decent thing to do.

On Sundays, he left his diocese to go to church. At first, he worshipped at the early, quieter services but eventually joined the family celebrations later in the morning. Worshipping with many adults and children made him feel better. The clergy in the other dioceses had heard about his troubles from his friends in their parishes. The older priests were welcoming and chatty. The younger ones kept their distance after a word or two. One young assistant, out of seminary for about a year, would turn and hurry away nervously when Joe appeared, as though avoiding a disease. Joe wondered whether someone had shown him a copy of LaBelle's and Porter's letter about him to his diocese.

After seven weeks, the Henleys returned late one night, several days early. Their son, who would meet them at the airport, alerted Joe early that morning. He removed his clothes and other belongings and cleaned the guest room and kitchen. He left a note of thanks and some fall flowers he had bought at an apple stand across the river, turned on the hall lamps and the porch lights, and drove away a bit before 9:00 p.m.

He had found a room in an inexpensive motel that catered to migrant workers and day laborers. The Palm Inn was run by a Mr. Patel and his deferential wife and daughters, mysterious ladies who went cautiously about making their fifty-year-old domain as tidy as they could. Because he would be staying for an indefinite time—until his funds ran out, although he did not feel it necessary to explain this to Mr. Patel—and he was willing to pay weekly in advance, Joe was given a favorable rate.

He wedged his winter clothing, suitcases, coolers, and boxes of personal effects into the tiny room, leaving narrow runways between the door, bed, and bathroom. If he met a roach on one of the paths, one of them would have to give way. His clothes, piled high on the opposite twin bed, obscured the window and blocked half the door. He shifted boxes around so he could see the antique television from the bed. There was no closet, but a few bent coat hangers dangled from a chin-up bar spanning a corner. Above the television, a ridiculous framed image of a Nordic Jesus with a Prince Valiant haircut gazed dreamily toward the stained ceiling. This would be home for a while.

He received a letter from Kirby Porter informing him that as a priest under prohibition, he should not attend the consecration service for Bishop Solenburger. He read it and smiled and tucked it in his file.

He had continued to receive mail at the rural post office near his former home, the postal manager going out of his way to accommodate him in his difficulties. But that manager, a huge pleasant black man who liked to talk with him about fishing and theology, would be transferred soon and no one knew whether his replacement would be cooperative. He could rent a post office box at Catoctin Springs but knew it was likely he would be moving on from there too.

He and Jim Edelman consulted every few days. He despaired of ever being able to show Jim the depth of his gratitude, and he became more and more reluctant to take up Jim's time. Jim continued to do everything he could for Joe, making room in his frantic schedule for everything that could resolve Joe's troubles. His appreciation for Jim Edelman, his wife, and his children increased daily, and he was increasingly embarrassed at the need to interrupt them. They appeared to sense his reluctance, and they reassured him at every turn.

Hank Biller was finishing his report, and it would be in the new bishop's hands within days. Biller was far too professional to say more than was authorized, but lawyers in negotiations learn to judge the movement and weight of disputed matters the way a trout fisherman reads a stream. The sense coming through his telephone conversations, letters, and facsimiles suggested to Jim that someone on the other side would be very hard to persuade that punishment enough had been exacted and that the time had come to relent. Andy Campbell, a retired priest whose perception of people had always intrigued Joe, telephoned a few times while Joe was still at the Henleys' and believed that "somebody on that executive committee has it in for you, my friend." He advised that many in the diocese figured that LaBelle and the committee had painted themselves into a corner. "Now they're stuck."

They're stuck, thought Joe as he typed letters at night in the real estate office of a friend. He was beginning the process of returning to the practice of law. It was very difficult for him to have to say in his letters that there was no telephone number at which he could be reached. He told the recipients that he was "moving from one residence to another" and that he would call them after they had had a chance to review his résumé.

Neither Solenburger nor Porter responded to his letters about ESGA or Dr. Zander. Until they answered, he felt justified and safe in continuing to go to Al-Anon meetings and leaving the matter of emotional groups and "intense psychotherapy with a psychoanalyst" alone.

In the long, troublesome days, he lay on the bumpy bed in his motel room and re-read *The Leopard*, drinking in the honeyed prose like wine and allowing the world of Risorgimento Sicily to occupy his mind. He listened to Ted Hughes's narration of *Four Quartets* a half-dozen times, and read Beevor's *The Fall of Berlin 1945*, plotting the movements of the desperate armies on the European roadmap he used as a bookmark. He re-read Kephart's classic *Camping and Woodcraft*, finding it had lost nothing of the power he had felt when he encountered it as a teenager. He stayed up all one night, reading Dashiell Hammett's *The Maltese Falcon*, marveling at its economy of prose and power. As always, he had *The New Oxford Book of English Verse* at hand. He re-read Hemingway's *Nick Adams Stories*. It was more reading than he had been able to do in the whole time of his marriage. He began to spot-read a huge *Encyclopedia of Dogs*. He put it away after a few nights because it made him think about Cory, who had resided with some good friends since the house was sold.

On every hand, the signs of care cut through his worries like shafts of sunlight in a forest. He had only to think of Jim Edelman to remind him of how blessed his life was, or see Harry Campos's smiling face, or hear Diana Boyd's upbeat voice on the phone. An old fishing companion from down on the Chesapeake called him every few days until he moved from the Henley's. Margaret Henley sent him a note every few days, telling him he was still calling and what he had said and keeping him informed of all the other calls he was still receiving there. It all made a difference to him. Each day passed in a small spell of caution and amazement that his intestinal pain continued in abatement or that it had been taken away because he had enough to deal with. His common sense had long told him that a man never realizes how blessed he is until he gets into trouble. Now his experience was adding new understanding to that old conviction.

Chapter Twenty-Seven

Dear people of Redeemer,

We would like to provide an opportunity for members of the Church of the Redeemer to come together in a safe place for folks to express their feelings during this difficult and painful time. Our role is to facilitate conversation. We want to assure you that what is said in these meetings will be confidential. We will not be reporting details back to either Bishop LaBelle or the executive committee. The diocese is sending us to Redeemer as part of its support ministry. The meeting times will be posted in the church. Know that you and the Stephenson family remain in our prayers.

Faithfully yours,
Mary Lake

T HIS LETTER WAS signed by Mary Lake, the bishop's assistant whom LaBelle had appointed as adviser to Kate, and by Leslie Culbertson, the diocesan deployment officer charged with assisting parishes in finding and employing priests. About fifteen people showed up "to express their feelings." Most of them spent the ninety minutes listening, confining their participation to asking when the diocese would end the whole mess and allow

Joe to return. A few were quite vocal in their opposition to Joe's return. A minister from another denomination, a man who had once been a missionary and was attending Redeemer services because his wife liked the liturgy, declared that Joe's conduct was unforgivable and that he would never enter Redeemer again if Joe returned. He was so personally hurt by Joe's criminal behavior that he had trouble sleeping at night. Several people spoke up to say they believed Joe to be truthful and sincere and wondered why the church was reacting so severely to a private family dispute. At this, the elderly minister, who was neither a priest nor a member of Redeemer, became quite flushed, shed a few tears, and delivered a short lecture on what a priest was supposed to be and what a fallen man Joe was, going on until even the moderators suggested that someone else should have a chance to speak. Most of the people went away more discouraged and angry than they had been when they showed up.

* * *

Joe,

My grandmother's crystal bowls were on my china cabinet, and I know you took them and I want 'em back. And the deacon's bench that was in the dining room that you didn't put on the plan of the house when you sent it to me, I want it and I want it now! The beach towel that is gray with colored lines, I want it back! I'm gonna use it next summer. You took all the good pictures and my good dishes from downstairs, and I want 'em back. And I want my money from the house. If you have it, I want it now. I don't understand how you could do me this way, Joe, after all I have done for you.

Kate

* * *

Dear Kate,

Your bowls were in the cabinet where you always kept them, except for one that you had filled with potpourri and placed on the coffee table. You used another one for candy, on the long table at the opposite end of the room from the fireplace. I left them all exactly where you had put them. I will give you the deacon's bench, but I must wait until I can get it out of storage, when I find where I am going. I do not know anything about a beach towel. I took only the hunting pictures. Since you had never liked them, I thought you would want it that way. I left all the others, and the mirrors, for you because I thought you would want them. The only dishes I took were the green and white set that I bought when I started to practice law, before we were married. I took some wineglasses but left all our wedding gifts for you, all your family china, and the Evesham set in the kitchen that we bought over the years that you had always liked.

I know your lawyer has explained to you that the proceeds of the house must remain in escrow until we are finally divorced. It is marital property and must be divided then. I cannot touch it and have never used any of it.

As to finances, I am still waiting for you and Ted to return to me the financial aid forms I sent you midsummer. The college financial aid people have not received them, and you did not send them back to me. You must still have them. Please send them to me right away. The time for the first payment is approaching, and I am not able to pay the whole amount. I have asked you for months to cooperate in this, and we are running out of time. Ted's signature is required on one of the forms (I marked the place in red). If he has not signed, you should complete the forms and send them to him right away, have him sign, and make sure he takes them to the financial aid office immediately. He must give them directly to Laurie Landsdowne. She is the one I have been working with, and she is expecting them. If he simply leaves them on the counter or gives them to anyone else, it will slow things down. We have only a few more days!

Kate, I need to know about Ted. He won't reply to me. He is my son too. I need to know how he is, about his start in college, so many things. I ask for your help in this again.

Love,
Joe

And he signed his name. The content of the letters to and fro had settled down to a pattern, always the same, the same issues, the same demands, the same pleading for action or information. He found himself explaining the same things week after week. Did she even read his letters? Did she honestly believe he had access to the sale proceeds? Financial aid for Ted's college education was in everyone's best interest. Why was she ignoring it?

After almost twenty years, he was still incredulous at her resistance even to routine matters and tasks that were clearly in the family's interest. In the eyes of many who knew them, the peculiar thing was no longer her resistance or resentment but Joe's surprise at it after so long.

* * *

Dear Joe,

This is a solemn warning to you. Based on the alleged domestic violence acknowledged by you,

based further on the recommendations in the eval-
uation by Dr. Frank McMahon, and finally, based
on the findings of the evaluations of you by Dr.
Williams and Dr. Casselman, the executive commit-
tee has directed, and continues to direct, you to enter
intensive psychoanalysis. Dr. McMahon has recom-
mended Dr. John Zander, and we concur and direct
you to enter into a year of intense therapy with him.
You will then be re-evaluated by Dr. McMahon to
determine if more therapy is needed. During this
time, you are to be completely disassociated from the
congregation of Redeemer, Catoctin Springs. You
may function pastorally or liturgically only with the
specific permission of the ecclesiastical authority. At
the conclusion of a year, another evaluation will be
done by Dr. McMahon to determine your fitness
to return to ministry. The executive committee has
issued this warning to you in its capacity as overseer
of the good order of the diocese.

We cannot emphasize enough that the time for
debate is over. You are to comply immediately. Any
further disobedience could be grounds for an addi-
tional charge against you resulting in a trial before
the ecclesiastical court of this diocese.

Sincerely,
Kirby Porter

Kirby Porter's barely legible signature ended in a dramatic flourish that was probably intended for emphasis. It was becoming as routine in Joe's bad dreams as the relentless references to McMahon's
counseling and Joe's anticipated disobedience. How would Porter
interpret his last letter, explaining that Dr. Zander would not be
accepting new patients for another six months? Why had he not
responded to it? Would he and his committee construe it somehow as another example of Joe's disobedience? It was a preposterous

thought, but these were the same people who now were using the positive evaluations of him by Williams and Casselman as a basis for ordering him into therapy.

Porter. A leader of the diocese, pastor of one of the diocese's few large churches, president of the executive committee, confidant of bishops, a man who fancied himself on the way to becoming a bishop too. In a world in which Alexander VI was pope and Jim and Tammy Faye Baker were televangelical celebrities, there was certainly room in the House of Bishops for the likes of prickly, pretentious Kirby Porter. Perhaps they would seat him next to their colleague who denies the virgin birth and resurrection of Christ.

In his dingy motel room, seated on the creaking bed, Joe shook his head and smiled and folded the letter and put it in his file with the other erudite communications from the church authorities. He could have seen it all as the stuff of low drama had it not been a threat to his future. After all his years of education, preparation, and conscientious service in the church, his future was being determined by ignorant little martinets who would have fussed and gossiped through the Sermon on the Mount. After diligent prayer and a careful assessment of the evidence, he had come to believe that it was not God's will that his ministry should be destroyed so recklessly. He was a sinner, and he knew it. He had acted badly. But he did not believe that God wanted him to spend years under the dictates of Porter, McMahon, LaBelle, and Solenburger. There was something withering about the thought of it. He would be derelict to allow his ordination and ministry to be destroyed by them.

"And in the whole church hierarchy, there is no one with the balls to stop it. Nobody to step in with mercy and common sense."

On the other end of the line, his friend Andy Campbell laughed heartily, a reaction that Joe recognized was philosophically appropriate to the circumstances.

"It's a comedy of errors. A comedy of errors."

"Except that my future depends on these…errors."

"You mean on these…assholes."

"Yes."

"Have you ever thought how different this all might be if you were a different person?"

I have. I wish I had been more patient, less worried about her, and a better father."

"No, no. I don't mean that. Look around you. Look at the times. You've got a handicap, Joe. Face it. You are not a female, not a member of an ethnic or sexual minority, and you're not a bishop. You are not pious. You are uncomfortably straightforward in a fuzzy vocation. You're a lawyer, on top of everything else. That alone makes you suspect. You are not dealing with theologians. They're businessmen and businesswomen, like your buddy Hervey. And your infraction falls squarely into a socially sensitive arena. All of which makes you, my friend, bad for business. A right volatile mixture. And the more you stir it, the worse it smells."

"And they feel perfectly justified because they can point to an unqualified doctor's damned evaluation. And he was recommended by their own damned expert."

"They got the bases covered."

Joe was quiet for a moment.

"You still there?" asked Campbell.

"Last night I re-read parts of Augustine's *The Spirit and the Letter.*"

"Good Lord! I'm all ears!"

"Grace does not find a man willing, but makes him willing."

"I'm listening."

"God gives us free will and then uses our free will to lure us forward, by winning over our will, seducing us, converting us. Then we can respond to God with joy. Then we do the right thing out of gladness, not from fear of punishment. That makes the right thing, when we do it, completely right. Right from the heart."

"So?"

"Then we can cooperate, of our own free will, with God's grace. Except that, being human, we are weak and will lapse unless we continue to receive God's help through grace."

"So—if I remember right—God gives faithful human beings the gift of perseverance."

"Yes, but not to every one of us. We can see that by looking at the world. There are a lot of nominal Christians around. But for the ones blessed with it, perseverance may be what reveals the true enormity of human sin."

Campbell thought for a moment and said, "You make me think of Karl Barth's words in his final moments. 'God be merciful to me, a sinner.'"

"How do we know? How do we know God's will for us, what God wants us to do?"

"Easy. Health and wholeness. The difficulty comes in discerning it in a particular set of circumstances."

* * *

Bishop-elect Solenburger and the executive committee received Hank Biller's report, but they would not reveal anything about it to Jim Edelman or Joe. Biller himself could only write to Edelman that the committee instructed him to keep his report and recommendations confidential. "Nonetheless, I can tell you that I formulated my conclusions and my recommendations having in mind the goal to seek some middle ground in this dispute that might enable the parties to achieve an acceptable compromise and avoid an ecclesiastical trial."

The executive committee had authorized Biller to "explore the feasibility of an agreed resolution of the charge pending against Reverend Stephenson." The proposal was that Joe voluntarily plead guilty, whereupon the bishop would suspend him "for a period." Joe would be prohibited from "any exercise of the gifts of ministry conferred by ordination and from the discharge of any priestly duties." During the suspension, Joe would be evaluated again, by a licensed professional chosen by the bishop-elect, "to determine whether he [was] suitable and fit to resume performance of his priestly duties at the end of the period of suspension." In their infinite wisdom, the church authorities would agree that the evaluation "would not involve psychoanalysis, would not be performed by a psychoanalyst, and would specifically not be performed either by Dr. McMahon or by Dr. Zander." If and when Joe returned to the active priesthood, he would be required to engage in "counseling by a licensed counselor deemed suitable to the bishop." Unless Joe agreed to all this, the executive committee and bishop would issue a formal presentment against him and he would be tried before the diocesan ecclesiastical court.

Hank Biller had completed his work for the diocese and would soon be out of the whole dreary business. Both Joe and Jim were sorry to see him go. He had been as straightforward as he had been allowed to be, reasonable, and professional. His departure would leave the field to others who played by very different rules. They both agreed that Biller had been the lone voice of fairness in the church's position and exactly the sort of lawyer they both admired.

Although Biller's letter and the church's proposal arrived in early October, the executive committee had received the report of his findings on September 24. By canon law, this meant that "the committee [would] have only until Wednesday, October 24, to decide whether to issue a formal presentment against Reverend Stephenson." Joe would have to decide before then whether to accept the terms or go to trial.

With no explanation, after almost a year, suddenly Joe was no longer a man requiring "intensive psychotherapy with a psychoanalyst" or participation in a twelve-step group for the emotionally out-of-control. He was certain LaBelle and Porter had their violent objections to this turnaround. Or as his friend Campbell opined, "They surely have their panties in a wad." And the year, at the very minimum, of leaving the ministry and separation from the church somehow was no longer necessary. That the church offered no explanation or reasoning and no comment on anything other than the take-it-or-leave-it punishment came as no surprise. Except for persistent references to McMahon's report, the church had offered no explanation for its vengeful choices since the beginning. Joe knew he had acted sinfully, and he had acknowledged it from the beginning. In all that time, the church leadership had given no indication of believing anything he said, no expression of concern into his circumstances, no compassion or mercy. The accusations and gossip against him, whatever the evidence and however contradictory to common sense, had been willingly excepted. In the estimation of the modern church, a slapped woman could not tell a lie. He could accept this attitude in the beginning, when she had left the house and his confession was fresh in the minds of LaBelle and Porter. Their position hardened conclusively after McMahon's evaluation of him, and he could accept that. And he knew that Kate had lied all the way through her interview with McMahon, who had accepted her story completely. But they had rejected all evidence that McMahon was not professionally qualified and that other medical experts were credible. He could imagine the church authorities' vigorous denials and self-righteous indignation in the face of criticism. He knew that other bishops would accept LaBelle's and Solenburger's position without hesitation. Looking behind their actions was just not done, regardless of their effect upon a common parish priest.

As astonished as Joe and Jim Edelman were at the abrupt turn-around, the manner by which it happened came as no surprise. They were used to it. In the overall context of ministry, what difference would it make to anyone? Who would even remember? An unknown parish priest who had dared to make a mistake deserved whatever the church authorities cared to dish out, regardless of the priest's conduct before and after the mistake, and his whole life's service notwithstanding. There was no one in the church willing to intervene or even take note of whether what was happening was fair or not. It was small stuff compared to the important things going on in the world. An expendable priest's reputation and integrity would be of no concern.

Theoretically, the executive committee could decide not to issue a presentment if Joe refused to plead guilty. Nothing in the committee's actions over the preceding months, or in the attitudes of the interim bishop or bishop-elect, suggested the slightest likelihood of this, however. An ecclesiastical trial would be fearfully expensive, what with payment for attorneys, travel, accommodations, and everything else. In a diocese afflicted with the direst poverty, the cost would be painful indeed, and much-needed ministry would suffer. No one with knowledge of the matter, however, doubted that the church would charge Joe and bring him to trial. After all, he had admitted in the beginning what he had done. And given the disruption he had caused, the vexation to diocesan leadership, and the secret maneuvering that had gone on for months, a trial before the ecclesiastical court would result in only one conceivable verdict. (Joe could close his eyes and see Ted testifying against him, "Don't trust him," as he had said to that bastard McMahon.) A verdict against him would place him entirely at the mercy of the church authorities. Ordering him into indefinite, expensive "treatment" with McMahon and company would be the least of the punishments he could expect. He would have to comply or be deposed and leave the priesthood in disgrace for the rest of his life.

As all this was being considered, bishop-elect Solenburger felt obliged to come to Redeemer for two evenings of "listening" to anyone who desired to tell him about Joe and his ministry. The diocese had long had in hand the Redeemer vestry's petition demanding Joe's return to their parish, signed by every member except Nancy Dodd. The position of these parish leaders required explanation, apparently, and he was determined to hear it with his own ears. Seated comfortably in the parish library with coffee, a legal pad, and pen in hand, he made available twenty-four five-minute interviews on a "first come, first served" basis. People duly signed up.

Joe's detractors came in quickly, and most of the interviews were assigned to them. As there were not enough of them to create an adverse balance, they signed up their children too. Thus it was that the teenage son of Don and Jane Ellen Rush spoke to the bishop about his dislike of Joe, although he had never participated in youth activities, never served as an acolyte, and rarely even attended services after the age of twelve. Lottie Bascomb's children, who had heard nothing at home for years except denunciations of Joe, had interviews too. Tom Downes and Ben Aster, the clergyman from another denomination who had spoken so passionately against Joe that tears came to his eyes, of course had interviews. News of what was happening began to spread, and the remaining slots filled up rapidly with Joe's supporters, or neutral people who wanted the diocese to end what was happening. Many who wanted to speak were unable to do so. Several of Joe's most vocal detractors were not entirely disappointed, however, because they had been in contact with the bishop-elect or other diocesan leaders by telephone or through letters. The Reverend Ben Aster, for instance, wrote a long condemnatory letter to Solenburger that was much talked about in town. From these people and others, many opinions were expressed. The bishop-elect made notes.

In addition to other worries, Joe was aware of the financial crisis at Redeemer. Many people, angry over the diocese's high-handed treatment of them, their rector, and the vestry, had concluded there was no other way left to express their anger than by their absence from the pews. Giving had diminished with attendance. Many who were determined to support the parish knew that part of their gift would have to be sent to the diocese as a portion of Redeemer's pledge. Faithful people who had supported Redeemer all their lives felt great guilt now in addition to anger and disappointment. Guilt over withholding funds caused many parishioners to write to Joe, whom they could no longer leave messages for on a telephone, asking what to do. He sent word through the vestry to make good their pledges to God. Meanwhile, the treasurer's funds dwindled as each bill and salary was paid.

Joe walked the neighborhood streets and sat up half the night, sleepless, remorseful, and humiliated. None of it would have made him feel so sick and lost if he could have spent some time with Ted. His son's presence and personality had always eased his anxieties, and he had thought Ted knew how much he loved him. Now he was beginning to doubt many things of which he had been so sure. "Don't trust him." The loneliness of an alcoholic marriage and the lonesome career of the priesthood had always given way at his son's bright disposition, dispelling shadows like sunlight. He had not seen Ted for months.

Anxiety in the voices and faces of his mother, brothers, and sisters and the look of pained expectation on the faces of his friends cut to his heart. None of his countless supporters, even those in his own denomination, understood the easily manipulated disciplinary canons of church law employed against him. His parish was slowing down, and the faithful were suffering. In most years, they would be halfway through their every member canvass at Redeemer. In another few weeks, it would be time to formulate the following year's budget. The canvass, begun by the deeply concerned parish leaders, was moving glacially. Attendance had all but dried up, even though the people knew that it was God they came to honor, not the diocese or Joe. The teenagers and younger children continued to send him cards and notes, each one delighting him and breaking his heart at the same time—a woeful combination of feelings difficult to describe. From the fall clergy conference to which LaBelle and Porter had not invited him, he had received a card signed by many of his colleagues. It came as a complete surprise, none of them having called or written before. No messages, just names. He was grateful for it and had tucked it under the top frame of the cloudy mirror in his motel room, where he saw it each morning, and felt a certain encouragement. He would have liked to hear his colleague's advice, to talk things over with them, but they had placed themselves off-limits. Bill Saunders said they were scared. He did not blame them; he understood. He supposed it was natural to avoid someone infected by the possibility of deposition. The mere thought of it made him want to vomit.

He had not heard from Bill Saunders since hearing him refer to Solenburger as "coach." "What makes you think I have any influence?" he had said. It seemed the arrival of a new man, one he could expect to serve under for as long as he remained in the diocese, had changed his allegiance from the days of "I'll do anything to help Joe Stephenson." But what could one expect? The clergy were not fighters. They had themselves to look after, and most of them had families.

It was getting colder and darker earlier. Seated on the chilly curb in front of his motel room—Mr. Patel had consigned the few Adirondack chairs to a storage room for the winter—squinting in the lights of town, smoking a Henry Clay, he missed the clarity of the evening sky. On starry nights, he drove out of town and walked on country roads and across the fields of friends who wouldn't mind. The autumn panorama overhead was giving way to winter patterns, and the great celestial drama shifted ever closer to the western horizon. Upward of Cassiopeia and northeast of her Ethiopian consort, he could make out the faint haze of Andromeda, the farthest humankind can see with the naked eye, night after night. South of Andromeda, the stars of Pegasus glittered high in the sky. On the especially dark nights of that late autumn, he could see the Milky Way passing high overhead, streaming through Cassiopeia's W like a flow of diamonds, ragged and relentless. He marveled at the night sky, at the whole creation, and what he did not know about anything. What had someone written? Berryman? Roethke? "Sole watchman of the wild and flying stars." What was it, and why couldn't he remember it? He thought of van Gogh's *The Starry Night* and the hoops of gold and silver against the cool and glittering blue. And Yeats. What was it? Stars "dancing silver sandaled on the sea…sing in their high and lonely melody." It must have been early Yeats, then. Stars. Silence. The end of knowledge. Or the extent, not the end. And we are never alone. Priests know that. He could look up and see the galaxy moving by, his galaxy, of which he was a part, a hundred thousand million stars, and our sun nothing in particular, nothing special. And our Milky Way, just one of a hundred thousand million other galaxies in only the part of the universe humankind can see. And God created all of it. God is bigger than all that. It always took him a step or two closer to a conception of glory.

His thoughts turned naturally to Job, humility, to knowing where—if *knowing* was the right word, if knowing had anything to do with it—he stood. "Where were you when I laid the foundations…?" "And to dust I shall return," he said quietly, almost silently, as if some presence in the cutover corn or icy soil might hear him and report his small moment of drama to anybody needing a good laugh.

Soon it would be Christmas. "The star of my life…in him there is no darkness at all, the night and the day are both alike."

He knew he had to settle. He must do it for everyone, the fair and the unfair alike. God had been good to him. Christ would stand by him.

There was much to do in the parish, and they needed to get busy. His mother and family needed an end to their anxiety for him. Diocesan time and funds that could have gone to worthy ministries had been wasted on punishing him. The people at Redeemer were worn-out. The wardens and vestry had done the best they could and done it nobly and willingly. He could not bring himself to accept another paycheck from them. His conscience was more and more troubled by the strain on Jim Edelman's time and legal practice. If he gave him everything he owned in the world, he could never repay Jim for his character and kindness. A final decree of divorce could be many months in the future, given the pace of Kate and her lawyer. If he stood fast and demanded a trial, he would, in good conscience, have to resign his ministry so that the people of Redeemer could get on with calling another priest. He did not think they could withstand more waiting. And how would he pay for a trial? Who would represent him? He would not consider taking up more of Jim's time. And how would he live, what would he live on, where would he live? His funds were gone. He would refuse financial help from friends. The money they had raised among themselves to pay for Casselman's evaluation alone had been thousands of dollars, which he would insist on repaying. But how would he support himself in the weeks or months leading to a trial? He was not licensed to work as a lawyer in this state. And how would he pay for the travel and accommodations for witnesses? He could no longer rely upon the charity he knew they were all still willing to provide. And all for what? So the court could sit listlessly through evidence of mitigating circumstances that even the bishops had been unable or unwilling to understand before finding him guilty on his confession? Then he would be wholly at their mercy, and everyone could guess what that would mean. He could be dealing with McMahon for years.

Agreeing to the church's settlement was the only way to return to Redeemer and guarantee himself some fairness. He would have left the ministry and moved to some other way of serving God, but that would have been treating the parishioners at Redeemer no better than the diocese and national church were treating them. It would be a wretched thing to do. And even if he did leave, however selfish and pretentious a thing it might be to do, he knew he would gradually die of the shame of being deposed. He thought he could live with a secular criminal conviction for theft in certain situations, or even involuntarily manslaughter. But guilt for moral or ethical wrongdoing was a different matter, especially in the church.

He remembered his friend Charlotte Payne's frustrated advice: "If they want your collar, let them have it." He gazed at the sky for another few minutes. Then he drove to a convenience store to call Jim.

Chapter Twenty-Eight

HANK BILLER REPRESENTED the diocese long enough to complete the negotiations for Joe's voluntary submission to church discipline. Bishop LaBelle had left for home, a departure for which many, for reasons that had nothing to do with Joe, appeared relieved. Joe never knew what other issues had grown up around the interim bishop, and he never inquired. He hoped he would never see him again. He knew he should pray for him, that he would manage other crises with more compassion and reason. That would have to come later, but for now, he did not want to think about him. The people at diocesan headquarters had grown rather close to LaBelle, a coziness that Joe now knew would affect him if he remained in the diocese. There was always a chance that Bishop Solenburger would make a difference. Joe was a hopeful man, but also a realist.

Donald Earl Solenburger was now the bishop. His ordination had been a festive celebration in a nondenominational college chapel with what seemed like half the diocese crammed in and joyfully taking part. A new spirit enthused the faithful now, a new hope, and all were ready to move forward with Bishop Don and build upon the good work of his predecessors. In a region eternally struggling with poverty and powerlessness, celebrations and new hope worked on the people like transfusions. In almost ten years among them, Joe had come to admire their character and appreciate the many good aspects of life in their state. To many decent, hardworking people who longed for better government and a stable economy, this new ministry could be evidence of God's favor and goodness toward them. The older and pragmatic, however, who had endured other promising starts, were more inclined to wait and see how this one would ride out the infectious apathy.

Jim proposed several changes to the diocese's demands. The suspension was to be cut to thirty days in view of the length of time Joe had already been officially shunned. Any evaluator the bishop chose must be a reputable, licensed, mainstream psychiatrist or psychologist qualified to administer and interpret the standard diagnostic tests recognized in the medical profession. There must be no more subjective, unprincipled evaluators. In formulating this demand, they consulted with health-care professionals in several states. Dr. Timothy Marshall, the diocese's own psychologist and a member of Redeemer, was particularly helpful. Like everything else that contradicted McMahon's nasty opinion, LaBelle and the executive committee rejected everything Tim Marshall had said on Joe's behalf.

Jim demanded that whoever the bishop chose must present a report about Joe by the first day of December. If the report found him competent for ministry, Joe could return to Redeemer as soon as the bishop had the report in hand, which should be by the third or fourth of December at the latest. Jim Edelman and Tim Marshall considered demanding a say in choosing the evaluator. They feared that this would again give the executive committee grounds for discrediting any findings that were too favorable to Joe. It would also prolong the process of choosing someone. As long as the doctor was qualified and unbiased, they were confident the evaluation would reveal Joe to be a healthy, competent man. So they kept quiet and let the diocese do the choosing.

To everyone's surprise, Solenburger and the executive committee would not agree to change except trimming the suspension down to thirty days. Jim and Joe knew that insisting on ninety more days was another act of meanness from whatever individual or group—maybe the whole committee—had been so set against Joe from the beginning. For eight months, he had been removed from his parish and officially shunned while his private marital issues and reputation were exposed to public gossip and ridicule. Anyone determined to punish him should have been satisfied. It was unfair of them to draw it out until spring, but someone was determined to get a full year out of him. The parish could not afford to pay him any longer, and he would not have accepted the salary anyway. He was determined to return by the first few days of December and begin to address the severe pastoral issues that waited. Hopefully, the important canvass could be completed before January. Having the parish together again for Christmas seemed only right. It would be spiritually and psychologically healthy for the parishioners and for him. While Joe and the parish leaders considered all this, they waited, allowing the approach of the October 24 deadline to exert its own influence.

He went to see Bishop Spencer again and told him what was happening. His former bishop was encouraged by the prospect of his return to his parish by early December and understood the urgency of the timing. He scrupulously avoided any comment on Joe's diocese, his bishops, or their executive committee. Talking about his troubles with a responsible clergyman familiar with the denomination, especially Bishop Spencer, was healing and clarifying. It had been impossible to speak with any clergy in his diocese since the letter sent out by LaBelle and Porter. And he had not wanted to trouble Bill Saunders since the meeting at Diocesan House.

During their conversation, he was aware of Bishop Spencer's face, gestures, and choice of words, just as he used to observe parties and witnesses in the law. In his former bishop, he read unbiased attention and sincerity. It was comforting for a change to speak with a church official who radiated no thinly masked contempt or indifference. He left Spencer's office convinced that his goals were valid, and began the long drive back to his motel room in Catoctin Springs.

On the road, he began prayer after prayer for continued guidance. He was too distracted to finish any of them and found himself in the midst of other thoughts before he knew it. As he drove into the night, he let his prayers go. God understood his needs anyway. He thought back to his observations of Bishop Spencer. There had been another reason for his careful scrutiny, and he recognized it now. In his loss of so much so quickly, and with no pastoral guidance except for his two trips to meet Bishop Spencer, he had been searching for a connection to the church he had grown up in. It was not that people should agree with him but that their disapproval should be just. If he was going to lose, it should be for the right reasons. He longed for the old pastoral sensitivity. He needed the reliable dignity and care of reason he had come to expect of his church early in life. He craved the signs of a restored creation, the grace that enlightens hearts and minds and strengthens wills. Grace would never end, but the particular means of its dispensation that had long nourished him was becoming harder to recognize. God's priceless gifts—so misunderstood by so many who followed other paths.

His church had molded his childhood and shaped his character and intellect as an adult. What was happening to it? It was not change he wondered about. He could understand change. Many accidentals must change for the church to thrive. And there were so many good people in it. The leaders who fumbled with his particular sin did not represent the whole church. It was still a place where truth resided, where the dignity of human nature reflected hope and glory. But why, in such a needy world, was it not flourishing? And why did he have to look so hard for fairness and common sense. Were his memories just misconceptions, misunderstandings of his immaturity and ignorance? Had his formation been something else all along? He felt it was too early to base long-term conclusions on his present straits. His situation could still be redeemed. People can change. In any case, his woes were nonessentials, crumbs under the table. He was an aphid, a flea on an elephant's tail. He knew his life was precious to God, but in all other senses, his problems paled when set against the vast brokenness of life.

He was much too astute to even think about drawing great lessons from his second or two onstage in the drama of life in the world. He thought of Constantinople in 1453 and the faithful watching their churches turned into mosques and armories after a thousand years. He thought of Jerusalem, Antioch, Alexandria, Armenia. He thought of the death of missionaries. He thought of Jews in Europe, Cathars, Native Americans. He thought of black teenagers in inner cities and elderly women of color raising grandchildren and great-grandchildren. He thought of Africa. He tried to imagine the Soviet Union, millions of murders, millions of orphans. He thought of the innocent who suffer everywhere, who have always suffered, whose cries a greedy world is conditioned to ignore. What were his vapid, nugacious afflictions laid alongside all that? When people were dying for want of food and medicine and clean water, were his prideful worries significant? And apart from his mother and siblings and friends, what difference did it make in the world? Yet he continued to believe, through feeling more than understanding, that God had room to care about him. He could feel the movement in his life. And when he considered those who loved him, what was happening around him made a difference to him too. He and his small distress were dust in cosmic time, a flyspeck against the great pain of the world. And yet in his miniscule existence, he felt the divine presence like an undertow, moving him around with power through the agitated surface of things.

* * *

With the deadline still a week away, Hank Biller began to email Jim Edelman every morning. It was evident that someone was leaning on him daily to extract an answer to the diocese's latest demand. Jim wondered whether the new bishop and his executive committee were beginning to consider the expense of an ecclesiastical trial. He could imagine Porter, his mustache twitching with anxiety, telephoning the new bishop daily to ask if he had heard anything. Whatever the reason for their urgency, the diocesan authorities' lethargy of preceding months appeared to be over.

One day before the deadline, Joe proposed that the church's ninety days of suspension should run from the previous September 1 and end on December 1, the same day the new evaluation would be delivered to Bishop Solenburger. Ten minutes after Jim emailed their counter proposal, they received word the bishop and executive committee would agree. Jim was elated, and he walked around the office in momentary relief. Joe was visibly glad, and he congratulated

Jim on his excellent representation and loyal kindness. He owed it to Jim to demonstrate all the obvious signs of relief and gratitude.

But inside it was different. He had thought he would feel great relief at laying down the weight he had carried for so long. He thought he would be happy, encouraged, moved. Except for the happiness he felt for Jim, there was none of that. For himself, for reasons he could not explain, he felt fresh grief at the loss of his wife and son and new irritation at the thought of yet another medical examination. And the thought of the stain that would soil his record forever filled him with nausea he knew was incurable.

* * *

He drove west through the mountains toward his fourth mental examination in six months. His was a diocese in which clergy salaries had only lately been increased to the national minimum standard, but there seemed to be unlimited funds at hand to prove that Joe Stephenson was emotionally unstable. This time the diocese had selected an examiner who ran a clinic and was quite well-known in her profession.

The weather was gray, and the roadsides, packed high with dirty snow, looked like the threatening terminus of an unending glacier. Even for the mountains, the weather was unusually severe for early November, and in every one of the high passes, he eased his car through squalls of blinding snow. He drove with the caution observed among the responsible locals for frozen winter highways, where coatings of dark ice were invisible until one's car began the sickening slide beyond control. After long drives over the winter mountains, his neck and shoulders remained tense for days and his hands and arms ached from the prolonged stress.

He had met Dr. Nadine Moncure several times at conferences and clergy workshops. He had no worries about her examination. He was satisfied that she was a competent professional. He knew himself to be a mentally and emotionally healthy adult, a qualified priest who had made a mistake and become the victim of a witch hunt. It was not the forthcoming evaluation but the ignorance and prejudice of the church officials who would review it that worried him. He had tried to be fair as a prosecutor, listening to both sides, weighing evidence with reason and conscience. His duty had not been to secure convictions, but to see that justice was done. As a lawyer, he was charged with avoiding even the appearance of impropriety. He had always felt that the same duty carried over into the priesthood, and he knew he had failed miserably at it. The church would except nothing in mitigation. Did he expect too much of the church leaders? Did the higher standard of ordination make him different from other men, or so different that he deserved no mercy? He was tired of thinking about it. In his present straits, he felt inadequate to determine the truth of anything on his own.

Joe thought of Cory. On their last night together at the house, he had arrived home after dark and spied his little dog creeping across the driveway in the headlights with his tail down. Unlike every other evening of his life, Cory was nowhere around when Joe got out of the car. He called and called but could not find him anywhere. He figured Cory was on a distant part of the lawn, investigating a mole hole or something. He brought out food and fresh water and left them between the picnic table and the doghouse. Later, while he was talking to his friend Jane Holloway on the telephone, he looked out the kitchen window and saw Cory eating. He did not look up at the window between bites, as was his custom, but kept wolfing down his food. When Joe next looked, Cory was gone again.

The next morning, when he went out to look for him, Cory was still nowhere around. Eddie and Jan Jackson, two of his best friends who ran a kennel near Catoctin Springs and built their life around dogs, would be waiting for Cory at 8:00 a.m. He walked around the property, calling and whistling. As he was beginning to think the clever little dog had jumped the invisible fence, he passed the sheltered place beneath a giant rhododendron where Cory used to take refuge when he was a pup. And there he found him. He had to pull him out and walk him to the car, holding his collar. Joe spoke to him as much as he could, but he could not look at him, and Cory kept his face averted. When Joe put him in the car, he curled up on the floor on the passenger side with his nose in the corner, pointing away from

Joe. He usually sat on the front seat, looking around at the scenery, glancing occasionally at Joe, and licking his hand when Joe reached for the gearshift. If they passed other dogs, Cory would stop panting and his ears would go up and he would stare until the foreigner was out of sight. But this time was different, and he remained on the floor. They drove in silence to the Jacksons' farm. Cory had grown to like the affable Jacksons over the years. Now he did not even wag his tail and only wedged his head between Jan's legs. They treated him as always, cheerful and welcoming and affectionate. They did not look at Joe out of kindness for him, and maybe as a gesture of solidarity with Cory. He got back in the car and drove away quickly without saying anything. He knew they understood.

As he drove through the freezing mountains, he remembered dozens of journeys over the same roads, recalling how eager he was to go home again and how he thought about Kate and Ted over every mile. It had been almost seven months, but it might as well have been seven years. Thinking of them no longer made him cry. It was deeper than that now. And when his thoughts turned to himself and to his own mistakes, it was very deep indeed, like a pit or a silent mineshaft, going down into thick darkness. How could he describe the depths? He had seen movies in which Japanese officers, provoked by a slight, that Westerners would have ignored, sat on the floor with thin knives and disemboweled themselves. Their weapons looked rather like the Scandinavian fillet knife he kept in his tackle box. He had gutted deer. He had cleaned fish, big goofy-faced red drum and gnashing chopper blues. He had dressed rabbits and snapping turtles and doves. There had been times over the months when his anguish had made him want to sit down like a crazy Japanese and do the same to himself. As thoroughly and painfully as he could, he would tear himself open in punishment. Even that would not be penance enough. Where were they? What were they doing? How could they hate him so, after all their years together? How could Kate have so little feeling for him that she would destroy his reputation and career? How could Ted...

But at this, especially, he had to stop to preserve his composure.

He turned on the radio, but the only station the mountains admitted carried an angry black academic raving about how the ancient Egyptians were black too. Strange for this part of the country. He had supposed he would hear a white evangelist identically passionate about one thing or another and with grammar equally as bad. He turned off the radio and put in a cassette tape of Bach's *Double Concerto for Two Violins in D Minor:* Issac Stern and Yitzchak Perlman and Zubin Mehta and the New York Philharmonic. Bach. After a few minutes, he took it out and carefully put it back in its small plastic box. He put in a cassette of Ella Fitzgerald and Louis Armstrong, catching them as they began "Stars Fell on Alabama." He listened until the end of the song and then took that one out too.

He had gotten better at offering up his grief to God. He must have said "I'm guilty," "I'm sorry," "Have mercy on me, a sinner," "Protect them, Lord," and "Let them know I love them" five hundred thousand times. He repeated them in his sleep. He would wake up, sweating and frowning, his heart pounding and his mind crazy with remorse. He began to intone "Forgive me, Lord" like a mantra, knowing that whatever in his words or method was wrong would be recrafted and made acceptable in the ear of God.

As a proliferation of billboards appeared, he concluded his prayers like a guilty student who knows after all his studies that he is still unprepared for tomorrow. On the outskirts of town, he pulled over and consulted his directions again and, fifteen minutes later, was parking his car down the street from Dr. Moncure's clinic. He put on his collar, which he always removed during long drives, wrapped an arm around his thick file case, and went in. He had arrived a half-hour early, just as he planned. He would have time to go to the men's room, maybe have a cup of coffee if there was any, and compose himself before meeting the doctor. One good thing about his disassociation and shunning—perhaps the only good thing—was the luxury of arriving at appointments ahead of time. In the law and in ministry, he was forever arriving just in time, or a few minutes late, or calling someone to explain he would be five or ten minutes late, rushing from place to place always with the feeling of holding somebody up or delaying this or that. And when he did begin on time, seconds away from the processional hymn or the moment the door of chambers opened and the judge appeared, there was always one of the self-absorbed oblivious, talking in his ear, demanding his attention, whispering of unrelated matters—although one had to listen to them to determine that they were unrelated—inquiring about future issues that could easily wait, insensible to his trying to sing or walk in procession or maintain eye contact with the court or call a class into session or a meeting to order. And no matter how important the subject of his attention, or how thoughtless the intrusion, he could manage interruptions well five hundred times and no one would notice. The one time he showed irritation, or spoke hastily or sharply to anyone, it would be remembered and commented upon for years.

He spoke to the receptionist, who offered him coffee. He accepted it with thanks and settled down at one end of a sofa and began to clear his mind of guilt and anxieties.

* * *

At one o'clock, the receptionist took him to a conference room, and a few minutes later, Dr. Moncure and her associate, Dr. Paula Kelly, came in and shook hands. Despite all his determination and confidence in their credentials, he was nervous. So much depended on the outcome of whatever happened here. Both doctors perceived his concern, although they might not have understood all the reasons for it. They tried to put him at ease, and he realized what they were doing and was grateful. Both women appeared to be in their early fifties. Dr. Moncure was short and slight, not petite. He thought he recalled her saying in a lecture once that she and her husband had twin sons, or maybe daughters, but he wasn't sure. He hoped so— that she had some personal experience with family life to go along with her training. Dr. Kelly was tall and buxom. Both were cordial. They offered him more coffee, which he accepted.

He was with them for four hours. They already had the reports of McMahon, Williams, and Casselman. The data of the extensive testing by Williams and Casselman was less than six months old, and they asked his cooperation in requesting it from both examiners.

He signed releases for it, and releases to allow them to speak with all three prior doctors. He went through his file with them, giving them documents that had not been part of what the diocese had sent them. They asked him many, many questions, and Dr. Kelly made notes as he answered. After two hours, they took a short break, and then the interview continued for two hours more. He told them everything, beginning with what he had done, and answered all their questions. As the afternoon ended, they asked him to come back in two weeks on a day when he could spend part of the morning and all afternoon there. They told him they would give him one, perhaps two, further psychological tests. He said he understood. They would give him a Rorschach test and wanted to know if he knew what that was. Joe was familiar with the idea of inkblots, but he had never had such a test and knew nothing about how it worked. They said that their testing would be short since he had already had most of what the profession recommended and they would now have access to that data. When they said goodbye, he was conscious of his own efforts throughout the afternoon not to be too friendly. They were professionally gracious people, and it would have been easy to feel too relaxed, but he needed the caution that his old professional strength had always entailed. He had tried to be himself, open and professional, without relaxing too much, and he hoped he had not overdone it.

It was dark when he left the clinic and began the long drive home. Home. His drab motel room. Not one thing about it had grown cozy or appealing. Merely thinking of going back there was depressing. And yet he needed to be there, alone, with the door closed, where mercifully no telephone could ring and nobody knocked, and he could lie down on the lumpy, sloping bed, put a pillow over his face, and perhaps sleep without dreaming. He needed all that. He had always been that kind of person, needing a dose of solitude to wind down, collect his thoughts, rest his intellect and emotions. In all their years together, Kate had continued to interpret it as a personal rejection. He just needed some time now and then to collect himself. How many nights had he come home craving peace, famished for rest, to have her unload on him from the moment he came in until she went up to bed, the whole time watching him and ready to pounce at the slightest flicker of disinterest or wavering attention, pouring out the gossipy minutia of her school day? Who was right? Who was wrong? If she had only gone with him to counseling...

The time with Dr. Moncure and Dr. Kelly had been painless enough, except for explaining yet again what he had done. He had told it so often now that he knew he might inadvertently come across as minimizing it somehow, and he did not want that. Thus, he had taken care to be accurate and complete without being rote.

* * *

In late November, Joe received the results of his final psychological evaluation. The day was icy and windy, and he sat in the freezing car beside the post office and read it immediately. More than the weather chilled him as he poured over the half-dozen pages, a copy of the original report addressed to Bishop Solenburger. After an initial reading, he started the car and drove to the nearby truck stop, where he sat in a booth and read it again.

Reverend Stephenson values others and has good perceptions about interpersonal relationships. He is not likely to behave in ways that others see as inappropriate. He is currently under great stress, but it has not overwhelmed him, and he can be expected to behave in ways that are consistent with how people see him. His desire to please and his need to do things as well as he possibly can will make him sensitive to the needs of others. He will occasionally project his own feelings upon others, but this is not problematic. He does not display on any tests the need to control others, difficulty controlling his hostility, or lack of concern for the feelings or welfare of others. These findings are inconsistent with any assumption that Reverend Stephenson is prone to abuse. In fact, it is far more likely he will attempt to please the people in his life to his own detriment, resulting in unmet needs that he will seldom voice. He is currently being hypervigilant in his relationship with others. This is to be expected, given the possibility that he will be judged and removed from ministry because of accusations against him. It would be more of a concern if he were not currently anxious.

"You wansa carfee?" The waitress with bright-red hair picked up his report and wiped the table vigorously with a wet rag and put it back on the table again.

"Yes, please. Regular. Black."

He closed his eyes and rubbed his forehead and let the words sink in once more. He re-read the paragraph again, flipped to the first page, and looked once more at the date and read the list again of the nine separate tests he had been given in the past six months. He browsed the intervening pages, spot-reading the cumulative observations of Williams, Casselman, and finally, Dr. Moncure and Dr. Kelly.

"S'cuse me. S'cuse me. Are you the reverend? The one down at Catoctin Springs?"

He looked up at the woman, dressed in a green tracksuit much too small for her and an Army fatigue jacket, unzipped and revealing a late pregnancy. She was about thirty, perhaps thirty-five. She was clutching the hand of a boy of about ten. Behind her stood a tall frowning teenage girl with her hair in tight cornrows. They all looked alike, and they regarded him in silence as she awaited an answer. He stood up and stepped away from the table, unconsciously careful to keep the report in his hand.

"Yes, ma'am," he said. "I am."

"Could I talk to you a minute?"

"When did you all eat last?" He looked at the tall girl. She scowled and immediately looked away.

"Yesterday, afore he made us leave out of the house. I ain't hungry, but my churtrin is."

"Where did you sleep last night?"

"They let us sit up in here."

413

"Have we met before? You'll have to excuse me. It's just that I meet so many people."

The waitress set a steaming mug of coffee and a handful of creamers on the table. He saw that the boy watched the cup intently.

"We ain't met, but I seen your picture in the paper with that column you used to write. People at our church reads it."

"Let's do it this way," he said. "You all sit at the counter and tell the waitress what you want to eat. I'll pay for it. After you've eaten, we'll talk. Can we do it that way?"

The woman nodded and, placing a hand on the backs of the girl and boy, herded them toward the long counter and its row of revolving stools. Joe spoke to the waitress and sat back down.

> *Having reviewed all the test data of the two previous evaluators, and data from our own testing, and the additional reports of Dr. Marshall and Reverend Clyde Candler, and over two hours of interview with Reverend Stephenson, we have come to the following conclusions:*
>
> 1. *All the information received and the test results, which are accurate, valid, and objective, indicate that Reverend Stephenson is mentally healthy and competent to serve as a parish priest in his diocese. Does he have personal problems right now that require individual counseling? Yes. However, this counseling can be conducted privately within the course of his ministry, as it had been done before. It is our opinion that Reverend Stephenson should be returned to parish ministry and the marital issues that remain be handled privately.*
> 2. *It is apparent that actions taken by his diocese during this process with Reverend Stephenson were not appropriate and that*

his personal well-being was not treated with pastoral sensitivity or confidentiality. Nor was his wife given the same evaluative tests to determine if her story was credible. As clinicians, we can only determine if one partner's story is credible by listening to both partners' stories and working with both of them to determine where lies the truth. Mrs. Stephenson's information was the only story the diocese believed, which seems extremely one-sided.

3. *When officials call our office to ask for referral recommendations for psychological evaluations, it has always been our policy to not recommend psychoanalysts due to the highly subjective nature of their evaluations. We only recommend psychiatrists, psychologists, or pastoral counselors, who utilize valid, highly normed, standardized psychological tests, which are objective in nature. Psychoanalysts are not trained to administer psychological tests, which is the reason they do not use them. They rely on subjective, personalized opinions for their analysis, which may not be reliable. Psychological tests are very reliable because they are normed on many thousands of people's answers.*

4. *Because we see many troubled couples from church conference, diocesan, and judicatory bodies, we find it disturbing that the entire diocesan churches and clergy were informed about Reverend Stephenson's personal and pastoral issues. It is not common practice to investigate sensitive personal issues in public. To enable Reverend Stephenson to*

proceed as leader of his parish church in Catoctin Springs, it would be beneficial if the executive committee sent a second letter with a statement either retracting the first letter or apologizing for making public a very personal pastoral matter. It might be stated only that it was necessary to launch such an investigation due to the serious-ness of the charges made against Reverend Stephenson.

5. *In our talk with Dr. Marjorie Williams, she informed us that her comments to Bishop LaBelle were rebuffed repeatedly by "But his wife says..." or "But his wife said..." This led her to believe that the bishop and the executive committee had already made up their minds about Reverend Stephenson prior to receiving her report. She indi-cated that Bishop LaBelle placed enormous importance on what Reverend Stephenson's wife said, and the bishop described Reverend Stephenson as "a classic wife-beater." Our test results and interview, and the test results and interviews of the other evaluators, do not support that statement. Apparently, Mrs. Stephenson's statements and opinions were taken at face value but what Reverend Stephenson said was taken as "being defen-sive." The diocesan authorities' opinion was highly influenced by a secret letter written by Mrs. Stephenson to Bishop LaBelle, which neither Reverend Stephenson nor his attorney was allowed to see. This further causes great concern that this was not a fair process from the beginning.*

*If additional information is needed, please do
not hesitate to call us at the above phone number.
We are pleased to serve your diocese in this capacity.*

He re-read it several times and drank his coffee. When they had
eaten, the woman and her children came over to his booth. He stood
up, and the boy slid across to the end of his seat and leaned against
the wall with his eyes closed. The tall girl sat opposite her brother
and glared at the tabletop. The woman slid in beside her daughter,
opposite Joe, and said, "Thank you."

He listened while she told her story. When she had finished,
he asked her several questions and listened to her answers. The boy
came to life only once, long enough to correct her on some detail,
and retreated again into his feigned nap. The girl never uttered a
sound and did not look at him. Something the mother said made Joe
think the daughter was pregnant, too, but he did not inquire.

He went to the payphone and found it was broken. The truck
stop manager was a decent sort who had called him in the past about
people who ended up in his restaurant, a clean, well-lit place on a
major road. He let Joe use his office phone and refused to let him
pay for the food. Joe telephoned the Abused Women's Shelter and
found it was full. The church the woman attended had a telephone,
but it rang and rang, and finally he gave up. He called a friend, a
social worker with whom he had collaborated on several domestic
matters, and she said she would send the worker on call but it might
take a while. He called the Public Health Clinic, and the people there
agreed to see the mother and daughter if they didn't mind waiting.
He called his social worker friend back, and she agreed to have the
caseworker on call meet the family at the health clinic. He called the
state police and arranged for an officer to meet them at the clinic
too. Then he returned to the table and talked with the woman some
more.

The back seat and trunk of his car were filled with things he
had no room for in his motel room. It would be impossible to get all
three of them into the passenger seat. He asked the manager to call
a taxi, but the manager came back and said that June, the red-haired

waitress, was going home to Catoctin Springs in a few minutes and would take them to the health clinic. Joe joined them again in the booth and asked them if they would like to pray. The woman said yes, and the children said nothing. He suggested they join hands, and the daughter reached out to her mother and brother and then began to cry. The boy looked at his sister and squeezed her hand across the table and took Joe's hand as though Joe had leprosy and shut his eyes again. Joe prayed for them, for the man they had been living with, for the caseworker and nurses they were about to see, and for their collective family, friends, and neighbors. He asked God's protection for them and asked God for justice and mercy on all people, and then he said "Amen." When June waved from the entrance, he walked with them outside and they all followed her red hair across the parking lot to a dilapidated Country Squire. The three got in the back seat without speaking or looking at him, and the big car, listing heavily to one side, chugged out to the access ramp.

* * *

After a promise that no names would be repeated, someone at Diocesan House told Sally Kelly, the state delegate, about the fit of rage that overcame Bishop Solenberger when he read the two psychologists' final report on Joe Stephenson. He had telephoned Dr. Moncure and, unable to challenge her findings about Joe's mental health, complained severely and loudly about how her report had been written. She had no right, he said, to come to so many conclusions, and recommendations on Joe's behalf. It had not been at all helpful for the diocese that had paid for the report and expected a different result. Amanda Rowland advised Joe about the bishop's temper tantrum. Harry Campos had heard about it and Margaret Henley too, and several others.

Margaret had attended seminars at which Dr. Moncure spoke and was alarmed by what the bishop had said to her. Joe replied that Dr. Moncure had spent a career dealing with scurrilous people, and while he was sorry about it too, he believed she could handle it.

Joe, Harry, Jim, the Henleys and many others wondered what in the world people must think of their beloved denomination.

The diocese sent out no letters of retraction or apology. When Joe wrote to the bishop concerning the report's recommendation, Solenberger replied that there was nothing he could do about it. Kirby Porter and other diocesan notables approached him with peevish faces and extended hands at meetings. Joe shook hands because he felt it was the Christian response but never engaged in conversation. The executive committee members, with the one exception who had stood up for Joe, kept their distance.

The agreement with the diocese's lawyer provided that Joe could return to Redeemer as soon as Dr. Moncure's report was in the bishop's hands, provided the report was favorable to Joe. This was especially important as it was almost Christmas, and the financial plans for the coming year had not even begun. Despite this urgency, the bishop kept Joe waiting for a full week, and then demanded that he come to Diocesan House for a meeting before returning to work. This was a few days before Christmas, and the visit required a twelve-hour round-trip drive. At the meeting, the bishop told Joe he was to leave Redeemer "as soon as you can wind up your ministry there." There was no room for discussion, and Joe agreed to depart in a timely way. He kept the bishop's order entirely to himself, fearing it would excite a furious reaction from his community. The Church of the Redeemer had suffered enough.

The Christmas Eve and Christmas Day celebrations were filled with people from all over Catoctin Springs, some of whom had stayed away since Joe's removal. They stood and applauded during the singing of *O Come, All Ye Faithful* as the procession came down the aisle. People who had not attended worship in years were there, and they celebrated joyously as befit the Christmas season.

Joe remained in his position as rector for a full year. He devoted himself to strengthening ministry and striving to build up the parish again. He reached out to the few who were still unsure of him, but never succeeded in relationships with Lottie Bascomb and her small detachment of spoilers, including dour, fussy Nancy Dodd and the lugubrious nuns. After a year, having stretched the bishop's patience as far as he dared, Joe left Redeemer, telling his flock that he had been there for ten years, had done the best he could to repair the damage, and that God was calling him to move on. Out of concern for the wider church and the people of Redeemer, who had suffered so much, he never revealed that the true reason for going was Bishop Solenberger's decision. He believed they would have a hard-enough time in the future with this difficult, dishonest man without his making it worse.

Joe's final service was happy and crowded to overflowing. Lottie Bascomb and her friends and children continued to refuse to receive Holy Communion from Joe, but he was used to it by then. The parish presented him with a gift, a fine, sturdy canoe, which they carried down the aisle singing "Row, Row, Row your boat."

With Bishop Spencer's blessing, he returned to his former diocese and began service as interim rector of a large church, whose longtime priest had recently departed. Whatever the leadership there knew of his past troubles ceased to be an issue because he came with Bishop Spenser's backing. Joe was so abysmally ashamed of his own conviction; however, focused by circumstances it was, that after long prayer and meditation, he concluded he should leave the ministry and return to life outside the church. After some months of searching, he was offered a position as assistant to the commonwealth attorney of a large jurisdiction. He was preparing to accept this generous offer when his time as interim rector was over. But Bishop Spenser was concerned about another parish, one that had experienced a time of turmoil, following the election of a gay bishop in New England and the resignation of its parish priest. So grateful was Joe to Bishop Spenser for his kind and generous support, that after much prayer, he accepted the leadership of this very old and troubled parish.

Joe continued to hear often from his heroes at Redeemer, Harry Campos, Jim Edelman and his wife, and the good people there, who still considered him one of their own. He prayed for them and thanked God that they had been in his life. The Henleys wrote to him often as he did his friend Amanda, the former warden of the parish. They were all grateful they had all survived the storm.

Ted continued as an eternal presence in his father's heart. Joe never heard from him again. From time to time, Kate wrote to him, wanting to "get back" certain things she coveted. When he could find them, he either sent them back to her by mail, or drove them to the home of her only friend. In her notes to him, she never mentioned Ted. Joe wrote to Ted every few weeks, for almost twenty years, apologizing in every way he knew how, for everything. He never received a reply. This loss of the son he loved was an anathema that seared his every waking moment and filled his dreams with tears. He gained some insight from his sister, Sally, however, as to what it meant.

During the early spring, before the Easter, when Kate and Ted left the house, Sally had arranged with Kate to visit her in Wicomico during the summer. After the separation, Sally, of course, decided to cancel the visit. But because Kate's bad behavior was not yet known (thanks to Joe's discretion), and because Sally and her mother wanted to see Ted before he left for college, despite their misgivings, they decided to go to Wicomico. It was during this visit that Kate received Joe's letter, encouraging her to cooperate with him in making financial arrangements for Ted entering college. In his letter, Joe provided the name of the financial aid director with whom he had been working, outlined the procedure, gave her telephone numbers and addresses, and urged again—they were running out of time—that they work together to provide the necessary money.

After reading the letter, Kate had stomped out to the beach where Sally was sitting (reminding Joe of the time she had stomped down the stairs to tell him that Ted and his friends had been saying things about him) and told Sally, "Well! I got your brother's letter! He refuses to pay anything for Ted's college. He will not pay for anything. He says it's all up to me, and that I can put Ted through college without any help from him. He will not contribute a dime. It's just like him to do us this way." Kate appeared livid with anger.

Sally was extremely upset and said, "There must be a mistake. Joe wouldn't act that way." Kate replied that maybe Sally and the family could see what Joe was really like. Kate said she had to leave to drive Ted up to Norfolk to have his computer serviced. They would return, she said, by dinnertime, and they could discuss it then.

Deeply disturbed, Sally had remained on the beach, thinking. Finally, she went into the house and did something she would never in her life have done otherwise. She retrieved Joe's letter from the shelf beside the telephone, where Kate kept her bills and read it. She was incredulous when she read what he had actually written. She went upstairs to where her elderly mother was resting and told her everything. They packed up, and when Kate and Ted returned from Norfolk, they apologized and told them that they had to leave early. Sally was too embarrassed to tell Joe, until much later, that she had read Kate's mail without permission. When he heard about it, Joe's first thought was that if Kate had lied to Sally, what lies had she told Ted in the car on the way to Norfolk? How had years of lies, from the mother on whom he doted, affected Ted's relationship with the father who loved him?

* * *

During his first year of return to Bishop Spenser's diocese, Joe was speaking on the telephone with his old friend, Andy Campbell, in his former diocese. His old friend's straightforward, commonsense voice soothed Joe as it had during the worst of his ordeal with the church.

"How's the depression?" Andy wanted to know.

"Getting better. I keep it to myself. Nobody here has guessed. I hope."

"What is God teaching you, Joe?"

"To forgive. It don't come easy as the Beatles say. But it is the only way. I've written to Bishop Solenberger several times, asking him to help me clear my record."

"Let me guess…"

"He writes back with the same choice of words each time. It's not possible. 'Even if I wanted to,' he says. By the way, how's that bastard Kirby Porter? Still a big man in your diocese?"

"Now, Joe. That doesn't sound like forgiveness."

"I'm working on it, brother. I truly am."

"Is it true Solenberger never showed Moncure's report and rec-ommendations to the executive committee?"

"It's true."

"So nobody in the diocese knows about her recommendations?"

"That's right. He wanted to save face. Look good. Look tough. To a man like that a meager parish priest is not worth loosing face for. He'll be the kind of bishop who will use every excuse imaginable to stay away from his diocese."

"What do you say in sermons?"

"I tell them the truth. That God is good. We are never alone. The universe was made to be inhabited. And we pray together that God *will deliver us from faithless fears and worldly anxieties, and that no clouds of this mortal life will hide from us that love which is immortal*...and we read together the definition of Grace on page 858 of the Prayer Book, and I explain agape love over and over, and we retell Bible stories, and..."

"God is good," said Al.

"God is good," replied Joe.

* * *

Weeks before he left Redeemer and moved from Catoctin Springs, Joe made a final Friday night visit to a place where he had always found friends. As he drove north on the familiar road out of town, the air and countryside, freshened all around him by a late spring snow, was a symphony of sensual whites. He thought of one of his favorite paintings, Monet's *The Magpie,* and its abundance of whites of every shade and value, a marvelous work he would, one day, see in person when he finally got to the Musee d'Orsay in Paris. As he parked in the gravel lot, a scrim of small blackbirds alighted beside his car, fussing and chirping in the fresh white powder. Thinking of Monet's lonely *Magpie* filled him with joy as he pushed open the heavy door and stepped inside, shaking the snow from his boots.

Instantly, they were on all sides, patting him on the back and shoulders, the heavy waitresses hugging him mightily like a ragdoll, men shouting his name, and a round of loud applause emanating from the poolroom and card tables. In his honor, someone cranked up the old Wurlitzer with John Dylan's *Knocking on Heaven's Door*. Raymond, exclaiming from behind the bar that he would not take "no" for an answer, produced a bottle of Old Forester bourbon, Joe's favorite (in years past so Joe had mentioned to him at one time), and poured him a stiff one. They were all friendly and happy to see him, and Joe felt as good as if Ted were there too.

He was escorted to a bar stool and practically lifted onto it. The general commotion was so great he could barely remain seated; it seemed that they all wanted to touch him or pat him on the back. He called for silence, and while they all waited with emotion, he raised the glass and said, "Praise the Lord. Here's to you." They all clapped heartily. As the warm whiskey settled in his throat, he thought—for a moment—how good it tasted after all these years.

"Joe, we know you been in the briar patch and all. We was pulling for you the whole time."

"It don't make no sense that your own church did you that way. Why, is what I wanna know."

"Yeah. Haven't any of them ever had a fight with their spouse? And why did they accept her word over yours? Seems they felt you was lying all the time."

On and on, the questions came, everyone talking at once, and all saying about the same thing. Arliss, a new waitress, said, "My old grandmother was a member of Redeemer years ago. She always was taking about how educated and intelligent folks were there, ministers especially. We was all Baptists at home, and she wouldn't go to our church. But that's what a lot of people think. How come they kicked you out?"

"When he heard you was living in a motel room, some of us came over there one night, but you wasn't there."

"Just tell me one thing, Joe. Answer me one thing. With people acting that way, how do we know there is a God, anyway?" The questioner was Benny, or Lenny, a construction worker, if Joe remembered correctly.

"The universe exists," said Joe. "Do you accept that, that this is true? If you do accept this basic truth, that the universe exists, there has got to be a maker. Someone, or somebody, had to make it, create it. That Creator is what we all call God. The Universe couldn't make itself. Can a refrigerator make itself, or a clock? No. There must be a maker, a Creator. That is God. God created everything. Even you and me."

"Well then, why do things go wrong so much of the time?" said Wilson, a young man who looked like he should still be in high school.

"The complex universe and all the things going on in it, moving in it, like planets, stars, galaxies, represent a plan, an ordered whole. God loves order. God hates the opposite of order…"

"Chaos," said a woman in the back.

"That's right," said Joe. "Chaos, disorder."

On and on, the questions came as in his first days in Catoctin Springs. He tried to respond to everyone, and gradually got around to asking about their lives, their families, health, jobs, and their faith. Everyone wanted to talk with him. Raymond poured him another drink, and as he wiped the bar surface, he asked about Ted, remembering the time Joe brought him in to visit, years before. And at the mention of his son's name, Joe found himself crying for the first time in many months. The tears flowed quietly, tears of the most intense joy at hearing his son's name. Joe didn't think that Raymond could tell. Or, if he could, he was too much of a gentleman to let on.

About the Author

EDMUND BURWELL IS a lawyer who lives in Virginia. He writes about the way people treat each other. Lovers in a Small Café is Part II of The Ice Meadows, which was published in 2019. He is also the author of a book of short stories.

CPSIA information can be obtained
at www.ICGtesting.com
Printed in the USA
LVHW030325030221
678219LV00001B/61

9 781662 412073